Dec

D0502512

EXTRACTION

EXTRACTION

STEPHANIE DIAZ

St. Martin's Griffin
New York

EXTRACTION. Copyright © 2014 by Stephanie Diaz. All rights reserved. Printed in the United States of America. For information, address St. Martin's Press, 175 Fifth Avenue, New York, N.Y. 10010.

www.stmartins.com

Designed by Kathryn Parise

LIBRARY OF CONGRESS CATALOGING-IN-PUBLICATION DATA

Diaz, Stephanie, 1992–
   Extraction / Stephanie Diaz.—First edition.
       pages cm
   ISBN 978-1-250-04117-3 (hardcover)
   ISBN 978-1-4668-3732-4 (e-book)
   1. Science fiction.   2. Survival—Fiction.   3. Love—Fiction.   I. Title.
   PZ7.D5453ex 2014
   [Fic]—dc23

                                                            2014008534

St. Martin's Griffin books may be purchased for educational, business, or promotional use. For information on bulk purchases, please contact Macmillan Corporate and Premium Sales Department at 1-800-221-7945, extension 5442, or write specialmarkets@macmillan.com.

First Edition: July 2014

10 9 8 7 6 5 4 3 2 1

For Julianne, my "odd sister,"
and Jennifer, my twin in spirit

EXTRACTION

1

Today I have to prove I deserve to stay alive.

I push the front door of my shack open a crack, enough to peek outside. It's dark and dusty out there. Soft pink moonlight falls on some of the shacks across the street. A small black ball hovers through the air with two red lights blinking on its metal surface.

I hold my breath, waiting for the cam-bot to pass. The red lights—fake eyes, we call them—double as motion sensors and cameras. They monitor our every move, relaying a live feed to the security hub in the city. Nighttime curfew isn't over yet, so I don't want to get caught.

But I hate waiting. My nerves have been on edge all night. Not just because of today, which is scary enough, but also because Logan should be here already. The wardens kept him late in the fields, but his extra shift shouldn't have lasted this long, or even half this long.

Finally, the cam-bot is far enough down the road that it probably won't notice me. I slip outside into the cold. Bitter wind rips at my red-orange curls. The wind is loud, but not loud enough to drown out the whimpers floating from the other shacks, from children having nightmares. Nor does it cover the constant hum of the acid shield in the sky.

Tonight the moon beyond the shield is only half an orb, but it still fills the sky, blocking many stars from view. Every night I see the pink acid clouds swirl on its surface and drip into the vacuum of space, pooling in rivers across the thin membrane scientists built around the edge of our atmosphere.

Every night I pray the shield won't break and let the acid through.

Dropping into the dirt, I lean against the front wall of my shack and dig my boots into the mud. I hug my knees to my chest. My heart hammers beneath my ribs. In my head, I recite chemical formulas—like LF for the moon's acid—and divide big numbers by other big numbers to stay calm.

Logan will be here soon. And I'll get through today.

The smells of sewage and decay settle in my nose. I try to ignore them. There isn't time today to regret the way the Developers have made me live for sixteen years.

There's only time to escape.

The sun creeps out. Security officials emerge from the haze of morning fog far down the road, a whole group of them with more cam-bots and the sinking moon at their backs. They tramp from one shack to the next, getting the other sixteen-year-olds outside.

The front door of the shack next to mine opens, and my friend Grady steps out. His brown skin glows in the pale sunlight. The bags under his eyes are puffy and swollen like he's been crying all night, but he'd never admit it. I don't blame him. It's normal to cry on the day we test for Extraction.

"Are you waiting for Logan?" he asks, forcing the door shut behind him.

I nod, glancing back down the road. He's still not here.

"Bad idea," Grady says.

"He won't be able to find me otherwise."

"They won't let you stay here." Grady nods to the officials in armor, who are still far down the road. They'll reach me soon, and they'll use their weapons to force me to get up and walk, if I won't do it myself.

"I don't care," I say.

I'm not sure I can face today without Logan. He should've been here last night. He would've snuck into my shack like he usually does. He would've held me and comforted me, and told me everything was going to be okay.

Even though that probably isn't true. He already took the test and failed. Our society's leaders, the Developers, are going to kill him when he turns twenty, if not sooner. Whenever they decide he's not strong enough for labor anymore. Whenever they have someone to replace him.

When I think about that, I get all crumpled up inside, and I shake so badly I can barely breathe. I'm afraid I'm going to crack and splinter into too many pieces for anyone to count—thousands, millions, trillions?

Grady nods, as if he knows all those things even though I didn't say them. He wipes his nose with the back of his hand. "I'll see you, then."

"Good luck." The words almost stick in my throat.

"Good luck," he says, his voice almost too quiet for me to hear him.

I dig my nails into my legs as he leaves. There are other kids walking past me down the road: a growing crowd of people. They're all heading the way Grady is, toward the departure station. Everyone is leaving the camp, not arriving.

I fight to keep the panic from rising in my chest. Logan has to be *somewhere*. He promised he would see me off this morning. He promised he'd walk me to the station.

He always keeps his promises. Unless—

"Clementine!" The voice comes from somewhere down the road, and I can't see who it belongs to.

But it's him. It has to be.

I push off the ground. Logan moves past a boy and hobbles into view. He was born with a defect in his right leg, which gives him a limp. His floppy, dark hair flutters about his shoulders. Even from a distance, I can see the weariness in his face and the flush in his cheeks. The wardens worked him hard last night.

I run to meet him. "Are you okay?" I ask, throwing my arms around him.

"I'm all right." He presses his lips against my forehead. His breath warms my skin, calming me. But only a little.

Some crazy part of me thinks passing the test today could save him, too. That if I'm picked for Extraction, if I get to leave, I can convince the Developers to let him leave, too. That maybe they'll listen to someone who's Promising.

My eyes trail across the shadow of stubble on Logan's square jaw as he glances over my shoulder and loosens his hold on me. The officials must be close.

"You ready to go?" he asks. He brushes under his left eye with a finger, as if he's wiping off a bit of dirt. But it's not dirt. It's a fresh bruise from some punishment a warden must've given him during the night.

He tenses from his mistake. He doesn't like me to notice these things.

I scowl. "Is that all they did, or is there more?"

"That's all, and I'm fine. Come on, you're gonna be late."

"Put some mud on it, at least." I crouch and gather a clump of puddle dirt in my hands. Straightening, I press it gently onto the skin below Logan's eye, ignoring his hand pushing mine away.

He grumbles, and I smile. "That's better."

"What, because I look like you?" He snorts and gestures to my mud-covered legs. "Did you sleep in a puddle?"

"No. Maybe then I would've actually slept."

"You look nice, though." He tilts his head and gives the dress I'm wearing a crooked smile. It's the only dress I own, light blue, speckled with faded pink flowers. Its hem frays at the bottom. The shoes I'm wearing are the pair my friend Laila wore before the Developers replaced her.

That was two years ago. The shoes still don't feel like they belong to me.

Boots squish in the mud behind me.

"Show me your arm," a voice says. It's deep, warped by machinery.

I spin and come face to face with an official in dark armor. Green light shines through the eye slits in his helmet, blinding me for a second. All officials have fixtures for night-vision and X-ray vision, so they can see if we have possessions on us that we're not supposed to carry. The remembrance always makes me sick. They can see other things too, if they want.

His gloved fingers close around my left wrist, wrenching it upward. He scans the number inked into my skin—S68477—with a device on his own arm. After a moment, he says, "You're eligible for testing."

As if that's news to me.

He drops my wrist. "Get to the station," he says to me, before reaching for Logan's arm.

"I know I'm not eligible," Logan says, his voice a little strained.

"You still need to get to the station," the official says as he checks Logan's Extraction status. "The work transport will leave directly after the testing transport."

"He knew that already," I say. I swear I don't intend to snap the words, but they spill out that way.

"Thank you," Logan says to the guard, forcing politeness into his voice and shooting me a look.

The guard grunts in amusement. "Looks like your friend here doesn't have much of a shot."

The green light shooting from his helmet feels, suddenly, like a hundred needle points on my skin. But I don't care what he says; he's wrong. I have a shot, even if it's a slim one. Of course I do.

Even if both Logan and Laila lost.

"Get going," the guard barks.

Logan tugs on my hand. I lower my eyes and move with him down the road.

We trail behind the others heading for the departure station. Red sunlight bakes the muddy road and heats my back.

There are twenty streets in total in the work camp, and a hundred shacks and two latrine stations in each row. Two more officials stand ahead of me on this street, on either side of the road, scanning the crowd for anyone who might threaten the stability of the camp.

I try not to make trouble. I try to cooperate with them. Obedience is a key component of what the Developers call Promise, along with intelligence and physical strength.

Promise is everything. It's how the Developers rank us according to our usefulness, and it's what the instructors will test me for today. The ten sixteen-year-olds with the highest Promise are the ones who will be Extracted away from here. They'll get to travel deep down through the underground sectors—Crust, Mantle, and Lower—to the planet Core, the fifth sector, the home of the high-class citizens.

There, they'll be safe instead of worthless. They won't be forced to labor. They won't be replaced.

"Maybe this'll be the last time you walk down this street." Logan bumps my shoulder.

I close my eyes for half a moment to steady my breathing. "We won't find out until tomorrow."

"Almost the last time, then."

My eyes trail over the shack doorways where the children who aren't old enough to work or attend school sit with swollen bellies in the dirt. I used to be like them, before I figured out how to find scraps of food and hide them so older kids couldn't steal them. Before Laila took me in one night, when I was bloody and broken from a bad run-in with an official.

The official had caught me trying to climb to the top of the school roof on a dare, even though it was off-limits. The butt of his gun smacked my jaw and gave me a horrible cut that turned into a scar. He was ready to take my already slim meal rations away for a week, but Laila convinced him to take hers away instead.

I thought she wanted something in return, but all she did was carry me home and lay me on her cot, and wipe the blood off my face while I cried into the straw of her mattress.

She said I could stay there if I wanted. She said I was a smart kid, but if I broke too many rules I'd be replaced early.

She said she'd like to see me get picked for Extraction.

But she can't. She's dead now. She can't even see me fail.

"Maybe," I say to Logan. My Promise is pretty high, but high enough to make me more than a body and a number in the eyes of the Developers?

Maybe.

We reach the departure station. The steel platform covers an old section of the rusted train tracks that still run through the work camp. The tracks are a remnant of the days before our planet's ozone layer corroded from pollution and the moon's acid bled into our atmosphere. The days before our leaders and their chosen people fled far underground and left the rest of us up here to fight for a rare shot at survival.

There's a line of people standing on the stairs on the left side, which lead to the top of the platform. Officials at the top make sure the sixteen-year-olds waiting for the hovercraft stay behind the boarding rail.

Logan and I push into the back of the line. I don't see Grady, but he must be here somewhere. I hope I'll run into him again soon.

The kids who can't test and the ones who already did, like Logan, have to stay on the ground and wait for the hovercraft to the fields. They have no choice but to work the farms for the Developers until they're replaced. Some are forced to procreate, to replace themselves. Logan hasn't been chosen for that yet, but it could still happen. I worry it will every day.

I worry it will happen to me too, if I don't do well today. We could run if we fail, but we wouldn't make it past the electric force field surrounding the Surface settlement. We could take our own lives—and some of us do try—but too many fail at that attempt. And most of us are too scared to try. Most of us still hold out hope that the Developers will make an exception. That they'll let us live even after we turn twenty, if we remain obedient and work hard.

But in all my years alive, I've seen them make only two exceptions—they Extracted two people at age nineteen, for whatever reason. Two out of several thousand people is not the best odds.

There's a loud, whirring noise behind me.

A scream erupts from the crowd.

I tense, but turn my head to see what happened. There's a flurry of movement among the group of older kids. A couple of them are suddenly frantic, tripping over their feet, trying to run, but there's nowhere to go.

My fingers dig into Logan's arm. A hov-pod has stopped in the street behind us. Two officials hop out of the back, pulse rifles in hand. Then two more officials, and three more after them.

They stomp through the dirt toward the crowd of older kids. They wrench people's arms into view, and scan the numbers on their wrists.

They're checking everyone's replacement status.

My breaths come too fast. They don't usually do this during the day. Usually, they take people away in the evening, so we don't even see. So we can almost pretend it doesn't happen—at least until it's our turn.

Logan pulls me against his chest. I squeeze my eyes shut and focus on the shaky rhythm of his heart, but it doesn't help. I can still hear the unlucky ones when they're identified. They scream and sob and fight against the officials as they're dragged into the back of the hov-pod, to be chained up and taken to quarantine. That's what officials call it, but we all know what it really is: a gas chamber in the detention facility. A death room.

Two years ago, officials took Laila there. She threw me the boots I'm wearing now as they dragged her away.

The more of us the Developers keep alive to work their farms, the more of a threat we become. So they keep us weak and hungry, trapped by guns and fences, until they decide fresher blood would be more obedient. More useful.

Twenty is the cutoff age, but many people are replaced sooner.

Logan tucks a strand of hair behind my ear. He hums the tune of a lullaby he made up the night Laila was taken away, when I fell asleep in his arms with my tears trickling onto his shoulder:

> *To the krail's caw, to star song*
> *In the field, love, we'll dance*
> *'Til the moon is long gone*
> *Until the world ends*

When all the people marked for replacement in this area have been collected, the back of the hov-pod closes, and the vehicle heads down the road.

The rumble of a sky engine reaches my ears. I don't have to look up to know it's the departure craft come to transport us to the city. But not all of us. Only those my age will be allowed on board.

Logan's arms loosen around me as the line on the ground starts to push up the stairs. "Don't be afraid, okay?" he says.

"I'll try," I whisper. But how can I *not* be afraid? I've dreamed about this day for years. I've longed for it. I've dreaded it.

Logan gives me a crooked smile.

Bodies bump me from behind. I force my eyes away from Logan and take the first step up the stairs. Clutching the rail, I focus on the red sun glinting on the surface of the hovercraft. With every step, I urge my legs not to shake so badly. I walk up these steps every morning on my way to school. I can pretend this morning is like every other morning; I can pretend everything is normal.

I won't look back at Logan. For days, I know he's been worrying about what will happen if by some miracle luck is on my side today. If I win an escape that he lost last year.

But I can't worry about that yet. This test is my only shot.

I won't mess it up, no matter what.

2

The faint smell of coura dung and wet hay fills the departure craft. I pinch the bridge of my nose. It always smells like this—like us, the only passengers of this ship.

The ship rumbles as we fly, sending vibrations through my already shaky body. I clutch one of the leather straps dangling from the ceiling so I won't fall.

There aren't any windows except in the cockpit, but by now I can guess well enough when we leave the work camp behind and fly over the first of the forest trees. Lumberyards where some of the older kids work sit below us. The woods stretch for miles and miles. We zip through the sky above them at breakneck speed, but it feels like nothing at all.

The hovercraft slows when we reach the Pavilion, the city that takes up the other half of the lone settlement on the Surface. Only adults live here, and they all come from the Core. Most aren't permanent residents; they travel to the Surface for research—top secret, so I have no idea what it is. The ones who stay in the city awhile work as instructors in our school, or wardens and guards in the camp, or nurses and doctors in the sanitarium. Governor Preston oversees everyone, acting in place of the Developers.

We settle with only a slight jolt on the landing platform atop one of the education buildings. The door opens, letting a gust of wind into the ship.

I search for Grady as I move with everyone else out onto the platform. But I don't see him. There are too many bodies. Their warmth does little to block the chilly air that seeps through my clothes.

Officials lead us down a short set of steps, onto a narrow roof of black and silver panels with a rail that blocks us from either edge. Ahead lies a set of glass doors leading into the main education complex, which has a few more stories than ours. I come here every morning for four hours of memorizing scientific theories and mathematics, and learning about why our world is the way it is. Most of my knowledge will only be useful if I'm picked for Extraction.

That's why only half of all children in the outer sector camps are tested. When we're born, doctors perform brain scans to determine how much Promise we have. Only those deemed worthy of possible transfer to the Core get to go to school and take the Extraction test. The rest are doomed for replacement.

To my left, dark buildings rise from the streets, most towering over us and touching the clouds. Sometimes I picture myself standing on one of their rooftops and sticking my arms out. I close my eyes, take a deep breath, and launch myself into the sky.

And I fly.

But even if I could fly, the towers are restricted for people like me. The only time we're allowed to move through any part of the city beyond the education complex is during school tours or on the day of the yearly Extraction ceremony. Tomorrow.

I glimpse the gravel road far below as we near the glass doors. A couple pods zoom by, whirring as they hurtle around street corners with giant CorpoBot screens that broadcast news from the Core, but are usually silent when I see them. The pods pass the oval-shaped sanitarium, where girls not much older than me give birth to babies they'll never see. They pass the spot on the gravel where Laila broke down after pictures of the new Extractions appeared on the CorpoBots, and her face wasn't shown.

"Keep moving," a guard says.

I turn away from the road. The glass doors to the education complex are already open, and kids ahead of me are moving inside. A small part of me wants to stay out here on the roof, to run far away from this test.

As long as I haven't taken it yet, I still have a chance. I could still be one of the chosen.

A guard stops me at the door. Even though it's not just me, even though the officials are stopping everyone to check us in, my heart quakes like someone jabbed an electric socket inside it. He grabs my wrist, digs his nails into my skin—I hide my wince—and passes his scanner over my citizenship number: S68477. Green light pierces my eyes through the slits in his helmet.

After a moment, he drops my arm and motions me along with a flick of his finger. My wrist throbs where he touched it. I keep my eyes trained on the floor as I move past him.

Two lines are forming in the fifth-floor lobby, one for girls and one for boys. They stand beneath a low, black-paneled ceiling. Officials patrol the room's perimeter, including the exit behind me and the entrance to the hallway ahead, where instructors wearing scarlet uniforms and knee-high boots stand waiting with smiles on their faces. Now I couldn't run even if I wanted to.

"Welcome to Extraction testing," a female instructor says, her voice rich and deep. She's darker-skinned than most and wears her ebony-colored hair in a sleek, high ponytail that falls halfway down her back. "We'll see you one at a time."

Words clump and tangle in my mind as I join the girl's line: It's going to be okay; it's just a test; I can pass this.

But the test for Extraction is different every year. No one knows what to expect or how to prepare for it.

I've done well in school. I got the highest score on my final exams for mathematics and quantum physics. My instructors have hinted several times that I'd make an excellent addition to the team of scientists in the Core.

I'm not sure that'll help me today.

I stand in line waiting for my turn with a trembling hand wrapped around my still-fragile wrist. I recite the prime numbers from one to five hundred to stay calm.

This year, one hundred and sixty-two sixteen year olds on the Surface are eligible for the test. Only the top ten will be picked for Extraction.

When I reach the hallway entrance, the instructor with the high ponytail steps forward, carrying a tablet. I notice a small, golden moon pinned to the neck of her dress uniform. "What name do you go by?" she asks.

The question catches me off guard. For years, adults have only referred to me by my citizenship number. "Um, Clementine."

Her eyes flicker to the scar along my right jawline. The reminder plastered on my skin of the night I met Laila. The night an official slammed the butt of his gun into my face.

I'm used to the stares, but it still takes everything in me not to lower my eyes.

"Follow me," she says.

Down the corridor and around several corners, she leads me through a door on the right.

In the center of the bright, whitewashed room, three instructors stand gathered around a machine: a leather chair enclosed by a cage of metal strips, adorned with knobs and wires. The walls to my left and right are made of glass. Through them, I see identical rooms running along the corridor. Kids climb into the caged chairs, while others climb out. The ones inside don't look quite right. Their bodies are almost seizing.

My eyes widen.

"This will help us determine how Promising you are," my instructor says.

No "it's all right" or "it'll be okay." If she'd cooed in that weird way the nicer instructors do—as if they think they're our parents, even though we don't have parents—it'd be easier to trust her.

But whether I trust her or not, I have to go through with this. This test might get me off the Surface.

I set my jaw and climb into the chair. The instructors approach and place black straps over my arms and legs. They don't tell me what they're doing, but I feel them push small, mushy balls into my ears that block out everything but my faster-than-usual heartbeat.

I focus on the air flowing in and out of my nostrils, urging it to steady. I have to make a good impression.

"I'd like you to try not to run," my instructor says.

Two pairs of hands place a lightweight silver helmet onto my head. It slides over my eyes, and the world goes black.

A soft hum fills my ears. The hum of the deflector shield in the sky.

Wind tugs at my curls. Desert dirt lies beneath my feet, though I still feel the leather of the machine chair against my back.

I breathe easy. This is a simulation. Whatever happens, it won't be real.

I spin in a slow circle, taking in my surroundings. I'm on the giant plateau that lies a mile west of the work camp. I can see the camp from here, with its sea of shacks on every street.

In another direction, a dark building looms much too close to me. It can only be one place: the quarantine facility.

I swallow hard and turn away. In the third direction, a row of figures stands in the distance. Children chained together. I hesitate before slowly walking closer to see them better. No one appears to be guarding them, but they aren't moving.

Maybe ten feet beyond them, the electric force field forms a hazy green barrier along the settlement perimeter. It runs from here all the way to the other side of the Pavilion, bordering the part of Kiel's surface where we are allowed to go. Making escape on our own impossible.

Beyond the force field and on the edge of the horizon floats the moon, a vast and terrible giant looming over our planet, Kiel. A pilot can reach the moon by ship in an hour if he's a fast flier. Pink gas drips from its surface onto the deflector shield built to protect us after pollution ate away our ozone layer. The technical term for the moon's lethal gas is *letalith acid*, but everyone, even the Developers, calls it moonshine.

The whir in my ears falters and starts zapping.

pew-pew

A flicker runs all the way across my vision. For a second the shield fails, and I glimpse the true golden color of the moon.

pew-pew

I twist my lips into a frown.

p-p-p-p-p-p

The sky flickers everywhere now like lines on the CorpoBots in the Pavilion, when their signal cuts out.

There's a flash, and the shield vanishes from the sky.

The moon sits on the edge of Kiel, a brilliant globe. Oozing pink acid.

I can't breathe anymore. I'm rock solid, and every inch of me is screaming, no, no, no, no, no, no.

Heavy fog stretches toward the line of chained children. The force field doesn't block the acid at all; it seeps right through.

I'm shaking and breathing too fast. Let me out, please, let me out, I want to scream. This isn't real, so I can't die, but I can still feel pain—I'll feel everything.

Moonshine reaches the children. I almost yell at them. I almost run and try to pull them out of the acid's way, even though they're not real. But it's too late.

Their clothes sizzle and disintegrate. Their bodies contort in unnatural positions, like they're burning insects instead of humans. Their mouths open in piercing screams—too many, too many— that make me want to fly out of my skin.

The acid is almost to me now.

I want to run. I want to be anywhere but here, even in quarantine, even staring at the muzzle of a rifle. Burning to death by acid is worse than any other kind of death.

But my instructor said not to run.

But I need to—I *have* to.

But there's no more time. The fog of moonshine clouds my vision. My face pulls away from my head like some hand is wrenching it. Then my hands and arms—everything. I burn like someone sliced me all over and drowned me in salt, and then set me on fire. The acid claws at my throat—I can't breathe. I can't think, and I sob and scream.

Let me die, I plead. But I don't die. Instead, I scream. Despite the fact that I don't want to give the instructors the satisfaction of having brought me to this level. The pain is too much, so I keep screaming, and soon I can't tell if it's me anymore. If I'm even real. Somewhere in the hazy darkness of my mind, I remember this isn't real. This is only part of a test.

But I'm still on fire, and I can't stop screaming.

click

The sickening feeling of acid corrosion zaps away like it was never there. The straps holding me down loosen and fall away. Hands lift the helmet off my head and remove the mesh things from my ears.

I still clutch the arms of the chair, and my knuckles are plaster-white. My teeth might fall out, they're so clenched.

My instructor's fingers fly across her tablet. She gives me a small, careful smile. "Great job, Clementine."

It takes me a second to understand what she means: I didn't run in the simulation. I followed orders, which is what she wanted.

This must've been a test of my obedience.

I'm shaking as she helps me out of the chair.

She snaps her fingers. "There's one more thing, and you can go."

A second instructor approaches with a tray. A thick metal syringe sits upon it.

My feet move to scramble backward, to run, before I can even stop them. If there's one thing in this world I hate more than officials and their cam-bots, it's needles. I don't even know why, really. My fear stems from vague memories, from my earliest days in the sanitarium: A flash of a glinting needle. A flash of pain. A flash of a nurse leaning over me telling me to *stop crying.*

But I force my feet not to run. I make myself stay put.

I can't run. This is still a test.

My instructor observes me. She slips her fingers around the syringe and picks it up. "Why didn't you run just now?" she says softly.

Honestly, I don't know. Officials use syringes like that on kids in the detention facility, to cripple them temporarily as punishment for their actions. Doctors use syringes to treat Unstables— people with ridiculously high Promise who fall off the deep end, whom the Developers want to fix. Needles scare the stars out of me.

But this is a test of my obedience.

"Because you didn't want me to," I say slowly.

The approval in her eyes deepens, though her lips barely part when she smiles. "You know, this isn't something that would hurt you." She flicks the metal. "This is a special injection that Core citizens are given to raise their health and stamina—to ensure they survive to old age and their Promise remains high and stable. If you are picked for Extraction, you'll receive it too."

I lick my chapped lips.

"What would you give for a way off the Surface, Clementine?"

Logan's face slides into my head. The one person I know I'd miss if they took me away.

Looking into my instructor's shining eyes, I push his face to the back of my mind.

"Everything," I say.

3

I still remember the night Laila learned she wasn't picked for Extraction. Logan and I stood in the crowd outside the building where the choosing takes place, watching the pictures appear one by one on the CorpoBot screens. Watching as the pictures switched to a video of the new Extractions shaking hands with the governor, relief in their eyes and smiles on their faces. Laila wasn't one of them.

Her body shook with sobs all night. Her cries kept me awake.

"I don't wanna do this anymore," she said. "They're gonna make me have babies, and steal them away before I can even see their faces. Why can't they just kill me now?"

My eyes stung and I clenched my hands into fists. It felt like the sky was falling on the two of us and we had no cover. Nothing I said would calm her down.

"Can't you just kill me, Clementine?" she said.

She came up with a plan. She'd break into a greenhouse and steal one of the shovels. She wanted me to smash the back of her head in.

"No, no, you can't," I said, really sobbing now, really choking. "Please don't leave me. You're my family."

Family. A word with three syllables that the instructors had defined in school. Sisters, brothers, mothers, fathers.

People who loved each other.

Laila didn't say anything for a moment. Then she sighed and pulled me onto her lap. I wrapped my arms around her neck, burying my face in her shoulder.

"I'm sorry," she said. "I won't leave you yet."

"You can still try to convince them you're Promising," I said. "Please try. They might still make an exception."

She didn't answer for a moment. I knew what she was thinking: The Developers don't make exceptions.

But she didn't say that out loud. Instead, she planted a soft kiss in my hair. "Okay, I'll try," she said. "I'll keep up my Promise. Maybe I'll even try to escape the settlement if I get brave enough. There's gotta be a way, right?"

"I hope so," I whispered.

But she never did get brave enough.

The field grass is still wet from yesterday's rain. It muddies Laila's old boots with every step.

I'm walking with a group of sixteen-year-olds, led by two officials and a cam-bot. A hov-pod transported us to the fields near the work camp after the test. We never get a day off work because there is always work to do. Today is no different.

"Did you run?" a girl beside me whispers to a boy. She fidgets and glances at the official, probably to make sure he can't hear her.

"When?" the boy asks.

"During the test."

He doesn't answer—we aren't supposed to discuss the test at all. But his cheeks flush red. He must have run.

"It's okay." The girl squeezes his hand. "So did I."

"I didn't," a voice to my left says. The girl who speaks has blond hair and a face that would be beautiful, if it weren't covered with dust and bruises. I've seen her in school, but we've never spoken.

"The instructor said not to, so I didn't," she says. "I didn't even scream."

The other girl narrows her eyes. "No one asked you, Ariadne."

The blonde, Ariadne, wraps an arm tightly around her body and stares at her bare feet in the grass.

My hands can't help trembling a little. Some of the others who tested didn't run. Some of them obeyed the instructors—of course they did. But how many?

No. Stop thinking about it. It's okay. It's going to be okay.

My eyes scan the workers in the distance, in the crop fields. I wonder how Grady did. He must've finished his test earlier than me, or maybe he's still in one of the machines, because I haven't seen him yet.

A big part of me is glad I don't have to see him yet, that I don't have to find out how he thinks he did. He's my friend, so of course I want him to be picked tomorrow. I want him to be safe.

But if the Developers pick him, that's one less chance for me.

We reach the greenhouses at the edge of the field, which sit near the packaging warehouse and the animal corrals. I'm grateful for the distraction. In the nearest corral, brown-spotted couras chew on tufts of grass.

Outside the warehouse, a warden shoves a plastic bucket into my arms and attaches a white tag to my wrist. The small dots along the tag flash green. If I tried to run, a warden would flip a switch and an electric current would pulse through my body, crippling me long enough for officials to capture me. The electric force field around the Surface settlement's perimeter is only a secondary precaution.

My eyes trail to where it sits in the distance, a green, shimmering wall beyond the crop fields. It stands at least thirty feet tall— tall enough that it's impossible to get over without a flight pod. If I had access to a pod and knew how to fly it, or if I could break into the security hub in the city and disable the force field, running might actually be an option.

But it's too risky. And even if Logan and I did manage to escape on our own, we don't know for sure what's outside the settlement, what fills the rest of the Surface. Instructors say there are oceans and mountains and fields—places Core scientists visit sometimes on research trips for the Developers.

But they could be lying. They tell us what's out there so we'll long for Extraction, which is the only future that might let us travel the rest of the Surface.

What's out there might be just as dangerous as life in the work camp, or worse.

I near the force field as we walk to the food crops. Hundreds of others are already working beneath the hot sun, pulling weeds or spraying fertilizer chemicals. Cam-bots hover here and there, providing extra sets of eyes for the wardens.

I slip away from the group to search for Logan. I squeeze between children and tall stalks of shir grain, cursing my short stature. Hoping the wardens and cam-bots don't notice me.

It doesn't take me long to spot him. He moves along a row of nage greens with a bucket in his hands, his sweaty clothes clinging to his body.

I watch him for a moment, not moving, not speaking. My heart thumps in my ears. I'm terrified to see him after what I said earlier, when I was in the testing room with that instructor.

But I'm sure he would've said the same thing. I'm sure he'd give me up, if it meant he'd win an escape. Wouldn't he?

Maybe I'm lying to make myself feel better.

I wipe dust and sweat out of my eyes, and join the row beside Logan's. Bending, I sprinkle coarse, smelly manure around the golden roots of a hoava plant.

He notices me, and his eyes search my face for some sign of how the test went. He wants me to say something first, but I don't because it's useless. What I think or feel, or want to say or do doesn't matter. Not when it comes to this.

"How'd it go?" he asks.

Two rows to my right, a girl falls to her knees from exhaustion. "Get up," a greasy-haired warden snaps. When she doesn't, he hisses through his teeth and stomps over the plants to reach her.

"I don't know," I say. "Not too bad, I hope."

Logan's forehead creases. He reaches out and laces our fingers. His hand is warm and steadying. I close my eyes and let it distract me from the girl's whimpering as the warden wrenches her from the ground. From my worry about tomorrow.

But only for a moment. Then Logan lets go and turns back to the nage greens, and I move to the next hoava root.

A moment is all we can spare with the wardens watching.

Beads of sweat gather on my face, neck, and under my armpits as we move down the rows. The sun overhead burns scorching red. Flies buzz around me. I swat at them, but they don't go away.

Logan works beside me, sometimes a few feet ahead, sometimes a few feet behind. I want to tell him about the test, even though we aren't supposed to. Last year, all he told me was that his limp hadn't helped him. He wouldn't say it straight out, but I think he guessed that was the only reason he wasn't picked for Extraction, since he's always been intelligent and obedient. He came home after the names were announced and didn't smile for days, even when I tried to comfort him.

He's mostly silent now. I wish I knew what he was thinking. But I'm mostly glad I don't.

My fingers tremble as I work. Every time I swallow, it feels like I'm swallowing rocks, my throat is so parched. My empty stomach makes me dizzy. I'm surrounded by food and it's tempting to eat something, but I can't be caught stealing. That's a form of disobedience, and it could earn me transfer to the detention facility and cost me my shot at escape tomorrow.

Of course, some kids, usually the older ones, manage to steal without getting caught. They hoard crops in secret places in their shacks and trade them to other kids. Sometimes I've joined in their market, but not often. It's too dangerous.

"Hey, Clementine," Logan says softly.

I glance at the warden to make sure he's facing away from us. When I see he isn't looking our way, I turn to Logan. He slips his free hand into his trouser pocket. "Yeah?" I say.

"I found something special earlier. Thought you might like it." He gives me a hopeful smile as he removes a small flower and twirls the green stem between his fingers. The petals glint silver like metal.

My feet falter. The breaths collide in my throat.

Of all the children in the camp, I like to think I'm one of the braver ones. Not all the time, of course. Some days the whippings and beatings make me want to curl up in a ball. When I dream of officials dragging Logan to quarantine, I wake drenched in sweat and trembling, but I calm down. I get over it. I have to be good at ignoring my fear, because how else will I prove I deserve to escape it?

This flower is different.

"Get that away from me," I say, panicked. I jerk away from Logan, bumping into the worker girl behind me. She makes a sound or says something, but I don't care.

It's been eight years since I've seen a flower with silver petals like this. But it seems like yesterday. I can still feel the ache slipping through my veins, the pinpoints of knives all over my body, the fever dragging me into a world of liquid fire.

About a hundred years ago, silver aster flowers were created by a Core scientist who injected a special kind of protein into the gene code of a flower, as part of some experiment. The protein released hormones in the aster pollen that relieved stress and slowed brain activity. The result was a pollen with a high calming effect on humans, that could be used as a stress or pain reliever for sanitarium patients. But I'm allergic to it.

"Wait, wait," Logan says, staring at me like I'm out of my mind. "It's just—it's not—oh, jeez . . ." He runs his fingers through his hair, looking at the flower with widening eyes. Realizing why I'm freaked out.

"Did you forget what happened last time?" I ask.

"I did—I'm sorry. But this is different. This isn't what you think." With a callused hand, he tears the petals. Thin, silver wrappings fall away, leaving behind the midnight blue of a common aster—a flower that will definitely not hurt me.

Nothing can stop the heat from spreading through my cheeks.

"I forgot, I'm sorry," Logan says, his eyes on the ground. "I was just trying to make it look prettier for you."

Out of the corner of my eye, I notice a curious cam-bot hovering over. I fix my bucket in my arms, swallow hard, and turn back to the hoava roots. I hope Logan will do the same. We have to keep working. We can't attract any more attention.

But I feel like such an idiot. That day eight years ago when we ran across real silver asters, they had spilled out of a hovercraft's cargo due to a security mistake. They don't grow on the Surface; they're genetically engineered in labs in the Core, in petri dishes under LED lighting. Logan couldn't have gotten hold of one.

My hand shakes as I reach for a rotten root and wrench it up from the ground.

"I'm sorry," Logan says. He's standing too close to me again—the cam-bot is sure to notice—but I can't bring myself to push him away. "I swear I forgot about the . . ." He sighs. "I just thought it might make you smile."

"On a normal day, if I thought it was a joke, maybe it would have."

"Right." The word comes out half caught between his lips. Almost as if he forgot today isn't normal, or maybe he was only trying to put it out of his mind.

Of course he remembers now. His lips press into a tight line.

I rip up another rotten root from the ground. Of course he was trying to be sweet and I messed it up. I mess up lots of things when it comes to him and me.

I realize he's stopped working again.

"What are you doing?" I hiss.

His brows furrow, and he stares at something I'm too short to see. "Do you smell that?"

I pause. I sniff the air. It smells like manure and musk and vegetation, but there's also something else. Faint at first, then stronger.

Fire smoke.

"Get working!" the greasy-haired warden yells.

But others notice the smell too. Muttering ripples among the laborers.

"Can you see anything?" I ask Logan.

He shakes his head. "The wind isn't bad. Hopefully it won't spread."

"Are you *deaf?*" the warden snarls.

I turn, and he's in my face, spewing saliva. The leather of his metallic whip rips the flesh of my arm, and I gasp, dropping my bucket.

Logan shields me with his body. The whip smacks his side. He winces.

The nearest cam-bots start beeping—a loud, obnoxious sound that makes my ears sting. In the distance, just before the electric force field, bright flames feed on crops and grass. Smoke blurs my view of the children who shout and stumble over each other to escape it.

The warden shoves Logan aside and staggers past us, realizing what's going on.

"Get water!" he yells over the beeping bots. "We need water!"

The emergency pods are already in the air. They come from somewhere near the greenhouses, and fly above the flames. Doors in their undersides slide open. Water spills out. I've never seen so much of it.

Logan pulls me to my feet. I'm trembling. "You're bleeding," he says.

I barely hear him, or notice the sting in my arm. Instead, I notice how officials are surrounding the workers nearest the force field and the fire. How they're dragging the kids into a line and roping their legs together with thin pieces of electric wire. They only use wire like that to handcuff people before taking them to the detention facility, or to quarantine.

Logan's arms wrap around me.

"Why are they doing that?" I ask.

"They must think it wasn't an accident."

My eyes flit again to the handcuffed children, to the smoke streaming across their faces. They're all older than me, and taller. One or two might be crying. But most don't look frightened. They hold their heads high and bite back their screams when the wardens snap whips at their ankles.

Some of the chemicals we use out here are flammable, but it takes matches to start a fire, or lightning, and there isn't lightning. The kids must've stolen matches. I bet they wanted to set fire to the whole field, just to cause trouble, or maybe to try to run in the commotion.

But the force field is still up. There isn't anywhere to run.

The officials near me and Logan are shouting, telling everyone to move. I guess we're quitting early.

I force myself to turn away from the handcuffed workers. I lean into Logan as we move down the crop rows toward the greenhouses, where officials will pass out our daily meal rations—the leftover food that didn't pass inspection.

They'll kill the rebels for what they did. They always replace people who don't cooperate. Some of them might be sixteen; some of them might not have even tested yet, but that doesn't matter. They've lost all their Promise now.

Maybe that's why they did this, though. Maybe they wanted to die.

4

Logan and I follow the old train tracks along the edge of the forest. The hov-pods and shuttles still run in the evenings, but officials don't care if we walk back to the work camp instead, if we want to. Sometimes it's nicer.

The tracks haven't been used since long before I was born, not since the days when everyone lived on the Surface and there were no lower sectors. The days before the Developers ruled and scientists had to build the acid deflector shield to cover the whole globe and protect our planet. The days before the upper class fled underground to survive.

Logan limps beside me over the tangled weeds and strewn rocks. He and I are alone, except for the spare cam-bot that floats past every so often to monitor the area.

"Are you still bleeding?" Logan asks.

"No." I quickly wipe the blood on my wrist onto my dress.

Frowning, he takes my wrist gently and touches the cut with a light finger. I wince. "It hurts?" he asks.

"A little." I pull away from him. It actually hurts a lot now that I'm not distracted by the fire, but he doesn't need to know that.

"I'll help you clean it when we get home."

Laughter echoes from somewhere not far ahead. The foreign sound makes my stomach twist. I squint to see who it came from, and so does Logan.

His eyebrows draw together. "Is that Grady?"

There are four figures in all, two standing and two on their knees between the tracks.

Grady stands unevenly, one foot on a track and one on the ground. The girl beside him is talking to the two boys on the ground, who are laughing. I tense. They're all in my classes at school, but they're not my friends. These three used to bully me all the time, whenever I scored higher than everyone on an exam. Throwing rocks was their specialty. My specialty was evading them.

Something about the way the boys, Larry and Carter, are kneeling now, clearly messing with something on the ground, makes my palms sweat. I check for cam-bots in the vicinity. There aren't any, for the moment.

"Grady!" Logan calls, and his head turns.

Dirt and sweat streak across his face, clumping in his eyebrows. "Hey," he says.

Larry and Carter look up too. Their eyes narrow ever so slightly. Carter whispers something to Larry, and they both snicker.

My eyes trail over them, from their arms to the rocks in their hands. They smash the rocks against the iron track, weakening the metal to mutilate it. It's already splitting into pieces that look like perfect weapons.

My heartbeat picks up, matching the rhythm of the *clanks*.

"That's dangerous. If a bot sees you—"

"You can run if you're frightened." The girl, Nellie, cuts me off, crossing her arms and smirking. Her black hair is shorter than it was the last time I saw her, and spiked a little with mud.

Logan glares at Larry and Carter, who are still smashing away and whispering. He turns to Grady. "Are you coming home with us?"

Grady shakes his head. The color rises in his cheeks. "I'm gonna stay here awhile."

I don't understand how he ended up here. I've never seen him with Nellie or these boys before. I've never seen him hanging out with anyone except Logan.

"If you get caught messing with the tracks, you won't have any shot tomorrow," I say. "You know that, right?"

Grady laughs, a sad laugh. There's red around his irises. "You really think I have a shot?"

Uncertainty drums in my chest.

Really, I don't know if he has a shot. He's always been obedient, willing to do just about anything without complaining. His scores and speeds in the genetics lab were excellent, but just average in his other subjects. The chances of him getting picked when competing against everyone else . . .

"Of course," I say.

Pain flickers in Grady's eyes, and my stomach drops to my toes. I took too long to answer.

"Yes, you do," Logan says firmly.

"You don't have to lie to me." Grady drops onto the track.

"Grady, we're not lying—" I reach for his shoulder, but he knocks my hand away. I feel the sting beneath my ribs.

"Maybe we'll get picked and maybe we won't." Nellie shrugs.

"We're just making sure we've got a backup plan," Carter says, smirking at me and holding up his rock.

"Dismantling a train track is your plan?" I ask.

"We're making weapons so we can fight the adults," Larry says, pausing to flex his almost nonexistent muscles. "Especially the officials."

Nellie gives me a hard look, challenging me. "I'd like to see you come up with a better plan."

I don't know whether to be mad or laugh. Of course I could come up with a better plan—try to break into the security hub and disable the force field, and escape the settlement that way—but I wouldn't be stupid enough to try. Getting caught would earn me an early trip straight to quarantine.

Logan focuses on Grady again. "Are you sure you don't want to come?"

"Will you just give it up?" Nellie says with an eye roll.

I ignore her. "Trust me, Grady, you've got a shot tomorrow. After all, you're competing against people like Larry and Carter."

Carter hisses through his teeth.

"Maybe," Grady mumbles. He doesn't look up.

"Grady, please—"

"He doesn't care what you have to say," Nellie snaps.

Logan tugs on my hand. "Let's just go," he says.

I don't move for another second. I watch Grady, pleading silently for him to come with us. He doesn't belong here with these people.

He wraps his arms around his legs.

Logan starts to walk away, still holding my hand, and this time I follow him. I pull my eyes away from Grady and try not to focus on the growing emptiness in my stomach.

This feeling that something unbreakable has jammed itself between us and Grady, and things will never be the same.

※

I sit on the straw cot inside my shack. Logan ties a strip of fabric around the cut on my forearm. His fingers move deftly in the dim light seeping through holes in the ceiling.

If the cut were bigger, I might worry about infection, but I've had worse. We've always had to sleep off fevers and bind wounds ourselves. If the sickness is bad enough, officials bring a medi-bot to assess the situation. A life-threatening illness usually lands a sick kid in the sanitarium. But even then, that's only if the kid has a high enough Promise that the Developers don't want to lose his skills just yet. Promise is everything.

In the Core and in the adult cities in each sector, where everyone has high Promise, things are different. No one ever gets that sick. They're vaccinated to prevent diseases before they happen.

Logan finishes tying the knot. "Is your side okay?" I ask.

"It's fine," he says, and stands and crosses the room. In the makeshift fire pit where Laila's cot used to rest, a muckrat roasts on a skewer over sticks and dull flames. The stale bread and salty soup the wardens gave us for our daily rations didn't fill my stomach, as usual. So we caught the rat in a ditch on our way home.

When we were younger, Logan and I made a game out of catching them. We would hide in the sewers, pretending we were statues, until the creatures scampered close enough for us to grab them. Whoever caught the fattest muckrat won. Then we would race home along the train tracks and kill the animal with a sharp stick before we showed it to Laila. I always did the killing because Logan was squeamish.

These days, he's gotten better at it. While he tests the meat and removes it, I stand and crack the door open to check how low the sun is. It's barely burning in the sky, a splotch of pale red in the approaching darkness. Officials send their bots to check the shacks an hour after sunset to keep the boys and girls separate, but we have some time. We have our ways of sneaking around after dark, anyway. All that matters is that we don't do anything stupid enough to get caught.

"Hungry?" Logan asks.

"Very." I shut the door and take half the muckrat from him. The tough meat burns my fingertips, and I gasp. But I don't drop it.

He smiles and rips into his portion. "Will this be your last muckrat? What do you think?"

"I don't want to think." I drop onto the cot again and pick at my meat. When I swallow, it doesn't settle well in my stomach.

Logan watches me. There's something soft and wanting in his gaze, like I'm just out of reach.

He takes a step. I push my free hand into the bed, ready to stand if he takes another. I'm scared. But I want him to.

Something scrapes at the door. We freeze.

It's not a cam-bot; they beep or buzz loudly before coming inside. Which means it must be a human. We don't have visitors, ever. Unless it's Grady—but he raps his knuckles twice every time—or officials. They only check inside shacks themselves when there's a serious problem. When someone is in trouble.

"Don't open it," I say.

"It'll be worse if we don't."

I'm not sure he's right, but I don't argue. He moves to the door. I slide my fingers under the cot for the sharpened stick hidden there.

Logan peers through a crack and frowns. Slowly, he pushes the door open.

A tiny girl with curly black hair stares up at him. She stands unevenly; one leg is shorter than the other. Tears stain her cheeks. Her face is so flushed, she must have a fever.

"Please?" she whispers, pointing at the bit of muckrat meat still in his hand.

I hesitate. When I was as little as her, I used to do this. I used to go around and ask people to share their rations or their extra food sometimes, until I got clever enough to catch muckrats myself. But we barely have enough food as it is, and there are two of us.

"I'm sorry, but there isn't enough," I say.

She whimpers.

"Here, you can have it." Logan hands her the rest of his portion.

"Logan—" I reach to stop him, but he grabs my wrist and pushes me behind him.

"It's okay. Enjoy." He gives her a smile.

She scampers off with her treat without thanking him. The other children lingering in the street turn to us, their eyes hungry.

I shut the door. "There's no use starving for them."

"They could die if we don't help them." The hollowness in Logan's voice surprises me. "I bet she hasn't got any friends, with that deformity of hers. I bet kids make fun of her. I was like her once. So were you."

"I know, I didn't say I wasn't."

"You should know better, then. You should be kinder." He turns away and kicks dirt onto the fire to kill it.

I stare at him, my fists clenched and my jaw trembling. How could he say that? If I'm selfish, it's because I want to survive. It's because there's no way I'll ever escape this place if I care too much about anyone else.

Sitting on the cot, Logan presses his fists into his forehead. The wind whistles over the roof. A krail caws somewhere in the sky.

I unclench my hands and force my jaw to be still. I force the anger away—I try to, at least. It's foolish to be mad at him tonight.

This could be our last night together, though I don't expect it to be. But it could be.

"I'm sorry," I whisper.

He sighs, staring at the ground, and runs his fingers through his hair.

I watch him for another moment, gathering my courage to sit beside him. Of all the things to be afraid of.

When I finally do, he slips an arm around me, pulling me close to him.

"You have nothing to be sorry for," he says.

I close my eyes and lean into his chest. His skin is warm against mine. His body is solid and present. Usually when we sit like this, I wish he would kiss me. Too many times I've thought he was about to, but something always gets in the way. Something always makes him stop, and makes me too nervous to follow through with it.

I wish I were brave enough. I wish I could fold into him until there was no space left, until there was nothing but our breaths and our lips and our clumsy hands.

But tonight is different. Tonight, even just sitting here in his arms makes me terrified—not of him, but of tomorrow. Of the announcement and what will happen afterward.

"I'm scared," I tell him, and my voice shakes

"It's going to be okay," he says, and lays down on the straw and pulls me close to him.

We lie side by side. His chest rises and falls against mine. His strong arms keep me secure. Safe.

Later that night, after the cam-bots have gone down all the streets in the work camp and checked that all the children are safely inside their shacks, Logan sneaks back in through the loose board in the wall and slips onto the cot beside me again.

Even after his breathing slows and steadies, I'm still awake, afraid to dream. The dark hides a tomorrow when I'm certain to lose something dear to me.

For a second night, I don't sleep.

5

We head for the Extraction ceremony at sundown.

Logan and I move hand in hand through the Pavilion streets with the others old enough to attend, escorted by officials and cam-bots. We've already passed the education towers and the sanitarium. Our destination lies a few blocks ahead of us, a block west of the security hub and two blocks east of the main flight departure bay, where the Extractions chosen tonight will depart for the Core.

I'm covered in sweat from working in the fields for twelve hours instead of eight. For the first time, I didn't have four hours of intensive study in school this morning. It's no longer necessary. Either I've learned enough that my Promise is high enough for Extraction, or my years of education were a waste.

The dirt on Logan's face makes the circles darker under his eyes, giving him a weary look. But his jaw is hard, his lips pressed together. He holds my hand with such a firm grip, I'm not sure he'll ever let go of me. I hope he won't.

Thunder rumbles in the distance. Spotlights sweep the city

streets. CorpoBot screens are lit up on every corner, spewing a crackling melody from their speakers and showing the symbol of the Core: a full moon embossed in bronze.

The real moon hasn't risen yet, though small dots of stars already shimmer through the acid shield. The red sun fragments into darkness at my back as it dips toward the world outside the settlement.

"What do you think is really out there?" I ask Logan.

He raises an eyebrow. "Out where?"

"Outside our settlement."

He laughs. "Don't you remember the maps in school? There are oceans, rivers, mountains, research facilities . . ."

I nod, biting the inside of my cheek as a small fear grows in the back of my mind. "And the lower sectors?"

"Work camps and cities, same as here. Except in the Core." His fingers squeeze mine harder. I'm sure he can feel my rapid pulse in my fingertips. "But you knew that already. What's this really about?"

A hovercraft passes by overhead, above the skyscrapers.

I take a deep, shaky breath. "They could be lying about the Core."

He's silent for a moment. Then he says, "They've shown us video footage of the people down there, including Extractions. Do you really think it's all fake?"

I remember the footage: smiling people and laughing children. Some of them feasted in crowded cafeterias, while others played simulation games and worked in laboratories.

Freedom. That's the word instructors use to describe that kind of life. I don't really understand what it means, but I'd like to.

"I guess I don't think it's fake," I say quietly. "It just scares me a little, is all."

"It's everything we dreamed about," Logan says. "Trust me. You'll see when you get there."

I glance at him. His smile is genuine. There's only a flicker of sadness in his eyes.

I think he actually believes he's going to lose me tonight. It makes my heart crack into a million pieces of something that feels like glass—whether because I think he's wrong or because I'm worried he's right, I don't know.

"Logan—"

A scream cuts me off. It came from around the corner of a nearby building. A girl's voice. She screams again, and the hairs rise on the back of my neck.

A pod engine roars in the distance.

"Get back!" officials shout. We all clump together, bumping shoulders. I grab on to Logan's arm.

The pod comes flying into view, a blur of silver. My eyes are wide and I'm clutching Logan and I can barely breathe because the pod's moving so fast, I'm sure it's going to hit us. I'm sure it's going to smack into us and smash us into a thousand worthless pieces. But it halts just in time, not ten feet from where I stand.

Steam seeps from the top of the pod as its side door zips open and a ramp slides out. The bronze insignia of the Core blazes on the pod's silver side. But the girl the officials drag through the doorway is the one who steals my attention.

Bone-thin, dressed in rags, her skin is pale and wrinkled, though she's only sixteen. I know her, or I used to. Before she was like this. When she was Rebecca, sitting in front of me in Sector History, braiding her hair and never saying a word but doing better than everyone on every test. She's the same age as me. She tested for Extraction yesterday.

Now, shackles bind her wrists, and black foam gathers at her lips.

I take three steps back, pulling Logan with me deeper into the crowd. Unstable. That's what she is—she must be.

The officials heave her forward. I clench my teeth when I see the torn flesh of her back, hanging in bloody strips. She shrieks and struggles against the armored men, but it does her no good.

In seconds, they get her through the door of the nearest building. They slam it shut behind them. The clang echoes in my ears.

Unstables have high Promise. They have to, or they wouldn't be marked Unstable—they'd be replaced. But these are people with high intelligence, high obedience, and high physical strength—until they snap. They turn insane and uncontrollable. No one knows why, but the Developers want to understand. They want to fix them, to see if the madness can be cured.

These officials must be prepping Rebecca for her trip to the Unstable treatment facility, Karum. It lies outside the Surface settlement, not far away.

"Settle down," the officials yell to quiet the mutters among the youth. "Keep moving."

"Come on," Logan says.

I turn away, ignore my tightening throat, and let him pull me past the others. It's awful, though. Rebecca was my partner in lab a few times. She never said very much unless she was answering my question or the instructor's, but she was almost better than me when it came to mathematics. She could solve Yate's Equation, the hardest and longest equation to solve, in forty-three seconds, only four seconds slower than me.

Now she's different—messed up and dangerous. I wish I knew why.

On the next street over, I recognize the structure across the road, and my stomach drops into the gravel. The top of the building has a dome shape similar to the sanitarium, but the whole complex is taller. Thick glass pillars lean against the building at an angle, as if they're keeping it from toppling over. A high pole stands near the door with a Core flag waving at the top, its fabric unfurling to show blue and black stripes, a silver circle in the center, and words running along the circle's bottom: INVENTION. PEACE. PROSPERITY.

I watched Logan enter this structure last year.

"All those who tested yesterday, please head inside the Extraction building," a loud voice crackles through hidden speakers on the street. The rich, deep voice of the woman who tested me yesterday. "The rest of you, follow the officials to the announcement plaza."

"Don't go yet," I say to Logan, tightening my hold on his hand as people move around us.

"I have to," he says.

Behind us, the sun dips down all the way, as thunder rumbles again and the wind picks up. There are several moments of only stars and dark sky above us, and then pink moonlight touches the roofs of the skyscrapers. I revel in this moment every night. Laila, Logan, and I used to climb up onto our roof sometimes to lie on our backs and stare at the stars. We went there the night before Laila turned twenty and they took her away.

"You know, it wouldn't be your fault," Logan says.

"What?"

His fingers slip from mine and close gently around my wrist. His other hand tangles in my curls, sending trickles of fire across the skin of my scalp. My breath falters on my lips.

"If they picked you, and you had to leave me," he whispers, "it wouldn't be your fault."

Rocks fill my throat, and my eyes grow watery. I blink fast. Moonlight trickles onto the street, over the skyscrapers.

"I might be back soon," I say. The instructors might eliminate me during the final processing, even before the announcement, like they eliminated Logan early last year. If they eliminate me, I'll be back with him in minutes. This will all be over.

I will have lost everything.

"I hope you won't be," Logan says, a sad smile playing around the edges of his mouth.

I hope I won't be eliminated, either. But when I think of hearing my name called, of Logan hearing it without me on the street, where he'll watch the announcement on a CorpoBot screen with everyone else, I remember I'll lose something either way. My heart trembles beneath my rib cage.

Shoulders bump mine as sixteen-year-olds push past me to head into the building. My shaky, sweaty hand slips away from Logan's. He steps back without another word and turns. The crowd soon swallows him.

I stand there for a moment, fretting. But the bodies still push past me toward the Extraction building. There isn't time to wait. The sooner I get tonight over with, the better.

Wiping the sweat from my palms onto my skirt, I follow the sixteen-year-olds through the double doors. I'm hyperaware of their body heat, their heavy breathing, their untrusting eyes. These are the people I grew up with and went to school with. We worked together in the fields. We shared worried glances when others were facing punishment.

Now we're fighting for ten spots on the pod that will depart for the Core tonight after the ceremony.

Now we're enemies.

✕

Ten minutes later, I'm in an elevator on my way to the fourth floor. My dress sticks to my skin. It's so hot in here, it feels like someone trapped the sun inside the ceiling.

The female instructor beside me keeps a hand around my wrist. Her hair is blond and curly, twisted into a high bun, and her dress suit is scarlet. "Final processing will be quick and painless," she says. "We're just going to take some scans of your brain for a final Promise check before the announcement."

I nod to show her I understand, but something twists inside my stomach. I can't even remember the last time I had brain scans. They're the safest way of determining a Promise score, though there are other methods, like the obedience test I took yesterday.

The elevator bell dings, and the door zips open. We move into a hallway with spare red lights here and there, splashes of color in shadow.

The last time I had brain scans, I would've been a new child in the sanitarium. It wouldn't have been long after my birth, not long after I was taken away from whatever girl in the work camp was forced to give birth to me. Whether she even knew what I looked like, whether she had any other kids besides me, I don't know and I never will. My mother, whoever she was, was replaced and killed in quarantine long ago. No one has ever told me her name. Or my father's name.

But I'm sure it's written down somewhere.

The stairs end, and my instructor pushes through a door into a corridor. Her boots squeak with every step. I realize she was talking, but I didn't hear what she said. "Sorry?" I ask.

"If you're one of the top fifty potentials after processing, you'll be shown into a private viewing room to watch the announcement, and you are allowed one guest. Who would you like to pick?"

My mouth feels dry all of a sudden. The answer is obvious, but I'm afraid to say it. She said *if*. Just because I give her his name doesn't mean she'll use it.

She presses her palm to a gel panel in the wall, and a hidden door slides open. There's a small, square room beyond. A man in a purple uniform and white lab coat taps buttons above a panel on the wall to my right. Beside him, a narrow white table juts out from a fluorescent-lit, gaping hole in the wall. To my left, a small CorpoBot screen shows the symbol of the Core and plays a quieter version of the melody I heard out in the streets.

"Here she is, Jeb," the blond instructor says.

The man in the lab coat turns. His fingers fly to his glasses, which he adjusts as he clears his throat. "Thank you, Dahlia," he says.

"So, can you give me a name?" Dahlia asks.

It takes me a moment to realize she's talking to me. "Um, yes." My cheeks grow warm. "His name is Logan."

"Do you know his citizenship number, by chance?"

I nod, rubbing the number on my wrist. I ran my finger over the same spot on Logan's wrist this morning, before we left for the fields. His skin was a bit too cold. It made me worried he was getting sick. "Z13729."

Dahlia taps the number into her tablet. "Thank you. I'll leave you two, then."

The door zips shut behind her. I'm left alone with Jeb, who stares at me with a slight frown on his lips. He has a splatter of freckles on his cheeks, and a waviness to his sandy-colored hair.

His eyes are pure blue, bluer than mine. A million oceans might be inside them—at least, if the Surface oceans really are as blue as the instructors say they are.

He turns away quickly, adjusting his glasses again. "If you'd please come over and lie down on the bed."

I stay put, my gaze returning to the gaping hole beyond the bed. The walls inside are a stark white color, except for the bottom surface, which is made of shiny metal. That must be the brain-scan machine.

"It won't hurt," Jeb says. "I promise."

"I'm not scared," I say. To prove it I step over to the bed, climb onto it, and lie down on my back. My body sinks into the soft cushion. It's far more comfortable than the straw bed I sleep on every night.

But I'm not comfortable, not really. My hands tremble again. I squeeze them into fists.

"I'm gonna slide the bed into the machine now," Jeb says, touching my wrist gently. "I need you to lie still. There's a strap I can use, but I don't want to unless I have to. Okay?"

He turns to the buttons on the wall and presses a big blue one. The bed slides back into the hole, carrying me with it. I breathe in and out through my nostrils. The music from the CorpoBot plays in the background. When the bed stops moving, I'm staring up at the stark whiteness.

"Here we go," Jeb says. "Lie still."

Air rushes over me. Freezing air that raises goose bumps on my skin. A steady hum fills my ears, growing louder and louder.

Something gelatinous presses against the sides of my head, latching onto my skin. Instinct screams at me to check what it is, to rip it off.

But no, it's not anything bad. It can't be. Logan would've said so, since he went through processing last year right before they told him he was out of the running.

The fluorescent light strengthens, blinding my eyes. I struggle to keep from blinking. Water trickles onto my cheeks.

Slowly, the gelatinous material pulls away from my face. The lights dim. The hum of the machine dies.

"You can relax now," Jeb says.

I squeeze my eyes shut as the bed slides out of the hole in the wall. My heart won't stop pounding. My hands hurt from clenching them so hard.

"I've sent the scans to the processors," Jeb says.

When I open my eyes again, he's wiping the small screen above the button panel blank. He glances at me. "Easy, wasn't it?" His lips soften into a smile that reveals his dimples.

I don't reply. It doesn't matter if this part was easy or not. It's the part that comes afterward I'm worried about. The part where I find out what the scans showed the Developers.

Jeb clears his throat. Turning, he heads for the door.

I sit up, swinging my legs over the side of the bed. "Should I come with you?"

"No, no." He quickens his pace, reaching for the gel panel. "They need me in another room now, but someone will come for you shortly."

He leaves like that, without further explanation. The door zips shut behind him. The click that follows after a second tells me he locked me in.

I dig my nails into the bed cushion and glance at the screen above the buttons, where my brain scans might've been a second ago. I don't know if the machine can figure out a Promise score on its own or not.

Biting my lip, I ease off the bed and move to the screen. Jeb didn't say not to touch anything, after all.

I tap the screen. A number pad pops up. It's asking for a passcode, nine digits.

I curse under my breath. I quickly type in a random combination.

"Access denied," the screen says.

I try another, then another. But of course they don't work. There are 387,420,489 possibilities, assuming the numbers can be repeated. Which they probably can.

With a sigh, I sit back on the cot and hug my legs to my chest. I stare at the bronze moon on the CorpoBot screen. The music, a soft trickle of bells, sounds almost ominous.

How long will it take someone to come? I hate being alone, especially now. The thought of death hovers too close to the edge of my mind. The thought of spending four more years working under hot sun out in the fields. The thought of being forced to get pregnant and give birth in the sanitarium, to assist with the Replacement system.

They don't let girls and boys pair up when they pick them to procreate; they use artificial methods. They take part of us away and don't give it back.

I squeeze my eyes shut, thinking how glad I am Logan hasn't been picked for that yet. I wish he were with me now. Instead he's freezing in the street, staring at a CorpoBot, waiting for the governor to announce the names. He's probably getting sick, if he isn't already. He's probably praying my name won't be called, though he'd never admit that to my face.

He'd never admit he's afraid of being alone. But I'm sure he is. Isn't everyone?

I realize the CorpoBot's music has stopped playing. I open my eyes.

The emblem of the Core is still up on the screen. But as I watch, it fades away and is replaced by a podium in a dark room. A strip of fluorescent red light runs along the back wall, where figures sit in shadow, in a row on benches. On the lower right-hand corner of the screen, the word LIVE is flashing.

A person steps up to the podium, and a spotlight comes on. Governor Preston smiles at me through the screen. He crosses his gloved hands on the podium. The sound of clapping comes from the figures sitting behind him.

"Surface civilians," he says. "It is time for Extraction."

My shaky arms loosen their hold on my legs. I'm still breathing, but I can't get enough air into my lungs. The ceremony's starting without me. This must mean I'm out of the running. This must mean I've already been eliminated.

The governor continues talking.

I stand and run to the door, fighting back tears. I press my palm to the gel pad. A voice says, "Access denied."

"Please," I choke. "Please let me out."

I wedge my fingers into the door crack, trying to force it open as Governor Preston explains the tradition of Extraction.

Five hundred years ago, pollution destroyed our ozone. The acid that's leaked from the moon's surface as long as history has been recorded entered our atmosphere, poisoning us and depleting our population. We had no choice but to escape underground until a shield could be constructed to protect the whole planet.

The four underground sectors—Crust, Mantle, Lower, and the Core—were built. When the shield was ready, the leaders assigned new homes to everyone, most on the Surface or in the other outer sectors, where natural resources remained. The upper-class retreated to the Core to continue ruling.

But those in the outer sectors grew angry with the rulers. Everyone wanted to live in the Core, too, where they would be farthest from the threatening moon.

So they rebelled against the Developers. They hoarded the resources they collected. They hijacked ships to infiltrate the Core.

They didn't realize how big the Core population had grown. They didn't realize the Core had developed much more powerful ships and weapons, and a military system that would crush them.

Soldiers slaughtered many of the working class. They exploded buildings with missiles. They threw the minors into internment camps. They weakened the system of labor and then slowly built it back up again, calling it a fresh start. A more efficient way to live.

But the workers in the camps needed something to fight for; a reason to work hard. And the Developers believed there were some people in the camps who would be more useful in Core society as scientists, doctors, and leaders. So they created the system of Extraction, to weed out the most intelligent, strong, and obedient from the rest.

At least, that's the story they tell us.

There's a click, and the door zips open. I snatch my arm back.

Dahlia blinks in surprise. "Clementine. What were you doing? I came to let you know you're still in the running."

I stare at her. I open my mouth, but no words come out.

"Your friend is waiting for you in your viewing room." She takes my hand. "Come with me."

She leads me toward the left, down the corridor.

The governor's voice continues through speakers in the walls, but I'm barely listening because I'm so relieved.

But that feeling splinters fast. I'm still in the running, but that doesn't mean they picked me. That doesn't mean I'm safe.

"Tonight," Governor Preston says as we climb two flights of stairs and enter an area similar to a docking bay, "we honor the most Promising among those who were born sixteen years ago."

Dahlia leads me down one of several short tunnels. There are three doors at the end of it. She presses a button on the wall, and the farthest one to the right zips open.

Beyond lies a small space—no more than six feet long by six feet wide. The far wall is made of glass. It shows me the dark room, with strips of red light on the walls, where the governor stands at his podium before a small audience of Surface adults. There must be other private viewing rooms to my left and right, where the other eligibles who made it this far wait for the announcement.

Logan sits in one of the two chairs in this room. He stands swiftly when I step inside.

I sink into the warmth of his arms, not caring that Dahlia is watching. I can feel his heart beating through his thin shirt, matching the rush of my own.

"You okay?" he says.

"Yeah," I say.

"Good luck," Dahlia says.

The door zips shut behind her.

I settle into the seat beside Logan's. A small CorpoBot screen sits in the upper corner of the glass wall, showing a close-up of Governor Preston's face, even though he's not standing that far beyond the glass.

"Those who are selected tonight will soon board a ship bound for the planet Core," the governor says, his voice loud through the CorpoBot speakers. "There, they will have the opportunity to choose their place and become a citizen worthy of remembrance."

A dull roar of thunder shakes the building. Logan closes the space between our hands. Instead of the usual comfort, all I feel is uncertainty.

"I will now pass the stage to Cadet Waller," Governor Preston says, "the Head Instructor of this year's examination."

The woman, Cadet Waller, takes the governor's spot before the podium. Her face fills the CorpoBot screen. I recognize her slick black ponytail, her scarlet dress suit, and the tablet in her hand. She's the one who administered my test yesterday.

I didn't realize instructors could also be cadets in the Core military. But maybe she's the only one.

"I'm honored to stand before you today and announce this year's Extractions," she says.

Pick me, come on. Please pick me.

"I am pleased to announce that fourteen Surface eligibles will be Extracted."

I can't help the small rush of joy through my veins. They usually only pick ten from each sector, to make forty total. The Core doesn't have unlimited housing space, so they can't take many more.

"I'll get right to it." Cadet Waller grips both sides of her tablet.

Her face disappears on the CorpoBot screen, replaced by the Core symbol again. The names and faces of the chosen will appear one by one in a moment, as this ceremony proceeds like last year's.

Logan lets go of my hand. Panic creeps over me again, until he slides his arm around my waist and some of my tension eases. But not all of it.

They should have picked him last year. He should have already gone to the Core, because I want to leave, but not without him.

"Citizen T67352: Andy."

On the CorpoBot screen, Andy's name and number appear along with his unsmiling face. His hair is black and messy, and his cheeks are caved in from lack of nutrients. They take pictures of all of us once a year, to keep a record.

"Citizen S98344: Hazel."

A girl's face replaces the first boy's.

Another face appears, and another. My chances get slimmer, and my heart rate doubles in speed. Soft rain patters on the glass ceiling.

Soon there are only four spots left.

"Citizen W12837: Flora."

My brows furrow as her face appears. I know Flora; she and I had Sector History together. She's a bully and a ditz, in the same crowd as Nellie, Carter, and Larry. She's not the least bit smart.

"Citizen X38197: Ernest."

I know him, too. He's gotten in trouble for stealing from the nutrition stockpiles before. Never serious trouble, but still, the instructors must know about it. What are they playing at, letting him get away with stealing and picking him?

I don't get it. Maybe these individuals were obedient during their tests, and maybe they're stronger than some, but they aren't intelligent. They aren't children I would assume have the highest Promise out of all of us.

"Citizen U43716: Samuel."

There's one spot left. I swallow, but it's more like gulping. Logan's arms pull me closer to him. His lips brush the side of my forehead.

Cadet Waller is taking too long to say the name. She won't say my name. I'm going to lose, and I'm going to die in four years. But that's okay because I won't have to leave Logan. I won't have to abandon him. I won't lose him until he dies.

Only, *I don't want him to die.*

Through the glass, Cadet Waller lifts her head, about to say the last number and name. My heart pounds so fast, it might explode in my chest.

I don't want Logan to die, and I don't want to die. I hate it here. I hate fear and officials and moonlight and muddy fields and teenagers in bloody pods being dragged to quarantine. I hate death. If there is any way to escape death, I'll take it no matter the price because I don't want to die.

But I don't want to lose Logan.

But I have to get out of here.

"Citizen S68477," Cadet Waller says.

I stop thinking. I stop breathing. I stop being.

My face appears on the CorpoBot screen.

There's a memory I always think of when good things happen, or bad things, or scary things. It's the first good thing I can remember.

It begins in a dark place, where I lie shivering. Dirt and dust clog my throat, my forehead throbs, and my chest tightens in pain. Cold blood dribbles down my temple.

"Help," I whisper.

I don't know where I am or how I ended up here, but I know the cold, reeking sludge around my body is mud mingled with disposed produce. When the ceiling scrapes open and pink light appears overhead, I know it's the moon.

And when a small, lanky figure with dark hair climbs into the trash bin beside me, I know it's a boy.

"Thought I heard something," he says. "Trash scraps don't usually talk."

"It hurts." I whimper.

He grasps my hand and eases me out of the trash bin into tall grass and moonlight. Above me, purple clouds fill the sky. Thunder rumbles, and lightning flashes.

"They got you good around your eye." The boy touches a hand to my throbbing temple.

I flinch away from him a little. I don't even know who he is. "Who did?"

"Those boys at school, right? I heard them talking about messing with you earlier. I tried to find you, but I guess I got here too late."

I scrunch up my face. There are boys at school who laugh at me and call me things like "Shorty." And they were mad earlier when I solved a math equation intended for someone twice our age in forty-seven seconds, but I can't remember them attacking me and throwing me in here.

The boy frowns at me. "You don't remember?"

I shake my head.

His forehead creases with worry. "You must've hit your head pretty hard."

I just stare at him. He stares back, his eyes wide and round, the color of a dark sky brimming with stars.

"I'm Logan, by the way," he says.

I realize I've been holding my breath, and let it out. "I'm Clementine."

"I know." He smiles. "They talk about you at school." His gaze shifts to my left ear, to the curls clumping beneath it. He sighs, reaches out, and touches them. I flinch again, but when his fingers pull away, they have blood on them.

My eyes widen. I touch the same spot with my own two fingers and feel a warm wetness.

"Here, I'll walk you home," Logan says softly. "Think you can walk fast enough that we can avoid the cam-bots?"

I swallow hard. "My legs are all right. Just my head hurts."

He nods, his forehead creasing with concern. He pulls me to my feet. "I'll help you clean off that blood too. Don't want those boys thinking they won their fight, eh?"

I shake my head. His hand squeezes mine into his grasp, and we step away from the garbage bin toward the street. "Thanks, by the way," I say.

His smile is crooked.

Moving through the door into the room with the podium is like stepping into a dream. Claps and cheers echo in my ears from the small audience. They're all standing, watching us Extractions enter.

My face warms and my palms grow sweaty. Bright yellow light flashes in my eyes. I blink to make the dots go away, and bump into the Extraction girl in front of me by accident.

"Sorry," I mumble.

Governor Preston steps forward to greet me. "Congratulations," he says with a kind smile. His gloved hand closes around mine in a firm grip.

"Thank you." I manage not to stutter the words.

He smiles wider. Another flash of yellow comes from behind him, from one of the cam-bots documenting the ceremony.

He moves on, but it isn't over yet. Bodies jostle me from every direction. It seems all the people in the audience want to shake my hand. Instructors, doctors, nurses, and officials too. People I've never spoken to or even seen before smile at me like we've been friends since birth.

I smile as best I can. But the walls close in tighter with every passing moment, and my heart rate quickens and my throat tightens.

I don't want to be here. I want to be outside where Logan's waiting. These people are stealing too much time away from me.

I notice Cadet Waller near the podium, looking as impatient as I feel. She speaks fast into an ear-comm, though I can't hear what she's saying.

Behind her, a small CorpoBot screen in the back corner of the room plays through the portraits of the new Extractions again. It shows not only our pictures, but the pictures of those chosen to-night in the ceremonies in Crust, Mantle, and Lower. Fourteen from each outer sector.

I stare at their faces and wonder who they are. I wonder why the Developers picked them.

I wonder why they picked me too, but didn't choose Laila. Or Grady. Or Logan.

Rain smacks the pavement outside. I move through the exit doors with the rest of the group, led by Cadet Waller and an entourage of guards. Cadet Waller said a transport will arrive any minute to take us to the departure bay.

My heart knocks against my rib cage. I swallow hard. I need to find Logan before the transport gets here. I need to say good-bye to him.

He's supposed to be waiting outside the door, but he isn't.

There's a big, loud crowd ahead, separated from us by a security rope and a line of officials. All the kids from the camp who came to watch the ceremony on the CorpoBots are still here, waiting to catch a glimpse of us. To say good-bye.

But something's not right. People are shoving against the security line. People are shouting—shouting at *us*. Like they think we're the ones who stole their spots away. Which I guess is true, but I can't believe they'd act like this with so many guards around.

The officials amplify their voices with their helmets so everyone can hear their orders over the noise: "Everyone, stay back. Do not touch the rope. Do not fight us or you will be sent to quarantine. You will be replaced."

"Let's stay close to the building, Extractions," Cadet Waller shouts over the noise.

Our escort guards push us away from the security line. I'm knocked back with the others.

The panic starts to rise, churning to a boil in my stomach. This shouldn't be happening. People have been angry after the ceremony before, but never this bad.

I need to see into the crowd. I have to find Logan. He can't disappear like this, with no warning.

The *whir* of an engine reaches my ears. My stomach flips as I turn toward the sound. The hovercraft speeds toward us from down the street, arriving much too soon. I need more minutes. I need more hours.

I turn back to the crowd again, fear and adrenaline coursing through my veins. I won't get on the transport yet. Not until I find him.

There's a smack in the crowd a few feet away from me. A scream pierces the air.

A guard steps out of my way, and I see an official beating a girl's head in with the butt of his pulse rifle.

She crumples in the gravel with blood pooling in her hair.

I'm gaping and shaking and screaming *no no no no no no* inside my head.

Everything falls apart. All the kids rush forward, slamming into the officials and knocking over the security rope. There are gunshots. Cadet Waller yells something. Guards scramble in front of me to block the kids from reaching me and the other Extractions.

I think they might want me dead, even though the Developers picked me and the official beat that girl's head in. I think they might kill me if they get close enough.

Someone knocks into me and I fall, my knees scraping the asphalt. I need a second to recover, but I don't have a second. Everyone's going to trample me if I don't get up.

I push off the asphalt, blinking fast to see what's happening through the rain. The guards are trying to create a new security perimeter. Cadet Waller's trying to steer the Extractions toward the hovercraft, which can't reach us anymore because there are too many people blocking its path.

My eyes water, blending with the rain. I can't get on the hovercraft yet. I can't. I can't. I need Logan. I can't leave without saying good-bye because I don't know if I'll ever see him again, or when.

Cadet Waller's voice reaches my ears—a shout of "Get on board. Hurry!"

Instinct pulls me in one direction. My legs carry me in another.

I slip under a guard's arm and into the crowd, letting it swallow me whole. Hopefully, I'll blend in. Hopefully, no one will recognize me. This is reckless and stupid and maybe it means the ship to the Core will leave without me, and I'll lose my spot on it, but this is too important.

Logan is too important.

Rain lashes against my face. More gunshots go off somewhere behind me. I don't look to see who went down.

I reach the part of the crowd where kids aren't trying to fight anyone. They're terrified instead. They're running away, tripping over each other.

I duck under people's arms and look frantically around for Logan's face. I blink tears out of my eyes and pretend they're part of the storm.

Where are you, where are you?

I'm almost to the other side of the crowd when I think I hear someone call my name. But there's too much screaming for me to tell where it came from. And I can't see anyone but the people right near me. I hate how short I am.

Thunder roars in the background. I count three seconds, and look up as lightning fills the sky. There's so much acid above the atmospheric shield, the bits of the moon I glimpse through the rain clouds look like they're on fire.

I'm always afraid when I look at the shield that I'm going to see some of the acid getting through, because it does sometimes. Scientists built the shield with strong ion particles to deflect the acid, since our ozone layer stopped doing that. But over time, the shield particles weaken and have to be replaced. I've heard of cases where some adult died from acid corrosion before the shield was fixed, their skin burned away by small amounts of gas that got through the shield. The adults try to keep it quiet, but word gets around.

It's one more reason we all want to escape the Surface.

I keep pushing forward, toward the road perpendicular to this one, where the crowd isn't so thick.

"Clementine!" someone yells.

I spin around, and Logan's there, shoving past two people to reach me. I fall into his arms. He's trembling.

"You have to go back," he says. "You have to get on that shuttle."

"I can't yet. I can't leave you."

"You have to."

"It's not safe, though." Officials are shooting kids over by the security rope. I might end up in the crossfire.

"Clementine . . ."

"Please. We can hide somewhere until the street clears out. The group won't leave without me," I say, ignoring how my heartbeat trips over the last sentence. Silently, I plead that I'm right. That they won't leave me behind.

Logan sighs, but his body relaxes a little. I'm pretty sure that means he's giving in.

I grab his hand. There's an alleyway nearby. We hurry over to it and slip inside, splashing in puddles in the dirt.

We wait until we're far down, around a corner and out of sight of the crowd before we stop. The other end of the alley is just ahead.

Logan lets go of my hand to lean against the wall and catch his breath. I run my shaky hands over the goose bumps on my arms. I look back in the direction we came from, toward where the Extractions were boarding the hovercraft.

Please, please, please don't leave without me. Please notice I'm missing.

Logan's eyes lift to meet mine. His face is unreadable; his lips are slightly parted.

My throat feels tight. It hurts when I swallow. I squeeze my eyes shut, taking a shaky breath. "This isn't fair."

He makes an odd, sad sort of laugh. "No, it's not."

"They should've picked you last year."

He shakes his head and stares off into the distance. "I'm not Promising enough."

I clench my fists in anger. "That's not true."

In my eyes, Logan has always been intelligent, obedient, and strong, all the qualities that go into a person's Promise and make a child useful to the Developers. But they don't agree. I bet they think his limp is too much of a weakness, which makes me want to throw things. Logan was born with his limp. He can't help it.

"I don't care what they think." I wipe rainwater out of my eyes. "You *are* Promising. They're idiots for not picking you."

"They know what they're looking for, and it's not someone like me. It's you." He steps forward and brushes his fingertips against mine.

"Once I'm down there I'll make them take you," I say fiercely.

That's what I *have* to do. I'll work my way to the top of Core society and convince the Developers that Logan is Promising enough, that they need him down there. I'll force them to make an exception. I won't let him die.

"That's a nice thought," Logan says, "but don't get too hung up on it."

I stare at him. "You don't believe me."

"I believe you'll try."

"I'll try and try and keep trying until it happens. I promise."

The corner of his mouth twitches, and something soft and sad fills his eyes. He lifts his hand and touches the scar on my jawline. I hold my breath, unsure what he's doing.

Slowly, his finger moves downward, gentle on my skin, and traces my collarbone. Eyes locked on mine, he takes one more step closer. My stomach drops and flutters in the same motion.

Feet crunch on dirt.

Logan's head snaps in the direction of the sound, to my left, back down the alleyway. We hear more crunches over the soft patter of rain; someone is coming. My body tenses. Inside I want to scream. Why is there always something?

A figure steps around the corner, followed by three others. Three boys and a girl with black hair, short and jagged.

One of the boys, I've known forever. Or I thought I knew him. Now I'm not so sure.

"Grady?" Logan says his name first.

7

Grady clutches a fragment of steel that might've come from a train track. His hands shake. An odd, mad look flickers across his face.

Nellie takes a step toward us, twirling her own weapon. Her lips curl into a smile.

One of these four must've seen me in the crowd. They saw us slip into this alleyway, and followed.

"Did you change your mind, Clementine?" Nellie asks. "Did you realize you don't deserve to be an Extraction?"

I press my lips together. She doesn't deserve an answer.

"What are you doing here?" Logan asks.

"We're here for her," Carter says. "Step aside, and we won't hurt you."

"I was asking Grady," Logan says.

"What do you think?" Grady's voice is hoarse. His raw, red eyes find mine. "The backup plan. Remember?"

My eyes cling to the steel weapon in his hand: a piece of the train track Nellie said they planned to use against the adults and the officials if they weren't picked for Extraction. But there are no adults here. There are no officials or cam-bots in this alleyway.

There's only me and Logan.

I clench my hands into fists so they won't tremble. I can tell by the look in Grady's eyes and the scowls on Carter's and Larry's faces that they blame me for stealing one of the spots. Even though they should blame the Developers.

"You think killing me will save you?" I ask, trying to keep my voice steady. "Because it won't."

"You don't deserve what you won more than any of us," Larry spits. "Why should we let you leave?"

"Grady, why are you with them?" Logan asks angrily.

Grady's bottom lip trembles, but he doesn't answer.

Nellie speaks for him. "He's never fit in with you, that's what he told me. He said you two are one thing and he's always sepa-rate, so why should he care what happens to her? She doesn't even care that he didn't get picked." She shakes her head at me.

My mouth has fallen open. "Of course I care—"

"Then why didn't you say something?" Grady cries. Tears spill from his eyes, and he's shaking so badly the weapon looks like it'll slip from his hand any second now. "You didn't even look for me earlier. I called your name in the processing building, and you didn't answer."

"What?" I ask. "I didn't hear you, Grady. I didn't—I didn't mean . . ."

But he's right. I was so worried about myself and about Logan, I didn't spare even a second to worry about him. Not even after the brain scans. But I shake my head, as if that will make it less true.

"Besides," Grady says, his voice growing steadier, "if you're gone, that'll open a spot. That'll open a spot for someone like me."

"No, it won't." I choke on the words, shaking my head fast. "They'll whip you for killing me. They'll send you to quarantine."

But would they? Would the Developers really care if they lost me? There are plenty of others who must've been almost as Promising. They could easily replace me.

"You won't kill her. I won't let you," Logan says, moving so he's a foot in front of me. I grab hold of his arm, afraid he might do something stupid.

"We'll blame him." Carter jabs a finger in Logan's direction.

"Notice how no one's here yet?" Nellie says to me. "If they really cared about you, wouldn't they have noticed you left right away and come looking?"

"There's still a riot going on, in case you forgot," I say, though my heart can't seem to find its normal rhythm.

She's right; they might get to the departure bay and leave without me. They might decide I'm not worth finding.

Please don't, please don't, please don't.

"Logan, leave." Grady swallows. "I don't want to hurt you, but I will if I have to."

"You think we can't fight you?" Logan says, his voice hard.

"There are four of us." Larry snorts. "And we aren't crippled."

"I'm serious." Grady's voice is anxious. "I'm giving you one more shot."

"Logan, you should go," I say. "I don't want you to get hurt for me."

"It'd be nice if you'd make this easy for us," Nellie says, closing the gap between us. "Taking care of two dead bodies might be a bit harder than one."

"Go," Logan says to me.

"What—" I start.

He shoves me to his right. Nellie makes for me, while the other three charge at Logan. He doesn't even try to get out of the way.

Someone's fist collides with his jaw. I scream.

Nellie gets in my face. She brings her weapon down, but I grab hold of her wrist. She snarls and wraps her other hand around what she stole from the train track. I don't have enough strength to stop her, so I let go and duck aside. A sharp bit of steel scrapes my cheek.

I slam my knuckles into her stomach. She groans and falters, giving me time to see Logan on his side in the gravel. Carter and Larry laugh as they kick him, while Grady mostly watches. With every grunt and slam, my heart shatters into a million pieces.

"Let him go!" I yell. "It's me you want, isn't it?"

Nellie lashes at me again. I jump out of her way, turning and racing toward the end of the alley.

"Get her!" Nellie shrieks.

Blood pounds in my temple as I run to draw them away from him. The rain makes it hard for me to see, but this street seems empty. I gnash my teeth together. Where are cam-bots and officials when I need them?

When I glance over my shoulder, relief fills me. They've left Logan in the alley. They're following me instead. Nellie, Carter, Larry, and Grady. The boy who I thought was my friend, who wants to kill me because he's selfish and afraid.

I stumble around a street corner, past a CorpoBot still showing the portraits of the newly chosen. A dark restricted building lies across the empty plaza. Made of glass and iron crossbeams, it towers over my head. Lightning flashes in the clouds, lighting up the rooftop.

A thrill of excitement rushes through me, mingling with my worry. All my life I've dreamed of scaling one of these buildings. They're so much taller than the shacks I'm used to climbing. But I bet I can climb this, if I try. Who cares if I break a million rules? I'm faster at climbing than I am at running. And if those four are really set on murdering me, this could save my life. That should be a good enough excuse.

I force my feet to move until I reach a spot to the right of the building entrance. The lowest iron beam attached to the glass becomes a handhold. I heave and swing my legs onto the beam, which is wide enough that I could probably sit on it without falling, if it weren't wet.

My footing isn't as solid as I'd like. But I reach for the next beam anyway, gasping for breath.

This is dangerous in the dark, especially with the beams slippery because of the rain. There are spare lights from the surrounding buildings, and light from the moon, but it's hard to see details. Even when I squint I can't see many cracks in the steel. But I'll have to manage.

Nellie and her gang stumble to a stop below me when I'm on the fourth beam, a good twenty feet off the ground.

"One of you go after her, will you?" Nellie pushes Grady toward the wall.

He sticks his weapon between his teeth and pulls himself onto the first beam. After he's up, he glances at me, his cheeks pale. I smirk as I get to my feet, though I feel a little sorry for him. He's afraid of heights, and he's always been a terrible climber.

"Bet you I can get to the top!" I shout.

"Bet your life, you mean," Nellie says.

"Sure thing."

She doesn't say anything to that. I take a breath and focus on my game. I don't know that there's any speed record to beat, but if there is, I'm going to beat it.

The seventh beam is a little harder; it's diagonal and slippery, and my fingers grope for a crevice or hold. I feel cracks here and there, but I can't see them, and most seem too small. I grasp one anyway and start to heave myself up.

My foot slips—

The bottom of my stomach drops out—

My fingers fumble and catch a bigger crack. I pull myself up, shaking, until I reach the flatter part. Below me, Nellie snarls in agitation.

The higher I climb, the more the icy wind and the rain rip at my curls. I glance down and my stomach squeezes. It's a long drop to the street. One slip and I'll turn to pulp in the gravel. I wonder if any kid has ever made Extraction and died before getting to see the Core, before getting a taste of safety.

I wonder again if Cadet Waller and the Extractions already made it to the departure bay, if they're going to leave without me.

My throat tightens, and I clench my teeth hard to keep from crying. I shouldn't have run away and gone looking for Logan.

But I had to. I never would've forgiven myself otherwise.

Five beams higher, I glance at the ground and pause, catching my breath and trying desperately not to think about the drop. My feet fit on the beam so I can stand, but just barely. I cling to a panel of glass by the tips of my fingers.

Below me, Grady has given up. Carter is taking his place.

I don't see Logan. I hope he's all right.

I'm about to continue up the ledges when I realize Carter isn't climbing anymore, either. He's scrambling back down to the street.

I hear a faint voice—Nellie, maybe. Before I can guess what she might've said, she's running. Carter hops down into the gravel.

He and the others race to my left, not the way we came but down a different road. They disappear around a corner.

Two officials stalk into view from around the corner we came from, their helmets casting green light in the dark. I lean instinctively into the glass. A cam-bot hovers beside them, its fake eyes two pinpoints of red.

"Is someone up there?" an official calls. His helmet magnifies his voice.

I'm frozen on the iron foothold, my heart knocking against my ribs. I wanted someone to come, but now I'm not sure anymore. I'm hanging off a restricted building and my attackers have disappeared, taking proof of the incident with them. These officials might not believe my story. They might not recognize me as an Extraction.

They might send me straight to quarantine.

Four more figures round the street corner before I decide what to do. One is a woman with a high ponytail and scarlet uniform dress, and two male officials are leading a boy who limps with every step.

Logan.

"Citizen S68477, we know you're up there," the first official says, his voice rank with annoyance.

They know. Logan must've told them. But what will they do when they catch me? The air I'm sucking into my lungs is cold, too cold for me to think properly.

Two fierce spotlights flood the gravel road, originating from the cam-bot's fake eyes. They hit the glass far below me and run along the iron beams.

I don't know if I can trust the officials. I just don't know.

So I do what feels natural: I keep climbing. I reach for the beam above and heave myself up with fumbling fingers.

I'm barely seven beams higher and getting to my feet when the floodlights from the cam-bot reflect off the glass in front of me, blinding me. I gasp and squeeze my eyes shut, clutching the window. My foot almost slipped just then. I almost fell.

"Stay where you are," the official says.

I open an eye. The lights flit away from me, so they're not blinding me anymore. I can see the ground below me again, so very far. There are more people down there: officials and even some adults who look like they just stumbled out of bed.

They're so far below me. I'm afraid to move an inch. I don't want to slip; I don't want to fall. I don't want to be up this high anymore.

A loud *whirring* reaches my ears. From around the street corner, a silver ball lifts into the air, its rotors spinning a cloud of dust.

A flight pod, come to rescue me. I hope; I plead.

I hold my breath as it nears my beam. I wish I'd climbed all the way to the top of the building, so I wouldn't be sitting here worrying about how I'm going to get from here into the flight pod without splattering in the gravel.

The side door zips open, and an official reaches his gloved hand out. "You'll have to jump," he shouts over the rotors.

I take two seconds. I take two breaths, and pretend the gap between me and the doorway is a centimeter instead of two feet.

I jump with a cry into the pod and stumble when my feet touch the ground. The patrol catches me as the door slides shut, silencing the wind's roar.

I expect him to release me right away, but he doesn't. His arms tighten around my shaking body, pulling me against his chest. It feels wrong.

"You all right?" he asks. "Those kids didn't hurt you, did they? I'll make sure they're sent to quarantine if they did."

My body tenses. He knows about my attackers. Logan must've told them what happened.

"I'm fine," I say, pulling away. "And they were just messing around—you don't have to send them to quarantine." *Please don't,* I want to add. They did hurt Logan, and Carter and Larry used to bully me all the time, but they don't deserve to die. Especially not Grady.

"Well, we'll see if they have other infractions," the official says. The slits in his helmet are open, and I can see his eyes. I've never seen an official's eyes before. They're wide with relief, almost a smile, and seem more youthful than I expected. He's maybe twenty-three or twenty-four.

"I'm vruxing glad you're fine," he says. "Commander Charlie would've blasted us all if you'd ended up dead."

The pod jolts me as it lands in the gravel. I clutch a ceiling strap like the ones we hang on to in the hovercraft, frowning at him. He means Charlie the Developer: the leader of our planet, who goes by the title of commander to set him apart from the other four Developers. But it seems rash for this patrol to assume Commander Charlie would kill his soldiers because they let me die.

"Before you go," the official says, "can I ask how you climbed so high?"

The pod door zips open. He slips his hand around the upper part of my arm to lead me out into the moonlight.

"I don't know, I just did," I say, distracted. I need to find Logan.

Cadet Waller steps in front of me. "Are you hurt anywhere?" she asks.

I shake my head. She observes me for a moment, her eyes narrowed slightly and her cheeks pinched, as if she doesn't believe me. Or maybe she doesn't believe whatever story she heard. But her face softens and she sighs, pulling me into a hug that feels a bit awkward. "I'm so sorry you got separated from us, sweetie. Everyone else is waiting at the departure bay. Do you need anything before we join them?"

Over her shoulder, I see Logan standing there. His arm is scraped and bloody, and the dirt running in a band along his jaw looks too much like my scar. I want to strangle Nellie and those boys.

Logan gives me a pained smile.

I close my eyes for a moment and take a breath. "I think I'm okay," I say.

"Great." Cadet Waller pulls away from me. "Let's get going, then."

I chew on my lip as she turns to say something to one of the officials.

"Wait," I say, and she stops. I hesitate once more. "Would . . . would it be all right if Logan comes with us? He could see me off at the shuttle bay."

Cadet Waller frowns a deep frown that forms several creases in her forehead. She opens her mouth to reply.

"Please," I add quickly.

She presses her lips into a line. She sighs and rubs the crease between her eyebrows. "All right. But he's not allowed far inside the station. You'll have to say goodbye near the entrance."

I nod, though that doesn't sound like enough time at all. I'm not sure there will ever be enough time. "Thank you."

She steps past me. "Well, come along, then, We'll take this pod to the station."

Logan glances at me, his eyes still weary, but focused now too. He knows this will be it.

I grab his hand as I turn back to the pod, so for a few minutes at least, I won't lose him.

8

The departure bay is abuzz with noise. Announcements play in an almost endless stream over the intercom.

"For Crust departures, please report to Terminal A. . . . All flight personnel, please check in with a commanding officer. . . . For Mantle departures, please report to Terminal B. . . ."

And so on.

We pause in the entrance terminal, near a counter with signs that read LUGGAGE COLLECTION and FLIGHT CHECK-IN. The place is darker than I'd expect, with dim red and blue lights flashing on the walls. Someone pushes through the door to the main terminal ahead, and I glimpse steam, ships, and personnel.

Cadet Waller glances at me and Logan. "I'll give you two a moment. Make it quick."

She snaps her fingers at the two officials who accompanied us inside, and they all move away toward the check-in counter. Cadet Waller speaks fast into her earpiece.

Logan turns to me, and every muscle stands out in his body.

His eyes are bluish-gray, starry-night and never-ending. They make my stomach squeeze.

"It's okay," he whispers.

"But it's not."

He'll die up here once I'm gone. They'll work him too hard. They'll take things from him he might not get back.

Unless I find a way to save him. If there's a way, I *will* find it. I'm Promising now, which means people might listen to me. The Developers might listen, if when the time comes that I'm allowed to pick a job, I pick one that will get me closer to them.

I'll convince them to make an exception. I'll do whatever it takes.

I take deep breaths to keep my eyes from watering.

Logan sighs and pulls me into his arms. I feel his heart beating fast through his wet shirt. "You'll love it down there," he says softly. "It'll be even better than we imagined."

Even if it isn't better, there isn't any choice for me here. The Developers picked me for Extraction and they didn't pick Logan. I have to live with that now. Unless . . .

"What if . . ." I swallow. "What if I stayed? What if we found some way to run, instead? What if we broke into the security hub and took down the force field and got out and found somewhere to hide—"

"Clementine, shh. We can't break into the security hub."

He's right; it would be near impossible. There must be a thousand security codes required to get inside. Not to mention all the systems we'd have to sort through to find the activation center for the force-field fence around the settlement, and all the skill it would take to shut it down. And that's without taking into account the officials who guard the hub 24-7.

A sound breaks free of my mouth, half a sob, half a sound of annoyance. I clench the bottom of Logan's shirt in my hands. "It's not *fair*. They're going to hurt you."

"Please don't be scared for me." He hugs me tighter. "You're leaving, you got that? You're getting out of here. There's nowhere else to go."

He's right, but that doesn't lessen the tightness in my throat. That doesn't make me feel any better about leaving him.

"Down there"—Logan pauses to take a shaky breath, and pulls away to cup my face in his hands—"you'll have a lot more opportunity. You should use it, since the rest of us can't. You should figure out how to change things on the Surface and in the other outer sectors."

"You think that's possible?"

Logan's thumb brushes my cheek. His hands are callused from fieldwork, but they feel gentle on my skin. "If anyone can do it, it's you."

I'm not sure he's right about that. Maybe I'm good with numbers and science, maybe I'm a fast climber, but I'm no smarter than anyone else who's ever lived. There've been hundreds of rebels in the past who've tried to change the system. They all failed. Rebellion is the reason the Developers make us live like slaves in the first place.

"I'll try," I say, "but you have to promise you won't do anything stupid. Don't rebel, don't try to run, just get through like we always have. I'm going to try to convince the Developers to make an exception for you."

His hands drop away from my face. "I said don't worry about me, Clementine."

"Promise me you won't do anything crazy." *Please don't kill yourself*, I mean. He knows what I mean; I can see it in his eyes.

But he doesn't answer. I wonder if I was right to bring up that option. Now, even if he says it won't be one for him, I won't know if I believe him. I'll always worry that he'll wake up one morning and decide he's done fighting.

I swallow hard. "Please promise."

"I promise I won't," he says quietly. "As long as there's any chance I might see you again, I won't. But that's all I'll promise."

"I'll save you, okay?" I wipe the tears off my cheeks. "I'll make the Developers save you."

"Okay," he says, but I can tell he doesn't believe me. He's trying to make me feel better, but he thinks he's going to die no matter what I do.

I have to prove him wrong.

The sound of someone else's breathing comes from behind me. "Time to go," Cadet Waller says.

Logan closes his eyes for a brief moment and nods. The two officials step over and place their hands on his shoulder.

"I guess I'll see you," Logan says.

It feels like a million needles are sticking into my skin, all over my body. But I force myself to nod.

Logan starts to turn away.

"Wait!" I say.

He pauses. I don't know what I'm doing. But I rush forward anyway and throw my arms around his waist. He pulls me closer to him, so close it's like he's trying to mold us together. He smells like musk and rain and hope. He feels like safety.

Without thinking, without realizing what I'm doing, I tilt my chin up to find his lips. Something feverish registers in his eyes.

His mouth moves to mine, and our lips brush. The particles between them are charged. Lightning shoots up every inch of my body.

Hands pull him out of my grip. Water blurs my eyes.

"I'm sorry, but he has to go," Cadet Waller says.

"I won't leave." I reach for Logan again.

"You have to," he says, blinking hard as the officials pull him away, toward the entrance doors. "I'll be fine."

The doors open. The officials pull him outside, into the rainy moonlight.

"No, you won't be." I should run to him. But my legs shake when I try to walk.

"Don't forget me, Clementine." The doors start to slide shut, and his voice becomes urgent. "If you don't know already, you should know, I—"

Closing steel drowns his words. His face is lost through the glass and the rain.

I know what he was going to say. I stumble to the doors. I don't care anymore. I don't care whether I get to leave or not; I can't leave him.

A hand closes around my arm. Cadet Waller.

I try to pull away from her, but she only grips me tighter. "Clementine, please. Control yourself," she snaps.

I stop fighting her. After a moment, she lets go of me. I stare at the doors and send my *sorrys* through them.

Cadet Waller shakes her head at me. "Come along. Everyone's waiting."

Tears stream down my cheeks as I follow her.

I run a shaky hand down the length of my arm and try to breathe. I have to escape because it's the only option for me—and also for him. It's the only way I might convince the Developers to save him too.

I will return for him. I will save him. I won't forget him or the feel of his fingers lingering on my skin.

He used to say he'd never leave me alone, not ever. Now I'm leaving him.

✕

I sit in my seat inside a rumbling hovercraft, the words *It's going to be okay* playing over and over in my head.

The ship is small and sleek from the outside. Inside, there are passenger seats behind the cockpit: six rows with three seats each on either side of the aisle, and luggage compartments overhead. But the compartments are empty. We don't own any possessions but the clothes on our back and the shoes on our feet.

After leaving the departure bay, we flew through a short tunnel that looked like nothing but gray streaks through the windows. Then we headed down into the Pipeline, the underground passage through the center of Kiel. I thought I'd fall out of my seat at first, we were moving so fast.

Now the ship doesn't jostle me as much. My seat straps hold me steady. I clutch the armrests and glue my eyes to the backs of the seats in front of me, and take deep breaths so I won't feel nauseated.

The Extractions in the other rows are chattering and laughing, talking about what the Core will be like. I've seen all of them in classes before, but they're not my friends. I don't usually talk to them.

The girl beside me is quiet, sifting through her long strands of blond hair with her fingers and running her teeth over her bottom lip. I don't really know her, either, but I recognize her from the fields yesterday. She's the girl who didn't run or even scream during the test. Ariadne.

There's a crackle, and Cadet Waller's voice comes over the ship-com. She's sitting with the pilots in the cockpit. "We're entering Crust, Extractions," she says. "We'll slow so you can catch a glimpse of it."

Holding my breath, I risk a glance out the window. Now there are lights on the metal walls outside: red, green, yellow, and purple. They're a blur at first, but they become clearer as the pilot slows the hovercraft.

Abruptly, the metal walls fall away and are replaced by glass. There's a dust-filled room beyond it with a rocky floor, though the way we're traveling, the floor is sideways. An official stands with a pulse rifle in hand. Pathways beyond him lead into tunnels made of the same grimy, blackening rock as the floor.

We pass another window that shows us more rocky pathways, and then another. These must be the coal mines, or near them. The parentless children in the Crust work camp collect the coal, which is Kiel's major energy source. They spend their days choking on dust and fire smoke in the mines. They spend their nights in cramped, rocky caves with no fresh air, while the adults of Crust live in the comfort and safety of steel walls in their underground city.

I don't envy Crust kids. Their home is worse than the Surface, where at least we can see the stars and pretend there's someplace better out there.

But I guess they're lucky in one respect: They don't have to fear the moon.

The Pipeline glass is replaced by metal walls with flashing lights again. "We're now approaching Mantle," Cadet Waller says over the ship-com. "Its biggest weapons manufacturing facility will be visible through the windows."

I see it in seconds: a facility filled with massive machinery and steam. I glimpse the dirty, wearied faces of the child workers. I bet the machines make noise all night—constant, high-pitched squealing. The kids probably fall asleep to it. I wonder if they have bunk rooms, or just blankets on the floor. Or no blankets at all.

It's hard to believe, but a thousand years ago, none of these sectors existed. Everyone lived on the Surface in three large settlements: one near the mountains, one near the desert, one near the ocean. When pollution weakened the ozone layer, and the moon's acid began seeping through, the scientists proposed underground expansion. There was nowhere else to go. The research facilities in the Surface cities offered some protection, but they couldn't hold all the citizens.

So the lower sectors were constructed, along with the acid shield. The planet became more like a spaceship underground. The scientists who led Project Rebuild were elected as the new government leaders, and they called themselves Developers.

"We're now approaching Lower," Cadet Waller says over the ship-com.

The textile factories appear through the window. This time, I avert my eyes. I don't like seeing the workers. They remind me of Logan and Grady. Some of them took the test this year too. They fought for escape just like me.

But they didn't win.

The windows disappear, and the Pipeline lights flash by. My heartbeat picks up with every passing second. My veins tangle. My lungs constrict.

Lower is the last sector before the Core, which means we're almost there.

I dig my fingernails into my legs when the ship-com crackles on again. "We've just entered the Core sector," Cadet Waller says, and an excited murmur slides down the rows of passenger seats. "We should reach the flight port in approximately five minutes."

Sixteen years I've spent fighting for this. Sixteen years I've spent longing for it, and now I'm sitting here and I can't breathe, and I wish I had more time to prepare myself.

I'm scared nothing is going to change. I'm scared everything is going to be different.

The hovercraft's engine stutters. We slow and fly into a tunnel horizontal to the Pipeline, and I grip my seat's armrests. Streaks of gray show through the windows. A blur of red lights comes into focus as the ship lowers onto a port dock.

The steel door at the back of the hovercraft slides open. Our seat belts unlatch automatically, while Cadet Waller emerges from the cockpit and rattles off commands, things like "Please walk carefully" and "Let's make sure our behavior is appropriate."

I'm half listening. I'm half shaking.

I tell myself, "It's going to be fine here," and, "You have to get up now; you have to walk; you have to be brave."

The other Extractions giggle nervously, standing and making their way off the back ramp, touching the seats they pass to steady themselves. Beside me, Ariadne pushes out of her seat with each of her eyes the size of the moon. I have to follow her or I'll be the only person left on the ship, besides the pilot.

So I do.

9

The night after Laila was taken to quarantine, Logan and I climbed to the roof of my shack. We lay up there watching the stars shimmer beyond the shield. Logan's arms were around me, and my head was buried in his shoulder. I'd used up all my tears already.

"Maybe she's the wind now," Logan said. "Maybe she's making us cold and laughing because we don't know it."

I almost smiled. I could see her doing that, if it were possible.

"She's not, Logan."

"You don't know that."

"I do."

"Well, maybe she's not. But she is safer now."

A hovercraft flew by overhead, heading somewhere beyond the force-field fence. "I guess so."

"You'll be safe someday too," Logan said, pulling me closer.

"When I die?"

"No, someone will fly you away before then. Wait and see."

"They'd better fly you away too."

"If they don't, you'd better come back and visit. You'd better tell me all about it so I can pretend I'm safer too."

I shook my head. "They can't take me without you."

"You still have to promise," he said.

"Fine. I promise."

It's harder to breathe underground. I know I'm sucking enough air into my lungs because I don't feel faint, but I clench my fists with every rise and fall of my chest. I taste air that's too sweet and smells like antiseptic.

I hope this will get easier.

"This is the flight port, as you already know," Cadet Waller says, gesturing to the deck around us. Red and orange lights flash everywhere. Steam spouts from vents in the floor here and there, blocking much of the hangar from view, but it seems massive. There are ships bigger than the hovercraft to my left, and a row of smaller flight pods to my right.

I glimpse a man in an orange worker's suit over by the flight pods. He holds a hand over his eyes. I think he might be staring at the group of us.

"Follow me," Cadet Waller says. "The Extractions from the other sectors are in the Pavilion. Commander Charlie is waiting for us to begin the welcome ceremony."

She leads us across the port—I glimpse two more workers along the way—and through a set of sliding doors into a hallway. Dim blue lights flicker on the curved ceiling, mixing with translucent colors. They're like stars, but a strange, fake kind of stars.

Of course the stars are fake here. The real ones are a million miles away.

I breathe in through my nose and out through my mouth. It's going to be okay; it's going to be okay.

We follow the same corridor for a long time, as it curves and bends in places. The other Extractions are talking around me. They talk about what our meals will be like, and our beds will be like, and our lives will be like. Cadet Waller explains that we'll divide our days between the various divisions of the Core. There are five primary ones, each devoted to a different facet of daily life. Nourishment is home to the kitchens and cafeterias; Slumber contains the living apartments; Training is where people receive education and job training; Invention is where most job centers, especially the science-related ones, are located; and Recreation offers fun and relaxation.

We're on one of the first floors of Invention Division right now, a few levels above Restricted Division, the sixth and final division. The core of the Core. It houses the Developers and their control rooms. It's the one place we're not allowed to go.

I learned most of this a long time ago in school, so I don't really listen. I count the doorways and elevator landings and stairwells we pass. I count the lights dotting the walls. I count the number of tiles on the stark white ceiling—278 so far.

I can't make sense of this place. It looks like just another building. It looks like just another skyscraper on the Surface with a hundred corridors and a hundred rooms, but it smells different and sounds different and feels different—not hot or cold, but somewhere in between. And it goes on forever.

I'm in a never-ending building with no exits.

Finally, we turn left. We take a different corridor, and walk up a flight of stairs, and then down another short corridor. I hear voices ahead—lots and lots of voices.

The doors zip open ahead of us, and we move through them into blinding spotlights. I have to blink and hold my hand over my eyes to make the glare go away.

When it does, I see the pods floating above us. At least, they look sort of like pods, and they would be floating if they weren't attached to the ground by spiral staircases. There are at least a hundred of them filling this massive room. The ones closer to the wall are higher than the others, so the group of them slopes downward like stadium stands. Each pod has about ten seats inside, and each is filled with Core citizens.

I think I've forgotten how not to stare.

I've seen adults before, of course. I've even seen lots of adults together. And I've also seen lots of children together.

But I've never seen lots of adults and children together—not like this, with adults and children together in each pod, when the adults don't look like officials. And the kids resemble some of the adults, and they're smiling and laughing and don't look skinny as sticks.

They're sitting with their families.

Something deep inside me loses a couple stitches. Some part of me that I thought was sewn tight and strong and whole, but now I'm thinking it might not be.

I wonder what it feels like to sit up there in one of those pods and know the woman on your right is your mother, and the man beside her is your father, and the kid next to you is your little sister or your older brother.

I wonder what it feels like to know you belong without having to ask.

Cadet Waller leads us across the floor beneath the viewing pods. The Extractions from the other sectors—fourteen from each—are waiting on the floor beyond the last viewing pod, near the far end of the Pavilion, surrounded by several officials and instructors. Waiting for what sort of welcome, exactly, I don't know.

To distract myself from the fluttery feeling in my stomach, I wonder how the Developers keep enough air in the Core for everyone. It gets recycled, I suppose. Or they grow plants in special laboratories that produce enough oxygen to replenish what people use.

When we reach the other Extractions, I'm pressed into their throng. The heat of their bodies makes me feel trapped. Boys and girls with torn clothes and sweaty palms press in from either side. They look as nervous as I am.

A flicker of light catches my eye on the far wall of the room, about twenty yards away from our group. There's a single glass box over there, about the size of my shack on the Surface. I'm not sure what it's for.

My eyes wander up from the glass box. A last, lone viewing pod juts out from the wall above the box. It's smaller than the others. This one doesn't have a staircase rising from the floor; instead, it's attached to the wall by a short ramp. It looks empty right now.

Above the pod is a large screen on the wall. It shows a faint image, the symbol of the Core: a full moon embossed in bronze.

"There are ten thousand one hundred and ninety-two people here," someone whispers.

I turn. Ariadne, the girl who sat next to me on the hovercraft, is standing beside me. She's scanning each of the viewing pods, her eyes wide, the clearest green I've ever seen.

"Six thousand nine hundred and fifteen adults, and three

thousand two hundred and seventy-seven children," she says, her voice soft, as if she's talking to herself instead of me. "Five thousand one hundred and twenty-seven females, and five thousand and sixty-five males. Two point seven percent are potentially Unstable."

My brows furrow. Is she counting everyone?

"Please quiet down." Cadet Waller hushes us with a hand.

Behind us, the families in the viewing pods quiet too. The lights in the room darken, casting everything in shadow except for the wall screen with the Core symbol. A solitary light comes on—a thin red beam pointed at the viewing pod beneath the wall screen.

A man in a slick navy uniform steps into view, followed by four other figures in white. These must be the five Developers, the descendents of the scientists who headed Project Rebuild. After the Developers quelled the people's rebellion and established the work camps to secure their power, they passed their rule onto their offspring when they died, instead of letting new leaders be elected. They didn't want new blood ruining their system.

The man in the navy uniform is the only one who stands beneath the light. His face and upper torso replace the symbol of the Core on the screen. He's older than I expected, with many creases around his mouth and on his forehead. His hair is a light shade of gray, flowing in waves down to his neck. His cheeks are a bit pale. He wears white gloves, and clasps his hands against his stomach.

Something magnifies his hoarse, cracking voice when he speaks: "Extractions, welcome to the Core."

His eyes are a dull shade, but they burn through the screen, and a stone settles in my stomach.

This must be Commander Charlie, the superior of the five Developers. The leader of the planet. He's the man who decided my fate, who picked death for Logan.

"Some of you," he says, "we picked for your intelligence—for your capacity to understand things the average person cannot, for your potential to become the scientists and physicians we need so desperately. Others we picked for your physical strength—for your stature and your build, for your potential to become the patrolmen we need to keep order and keep everyone safe. We've observed you your whole life, both in the classroom and in the work camps."

I bite my lip, thinking of the cam-bots that monitored us all the time back on the Surface. I wonder how much Commander Charlie has seen of all that footage.

He continues: "Your reactions to the situation you experienced during your Extraction test, as well as the brain scans we collected, were a final checkpoint, an assurance of the qualities we already knew you possessed. We have high hopes that you will offer much to our society."

His words draw applause from the people in the viewing pods, and mutters of relief and excitement from the people around me. But Commander Charlie's lips stretch into a smile that sends an icy shiver down my spine.

When the clapping dies down, he continues, "Of course, you've all come from societies very different from this one. You have much to learn, and many skills that need to be strengthened. Over the next week, you will participate in training sessions that will help with this. They will elevate each area of your Promise— intelligence, strength, and obedience—and raise you to a level of worth that will stay with you for the rest of your lives. We will mold you into perfect citizens. And you will reap the rewards: safety, nourishment, and the freedom to help us decide what your place will be in this society, based on your particular skills.

"Traditionally, Extraction training begins in this room." He gestures below him. "Notice the glass box in front of you."

I glance at the box against the wall. The glass lights up, a soft blue color, that helps me see inside better. It has a metal door at its back wall and a small square of red glass on its front.

"In a moment," Commander Charlie says, "the box won't be empty. Through its back door, two officials will lead in an Unstable, fresh from the Karum treatment facility on the Surface. This is your chance to help us cleanse our society of their dangerous presence. There will be one Unstable for each of you to shoot."

I'm a statue made of steel. He doesn't mean . . . he can't mean . . .

"We strive to cure all Unstables," he says. "We strive to make them better. We do everything within our power, but some people who were once useful to our society endanger us. Some we cannot cure. Hopeless cases . . . must be exterminated. I ask you, my dear Extractions, to assist me in sending them on their departure. It is for the safety of all, and it is an honor."

The Core crowd hoots and hollers.

I don't want to believe him.

"Each of you will receive a gun," he says. "A small part of the box will open, allowing you to aim your gun inside. All you must do is pull the trigger. This will be your first contribution to Core society."

The other Extractions mutter in worry, their faces pale again in the dark. Across the floor, more instructors and officials are descending from a pod stairwell, carrying crates with the guns they'll pass out to us.

"If you refuse to do this," Commander Charlie says, "then it is possible we were mistaken about your Promise. Maybe you are intelligent or physically strong, but if you cannot understand that this is the safe and right thing to do, it's possible you are one of them. It's possible you are Unstable, and therefore a threat to our society." He sighs and rubs his temple. "Regrettably, in the case of your refusal, we will not be able to send you home. An . . . alternative method of departure will have to be used. I truly hope you will make the right decision."

No one says a word. No one moves an inch.

My heart beats fast—fast—faster.

He's going to kill us. I thought he'd send us back to our old sectors. Then I wouldn't be alone anymore. I'd die at twenty, but at least I'd have a couple more years with Logan.

Now I wouldn't have any more years. I would become nothing, because that's what death is. We don't go somewhere better when we die; we go nowhere. We become *nothing*.

I ball my hands into fists. I have to do what he wants. I can't die tonight.

Beside me, tears sparkle in Ariadne's eyes. "It's not fair," she whispers.

I almost ask her what she really expected. Our whole lives have been unfair.

"Let's form a single-file line," Cadet Waller says, directing us to move with the help of the other instructors and the officials.

I don't want to move, but shoulders bump mine and jostle me, separating me from Ariadne. I don't want to kill, not now, not ever. But I have to do this or I'll die.

So will Logan. I won't be able to save him.

Someone presses a gun into my palm. An instructor, I think. She's a young woman with short black hair and a metal stud in her nose. "Don't be scared, sweetie," she says, and smiles.

I swallow, staring at the weapon in my hand. The barrel is thin and dark.

I'll pretend it's fake. I'll pretend this is a dream.

A boy from another sector knocks his shoulder into mine as he gets behind me in line. "Sorry," he says quickly, and gulps. His clean, pale palms are different from the callused fingers of Surface kids.

"Are you nervous?" I ask.

"Aren't you?"

I press my lips together. Give him the slightest nod of my head.

I'm terrified of the guilt, of the ache in my gut, and the shaky hands. Of not being able to breathe because I will have killed someone. I'll have killed a person.

"But . . . we don't have a choice." My voice cracks a little. "We have to do it, even if we're scared. We have to save ourselves."

The boy looks at his gun and doesn't say anything.

The door at the back of the glass box opens, and pain stabs at my chest. Two officials with green light beaming from their helmet visors lead in the first Unstable.

This one is a man, probably middle-aged. Cloth covers his eyes and nose and part of his mouth, but he's bitten through most of it.

Bruises and mud cover his bony legs. His torn clothes reveal places I don't wish to see on anyone. And there is blood: on his fingernails; on his raw, bare feet; and trickling from cuts on his wrists and calves.

Bile threatens to fill my mouth. I swallow again and again to make it go down.

His wrists are already clasped in chains. One of the officials attaches the shackles to a small brass ring in the roof of the compartment, chaining him to the ceiling so he can't move much at all. But he's still trying.

The square of red glass on the front of the box slides to the left, leaving an opening for a gun. I can hear him sobbing.

"Whoever would like to go first may begin," Commander Charlie says. "Impress me."

Please don't make me do this.

The girl at the front of the line waits several moments, then steps aside to let someone take her place.

A boy takes a hesitant step closer to the glass box, lifting his gun to shoot. But his hand shakes. He's too afraid.

I wonder if I should go first. I wonder if I should shove my way to the front, aim, and fire, so I'll be remembered. So I'll prove my obedience in front of everyone and in front of Commander Charlie.

But my feet won't budge.

My hands won't move.

My heart won't stop fluttering.

Crack.

Red splatters all over the glass. My eyes widen.

The shot didn't come from one of the Extractions at the front of the line. It came from a boy standing well off to the side, a solid fifty feet away from the small hole in the glass. Yet he made a perfect shot.

The Unstable inside the box is limp as a wet rag now, hanging from the ceiling by his shackles.

The shooter turns and grins at us, a sly, cocky grin. He's wearing a tight gray suit, a belt with gun holsters, green gloves, and knee-high black boots. His blond hair sticks up a little. His gun still smokes.

"See? That's how you do it," he says.

He must be an official-in-training. That's the only way he could shoot like that, kill like that, and still smile like that.

"Thank you, Sam, for that lovely demonstration," Commander Charlie says on the wall screen, his eyes full of approval. "Extractions, it's your turn. Prove you are Promising."

Cadet Waller and the other instructors move to the front of the line, and direct the kids to begin. They have to wait for an official to bring in a new Unstable first, though. They have to wait for the dead one to be taken away.

I tighten my hold on my gun. I don't want to shoot, but I have to. It's my life or the life of an Unstable.

They're dangerous, anyway. It's like Commander Charlie said: It isn't safe for them to be allowed to live.

One by one, each Extraction in line steps forward, pulls the trigger, and flinches at the gunshot. The glass box turns into a river of red and black chunks. Officials drag bodies away and return with fresh, living ones. The Unstables slip on the bloody floor as they're chained to the brass ring in the ceiling.

People are talking, laughing, cheering in the viewing pods. The sound makes me sick to my stomach.

Ariadne fires. Her arm shakes so badly she nearly drops her weapon. But her fire blasts a man's head to bits. She's led away by an instructor to one of the nearest pods, where all the Extractions are going once they've finished.

The girl in front of me walks away, and it's my turn.

"As soon as your Unstable is inside, you can go ahead," Cadet Waller says to me. Her smile isn't as warm as I'd like it to be; it's full of expectancy.

I hold my breath as two officials bring in a new Unstable. A woman. I stare at the brass ring where her chains will go, afraid to look at her face too closely.

Behind me, the boy with the glasses is breathing loud. Heavy. I risk a glance at him. His face is white as a cotton sheet.

"What's your name?" I ask, to distract myself.

He takes a hoarse breath. "Oliver."

"Clementine, your Unstable is ready," Cadet Waller says.

I take a shaky breath. "Don't think, Oliver."

I take a step forward. Then another, until I'm only three feet away from the hole in the glass.

Gritting my teeth, I raise my weapon. Now I can't help but stare at the face of my Unstable. She's bitten off so much of the cloth, I can see one of her eyes. It's the color of the sky, and tears trickle from its corner. She struggles to get her hands out of the shackles, but they're too strong for her.

I squeeze my eyes shut. I can't do this if I'm looking at her, if she seems real and not dangerous at all.

I have to do this. I've come all this way.

I open one eye, only enough to check that my gun is still aimed at her face through the hole. When I shut it again, I block out her sky blue eye from my mind and focus on the crowd's voices echoing in my ears. My heart's beating a thousand times a minute, and my hands are sweaty, but I have to shoot. It's the only way I'll be allowed to stay here, and that's the only way I might be able to save Logan. I have to save him. I *have* to.

My finger almost slips when I pull the trigger. But not quite.

The shot rings in my ears. The recoil makes me stagger back two steps, breathing fast.

My Unstable screams. I force myself to look at her.

Blood trickles from her side, so the bullet must have grazed her. But she isn't dead. She's slipping out of her shackles somehow. My limbs freeze up.

One of the officials who brought her moves to stop her, but he's not fast enough. She breaks free all the way and half-stumbles, half-lunges for his neck.

Mutters and shouts peal through the crowd. I can't say a word. I can't do anything.

A second shot rings out. Her body slumps to the floor behind the glass. The official tucks his gun back into its holster, looking disgusted.

The crowd all around me is silent. On the balcony, Commander Charlie purses his lips.

I didn't kill her. Someone else did.

He's going to kill me.

"What a shame," Charlie says. "Your fellow Extractions played a key role in the protection of our society, while you failed."

He's going to kill me.

I'm shaking so badly, I don't think it's ever going to stop. This can't be it. This can't be over.

Please.

You have to let me stay.

"Still, your efforts will be rewarded." He gives me an odd smile that doesn't reach his eyes. "You were willing to shoot her, at least."

The crowd goes wild. Relief stills some of my trembling, but not all of it.

"Come on," a voice says. The young woman with the metal stud in her nose slips a hand around my wrist to guide me to the stands.

My legs feel like rubber when I walk, and every breath trips on its way out. I'm safe. I didn't kill her.

But I still feel sick. I almost did.

10

I shoot Logan in my dream.

It's the day he turns twenty, and I'm one of the officials who has come to take him away.

He's already awake when we break down the door. He's already crying.

"Please go away," he says.

A small voice in the back of my mind says that I should leave, I should let him go.

But I have my orders. I help the other official haul him out the door.

"Clem, what's wrong with you?" Logan says, his voice choking as it grows louder. "You promised!"

You promised.

You promised.

"Shoot him," a voice says in my ear.

I pull out a gun and I shoot him. Logan falls limp in a puddle of his blood in the dirt.

⚹

I wake to a burning feeling in my throat. I'm breathing fast, and there's wetness on my cheeks. My shaky hands fly to wipe the moisture away.

It was just a dream, I assure myself. I wouldn't shoot him.

But why would I dream something like that? I wrap my arms around my stomach, squeezing my eyes shut.

I'm glad there's no one here to see me crying. Ariadne slept in the other bed in the room—we were assigned to be roommates last night after the welcome ceremony—but that bed is empty now. Its blankets are in a heap, trailing on the thick carpet.

My own, oval-shaped bed has a foam mattress that molds to my body. The room has a domed shape to its ceiling. My nightdress is made of soft cotton fabric and my blankets are warm, but a shiver runs across my skin. There's an unnatural silence, except for the low hum of the blue ceiling lamps. There are no screams outside, no cam-bots buzzing, no pounding footsteps. Usually, I wake beside Logan with his breath on my face and his arms holding me against his chest.

Nausea constricts my stomach. Only yesterday, I was with him. His fingers lingered on my cheek and his muscles softened against mine. He told me not to forget him.

He had other words he wanted to say, words that might've meant everything. There's a chance I'll never be able to say them back. He might not last much longer; he might give up before I can go back for him. And I'll be left with too much regret to bear.

A clattering noise comes from the bathroom, startling me. Ariadne peeks her head around the corner. "Sorry," she mumbles.

"It's fine." I sit up, rubbing my eyes. "What time is it?"

"Eight o' clock."

It's funny how I feel tired, since I usually get up for school before the sun is even out. But then, it took me a lot longer than usual to fall asleep. It was hard to forget those gunshots.

Ariadne ties her hair into a ponytail. Her eyes meet mine, then lower. "We have new clothes."

"What?"

She points to a black slot in the wall near the foot of my bed. I push the covers back, get to my feet, and move to the slot, curious. My finger barely touches the red button beside the wall slot and it whirs open, revealing a pair of shiny black boots, fresh socks, and a folded outfit: a pair of skintight gray pants and a matching shirt. Ariadne's wearing a matching outfit.

Last night I folded my old dress and left it on the floor, on top of Laila's boots. Did someone come in and take them away during the night? The thought makes me tense, because I should've heard them if they did. I shouldn't be letting my guard down.

I wish they'd given Laila's boots back. They were old and tattered and smelled of mildew, but they were still hers. They were the only thing she left behind.

"I expected something nicer," Ariadne says, picking at the thin fabric of her shirt.

After last night, I have no idea what to expect.

I slip the slacks on under my nightdress. "Do you know where they want us?"

"Nourishment Division for breakfast." She points at a small blue screen on the wall over by the door, which Cadet Waller said will relay important messages about our daily schedule.

"Does it say what comes after that?"

Ariadne shakes her head.

I slip socks onto my feet. Cadet Waller said last night that the worst is over, that Commander Charlie wanted to be certain of our obedience to him, of what we were willing to do to stay alive. He wouldn't want to waste resources on Extractions who care more about the lives of dangerous Unstables than their own.

She said we don't need to be afraid anymore.

Ariadne meets my gaze and then pulls away from it. "Are you ready?" She bites hard on her lip.

"Almost." I pull on my new black boots and tie them.

I wonder what they did with Laila's shoes. I wonder if they were given to a new owner, or recycled, or thrown away, like the Developers threw away Laila.

Rows and rows of glass tables fill the Nourishment Division cafeteria. The room has a rounded shape and a domed ceiling like most of the rooms I've seen so far in the Core. Extractions dressed in gray sit on the right side and Core citizens sit in clumps of color on the left. Many people are still up and about, balancing breakfast trays and placing orders through an array of buttons and touch screens on silver panels on the walls.

An instructor guides Ariadne and me through the steps of picking our meals. There are main dishes and side dishes, drinks and desserts. I don't know what a lot of the words mean until the instructor explains them to me. Hodgori is a baked custard made with caramelized brown sugar and shir grain. Bansa is a stew. A raerburger is a coura patty topped with spicy beans and cheesy sauce, served between two wheat patties.

I've never had a choice of food before, and it's daunting.

We find open spots at an Extraction table. It might just be my imagination, but some of the Core kids at the table next to ours look like they're pointing and whispering at us. Maybe even laughing.

Memories come rushing back to me: boys knocking me down in the streets; kids throwing mud at my face; people making fun of me and bullying me because I was short and better than them in school.

I hoped I'd escape that here. I hope I'm imagining this.

I duck my head and slip onto the bench, setting my tray in front of me. I picked slivers of hoava root and woreken sausage in a thick, sugary sauce. I've never tasted woreken before, though I fed the snorting, fat creatures many times on the Surface.

I take a bite of the sausage. Sweet and tangy juices fill my mouth. The meat is delicious, but so different from the tough muckrat I'm used to eating that I have trouble swallowing it.

Across from me sits Oliver, the boy with the glasses. His eyes are on his plate. He has a strip of butter-soaked coura meat half way to his mouth when he lifts his head and notices me. "Oh, hello—Clementine, is it? You look different without the . . . gun."

I smile. "So do you. Less shaky."

A light shade of red rises in his cheeks.

I introduce him to Ariadne, who gives him a shy smile. "It's nice to meet you," she says. "Where are you from?"

"Crust," Oliver says.

I think back to what I saw of Crust through the window on our way here: the dusty, rocky caves. The coal mines.

Oliver nods, and his glasses slide forward. He pushes them back up the bridge of his nose.

Ariadne's eyes meet mine for half a second. I wonder if she's thinking the same thing as I am. On the Surface, those with poor vision rarely make it past age five or six. Their lack of vision usually makes them ineligible for high Promise, and since they can't see well enough to be much use in the fields, they're usually replaced early.

I wonder how Oliver survived, let alone got picked for Extraction. His intelligence, maybe. I study his face, wondering how fast he can solve a chemical equation or divide 201,388 by 23.

"This food is good," Ariadne mumbles, more to herself than anyone. "It doesn't taste like rocks or paper or dust."

"Shh." Oliver cuts her off, his eyes widening like he's trying to point something out.

The cafeteria has fallen silent.

Commander Charlie stands inside the entrance doors, two officials flanking him. His eyes sweep the tables, and a smile plays around the edges of his mouth. It seems almost possessive. "Don't mind me," he says.

The chattering slowly picks up again, but remains quiet.

He inspects us from the entrance doors for a moment, and then turns and walks away. Only after he's gone do I realize I wasn't breathing.

I shouldn't be afraid of him anymore, but I am, because he's the one who can still save Logan. He can make an exception.

I don't know how I'm going to convince him yet, but getting close to him seems key. The thought of doing that, of pretending I admire him and will do anything he says, makes my stomach churn.

But it's my only option.

After breakfast, Cadet Waller leads us down a long stretch of corridor outside the cafeteria. We're all quiet, unsure where we're headed. Ariadne chews on her fingernails. Oliver frowns at everything, from the floor that makes our footsteps echo to the walls without windows.

That's the strangest thing about this place: the confinement.

I'm free here, but if I were to run, I wouldn't be able to find a way out.

The corridor ends, and we step into air that's more open than before, onto a curved path with a left-hand railing. I set my palms on the railing to peer over the side.

"Welcome to Training Division," Cadet Waller says.

The deck below us is a bit far, but not so far that I can't make out details. It's a wide-open space set up like a maze. Every compartment seems to be designated for a different activity.

In one corner, a group of people in gray and green—officials-in-training, maybe—throw knives at lit-up targets and wrestle each other on mats. In another compartment, the floor is a screen, and people walk across the screen directing small rectangular bots in some sort of battle scenario. In a third area, children sit wearing steel helmets inside glowing blue, see-through capsules, probably reciting statistics and chemical equations. I've seen pictures of capsules like these in school.

"Intelligence machines," Oliver whispers, noticing them too.

The machines interact with their passengers, feeding knowledge straight into their brains as if they're injecting a smart gene. Students here don't have to memorize facts like we did. They sit through sessions on various subjects inside these machines, and when they're finished, they remember everything.

"You'll find facilities for youth education and career training in this division, which spans multiple decks." Cadet Waller points to rows of identical holes in the wall far across from us, which must be windows into rooms. She gestures for us to follow her along the path.

"Today is the first day of your Extraction training," she says as we step off the railing path into another corridor. "As Commander Charlie explained last night, the purpose of training is to make you useful Core citizens. You were each picked for a particular skill: half of you, for your intelligence; the other half, for your physical strength. But those aren't the only skills we want you to cultivate."

I glance at the other Extractions, categorizing them in my mind: the brawnier ones—though they still seem starved and skinnier than they should be—in the physical group; the skinnier, shorter people in the smart group. I'm willing to bet the Developers didn't pick me for my physique.

"For the upcoming week," Cadet Waller says, "each half will focus on the skill you were not picked for during your training sessions. We want all citizens to be well-rounded, no matter what working position you end up in.

"At the end of the week, your Promise score will be tested to determine whether you are ready to begin your work as a citizen. This is a score of your well-roundedness, which helps us identify your skill sets. For example, whether you'd be more useful as a scientist or as a soldier. Your score can even help us know how genetically advanced your offspring might be, depending on what sort of person you procreated with."

A couple girls giggle at that.

"An overall Promise score can fall between zero and a hundred, though there are many layers to consider," Cadet Waller says as we move through a pair of doors. "The average score in your group is forty-three. By the end of the week, you should all have scores of eighty or higher."

I run my teeth over my bottom lip. Instructors have never told me my score, though it must've been somewhat high to get me down here, to the Core. But I can't be sure I'm anywhere close to eighty.

We move through a set of sliding doors. "Sit wherever you like," Cadet Waller says.

Rows of identical chairs fill the room, facing a wall with five evenly spaced doors. I sink into a chair between Oliver and Ariadne. The leather sticks to my legs.

"What happens if our score doesn't hit eighty?" Oliver asks under his breath.

My eyes flit to Cadet Waller. She didn't say, really. She said we *should* have scores of eighty or higher, but what does that mean? I'm afraid to ask.

"I don't know," I say. "But the Developers wouldn't have picked us if they didn't think we could raise our scores that high."

"They make mistakes sometimes," he says.

I think of Logan. Of Laila. Two people they should've saved. "Yes, I suppose they do," I say quietly.

Cadet Waller clears her throat to get everyone's attention again. "For today," she says, "your training session will be a bit different from what I described earlier. We won't be splitting you up. You will participate in something that's available only to Core citizens. It sets us apart from those who reside in the outer sectors. It will, we hope, help you feel more like you're one of us."

She smiles before glancing down at her tablet and tapping the screen. "I will call you in groups of five. You'll each enter your own door. Jude, Ariadne, Ron, Karen, and Stephen are first."

Ariadne grips the armrests of her chair. She swallows and stands, not looking at me. The five doors slide open, and she moves through the second one on the left and is gone.

"I hope it won't be like yesterday," Oliver says. His face is a bit pale.

"I don't think it will be," I say, though *hope* is a safer word. I twist my hands in my lap "We're safe now," I add. I don't know whether I'm saying it to convince him or myself.

He presses his mouth into a line and doesn't reply.

✕

Cadet Waller calls my name in the next group of five. I take a breath and push off my chair. Oliver watches me leave with a glossy look in his eyes.

Through one of the doors, I find myself alone at the end of a corridor. The hum of fluorescents grinds in my brain.

This will be fine, whatever it is. I'll handle it. The first step to getting anywhere in the Core, before I can even think about gaining an audience with Commander Charlie and convincing him to make an exception for Logan, is doing well in training. Proving I can be a useful, obedient citizen.

Click. Chirp.

A panel in the wall in front of me slides to the left, revealing an empty, stark white chamber.

"Enter," a sweet, computerized voice says.

I hold my breath and step inside. The panel slides shut behind me.

A metallic, antiseptic smell fills my nostrils. I scan the rounded chamber for a crack, a handle, a button. Nothing.

There's a *whirwhirwhir,* and a green hue slides over my body, giving my skin a tingling sensation.

"Scanning for imperfections," the sweet voice says.

I don't know what that means, but it doesn't give me a warm, fuzzy feeling inside.

"Scan complete."

The green fades, and a crack appears out of nowhere in the wall in front of me, splitting open the chamber. Beyond lies a new room with the same blue fluorescent lights as the hallway behind me.

I take a small, cautious step forward.

Two figures step in front of me, blocking my view. They are almost identical. Both female, both with blue eyes and black curls, both wearing white surgical caps and gowns. My heartbeat stumbles. They're nurses.

"Welcome," Nurse One says with a smile. She slips her fingers around my wrist and pulls me into the room. "You're Clementine, right? You have such lovely hair."

The second nurse brushes my jawline with her thumb. I flinch. "Your skin would be nice without that nasty scar," she says.

I don't know what to say to that.

The room I've entered is small, with a blue hue and a domed shape to the ceiling, similar to my bedroom. Steel cabinets and a sink lean against the left wall. Silver medical instruments rest in containers on the sink counter, and a metal examination table sits straight ahead of me.

I swallow hard, fighting down the worry rising like bile in my throat.

My whole body tenses.

"You're a bit quiet, eh?" Nurse One smiles wider. "No need to be shy!"

"Sorry," I manage. "I just . . . Why am I here? What's going on?"

"We'll let Surgeon Pond explain," the second nurse says. She shouts over her shoulder, "Sir!"

I clench my teeth. Needles and examination tables are only used for treating infections and Unstables on the Surface. But things are different here, so I shouldn't be afraid.

There's a click in the wall.

Nurse One spins to a slot like the one in my bedroom. She removes a see-through, green tablet. On the opposite wall, a door slides open, and a man in a white coat who must be Surgeon Pond steps into the room.

"Welcome to the Core, Clementine," he says, his voice too cheery. "How do you like it so far?"

No one starves here, and I'm far from the moon, and everyone lives a long life. But there aren't any windows, either, and every door leads to another corridor. This place is freedom and suffocation at the same time.

But all I say is: "It's wonderful." This feels like another test, and that's what Commander Charlie would want to hear, if he were listening. There's no way to be certain he isn't.

"We're glad you think so." The surgeon moves to Nurse One, who hands him the tablet. "Let's see what we've got here. . . ."

"It's mostly standard," the second nurse says. "Though I'm sure you'll want to do something about that scar."

"Definitely."

"Um." I clear my throat. "What's going on?"

"Don't worry, it's nothing to fret about," Nurse One says.

"We're here to help clean you up and make sure you're healthy," Surgeon Pond says, handing the tablet back to Nurse One. "Every new Extraction receives a special procedure—a simple one. The most important thing we do is speed up growth of your muscle fat so you'll be a healthier weight, and stronger."

"What about my scar?" I ask.

"Well, we also use the opportunity to clear up slight imperfections, things like bruises and birthmarks. Scars you shouldn't have anyway. Because who likes scars? We'll help you look as beautiful as you were meant to be. It will help you feel that you belong here."

I force my lips into a tight smile. But I don't want to change; I want Logan to recognize me when I see him again.

Plus, something tells me there's more to the reason behind the procedure than making us feel like we fit in here. I want to press the matter, but Surgeon Pond is already heading back out the door.

"Show her in the mirror, will you?" he says. "And help her into a surgical gown. I'll be right back."

He exits. Nurse Two moves to a cabinet and returns with a rectangular mirror the size of a textbook.

Nurse One helps her slide the tablet into a slot in the mirror.

With the press of a button, the mirror hums and glows red around the edges.

Nurse Two places it in my hands, not seeming to notice they're trembling.

I stare at my reflection. The bags under my blue eyes are prominent. I bite hard on my pale, flaking lips. My red-orange curls are wound with old, crusted dirt that won't come out with water. The scar trails along my right jaw line. For now, I'm still the small girl with mud on her cheekbones, who somehow got lucky.

Nurse One taps the edge of the mirror, and the image dissolves into another. "*This* is how you will look after."

Now my skin appears smooth with a soft pink hue, no longer covered with a layer of dust. My lips aren't chapped anymore. My curls seem fresh and elegant, flowing about my shoulders. The scar has disappeared. When I part my lips, my teeth are half a shade whiter.

The changes are simple, but it still looks like someone else. A girl who never felt the butt of an official's gun slam into her jaw when he caught her trying to climb to the school rooftop. A girl who doesn't know what it's like to live on almost nothing, afraid her nightmares about the moon will come to life, afraid she'll die in a gas chamber at twenty.

I'm not this girl.

But . . . deep down . . . I almost want to be.

"It's all right to be nervous," Nurse One says, sliding the mirror out of my grasp. "I promise, you'll feel wonderful, and it won't hurt a bit."

I'm not sure I believe her.

But refusing to do this would make me seem disobedient. I have to do what Commander Charlie wants. I have to get on his good side, or he won't listen when I beg him to save Logan.

And . . . maybe this will be worth it.

I tuck a curl behind my ear. This isn't a big change, after all. I'll always be Clementine, no matter how I look. And if Logan is the boy I know, he won't care if my appearance is a bit different when I see him again.

"Here, let's get you into a special gown for the procedure." Nurse Two moves to a drawer in one of the cabinets. "You can leave your shirt on."

When she comes back with the gown, I let her ease it over my head. I don't know if I'll love how I look after this, but I'll have to learn to love it. This is the life I won and the life I wanted.

The nurses tie the back with easy, quick movements.

"If you'll please climb onto the table," Nurse One says.

I lie back on the metal. A small mesh pillow cushions my head, but the comfort doesn't ease me all the way. My heart pounds in my chest, but also in my arms, legs, hands, and head.

Surgeon Pond hums as he reenters the room. Cabinets open, and metal instruments click and clang. Water runs in the sink.

"We're ready," Nurse Two says.

I hear the sound of suction. Nurse One appears, holding a clear mask in her gloved fingertips with a wide, purple tube attached to its end. She fits the mask over my nose and mouth, trapping my lips with plastic.

"Deep breaths," she says.

A sweet smell fills my nostrils.

"Scalpel." The surgeon's voice.

I press my hands into the metal, so I won't decide at the last second to rip off the gas mask and not go through with this. But my limbs are already softening, my eyelids drooping. I couldn't fight if I wanted to.

It'll be worth it, I tell myself as the edges of my vision blur.

Pond's face leans over me.

I see a flash of silver, a surgical mask, blue lights.

They darken . . .

. . . darken . . .

. . . darken . . .

Then nothing.

11

Fingers guide the rim of a cup to my lips.

"Drink up, honey."

The liquid is pink and sweet.

Dots speckle my vision. I blink, and the world clears a little.

Two drip bags hang on poles to the right of me, one with blood and the other with clear fluid, both connected to IV lines. My legs hang over the side of a thin mattress, but I don't remember sitting up.

I'm wearing a purple bodysuit made of stretchy leather fabric. One sleeve is rolled up to my shoulder, revealing a thin strip of gauze in the crook of my arm. A blue curtain hangs around my bed, and quiet speech and movements come from beyond it, all around me. They must have moved me to a different room after the procedure.

Nurse One takes the cup away and smiles. "How do you feel?"

With a hesitant finger, I touch the skin of my face. It feels soft, smooth, and shiny. Unnatural. The heartbeat is loud in my ears, a touch faster than usual.

"How do you feel?" the nurse asks again.

"Awake," I say.

"No hurts? No aches?"

I take a breath and stretch my fingers and toes. But there's nothing. My body feels normal—better than normal, even. . . . Stronger. Adrenaline flows in a calm, steady stream through my veins.

"I feel fine."

"Wonderful!" The nurse pulls my sleeve down. "You're free to go, then. You have free time for the rest of the day. I can bring you a mirror if you'd like to see how your surgery turned out. You won't find any scars on your face."

That makes my stomach squeeze. I'm not sure I'm ready just yet to see what I really look like without my scars.

"I think I'd like to wait," I say.

"Whatever you'd like, dear."

When I stand, my legs are steady. To my body, it's like I was never asleep. One second, my eyes closed; the next, they opened.

"How long was I out?" I ask.

"The main procedure lasted three hours, but we kept you overnight to fix more minor concerns."

I momentarily forget how to breathe. "I thought it was a simple operation. That's what you said."

"It was. The muscle growth takes time, that's all." She gives my head a light pat.

I forgot about the muscle growth. Still, I can't believe they used the word *simple* and then kept me all day and night.

It makes me wonder if they lied about something, or left out part of what the operation involved. It makes me wonder if I look completely different.

The nurse pushes the curtain back, and I see that there are other curtains in the room, each probably hiding another bed with another Extraction. She tucks her arm through mine and leads me through a door into a hallway.

It's okay, I tell myself. Whatever they did to me, everything is going to be okay.

Please, please, please be okay.

"I hope I'll see you again, Clementine!" The nurse waves me off.

I don't say anything to that.

Down the corridor, I come to a glass window. For a moment I pause, staring at a spot to the left of the glass. If I flit my eyes less than an inch to the right, I'll see myself. I'll see my new face, a face Logan might not recognize.

I run, even though it makes me feel like a coward.

I take a staircase down and pick a corridor that should lead to an elevator. But every corridor looks the same, and I don't know where I'm going.

I end up lost in the maze that is the main floor of Training Division. Blue lights flash everywhere, reflecting off the stark white walls. I pass doors and sections of glass wall that show me some of the training areas I saw from above: the room with the intelligence capsules; the room with the battle screen for a floor. But they're empty now. I don't see students, let alone instructors. Small, rectangular bots hover on the sidelines in the battle room, but they can't help me find an exit.

I recite all the digits of pi I have memorized to keep calm: 3.1415926535897932384626 . . .

Around a corner, I reach the end of the pathway, the last door to the last room. I'm definitely moving in the wrong direction.

I'm about to turn back when I realize where I've ended up.

The last doorway leads to another empty training room, but this one has fighting mats on the floor, and knives lining the far wall.

This must be one of the places where officials learn how to fight. All of the officials in the outer sectors grew up here in the Core, which means they trained here too. That patrol I met when I climbed the restricted building trained here. And so did the man who gave me the scar I had before I lost it during the surgical procedure.

Red light floods the entrance to the training area. I take a step forward. The entrance makes a sound—a soft hum that reminds me of the acid shield, and the moon.

Frowning, I stretch a hand toward the red light. The instant I touch it, a shock reels through my arm. I pull it back with a gasp.

"Sorry, officials only," an amused voice says behind me.

I whip around. A boy smirks at me, flanked by two others.

"Ah, an Extraction," he says. "Are you *lost*? You're short, so I guess you can't see the exit."

His snickering friends move through the entrance and head to where the knives glint on the far wall, but he just stands there, smiling at me.

I take in his blond hair that's sticking up a little; his tight gray suit with the Core insignia on his chest pocket; his belt with several gun holsters; his green gloves; his knee-high black boots. The sound of a gunshot rips through my memory.

His name falls into my head: *Sam*. This is the Core boy who shot an Unstable two nights ago, in some sort of demonstration for Commander Charlie. The killing didn't even faze him. He stood there smiling when it was finished.

"Can you talk, Shorty?" he asks.

I press my lips together. I don't want to talk to him, but now I'll look stupid if I don't. "Can you help me find an elevator?" I ask.

"Sorry," he says, bumping my shoulder as he moves past me and through the red-lit doorway. "I'd love to help, but it's training time. Gotta practice throwing knives."

I narrow my eyes a little as he heads to the weapons wall. Commander Charlie likes this boy. He loved it when he killed that Unstable.

Sam trails his fingers over the options for weapons, then picks one. He turns back around and walks straight toward me, knife in hand. "You any good at throwing knives?" he asks. "Did they teach you that wherever you came from?"

"No." As if officials would teach us how to throw knives so we could throw knives at them.

"Figured." He stops in the doorway and gives me a smug look. The kind of look bullies used to give me in school when I was little, when they thought I was short and small and afraid. The red light glints on the sharpest edge of Sam's blade.

An idea hits me. A bad one, maybe. But before I can stop myself, the words come spilling out: "I meant, no, they didn't teach us. But I learn fast. I bet I'd be good at it."

"Oh, really?"

"Yeah."

"Huh." He twirls the knife's hilt in his fingertips, then holds it out to me. "Show me."

This isn't smart. But I grab the knife from him anyway and take five steps back, giving myself some space between me and the wall. I'm not sure where to aim. The actual targets are around the corner in the training area.

"Hit the very edge of the door frame," Sam says, stepping behind me, "and I'll help you get out of here."

The door frame? The edge is thin—a couple centimeters wide. But I'm not about to back down, so I hold the knife out in front of me and close one eye. I've never done this before, but I've seen an official throw a knife, and I think they did something like this. I line the tip of the blade up with the left edge of the door.

Breathe in, breathe out.

I pull my arm back and bring it down.

Sam's boot kicks my ankle, knocking me off balance as the knife flies from my fingertips. The weapon sails into the training room, a good fifteen feet from where I aimed it. It clatters on the floor near one of the fighting mats.

"You messed me up!" I say.

"Oh, did I? It looked to me like you lost your footing. Might want to work on that." Sam saunters through the doorway and disappears around the corner. I can hear his friends laughing.

I glare after him. If I could walk into the room without getting zapped, I'd grab that knife and aim it at his throwing hand. He thinks he's stronger and smarter because he's lived here forever, but Core kids aren't any smarter than those who live on the Surface. We have just as much potential. We can be just as Promising, if not more.

I have to be. I have to make Commander Charlie like me.

"Clementine?"

"What?" I snap, turning around. "Oh. Sorry." It's only Oliver.

"You okay?" he asks, raising an eyebrow.

"I'm fine," I lie. The *plunk* of a knife hitting a target reaches my ears, followed by a catcall. I try to ignore it. "Where were you?"

"Looking for you," Oliver says. His eyes are a brighter shade of blue, a clear sky behind his spectacles. I frown, unsure why he still has glasses after the operation. He stares at me.

Heat floods my cheeks. "Will you cut it out?"

"Sorry." He blinks. "You look different, is all."

"Thanks for reminding me."

"I don't mean it in a bad way."

I ignore that statement. "Are you lost too?"

"I found a way out," he says. "But I saw you down here."

He must not have seen Sam or my knife-throwing experiment, since he doesn't mention them. I decide not to tell him.

"Which way, then?"

He leads me back the way I came, past several training areas and around a corner I didn't try before. I curse under my breath. If I'd seen it before, I could've avoided that run-in with Sam.

The path turns into a steep set of stairs and then a corridor. The corridor becomes an elevator landing. Oliver presses the call button.

I drop onto the metal bench across from the elevators and run sweaty palms over the purple leather covering my legs. Above me, a fake window is built into the ceiling. Black frames surround silver panels that could almost slide off and reveal the sky if they weren't screwed on. If we weren't a million miles underground with brand-new faces and suits getting tighter by the second.

I grimace, feeling trapped again.

"I don't look weird, right?" Oliver asks, twisting his mouth. His skin is fresher and shinier, and his hair is cleaner.

"You don't look that different," I say. "I don't get why they kept us overnight."

"My nurse said they did muscle repair and gave us nutrients through injections, so we wouldn't be so skinny."

"Yeah, I know they did. I guess I just don't trust them yet, that's all."

"I don't blame you."

We sit in silence for a moment. I chew on my lip and glance at my body in the tight purple suit, curious to see if the muscle growth is obvious. The leather makes my thighs more pronounced, showing curves where I've never had any before. I wonder what Logan would think of them.

I shove that thought away. "How come you still have glasses? I would have imagined they'd fix your eyesight."

Oliver blushes a light shade of red. "I wouldn't let them. I like my glasses."

"They let you keep them?"

"They said choice is important here, and once we're citizens, especially, we'll have lots of choices. They wanted me to feel comfortable."

"I didn't want to get rid of my scar, but they made me do it."

He observes me, a smile teasing his lips. "I bet you wanted it."

I scoff. "How would you know?" He's not Logan. He barely knows me.

"We all want to look more Promising."

The elevator dings.

The doors zip open, and Oliver moves inside. I push off the bench and follow him, trying to quell my resentment. He isn't the one who made me undergo a beauty operation, or laughed at me because I couldn't hit a door frame with a knife.

The elevator walls are made of glass. Without meaning to, without intending, I catch a glimpse of my face. My cheeks flush.

The door closes, and Oliver scans the map of the Core on the wall. "Where do you want to go? It's a free day."

"Wherever," I say, only half listening.

The change to my complexion is subtler than it looked on that tablet when the nurses showed me beforehand. But my skin still looks smoother, and my curls do look nice without dirt in them. I don't know whether I'm "as beautiful as I was meant to be," but I do feel prettier. I do look more Promising. Only the missing scar makes my brow crease.

Still, I'm not a different person. Logan will recognize me when I see him again.

I wring my hands and force down the winged creatures fluttering in my stomach. I would worry about him always, but I can't, because I need to focus.

I take a deep breath and run through the steps in my head:

I have to raise my Promise as high as possible during training.

I have to become someone who is useful here, and needed, maybe even special.

I have to pick a career that will earn me an audience with Commander Charlie.

I have to convince him to make an exception for Logan. I don't know what exactly I'll need to say or do to convince him. But I will do whatever it takes.

Oliver jabs a button. A *whir* rises in my ears as we pick up speed, moving to the left in a smooth fashion.

Yellow dots on the Core map inside the elevator light up, showing where we are. We're on the eighth floor of Training Division. I can't see anything but steel walls through the glass of the elevator. But there must be a hundred training rooms, at least, that I haven't seen yet, since there are twelve floors in this division and an average of twenty rooms on each.

As we speed along the elevator track, the dots on the map show us departing from Training Division and entering Invention. The steel walls outside the elevator are replaced by a long stretch of window.

We're passing one of the science laboratories, this one for food production. Most of the food people eat in the Core comes from the Surface fields and greenhouses, but down here they're able to grow certain crops hydroponically, without soil. Plants grow in steel reservoirs under harsh lights that serve as the sun.

Oliver is quiet beside me, his eyes drinking in the view. There's a short break in the window, and then we pass into another laboratory. This one has more adults than the last. They wear blue coats and tap on screens in the wall, or work with test tubes and petri dishes. A couple of medi-bots hover in the corner, where a young lab assistant slips a slide under a microscope. This lab must be related to medicine. Perhaps they're developing a cure for an illness, or even a cure for the side effects of the moon's acid, in case it seeps through the shield again.

But even if they discovered that cure, most of the kids in the work camps would never see it. Cures for sickness are reserved for those with high Promise.

We pass another stretch of steel wall before we come to the next window. This time, there's not a room right in front of us, but a massive deck of steam and darkness far below: the flight port. The first room we saw here in the Core.

From above, the steam hides most of the ships, but their flashing lights are visible. I can see the biggest ships clearly, the hovercrafts like the ones they use on the Surface. Down here, Core pilots use them to fly through the Pipeline to visit the other sectors, for passenger or cargo transport. Sometimes they fly to the Surface on research missions for the Developers. I've seen ships careen through the sky toward the world outside the settlement—even, once or twice, to the stars.

I don't know what they were looking for.

"Did you know they made spaceships so big?" Oliver asks, his voice filled with wonderment.

I smile a little. "Yes. Are they smaller in Crust?"

"We don't have ships, really," he says. "Mostly everyone just walks everywhere. Even the smaller pods aren't that efficient to travel in underground . . . but I've always wanted to fly one."

Beyond the elevator glass, steel walls replace the view again, and then drop away. The flashing lights of the Pipeline appear. Only for a moment; then there's steel again, and the elevator shifts to a vertical shaft to carry us up a few decks.

"Well, I bet they'd train you to be a pilot, if you wanted," I say.

"I hope so," Oliver says, and smiles.

The elevator slows to a stop. *Ding.*

"Recreation Division," a cool, female voice says.

The doors open, and we step into what looks like outer space.

My breath leaves my body like it's been sucked into a vacuum. My eyes widen.

There are lights all around and above me, flashing in the dark, some the size of normal lamps, others big enough that they look like small planets and stars. Reds, yellows, greens, and purples flash in the dark of a compound so high and wide I can't see where it ends. It might not have an end. We might be floating in the sky, somewhere far out in the universe, though the ground feels solid.

And there are people. Civilians of the Core, mostly children, but also adults. They wait in line and chatter and stomp and holler, waiting for their turn inside lit-up game stations.

There are hundreds of these stations. Blue and green lights flash across the surface of a nearby one that's round and shaped like a pod. Three gamers inside shoot blast pistols at fighter ships on a screen that covers half of the interior glass. In another station, people swim inside a giant tank of bubbling water, lit up by purple fluorescents. On the far side of the room, there's a giant steel dome with the word PHANTOM lit up on its side. I wonder what's inside it.

There are floors above us too, made of glass. The people up there look like they're flying as they run between the lights from station to station. Some of them really are flying, racing in small hov-pods through the flashes and darkness in a flight arena on what seems to be the highest floor.

Logan and I used to make up stories about what people do all day when they're not stuck laboring in fields, when they don't have to prove they deserve to live past twenty. I wish he were here to see it.

"Clementine?" Oliver asks. His eyes reflect fake stars. "Does the real sky look like this?"

I almost laugh, but bite it back. Of course he wouldn't know. "No, it's bigger," I say. "Real stars are tiny, and the moon is giant and pink." *Dangerous*, I should say. "But this might be prettier." *Safer*.

"I still hope I see it someday," he says. "From a spaceship or something."

I smile at the hopeful look on his face. Part of me hopes I'll see the sky again too. There's something free and beautiful about the stars especially—even the moon, though it's deadly.

But we're still safer below ground.

"So, what shall we try?" Oliver asks, pushing his glasses up the rim of his nose.

I twist my mouth, staring at the deck before me. I don't know where to begin.

His eyes flit through the crowd. "I wonder if they have . . ." Instead of finishing his thought, he grabs my hand and pulls me past game stations. His palm is soft and warm in mine.

We come to a compound of large, glass capsules. Four of these capsules are connected by giant tubes, so they all form a square. In the center sits a fifth attachment, the biggest, and shaped like an egg. Children float inside the compound, but unlike the swimming tank, this one has no water.

"Zero gravity." Oliver grins.

"There you are!" a voice calls, to my right. "I was looking for you."

Ariadne slips through the crowd to reach us, her fingers pressed against the purple leather on her thighs. Her hair was tangled and messy before, but it's ravishing now. Oliver stares at her.

"Clementine," she says, her voice filled with awe. "You're beautiful."

I shake my head, laughing. "Thanks. But you're prettier, Ariadne."

Oliver seems to realize what he's doing, and blinks and clears his throat. "Hey," he says. "We were gonna go inside. Do you want to come?"

Ariadne looks at the capsules. She frowns. "What is it?"

"It's not scary," Oliver says. "Trust me."

He tugs me after him into a small glass box connected to one of the four outer capsules. Ariadne follows us, biting her lip. The door closes behind us and makes a loud suction noise, trapping the three of us inside the box. A moment later, the door before us zips open.

Oliver takes a step, and I take a step, and Ariadne takes a step.

We've already left the ground.

I move my feet, seeking something solid, but find nothing.

For a moment, I panic. I'm not used to this. Gravity is stable and strong and dependable, while this feeling of weightlessness is not.

But I'm okay. I'm okay. I suck air in through my nose and out through my mouth. It's silly to be afraid of this. I've always wished I could fly.

My eyes close. I breathe in and out.

In and out.

I forget about things that used to matter. Things that hurt me, scarred me, and worried me. Floating here, I could be a cloud, a krail, a wanderer among the stars. Or maybe I am a star.

Whatever I am is a small thing with little significance in a universe as wide as this one, but in this moment, I feel big. I feel like nothing can break me.

My eyelids flutter open. Oliver flaps his arms and rises higher and higher, until his head bumps the glass ceiling. Ariadne's laughter peals through the capsule. Oliver laughs too, and then so do I.

We pretend we're swimming through the air, though none of us have ever swum before. We pretend we aren't trapped inside glass. We pretend the fake sky overhead is the real sky, but a safer sky. We pretend life stretches on forever, that it doesn't end.

We pretend we're invincible.

I don't know how long we float, for seconds or minutes or hours. No one makes us stop. No one slaps me awake, so this must not be a dream.

It's the first time I understand the meaning of the word *free*.

12

"If I call your name, you're in the physical training focus group today," Cadet Waller says.

We're standing in a lobby area in Training Division, floor twelve. A female instructor sits behind a high counter to my right, tapping away on the monitor in front of her and glancing at the group of us Extractions occasionally.

I feel a yawn tingling at the back of my throat, and try to stifle it by pressing my tongue to the roof of my mouth. I shouldn't be tired. I slept in until eight thirty and almost missed breakfast. But we stayed out too late in Recreation Division last night, and when I tried to fall asleep, there were suddenly knots in my stomach.

I had fun last night. I was happy, and that doesn't seem fair. Why should I know freedom when almost everyone I left behind won't ever get to?

Cadet Waller has already started reading off the names. "Andy," she says.

The name belongs to a Surface boy with freckles and hardly any muscle on his biceps. The brawny boys beside him snicker.

"Hazel," Cadet Waller says, not seeming to notice.

Hazel is another person who looks like she's more suited for acing exams than throwing knives at the center of a target.

Cadet Waller's going to call my name soon, I can already tell. I take a breath and force my worry about last night into the tiniest compartment of my mind. This is my first real day of training, and I have to be ready.

Besides, beating myself up won't do any good. I'm not the one keeping freedom from those in the work camps.

Commander Charlie is.

"Stanley," Cadet Waller says, calling the name of a dark-skinned boy. "Oliver."

Oliver shifts uncomfortably.

"Drew . . . Ariadne . . ."

Ariadne blows the hair out of her eyes. "Knew it."

"William . . . Clementine . . ."

I'm not the least bit surprised. The thought of running or lifting weights or doing whatever it is this training session will require of me doesn't make me ecstatic. But there's one good thing: I already know I'm fast when it comes to climbing buildings. So I must be a bit stronger than the instructors think.

When Cadet Waller has called off the rest of the names, she looks up from her tablet with a crisp smile. "Physical group, you're working with different instructors today—some special guests, if you will. Head through the door over there."

Over by the counter, the instructor who was sitting stands up and presses her thumbprint onto a small pad in the wall. A door zips open.

"The rest of you, follow me to intelligence training," Cadet Waller says, waving the other half of the group after her as she heads down the hallway.

I start to follow Ariadne to the door, but my eyes skim the other group walking away. Every single person has a similar build: big and muscular, though I bet the beauty operation amplified what they already had.

I recognize some of them—Ernest, the boy who was caught stealing from a food stockpile on the Surface; Flora, the girl in my Sector History class who liked to bully younger kids. They throw us looks of amusement as they saunter after Cadet Waller. As if their physique makes them special, when the Core needs scientists, doctors, and teachers just as much as officials, if not more.

I turn away and put them out of my mind. Through the door, we enter a short corridor that ends with a steel archway. A boy stands just beyond it. With sandy-colored hair, knee-high boots, and a smirk tugging at his mouth.

Sam.

My feet falter. Oliver bumps into me from behind. "Ow," he says.

"Sorry," I manage.

"Welcome, welcome," Sam says. "Step through the archway one at a time."

My heart bumps fast against my ribs. *He's* one of the special guests? It makes sense, I guess. Officials do have lots of experience with physical training.

But I don't want Sam here. He made a fool of me yesterday. And no, it didn't really matter—it was just me and him and two of his buddies. But what if he tries something again? If I mess up or lose focus and he says something about it, this time lots of people will hear, and might make fun of me.

My face warms and I want to hide on a rooftop or in my bedroom. But I can't do that. I can't run away. I can't let him be the reason I don't do well in training.

People pass ahead of me under the arch. It's almost my turn.

Ignore him, I tell myself. Stop caring what he thinks.

Ariadne moves ahead of me through the archway, which lights up blue in recognition, and into the training area beyond. Sam's eyes trail after her.

I walk quickly forward. Maybe he won't even notice me. Maybe I'll get lucky.

But of course he glances at me at the last second. The smile widens on his face. "Shorty. I was hoping you'd be here."

"I was hoping you wouldn't be," I mutter, giving him a wide berth as I walk past him, in case he tries to touch me or something. He doesn't. He just laughs.

I force the sound out of my head.

The training area we've entered reminds me of the knife-throwing arena, except it's much bigger and there are no targets or weapons on the walls. Half of the room is taken up by an elaborate obstacle course, while the other half is a smooth running track with floor mats in the middle, and some weights.

Ariadne and the others stand on the track before five males wearing the same outfit as Sam's. They seem older than him, though. More like actual officials than officials in training.

I slip next to Ariadne while the last of the Extractions file into the room. Oliver joins us a second later.

"Do you know him?" he asks, cocking his head at Sam, who's walking over to join the other officials.

My face warms. What am I supposed to say? Yes, I met him yesterday and made a stupid decision, and he embarrassed me. "Uh . . ."

"Good morning, Extractions," one of the officials says loudly. I've never been more grateful to hear one of them talking.

He rubs his thin black mustache with his thumb, his blue eyes piercing the group. His hand rests atop the small pulse gun in his belt holster. "Can anyone tell me the square root of 2,815,684?"

I frown, not sure if he's serious.

"Is it 1,652?" a tall boy with curly blond hair says. Drew, I think is his name.

"No, it's 1,678." Ariadne says.

"Correct," the official says. "What's the Armanahan Principle?"

There's an awkward silence. That's one of those principles instructors mentioned in passing during genetics lab.

But I remember: "Allele and genotype frequencies remain constant in a population from generation to generation unless specific disturbing influences are introduced."

Sam eyes me curiously. Oliver stares out of the corner of my eye. Drew and a couple other Extractions mumble something.

The official smiles, though it doesn't soften his face. "Very good. Just wanted to make sure I'm working with the right group. My name is Colonel Parker. I'm the leader of Core patrol Squadron A, and these are a couple of my lieutenants."

I glance at Sam, my mouth falling open a little. He's a lieutenant? I'm pretty sure that's the highest rank for officials below colonel. He seems too young, maybe a year older than me at most.

His lip curls when he catches me watching him. I look away, my cheeks hot.

"We're working on physical conditioning today, as Cadet Waller already told you," Colonel Parker says. "Now, I know some of you think exercise will be completely irrelevant to your future occupation, since most of you would prefer laboratory work over work as an official or a general for the military corps. But you're gonna have to get over it, because this is how we do things here. Exercise is a frequent part of daily life. We don't want you to be as weak as those kids in the work camps. We want you to be stronger. Fiercer. Better."

"Aren't we better already, sir?" the dark-skinned boy, Stanley, asks.

Sam grins. "Of course."

Colonel Parker doesn't argue. Neither does anyone else.

I want to say something. I want to tell them they're wrong, we're not better than anyone in the camps. The only difference between us and them is the clothes we're wearing, and the food we eat down here, and the lack of scars on our faces.

The only difference is we got lucky, and they didn't.

"Let's get started," Colonel Parker says. "Give me ten laps for a warm-up."

"*Ten?*" a girl protests.

The track is pretty big. Ten laps seems like well over a mile.

"Get moving," Parker barks. "I don't tolerate whiners. Keep in mind we're not the only ones watching."

My eyes flit to the room's perimeter, looking automatically for cam-bots. But I haven't seen any of those in the Core. That doesn't mean Parker is lying, though.

I start to run alongside Ariadne and Oliver. Slowly at first to get used to the feeling, and then I pick up my pace, breathing in through my nose and out through my mouth. I can't slow down, no matter how tired I get. I have to impress Commander Charlie.

And I won't give Sam one more reason to laugh.

Ten laps, twenty push-ups, and one hundred sit-ups later, I'm pretty sure Sam is laughing. I refuse to look at him to check. I'm leaning over a mat, my hands on my knees, trying to catch my breath. My calves are screaming, and my clothes are soaked with sweat.

"Now that you're warmed up," Colonel Parker says, "follow me."

He and the lieutenants make for the obstacle course.

"They can't be serious," Oliver says, stumbling after them. He has an arm around his stomach, and his face is almost green.

"Remember the surgery?" Ariadne says. Her face glistens with sweat, but she's standing a bit straighter than I am.

"What about it?" I ask.

"I think it made me stronger."

Wiping my forehead with the back of my wrist, I do a quick glance over my body. She might be right. My leg muscles are on fire, but I can walk all right, and my arms don't actually hurt that much. My biceps and pectorals—the muscles I use the most for climbing and wrenching up bad crops in the fields—sting, but they don't ache. I can flex them fine.

"Maybe a little," Oliver mumbles. "But not much."

"Maybe you were just weaker than everyone to begin with," Ariadne says, sticking her tongue out.

Oliver's cheeks flush.

We're almost to the obstacle course. It's an enormous complex surrounded by a high steel wall that hides most of what's inside the course. I glimpse high handlebars and rope swings. Part of the course is a climbing tower that stretches far up to the ceiling. There aren't any ladder rungs or ropes attached to it, as far as I can tell. It seems impossible to climb.

But part of me itches to try it.

Colonel Parker, Sam, and the other lieutenants stop next to the entrance to the course, a ladder leading to the top of the outer wall.

"This course is the final segment of CODA, a test for incoming patrolmen—the Core Official Development Aptitude test," Parker says. "Anyone who wants to be an official must finish this course in under four minutes and thirty seconds in order to complete their training. The fastest time recorded is three minutes and seven seconds, held by Sam here."

Sam folds his arms and scans the group of us with that smugness in his eyes.

"Since this is your first day of physical training," Parker continues, "I don't expect you to do it that fast today. But you should aim for under seven minutes. The most difficult part of the course is the final stage, that tower you see over there. You can't see them from here, but there are thin, sturdy ropes designed to help you reach the top. Some of you might not be strong enough yet, and that's okay. I do want you to attempt it. Once you reach the top, there are ladder rungs to help you get down on the far side. Some people prefer not to use them. There is a system in place that will keep you from injury if you fall or jump. And jumping might get you down faster."

"What sort of system?" someone asks.

"I'll let you figure that out for yourself," Parker says with a smile. He removes a small scanner from his pocket, like the kind Surface officials wear as part of their uniforms.

"Go ahead and line up," he says. "I'll cue each of you when to start. Hold the number on your wrist out for me when I tell you. We'll keep track of your time."

Stanley, Drew, and others rush to the front of the line. I'm not so eager, since Parker didn't say it matters if we go first or last. I'd rather see how the others are doing. I end up near the back behind Oliver and Ariadne.

Three of the lieutenants slip through doors into different areas of the obstacle course, probably to keep an eye on us from the inside. Sam heads for the end of the course, over by the tower.

"Begin," Parker says at the front of the line, and Drew waves his wrist over the scanner Parker had in his pocket. There's a beep and he's gone, heaving himself up the ladder to the top of the high steel wall. He swings one leg, then the other over the top, and disappears.

Five seconds later, Parker cues Stanley, and he takes off.

"You think they really just want to make us 'well-rounded' citizens?" Oliver asks, his ragged breath betraying how tired he still is from the warm-up. "This seems a little much."

"Begin," Parker says to the girl in line after Stanley.

"Maybe they're trying to turn us into soldiers," Ariadne says, twisting her mouth in contemplation.

I almost snort, but stop myself. She's sort of right. We're training in the same arena as officials, after all.

But they can't actually be turning us into soldiers. They need those of us with high intelligence to be scientists and medical personnel, like Commander Charlie said. It's not like we're fighting a war.

"Next," Parker says. It's Oliver's turn already.

He slides his arm over the scanner. I can't see his face, but I bet he's avoiding Parker's stern gaze. I know I would be.

Beep.

He starts up the rungs.

Ariadne moves to the scanner.

Beep.

She takes off.

It's my turn. I take a deep breath and step forward, holding my wrist up to Parker's scanner. My eyes skim the top of the wall. I wish I could see through steel, so I could tell what's on the other side. This is my first opportunity to prove myself, after all.

Three minutes and seven seconds. That's how long it took Sam to finish this course. That's the time I have to beat.

My citizenship number pops up on the scanner: S68477.

Beep.

The timer starts. I grab the highest ladder rung I can reach and pull myself up, already counting the seconds in my head. *One, two, three* . . .

My legs aren't happy with me. My calves strain with every step, but I do my best to ignore them.

At the top of the ladder, I swing my leg over the wall and give myself two seconds to take in what's on the other side: A platform sits about three feet below me, some ten feet above the ground, where one of the lieutenants stands with his arms folded. The platform leads to three sets of handlebars. Oliver is almost to the end of the middle set. Ariadne is halfway across the set on the right.

I swing my other leg over the wall and drop down, bending my knees when I land so I won't hurt my feet. Pain slices through them anyway. I clench my teeth. *Focus.*

Two steps and I'm gripping the first bar with one hand. I reach out to grab the next. I should've wiped my palms on my clothes first. They're sweaty. I'm breathing hard, and I'm afraid I'll slip, but I reach for the next bar anyway. And the next, trying not to think about whether the bones in my legs will snap if I fall and hit the ground.

I reach the end platform at the same time as Ariadne. This time there are ropes to help us climb the next wall, which looks about twice my height.

But there are no footholds. I'll have to depend entirely on my arms.

I grab the rope, heaving myself up. Ariadne does the same beside me, her face pale, her eyes focused. I try to keep holding on so I can push my feet against the rope and move higher. The rope sways from my weight. I lose my grip and fall hard on the platform.

Wincing, I push off the ground even though I haven't really recovered. I can't quite remember why I'm doing this. But I can't afford to waste any time.

I try to climb the rope again, visualizing all the strength in my body seeping into my arms as if strength were made of liquid. After too many seconds, I manage to pull myself up to the top, and then reach and grab hold of the wall's edge and drag myself up the rest of the way. I'm breathing through my mouth instead of my nose.

I see what's on the other side of the wall, and my heart's rhythmic beating speeds up about 10 percent.

This time, there's a thick steel pipe—one of five in total—about three feet below me instead of a platform. Below the pipes lies a pit of murky water instead of the ground.

Oliver crosses the pipe next to mine, shaky. Three other Extractions are also still crossing.

There's a splash. A girl slipped off one of the pipes and fell.

I watch her come up for air, sputtering, and flail her arms about. A lieutenant pokes out of a hole in the wall and reaches to help her.

My eyes are wide, and I'm pretty sure I've been clinging to the top of the wall for fifteen seconds too long.

Swallowing hard, I swing my legs over, one at a time, and drop down. The pipe is wide enough that I land easily. But it narrows in a few feet. And I can already tell it's slippery.

I don't know if I can do this. I don't know if I can cross without falling.

But the tower is on the other side.

Eyes wide, I take a step. And another.

By the fifth step, I'm breathing easier. This isn't so bad, as long as I don't look down. As long as I don't think about how cold the water might be, or the fact that I don't know how to swim, and therefore might drown if it's deep.

When I'm almost at the end, I run the rest of the way. My boots slide on the pipe once, and I gasp but recover. I don't stop running until I hit the final platform and grab a rope hanging from the looming tower.

The Extractions who aren't still behind me on the course are already attempting the climb, some only a few ledges up, some nearly halfway. One person is almost at the top.

My lungs feel like they're going to explode in my chest, but I do my best to suck in air and ignore them. I grip the rope with one hand and find a hold on one of the thin ledges of the tower with the other, and pull myself up. My forearms tremble—oh no, oh no—but they hold me steady.

My mouth twists into a smile. This is familiar. This is what I'm good at.

On the sixth ledge, my foot slips.

I cry out and clutch the rope. My feet dangle in the air, leaving me suspended. Sweat dribbles down my cheeks, and I can't let go but I'm losing my grip. I need a foothold—I need one fast.

My boot digs into a crack. I put all my weight on it and push off, climbing up to the next ledge.

I stay there for a second, catching my breath. I can't let that happen again. I'm already high up from the ground, and I'm only going to get higher.

Colonel Parker said we won't get hurt if we fall from the tower, but I don't want to risk it.

I keep moving, fast. There's no wind here—not in this room or anywhere in the Core—but the air grows colder as I reach higher ledges. It nips at my skin through my leather suit.

I pass the Extractions who haven't reached the top of the tower yet, which is most of them.

Soon I'm at the top. I clench my teeth hard, and use what's left of my breath to crawl onto the roof. My whole body is on fire, but it's a good kind of fire. It makes me feel capable of anything.

Standing, I lean over the edge and glimpse the people still struggling up the ledges. That might be Ariadne near the top, but I can't tell for sure.

Adrenaline warms my veins, though the air is freezing. I turn away to cross the rooftop to the other side. I still have to get down. I've lost track of counting seconds. I have no idea how long it's been.

Five sets of ladder rungs stretch from here to the ground. Three of them are already in use by Drew and Stanley, and a girl whose name I don't know.

For a second I hesitate. Should I jump? Colonel Parker said that would be faster.

But it's a long way down. And I don't know if I trust him when he says we won't get hurt.

The ladders look less scary to use. I lower myself onto a rung, slowly at first, to test the strength. It holds me, so I drop to the next. There's pressure in my lungs from controlling my breathing for so long, but it eases as my altitude decreases.

I shift my weight to the rung below me, and it snaps.

I hang suspended, gripping the metal bar above me, my heartbeat in my fingertips. My toes stretch, seeking something to touch, but my legs aren't long enough. The next rung is barely three inches from my toes, but I can't reach it without letting go.

My teeth clench so hard, I might break them. I'm going to fall.

I strain my arm muscles and try to pull myself up to stand on the rung I'm holding. I can't do it. Adrenaline rushes through me, but my biceps are too tired. I'm not strong enough.

I squeeze the bar until my fingers hurt. I'm okay. I'm okay. I'm *not* okay.

Parker said if we fall, something will keep us from getting hurt. Which means I won't die, but what if he's a liar? I don't think he wants me to die; I think the Developers want me alive, but I'm not certain. I don't know if I trust him.

My fingers are slipping, and my heart is racing, and I'm going to have to do something. I can't reach the next rung, and I can't hold on much longer.

I have to trust him. I don't have another option.

I squeeze my eyes shut and let my fingers slide off the rung.

My nerves scream. Wind rushes past me, ice that chokes me. I'm falling, tumbling from the sky, and nothing will catch me. I will splatter, and then *nothing*.

But something soft surrounds me, like a breeze or a bed of feathers, and I float. I'm still high, still sinking lower, but no longer in danger of breaking. I'm a leaf on the wind, falling slowly until I land on the soft mat on the ground.

I close my eyes, my chest still heaving, trying to get more air in.

I open my eyes and Sam is standing beside me, a small scanner in his hand. His eyes are narrowed.

I push off the mat, glancing around. Drew is here too, leaning over and coughing up saliva. And Stanley is almost down. But I don't think either one of them jumped—they didn't have to.

"What was her time, Sam?" a second voice says. I turn to see Colonel Parker.

"Four minutes and twelve seconds." Sam's voice is stiff.

Colonel Parker observes me, his eyes saying something I can't read. "And that was her first time. Incredible." He pulls a small tablet out of his back pocket. His fingers tap the screen. "Commander Charlie will want to hear about this."

My eyes flit to Sam. He scowls at me from behind Colonel Parker. I can't help smiling a little. I didn't beat his time today, but maybe I will tomorrow. I proved myself like I wanted to.

Now Commander Charlie will know my name.

13

I stand in Recreation Division with Oliver and Ariadne, watching two boys who look like they're ten years old fight each other on a floor mat, while their friends cheer them on. The bigger boy aims a kick at the other's stomach, knocking him to his knees. He shoves his head to the floor and pins him for three seconds.

Ding.

A screen on one side of the mat adds a point to the bigger boy's score. He's winning four to one.

Seeing kids hit each other like this for fun makes my mouth taste sour.

"See?" Ariadne says beside me. "Soldier training."

"It's just a game," I say, turning away. "They want to be officials when they grow up, so they're practicing."

"Since when are you okay with them growing up to be officials?" Oliver asks, his voice almost spiteful.

I falter, biting my lip. He's right. Why am I defending them? "I'm not."

"Good." Oliver moves past me into the crowd, his shoulder

bumping mine a little too hard. "Since you're the only person who passed the officials' obstacle course the first time, I wasn't sure if you'd decided to become one of them. You and Sam seemed pretty tight, after all."

I stare after him. "Excuse me?"

"Just saying."

I glance at Ariadne, who twists her mouth. Her blue eyes reflect the flashing lights.

"I wasn't trying to pass because of that," I say, trying to keep my voice steady. "I don't want to be an official. I have to do well in training because . . ." I swallow, unsure if I want to tell them. "Because there's someone I'm trying to save."

"Who?" Ariadne asks.

His face flashes through my head: his starry eyes, and the scars on his skin, and those lips that turned me into lightning. "Just someone," I say, blinking fast because my eyes are watering.

Oliver turns around. "I'm sorry," he says. Pain flickers through his eyes.

I duck my head so he won't see my face. "Do you miss anyone?" I ask. "From where you came from."

"No," Ariadne says without hesitation. When I look up, her lips are pressed firmly together.

"I do," Oliver says. He runs his fingers through his hair, his eyes on the ground and his forehead creased. "But it's pointless, you know? We're not going to see them anymore."

"Thank the stars," Ariadne whispers.

They're wrong, but I don't want to argue with them. I turn away and take a breath, and remind myself that everything is going to be okay. Commander Charlie already knows my name. I just have to keep this up. I just have to show him I'm useful and that he can trust me.

I just have to convince him to make an exception for Logan.

I wipe the wetness from my eyes and glance back at Ariadne and Oliver. "Come on, let's do something, yeah?"

"Sure," Oliver says.

We push into the crowd, past the tank where people are swimming. We pass the zero-gravity capsules and a giant system of glass-and-steel tunnels where children are crawling. None of them appeal to me at the moment, and they must not appeal to Oliver or Ariadne, either, because we keep on walking in silence.

"Hey, Shorty," someone says.

I know who it is before I turn around. I stiffen.

Sam pushes through the crowd with those two boys he was with yesterday. There's a smirk on his face, as usual, but something colder in his eyes. The same glare he gave me earlier when Colonel Parker congratulated me on my time.

"What do you want?" I ask.

"We thought you three might be down for a little game," he says, sticking his hands in his pockets.

"Why would we be?"

"All the cool kids are playing it. We're about to go pick teams. See that dome over there by the wall?" He points behind us.

I turn and look. He means the massive steel dome with PHANTOM flashing on its side. The dome stretches through a hole in the glass floor above ours.

"What's the game?" Oliver asks, frowning.

Sam's lips spread into a grin. "Come see."

⚹

I'm not sure why we agreed to this. Beyond the entrance to the dome, the room is small and round, brimming with unfamiliar weapons in glass cabinets and steel fixtures. Static sounds and low hums fill the air.

"Phantom Preparation Deck," a computerized voice says. "Pick your weapons."

There are quite a few people in here already—ten or twelve of them around my age, I'd guess. They wear leather suits like mine, but in shades of red, gray or green. Ahead of me, a muscular boy in gray snatches an orange mega-gun with double barrels. It's the biggest weapon I see.

"Everyone, gather up," Sam yells. He and one of his buddies march to the far side of the room, to a round door I imagine leads into the main part of the dome. They face the rest of the group.

"Captains are me and Riley," Sam says. "We're doing two teams, nine people on each. It's gonna be tough today. If you don't think you can handle it, better leave now. There are plenty of easier training modules. Go test those out. Riley, take first pick."

"You in the red." Sam's crony, Riley, points to a well-built girl who cracks her knuckles and smirks.

"Joe." Sam makes his first pick.

The muscular boy with the orange mega-gun nods.

"What a surprise," a girl standing a couple feet in front of me mutters.

Riley picks another person. Sam picks another.

Finally there are only three people who haven't been chosen: me, Oliver, and Ariadne.

It's Sam's pick first. He rubs his chin and smiles. He whispers something in Riley's ear.

"Fine," Riley says, rolling his eyes.

"Shorty and Blondie on my team," Sam says. "Riley's taking Glasses."

"Two minutes to launch," a computerized voice says, echoing through the room.

"Let's hurry." Sam moves toward a weapon's cabinet.

I turn to Oliver, who's grimacing. "Sorry," I say. "We can still not do this, if you want."

"Nah, it's fine," he says. He adjusts his glasses and moves to inspect a case full of small bots that remind me of cam-bots, but they're shooting lasers. A girl sticks out her foot, and he trips flat on the floor.

"Hey," I snap.

She smirks and walks away. A few other girls giggle.

I help Oliver to his feet, narrowing my eyes at the girl's back. What's wrong with her?

"Thanks," he mumbles.

Beside me, Ariadne braids her hair and inspects the weapons compartments with curious eyes.

"You okay too?" I ask.

"Yeah."

I guess I'm the only one who's not sure about this. Maybe because Sam hasn't even explained the game yet.

I turn to search for a weapon and realize he's coming over.

"You know, Extractions never get to do this before they complete their initial training," Sam says with a wide, mischievous smile. His teeth are a perfect, polished line. "You should be happy I'm allowed to make exceptions."

"How touching," I say.

"Blondie's grateful," he says, taking a step closer to Ariadne. "Aren't you, love?" He reaches for her hand.

She snatches it away from him, looking disgusted. But the color rises in her cheeks.

Amusement sparks in his eyes.

"Ignore him," I say, and step to one of the cabinets. Round purple guns sit behind the glass, under a sign that reads DEATH RAYS.

"Stick with the coppers." Sam stretches a hand to reach into a black net strung above the cabinet beside me. He removes a small copper-colored laser gun. "They have knives too." A blade pops out when he clicks a button. "You can blast an enemy or stick one in the gut, and it's just the right size for you." He tosses it to me, his eyes dancing with malice.

The girl who tripped Oliver giggles. Several others glance at me, some smirking, others whispering to each other.

I tuck the copper between my legs and work my curls into a bun, ignoring the girls. "Tell me what the game is."

Sam grins. "You don't like surprises?"

"I want to be prepared."

He tosses a copper to Ariadne, who blushes a deeper shade of pink. He turns away and squats to find something in a giant steel drawer. "We're going to fight Unstables."

Beside me, the copper Ariadne was holding a moment ago clatters to the floor.

I stare at Sam. "They're not real," I say, hoping he won't correct me.

"They can't be," Oliver says, coming back over with a frown. He snaps on an armored vest. "We shot all the ones in the Core."

The gunshots from the other night echo in my ears, and I flinch. But Oliver's right. Unstables are usually kept in the Karum treatment facility on the Surface. That's where they're killed too, unless Commander Charlie decides to use them for an Extraction welcome ceremony.

"Of course they're fake," the annoying girl snaps. "It's a simulation."

"Be nice," Sam says. He straightens with a silver gun in his hand that has a rounded barrel and lots of buttons on its side. His eyes meet mine. "An army of Unstables attacks both our teams. The team who kills the most wins."

"How much time do we have?"

"It's different every game."

The computerized voice breaks in: "Thirty seconds to launch."

The annoying girl and the others adjust their weapons and move toward the round door into the main dome, pushing against each other to get closer.

"Follow orders in there," Sam says. "Do whatever I say. Got it?"

I lie and say, "Yes."

"One more thing." He takes a step closer to me, and his hot breath touches my ear. It smells acrid and smoky. "If you and Blondie make us lose," he whispers, "my fingers might accidentally tap a button on my gun when the muzzle's pointed your way. Any injuries you get in there will hurt like krite. So I wouldn't make us lose if I were you."

My stomach clenches.

"Ten seconds," the voice says.

I grit my teeth, shove Sam away, and snatch two laser-proof vests. I throw one to Ariadne, who fumbles for it, but catches it.

Sam's kidding. He's angry I passed Colonel Parker's test earlier, and he's joking to mess with my head. But he still watches me, and the fire in his gaze makes my legs wobbly.

The lights dim, and a *whir* picks up. A round door in front of us slides open.

I snap my vest into place. I grip my copper.

The computerized voice offers two more words: "Launching Phantom."

14

We step into the pitch blackness of the dome.

There's a flash. Giant letters type their way onto a screen overhead: MISSION OBJECTIVE: DESTROY UNSTABLES. MISSION TIME: TEN MINUTES.

"Ten minutes?" Oliver's voice cracks, somewhere to my right.

I hold my breath.

The letters disappear and the blackness warps. Thick green stems rise out of the ground, higher and higher, sprouting purple petals that form curly and spiral shapes. Other plants and trees grow with spiny limbs and weeping veils of leaves. Mud squishes beneath my boots where water seeps into the dirt, more and more of it, flowing and flowing.

"Move it!" Sam shoves the butt of his gun into my arm.

I splash into the trees and bump into Oliver. Huffing, I narrow my eyes as fire slides through my shoulder. "You didn't have to—"

"Shut up," Sam says, stopping on firmer ground and scanning the jungle.

Where the water seeped into the dirt, there's a river now, deep and murky. Members of both teams stand on the other bank. Ariadne's over there. She's looking wildly around, backing up into a tree. I have a bad feeling she won't be okay over there. Some of the boys give her strange looks.

But the river looks too deep, and I can't swim. I can't cross it.

"What now?" Oliver says. He's the only member of the other team on our side.

"You stay away from us." Sam moves past him roughly. "Joe, you cover inside."

The brawny boy with the giant orange gun nods and tramples off into the trees.

"Marcus, take the left," Sam says. "Shorty, stick with me."

"When does the timer start?" I ask.

"As soon as the Unstables appear."

I clutch the copper to my chest and glance at Oliver. He's a little shaky now.

A hollow choking sound reaches my ears, coming from behind.

I spin, pressing a knob on my gun so it's ready to fire. Overhead, red numbers appear in the sky: 10:00:00, and the team scores: 0:0.

The clock has started.

"First kill is yours, Shorty," Sam says with a smirk. "Think you can handle it?"

This is all in my head. All of this is fake.

"Of course," I say.

Sam narrows his eyes. Guess he doesn't like my confidence.

A broken, strangled sound bubbles up from the river. Strands of hair emerge, then the top of a head, dripping wet. Dark fingers stretch from the water, reaching for the mud of the bank. Eyelids, nose, and a mouth appear, grayish and wrinkled.

"H-help me," a voice cries.

I freeze with my finger on the blast button. The bags under his eyes are dark, even darker than mine looked before my operation. When his eyes open, they're the color of dusk. His limbs shake as he digs his nails into the mud and drags himself out of the river not five feet away from me, his bony chest heaving.

I've never seen an Unstable this close before—not even the woman I shot in the glass compartment. They're dangerous, and we aren't allowed to get this close to them. So why make a game where we have to fight them?

"Kill it," Sam orders.

Pressing my lips together, I touch my finger to the blast button and start to press.

"P-please . . ."

The Unstable coughs, choking on phlegm.

An awful realization hits me—

Slaps me—

Shocks me.

He sounds like Laila did when the officials dragged her into the hov-pod, that day they took her to quarantine. She begged them to let her stay. She swore she'd try harder to raise her Promise, but they didn't care. They dragged her away while she struggled to give me her shoes. Her shoes, her ripped up *shoes*. That's all they let her leave behind.

"I said kill it," Sam hisses.

"What if we can help him—"

"He's not real, you idiot. *Kill it*."

I ease my finger over the button, readying to press but still staring at the Unstable.

Why does he look so real? His dusk-colored eyes lift to mine, and I see the sky in them. Vast, never ending, gray-blue. Starry-night eyes, like Logan's.

Sam's elbow knocks into my face.

Dots—dots—

Teeth clenched—

Stumbling—

A gunshot goes off in the distance.

Oliver catches me with clumsy hands. "Sam, stop it!" he says.

Another gunshot.

When my vision clears, I'm gasping for breath, and Oliver hasn't let go of me. Sam is in my face. "You shoot them, for krite's sake, or I will kill you."

"It's only a game." Oliver tightens his hold on me.

"Phantom isn't just a game," Sam spits. "It teaches us how to strategize in combat. It trains us, like most things here do, in case there's ever another rebellion in the outer sectors and we have to fight them."

I stare at him. He said most things here train us for that. Extraction training, too? Colonel Parker's obstacle course?

But it makes no sense. There won't be any rebellion. Every person in any of the sectors who disobeys or seems like a rebel ends up in a detention facility, or marked Unstable. The officials take care of that.

Before I can reply, Sam wrenches me away from Oliver and throws me to the ground. I land hard on my hands and knees in shallow water. His boot smacks into my side.

"I said I'll kill you if you don't shoot. Do you think I'm joking?"

"No," I sputter.

"Then shoot them."

Through the curls falling over my eyes, I see Unstables everywhere. Piling like dead bodies in the river, staggering from the trees, all of them coming for us, moaning and crying. Lasers and cracks and zaps of guns fill the air on the opposite bank. The Unstables turn to mist when their hearts stop beating. Real people don't turn to mist, so these definitely aren't real. This is only a game.

I push off the ground and get to my feet.

"I said shoot them," Sam says.

I'm already aiming. I press the blast button on my copper. The recoil makes me stagger back several feet, but I get an Unstable in the face. The laser blows her to bloody chunks that sink with a gurgle into the murky river before vanishing.

"Finally." Sam growls, blasting his sixth or seventh to smithereens.

I stare at the copper in my hand, at the metal barrel that's smaller than the gun I used to shoot a real Unstable. The welcome ceremony. Would Sam say that was supposed to train us for rebellion, too?

I remember what Ariadne said earlier before we entered the obstacle course: *They're training us to be soldiers.*

I laughed at her then. Commander Charlie trains some people to be soldiers, to keep order in the outer sectors. But he doesn't need to train everyone because there isn't any war. There's no one to fight.

And even if there was, I could still refuse. He can't train me to be mindless.

I don't know why my hands are trembling.

Stumbling out of the water, I aim at another Unstable and hit it in the leg. It's much easier when I don't look at faces. When I don't see Logan in their eyes.

"Clementine!" Oliver says. Two Unstables lurch toward him. He tries to back up from them and almost trips over a rock. His arms shake when he fires his gun, and his lasers keep missing.

I got him into this. I can't let him get hurt.

"Duck!" I yell.

He obliges, and I aim at one, then the other. Their blood splatters on his face.

A searing pain shoots through my elbow. I cry out, spin around, and slash an Unstable's face with my copper's knife until its teeth loosen their hold on my skin.

"Speed it up!" Sam shouts. "Clock's ticking."

The timer overhead is already down to five minutes. The score is 34 to 47 with team one in the lead. We are losing.

Ignoring the soreness in my arm, I turn my head and concentrate on our environment. Giant flowers, jungle plants, turbid river water, weeping trees. There has to be something in here that can help me eradicate a bunch of Unstables at once. Something the other team won't think of.

A child-size Unstable lunges at my leg. I jump back and blast him. Turning, I knock the butt of my copper into another Unstable and make for the trees.

I don't know what I'll find, but I will look regardless.

"What're you—" Oliver starts, but something distracts him, and I don't hear him anymore. Moss and jungle leaves muffle gunshots. I hope he'll be all right without me.

The canopy of branches overhead makes it darker, harder to see where I'm running. I stumble; I pick myself up. A body appears behind a tree trunk, teetering toward me. Then another with an arm outstretched, reaching for my face. I try to shoot it down, but I don't wait to see if it works.

I search for the tallest tree.

Branches snap beneath my feet. Vines slap my cheeks when I fail at ducking under them. Jungle smells seep into my nose: musk, stuffy air, and the sweet and tangy scents of pollen. If there are silver asters in here, I'll be crippled and knocked out with fire bleeding through my body when Sam finds me and shoots me.

Maybe that would be for the best.

I duck underneath a web of leaves and spider silk, and the muzzle of the orange mega-gun points straight at my eyes. A scream escapes my lips before I even think it.

"Oh, krite. Sorry." The muscular boy with the gun, Joe, quickly lowers his weapon.

"*Think* before you fire," I say through gritted teeth.

"I think I just did."

"Barely." I wipe saliva off my mouth with the back of my palm.

He frowns at me. "What're you doing here? Sam told you to stay with him."

"I'm looking for something."

"Vrux." He pushes me out of his way, and a loud whooshing sound peals from his gun. A shriek, then the slam of a body hitting the ground.

"Come on, we've got like two minutes left." He tramples off again.

Two minutes, and through cracks in the canopy, the numbers in the sky say we are falling further behind. I press my hands into my knees, doubling over. What can I do? Even if Sam doesn't kill me, he's going to hurt me if we lose. I don't have any doubts.

Think, I tell myself. What do I know?

We're in a simulation. I don't know much about this game, but I know simulations of this size often have hidden functions in them—buttons or levers that blend into the environment, which could turn off a simulation or switch it to a different mode.

We're still inside a dome. If there's a secret button or lever, the best place to hide it would be some part of the wall or ceiling, since neither is visible while the game is in motion. Maybe, maybe, a different mode would help my team win. If I can even find the switch and set it off.

"Joe!" I yell, stumbling after him.

I'm wrong, no doubt, but I'll try regardless. I have an idea where a switch might be. However, I need a stronger weapon.

"What?" Annoyed, Joe slows and turns to me, sweat dripping down his forehead. "We're gonna lose!"

"Switch guns with me."

"What?"

"Switch guns with me!"

He looks at me like I'm crazy.

"Joe, trust me. Switch with me!"

He growls, but his grip loosens on the mega-gun. I grab it from him and push my copper into his fingers.

Turning, I look to the tallest tree in the vicinity. It looms over my head, some thirty feet tall, at least. I heave myself onto the lowest branch. Moss tangles in my eyes, my hair, my face. Back, I tell it.

"What're you doing?"

I don't answer.

It's hard to climb with only one hand. I manage because I have no other choice.

Logan used to say I'm the best climber there is. One time, he tried to race me up one of the trees on the edge of the forest. I told him not to try, because of his limp, but he did it anyway. He was taller; I was faster. I beat him, and he didn't scowl or laugh or chide me for it. He hugged me. He wrapped me in his arms, in his warmth, like he would never let me go.

Branches scrape my hands. Sweat gathers on my face and under my armpits. With every step, the gun feels heavier and heavier in my hand.

Thirty seconds left, the sky says.

The weapon slows me when I want to fly, but I need it or this won't work.

Please work. Please work. Please work.

Above, through a break in the weeping leaves, a pair of red-gold wings flies past over the treetops. I can't see the steel of the dome, but it's there. I know it is.

Fifteen seconds, the sky says.

There's no time. I clear the last of the branches that are heavy enough to hold me. I grip the barrel of the orange gun and aim at invisible steel. My finger brushes the biggest blast button.

Ten seconds.

I smash the button.

Squeeze my eyes shut.

There's a rushing sound and a blast so loud its vibrations rip through my skull. I open my eyes and block out the jungle fading away. I block out everything but the scores in the sky: one is 72, and the other is 97 . . . 105 . . . 117 . . . it's still rising.

It worked. *It worked.*

The branches of my tree turn to mist, and my relief shatters in my throat. I have nothing to cling to.

I fall through nothing but air, screaming

15

Lights flicker on overhead like stars.

I'm shaking. I'm shaking so badly, air can't even reach my lungs. Fire shoots through my legs and arms and chest, and I gasp for breath. I need that adrenaline back. But the pain in my body mingles with relief. The ground could have been linoleum or stone. I could have died when I slammed into it.

What a funny thing that would be, to escape death only to find it in the place where I'm supposed to be safe.

I heave myself onto my elbows. It's dark in here, even with the lights like stars. Shadows make for the exit door. Boots and legs stumble past one another. The scores have disappeared from the sky.

A shadow drops beside me. Oliver's glasses glint where they aren't smeared with blood.

"What happened to you?" His voice is anxious.

"N-nothing." I try to get up. "Did you see who won?"

"Not yet. They took the scores down."

I bite my lip. I want to tell him what I did, but at the same time I'm afraid I dreamed it.

He grasps my wrist and pulls me to my feet. My leg screams in pain, and I gasp and lean against him heavily.

He frowns. "You don't seem fine."

I clench my teeth so I won't cry out. "Really, I'm good. Let's go see the scores."

He grumbles something, but helps me walk.

The outer rim of Phantom has shifted. I can tell as soon as we step through the door because the place is different. The weapons are gone, and the room is smaller, with black walls and pale lights. This must be what it looks like pre-game. My teammates and opponents crowd before a gray hologram displaying the words:

SCORE PENDING

To my right, a WEAPONS AND ARMOR DISPOSAL slot in the wall flashes red. Oliver eases the laser-proof vest off me, and I slide it in after the mega-gun. The slot makes a crunching sound as if it's eating the metal.

I shift my weight to the wall and dig my nails into my arm to distract me from the pain in my leg. I notice that mud coats Oliver, like he rolled around in it. Blood soaks spots in the fabric of his leather suit, but I don't think the blood is his. I hope it's not his.

He frowns and pulls a clump of leaves out of my hair.

"Did you kill many Unstables?" I ask.

"A few. Sam kept knocking me out of the way."

"I'd like to punch him. Where is he?"

"I don't know." Like me, Oliver is too short to see him.

Ariadne steps into the room, running her fingers through her braid and glancing around nervously. She spots us and hurries over. There's a small cut on her left cheek where a strand of hair is plastered to dried blood, but that's the only wound I see.

I open my mouth to ask if she was okay in there, but her eyes widen, and she speaks first. "Clem, what happened?"

I touch a hand to my face and feel my mouth. My upper lip feels fatter than it should, and my forehead stings, but that's all. "Is it that bad?"

"It looks like they reversed the beauty operation." Oliver grimaces.

I snort. "Oh, really?"

Ariadne frowns. "No, you just have a couple scrapes."

"Thanks, Oliver." I hit his arm.

"Ow." He rubs his elbow. "I was joking."

I shrug and smile. He shakes his head, but his eyes catch mine, and he smiles too.

A flicker runs across the gray hologram.

The scores pop up:

TEAM ONE: 72   TEAM TWO: 286

Gasps fill the room. I stare at the final score. It's higher than I ever imagined it would be.

The scores slide to the top of the hologram, and two columns appear, one with individual scores and one with a leader board.

LEADER BOARD

FIRST:	CLEMENTINE	178
SECOND:	SAM	58
THIRD:	BEECHY	56
FOURTH:	RILEY	44

Relief runs through me again, and this time nothing stops it. I don't know how my plan worked—it doesn't actually make any sense, now that I think about it—but I don't care. I didn't make us lose, which means Sam won't try to kill me.

My lips spread into a smile. I beat his score. I beat *every* score.

Ariadne gapes at me. So does everyone else.

"What did you *do*?" Oliver breathes.

"She must've shot that thing Sam was trying to find," someone says. "Every game, there's a spot that explodes everything. They say you have to be ridiculously smart to find it."

"That doesn't exist," a boy says flatly.

"She must've cheated," another says.

"I didn't cheat," I say, but maybe I did. No one explained the rules to me.

"Oh, yeah?" The annoying girl from earlier crosses her arms. "Then how'd you do it, huh?"

"It could be a Phantom glitch," someone offers.

"Phantom doesn't glitch," Joe cuts in, grinning at me. "She found the spot. She's vruxing brilliant."

"Uh-huh, sure, Joe, that makes *so* much sense." The girl rolls her eyes.

"Shut up," Sam says, and I'm so short I can't even see where he is. "All of you, *shut up*."

He shoves through the group, past Ariadne and Oliver, and stops two feet in front of me. Tension flickers in his jaw, his body, and his clenched fists.

"Get out," he says. "Everyone, get out."

The girl starts to say something, but everyone complies, heading through a glass door that slides open and reveals the main floor of Recreation Division. Ariadne shifts on her feet. Oliver mouths "Come on" to me.

Sam's eyes turn me to ice. I purse my lips and move toward my friends. He blocks me with a strong arm.

"Everyone but you," he says. His face is too close.

"No way," Oliver says. "We're not leaving you alone with her."

"Clem?" Ariadne's voice is uncertain. She glances at Sam with wide eyes.

"Get out," Sam says again. His gaze burns me.

It hits me that my plan was a bad idea. He doesn't like that I beat his score—which almost makes me smile. I did beat him, finally. That makes me feel stronger. More Promising.

I don't want to run away from him. I don't want him to think I'm a coward, not after all of this.

I take a breath. "Both of you can go," I say. "I'll be there in a minute."

"No." Oliver reaches for my arm.

Sam knocks his hand aside.

"Just go," I tell Oliver, my voice hard. He doesn't need to get hurt for me.

Oliver looks at me like I'm crazy.

I set my jaw. "I mean it. I'll be fine."

After a moment, he presses his lips together and grabs Ariadne's hand. "Fine. Come on."

He pulls her through the glass door. It slides shut, and I'm alone with Sam.

I cross my arms. "Well?"

He grabs my shoulders and slams me against the wall. "How'd you do it, huh?" Sam's voice is fierce and strangled. "How'd you do it?"

"I got lucky—"

"Tell me what you did."

He slams me back again—my head hits the steel. My vision spins, and I try to catch my breath. I think someone's pounding on the glass, trying to get back in.

"Tell me!" Sam says again.

"I-I blasted the ceiling," I manage. "I went crazy and blasted the ceiling to find some cheat for the simulation, and it worked, okay?"

He releases his hold on me for half a second to run his fingers through his hair.

I'm still recovering. I set my palms on the wall and start to push off.

He kicks my wounded leg, hard, and I cry out. His hands press me to the wall again.

"First you beat the vruxing test, then you come in here and beat my score." His eyes are glossy. I must be imagining it. "That is *not* okay. Do you know how long it took me to beat Beechy? Commander Charlie's gonna think you're better than me, but it's a *lie*, you vruxing cheat. I'll get you for this—I'll make your life hell—you won't even see it coming."

There are needles, a million needles slicing through my leg. "I can't believe"—I struggle to breathe—"you're threatened by *me*. You must be really insecure."

"Shut *up*."

Again, my head smacks the wall. Stars speckle Sam's face in my vision, and I feel wetness in my hair and on my cheeks. Oliver yells something but the glass muffles it.

"I'd kill you right now," Sam says, "but I'd miss out on so much fun, making you suffer." He lets out a shaky laugh. "If you even get through training. To be honest, I doubt you'll do well enough in the next stage. Commander Charlie will realize he made a mistake when he picked you, and he'll ship you off to quarantine, where you belong. You and everyone else who is worthless."

"You're wrong." My temple pounds with fire, but I won't cry for him.

A smile tugs at his lips. "You think you're safe now, but are you, really?" His voice softens. "Maybe I should take advantage of the situation, if they're going to kill you soon. Remember, I'm a lieutenant. I'm the one with authority here."

His fingers trail along my collarbone to the back of my neck and my suit zipper.

"Let go of me." I struggle against him. He's too strong. "You'll get in trouble if you touch me," I say, but in my mind I'm screaming because I don't know if he will. He's a lieutenant—he's one of Charlie's people.

"You really think so?" His breath is hot in my ear. "I used to be like you, you know. An Extraction with high Promise. But I came here when I was ten. Commander Charlie transferred me early because he knew I was special, and I've been training to be one of his army leaders ever since."

Through the glass, I can't see Oliver or Ariadne anymore. I'm alone and no one can help me. If I could slip away, if I could *run*—

He pulls my suit zipper down and skims his fingers over the small of my back, lower and lower until they are too low.

"I'll kill you. I swear, I'll kill you."

"I'd like to see you try," he whispers.

He presses his shoulders and hips against mine, and it feels *wrong*. This happened to me one time back on the Surface with an official—a bad, bad night, but not the worst, because Logan got there before the man could take it too far. I was halfway out of my dress and sobbing, but Logan found me and made him go away.

Now Logan's not here. Now I can't even speak, and my wrists and legs are pinned. I want to murder Sam. I want to strangle him, but I can't.

The glass door slides open. "Sam, back off," a voice says.

Sam's eyes narrow. He digs his nails into my back—I cry out—and pulls away, leaving me sickened and trembling against the wall.

A young man stands in the doorway, his muscles showing through his dark leather suit. He looks older than me, but not more than twenty-two or twenty-three. His black hair is tinted green.

His eyes lock with mine, and all the color drains from his face. "You . . ." he says.

I've never seen him before in my life. He moves toward me abruptly. I make a noise and press against the wall, but there's nowhere to go.

He hesitates. "You're not . . ."

"Not what?" I ask when he doesn't finish.

He sighs and rubs his temple. "Sorry. I mistook you for someone."

"And they say you're smart," Sam says.

The boy turns to him with narrowed eyes. "What the vrux were you thinking?"

Sam crosses his arms, but he doesn't answer. If he thinks refusing to speak makes him superior or clever, he is wrong.

Oliver stumbles toward me out of the flashing lights, Ariadne two steps behind him. "Are you okay?" he asks. "I'm sorry, I tried to get back in."

I still feel Sam's nails in my back, his fingers trailing across my skin, his breath in my face. Worse, I feel the Surface official's grimy hands ripping through my dress. I want to drown myself in shower water until the memories go away. I want to throw a knife, or maybe ten knives, at Sam's face.

"I'm going to kill him," I say.

Oliver shoots Sam a dirty look. "You won't have to do it alone."

I wipe the moisture out of the corner of my eyes and reach a shaking hand behind my back to pull up the zipper, but Ariadne moves my hand away. Her fingers zip me up, closing the path to my skin. She brushes the curls off my neck.

"I asked you a question," the boy in the doorway snaps.

"It's none of your business." Sam shoves past him, but the boy grabs hold of his arm and doesn't let go. He's stronger.

"What are you even doing here, huh?" Sam snaps. "Stalking me again?"

I wish I were stronger. I wish I could make him hurt.

The boy snorts. "You're paranoid. I wanted to check if you beat my score." He glances at the hologram and smiles. "Ah, you did, by two points."

He must be Beechy, the one in third place.

"But wait," he says. "Someone beat *your* score? Who's Clementine?"

I swallow. "Me," I say.

Beechy looks at me. Recognition flits through his eyes again— it looks almost painful this time. I don't understand it.

"Ah," he says, looking away from me. "Jealous, as always. You really need to work on that, Sam. Fight the insecurities, and maybe some good will come of it."

Sam wrenches away from him and makes for the door.

Oliver's nostrils flare. He's in Sam's way, but he doesn't move aside to let him pass.

A fist flies, and there's a crack.

Oliver is on the floor, clutching his arm. The glass slides shut and Sam disappears.

My heart might've stopped beating, but now it starts again, way too fast.

"Vrux." Beechy moves to Oliver.

I can't move, and then I move without thinking, stumbling to drop to my knees beside my wounded friend. Ariadne follows, holding on to me.

Beechy tries to touch Oliver's arm, but Oliver pulls back. Tears trickle down his cheeks, and my throat clenches. This is my fault. If I hadn't beaten the test earlier, Sam wouldn't have been mad and asked us to play Phantom in the first place. Or if I hadn't been stupid enough to stay with him afterward, if I'd just *run*, this wouldn't have happened.

"I'm sorry," I say. "I should've listened."

"No, it's not your fault." He shakes his head. "I shouldn't have left you alone with him, I really shouldn't have."

"Shh." I squeeze his sweaty palm.

"And you?" Beechy says to me in a hard voice. "Did Sam touch you?"

A stone fills my throat, making it hard to swallow. In the way Beechy means, he almost did. He made me think of that other time, which I'd tried to forget, but now I can't. I can't forget the roughness, the weakness, the fear, and how safe I felt when Logan finally found me and buried me in his warmth again.

"He was going to," I say.

Beechy presses his lips into a line. "I thought so." He keeps looking at me, and I think he's going to say something else, but he doesn't. He turns back to Oliver. "Come on, let's get you to a doctor."

Oliver protests, but Beechy ignores him. He eases his arms under his body and lifts him up, then sets him carefully on his feet but doesn't let go of his good arm.

I stand and clench my fists at my sides. Stop shaking, I tell my body. *Stop it.*

Oliver is shaking too. His face is ashen, and I wish I could do something to make him better.

"Let's go," Beechy says, glancing at me again.

Ariadne tugs on my arm, and I lean on her and limp out of Phantom, following Beechy and Oliver.

We pass through Slumber Division to reach the health ward. It sits below the Nourishment Division cafeteria and above Restricted Division, the part of the Core where only Developers and high-classified personnel are allowed to go.

I lean against the wall of the elevator between Ariadne and Oliver, who clutches his arm and breathes heavily.

I glance at Beechy. His eyes shift away from me. "So who are you?" I ask.

He smiles. "Right. Sorry. I'm Beechy, mechanical engineer. I fly ships and teach people how to fly them." He offers a hand.

I take it and force a smile. "Clementine. This is Oliver, and that's Ariadne."

"You're a pilot?" Oliver asks, his voice a bit hoarse.

"Mhm."

"Could you teach me?"

Beechy chuckles as the elevator dings and the door zips open. "Let's get your arm better first. Then we'll see."

We step out into the health ward lobby. Beechy goes to the desk to talk to the receptionist, while we sit in the waiting chairs.

A couple minutes later, a nurse arrives with a tablet in hand. "What happened to you three?" She eyes our muddy figures.

"Phantom." I grip Oliver's arm to steady him as he stands.

The nurse glances at him and then at me, her forehead creasing. "Which one of you got hurt?"

"Both of them," Beechy says.

"No, just him." I wipe dried blood off my forehead. The back of my head hurts, but I don't have dizziness, amnesia, or fatigue, so I don't think I got a concussion. Anyway, Oliver's arm needs more attention.

The nurse makes a tsk sound and gestures for us to follow her. She leads us into a small, round examination room just down the hall.

"You." She points at me. "Wash that blood off in the sink." She turns to Oliver and looks him over carefully. "You'll need a steam-clean. It's just through there." She points at a sliding door in the wall that's not the one we came through.

Oliver looks like he swallowed something sour.

"It won't hurt, dear," the nurse says, giving him a light pat on the shoulder. "One of your friends can help you walk in there and wait just outside, if that makes you feel better. You can keep your clothes on."

He looks over to me. I shift my weight to my injured leg in order to walk. Pain shoots up my calf muscle. I muffle my cry with a cough.

"I'll go," Ariadne says.

Oliver takes a shuddering breath and winces, but lets her help him walk. They move through the sliding door, and they're gone.

"A physician will be here shortly," the nurse says to me and Beechy, and leaves the way we came in.

The smell of antiseptic makes my stomach sick. I grit my teeth and wrap my arms around my waist.

In the silence, Sam is in my head again. Sam's hips pressed against mine in that way that was *wrong*. Sam's fingers skimming the small of my back. Sam's lips too close to mine.

My eyes seek Beechy, for a distraction. He's watching me again. His eyes are the color of sunlight in the breaking moments of the day, before the stars hide.

"You think you can manage without me?" he asks.

"Yes." He probably means with Oliver, but I mean the next time I face Sam. I'll have to manage alone. I'll have to get stronger, somehow.

Beechy nods. "Good."

I look at my feet. *Good*, I think.

I wet my lips and turn to go to the sink, but I stop because he's still looking at me. A crease appears between his brows.

He takes a step toward me and brushes my upper lip with two fingers. I flinch away from them, but his hand follows.

"You should clean this off," he says. "It might bruise."

"I don't mind bruises."

His lip twitches into a smile. "I'm not surprised." His hand drops away.

"See you," he whispers. The main door slides shut behind him. I stare after him. I swallow.

The other door opens, and I jump.

Ariadne leads Oliver back into the room. He's not muddy anymore, but the pain is heavier in his face, in the way he struggles to breathe. Ariadne helps him into the examination chair. I squeeze my arm with a hand, fighting the urge to help him too. I'm afraid it'll hurt my leg.

When Ariadne finishes helping him, she brushes the hair out of her eyes and sits in a chair beside the sink, to the right of Oliver.

"Does it hurt a lot?" I ask him.

"Not bad," he says, but he doesn't let me see his eyes.

The main door zips back open.

Dim blue light casts shadows on the doctor's face. She doesn't say anything, but pauses a moment to let the door close. She snaps on gloves and leans over Oliver's exposed arm and shoulder. Her hair is dark and her lips are a bright pink shade.

"Oh, sweetie." She clicks her tongue and presses two spots on Oliver's arm where a bruise is forming. He grits his teeth and squeezes his eyes shut. "Small fracture, I'd say. Did you fall in Phantom?"

I ease into the chair beside Ariadne. "He was attacked."

She blinks at me behind her thick lashes. "By whom?" She moves to a silver cabinet.

Sweat trickles down Oliver's forehead. "A boy named Sam," he says.

The doctor laughs lightly. Her fingers snatch a syringe, a plastic dish, and a vial of cloudy blue liquid from the cabinet. "Sam who?"

I dig my nails into my thigh. I don't want to have to use his title. "Lieutenant Sam," I say stiffly.

"Ah, of course. Well, I'm sure he had a reason." The doctor fills the syringe and drops the empty vial into the plastic dish. She moves to Oliver, whose face turns chalk white.

I stare at the doctor, at her slightly pursed lips. She knows who Sam is. He must not have been lying, then, about the kind of status he has here. He's a brute and a bully, but Commander Charlie transferred him here early and gave him special rank in the military. *Why?*

Commander Charlie must be like him. That's the only logical reason.

The doctor wipes Oliver's shoulder with a small patch of fabric and pushes the syringe's four-inch needle into his skin. A strangled sound comes from his throat.

"This will ease the pain and help the bone heal faster," she says, pulling the needle out and pressing a square of gauze over the spot. She drops the syringe into the sink and strips off her gloves. "I'll be right back."

The door slides shut behind her.

I need to breathe. It's too hot in here. I push off my seat and limp past Ariadne to the sink. I run a fierce stream of water onto my hands and wipe the dried blood off my face.

"I feel so weak," Oliver whispers. "All Sam did was punch me, and look at me. I'm way too weak."

"You're not weak," I say, switching off the faucet. "We came here three days ago, and Sam's been here for years. He's stronger than you, but you're smarter. You can get stronger."

"I'm not sure I can." Oliver runs his hand over his forehead. "They tried to kill me back in Crust, you know."

"What?" Ariadne says.

"They did." Oliver laughs a little, but it's cold. It doesn't sound right coming from him. " 'Cause of my eyesight. I could still make out faces and coal and stuff at first, but it kept getting worse. I overheard the instructors talking about me at school. They were gonna send patrolmen to take me away in the middle of the night." He pauses.

When he doesn't continue, I say, "But they didn't."

He shakes his head. "They caught me disabling a cam-bot. I'd managed to hack into their security system. Guess they were impressed, or something. So they let me live."

I smile to myself. That's the sort of thing I always wanted to try when I was younger.

"What does that have to do with you not being strong, though?" I ask.

"Well, they told me I wasn't," he says. "They told me my genes weren't built for physical work, but that I was smart enough so it wouldn't matter. They pulled me out of the mines and made me an assistant in their security hub. They kept me away from the other kids, so I wouldn't make friends or care about them. I was ten."

My eyes widen. I've never heard of something like that happening before. Those under age sixteen in the outer sectors are never given special jobs—unless, it seems, they're as smart as Oliver.

Or as brutal as Sam.

"They talked about letting me stay in the hub and just work there forever," Oliver says quietly. "But they ended up deciding to transfer me here instead. Commander Charlie requested it."

Oliver says it as if part of him wishes Commander Charlie hadn't. Like he wishes he were back in Crust working in the security hub, where maybe he felt safe and happy even though most of the kids in that sector aren't.

I think of Logan's fingers lingering on my skin that last rainy day on the Surface, and I almost agree.

That night, I dream I'm trapped with Sam inside four glass walls. Logan stands outside, pounding on the glass, trying to break in. But he can't get in, and I can't get out. Sam presses the barrel of a copper against the skin between my eyes, and smiles.

I wake on the floor drenched in sweat, tangled in blankets.

Ariadne sits up in her bed, the covers pulled to her chin. "Are you okay?" she whispers. "You were screaming."

My cheeks grow hot as I sit up. Did I *fall off*? "I'm fine."

"Are you sure?"

"I'm fine," I say again, snapping the words, because I want to be fine. I *should* be fine.

Ariadne presses her mouth into her sheets. "It's not a bad thing." The fabric muffles her voice.

"What?"

"It's not a bad thing to be afraid."

She watches me, perhaps waiting for me to say something.

When I say nothing, she gives me a sad smile and turns away, rolling onto her other side. Her breathing slows and steadies.

In the dark, I fiddle with the hem of my blanket, wondering what she means. Maybe there's something she fears that's so terrible, the fear keeps her safe from it. It protects her from getting hurt.

But I don't think fear is a good thing for me. It makes me weak, and I don't want to be weak. I don't want to be afraid of Sam or officials or anyone ever again.

16

I don't have any more dreams that night, but I wake too many times.

After a while, I stop trying to sleep, though I have a good hour left before they'll serve breakfast in the cafeteria.

In the bathroom sink, I wash my face with warm water. There's a blackish-blue cut on my upper lip, as Beechy predicted. Another forms a small line above my left eyebrow. I wonder if they'll leave scars like the one I used to have before the surgeons fixed me up to make me feel like I belong here.

I pull on my clothes and tie my boots. My leg throbs a little, but it doesn't hurt as bad as yesterday. I can walk without limping.

Ariadne is still sleeping, curled up on her side with her hands clutching her pillow. She looks so peaceful, I don't want to wake her. Anyway, I think I want to be alone.

In an empty corridor in Invention Division, I sit with my back against reflective steel. In front of me, a strip of glass in the wall reveals the Pipeline's flashing lights. I've already seen one pod fly by, so fast it was really more of a silver blur. I wonder where it's headed. To Lower, Mantle, Crust, or the Surface. If Logan sees it, I wonder if he'll think of me.

We used to watch ships pass by on their way outside the settlement. Before I got lucky one day and found a wooden plank to patch up the giant hole in my shack roof, we had a perfect view of the sky. On nights when pilots flew over our camp, Logan would lift my hand and try to pinch my fingers together at the right moment, so I would squish their ship. If they weren't going to take us with them, we didn't think they had any right to escape.

My intestines twist into knots. I've been without him too long. Four days have passed, and he's already starting to blur in my memory—not all the way, but enough so that I'm worried. My hands shake when I try to picture him.

Maybe I'm a blur to him too. Maybe he's already forgotten me, or given up. He promised he'd stay alive as long as there was a chance he'd see me again, but he might've changed his mind. Or maybe he lied when he promised. I don't know anymore.

If he dies, will I know? Will something shift inside me?

"We have the same hiding spot," a voice says.

I turn my head.

Beechy's boots make soft taps on the floor. He walks toward me with his hands in his pockets and a light smile playing on his lips.

"I'm not hiding."

"Not doing a very good job of it, anyway." He stops beside the glass, training his eyes on the Pipeline. "Guess there isn't really anywhere to hide."

We're quiet for some time. "Did you want something?" I ask.

"No. I'm waiting."

"For what?"

"Doesn't matter." He faces me. "Is your friend Oliver feeling better?"

"I think so," I say, but I don't really know. Last night before we went to bed, his cheeks had more color, and he wasn't shaking anymore. But his eyes didn't have that spark in them as they usually do.

After a moment, Beechy says, his voice softer, "What about you?"

I remember the dream from last night and hug my legs to my chest. "I'm fine."

"You don't have to lie."

"I'm not lying."

He frowns.

An odd feeling tangles my chest. I swallow to make it go away, but it doesn't.

I lie too much, really. Even with Logan, I lied. It was a habit, a way to keep him from worrying. Because he had his own problems to worry about, so why should I bombard him with mine?

But Logan could always tell when I lied. That was the way things were with us; we pretended things were okay even when they weren't.

But I'm not sure I want to lie anymore, to anyone. Especially not to Logan. If he were here, I'd tell him that. I'd tell him I miss him and I don't want to lose him, and I'm sorry for leaving. I'm sorry I can't go back for him yet. I'm sorry I'm not sure I'll be able to convince Commander Charlie to let me.

I push off the ground. He's not here, and I'm going to cry. I don't want Beechy to see me cry. So I'll run. Running is much easier.

"I'll see you." I turn to go.

He reaches out and touches my shoulder, and I pause without even thinking. Like he's a magnet pulling me back. His hand is warm through the leather of my suit. Warm and real and comforting.

"It's important you understand that Sam isn't kind to anyone," he says. "He gets away with it because of his position, because Commander Charlie sees something in him worth encouraging."

I clench my teeth. I don't want to think about Sam anymore. Why did Beechy have to bring him up?

"Why did Charlie even pick him?" I ask. "Officials are supposed to protect us, not hurt us."

"It's complicated."

"It shouldn't be."

"Just . . . please don't give him any more reason to be angry with you."

"I won't. Why would I?"

He turns me around to face him, and gives me a conflicted look that makes me fear he cares too much. Or, he cares too much for whomever I remind him of. "I don't mind saving you," he says, "but I'd rather not have to."

I look away from him, my breathing shaky. I don't like that he thinks I need saving. In the safety of my head and heart, I know I'm strong and brave, but not everyone sees it. I need them to see it, to believe I can survive without their help, because that's the only way I'll learn to survive on my own.

"I should be stronger," I whisper. "I shouldn't need you to save me."

A smile tugs at his mouth. He stares at me, and I stare back. Hesitation fills his eyes, but he doesn't blink or alter his gaze.

He makes me feel strange, both warm and cold at the same time. Maybe I don't have to be afraid.

"You don't have anything this afternoon, do you?" he asks softly.

I shake my head. "Just physical training this morning."

"There's something I'd like to show you. It's not entirely allowed, but . . ." The smile reaches his eyes. "I think I can get away with it. Will you let me show you?"

I bite my lip. I want to let him, but my heart's beating fast. It scares me. "Can I bring Oliver and Ariadne?"

"They can come, if they'd like."

His fingers release my shoulder, and something inside me deflates. "Meet me back here after lunch," he says, and walks away.

I avoid Sam during training. Every time I glance over at him and the other lieutenants, he's watching me with subtle anger in his eyes. There's something else there too: intrigue. As though he's plotting something.

I stay near the middle of the group of Extractions, and hope he won't come near me.

We don't do the obstacle course again. Instead we have two hours of sprints and lunges, while Colonel Parker observes us from the sidelines. I wince with every sprint because my leg still hurts, but I try to hide it. I don't want Sam to know my cheat in Phantom left behind a scar. Thankfully, this is our last day of doing physical work. Tomorrow will be easier.

But by the end of the session, I can't walk without clenching my teeth, and I feel like puking. I wish I'd skipped breakfast.

We shower afterward in a bathroom facility near the training arena. The hot water and steam eases the ache in my leg, until there's no more pain. I stare at my calf, flexing it to test it out. But there's nothing. These showers must have miracle water.

Outside the facility, I meet Ariadne and Oliver.

"You hungry?" I ask.

Ariadne shakes her head.

"Me neither."

"I am. . . ." Oliver says, almost embarrassed. He was told to take it easy during sprints because his arm is still in a sling, so he's not as tired as the rest of us. "Can I just grab something? And then we can go wherever you want."

"Sure. Beechy wants us to meet him afterward, actually."

"For what?" Ariadne asks.

"He didn't say."

We find an elevator nearby. "Where were you this morning, by the way?" Oliver asks when we're inside. "You were late to breakfast."

I stare at my reflection in the glass. The steel wall beyond it looks like gray streaks as we speed along. "I couldn't sleep. I just went for a walk."

"Bad dreams?"

"Yeah." I take a deep breath, hoping he won't ask what they were about. But he's quiet beside me. Ariadne doesn't say anything, and I'm grateful.

The steel wall turns into a window outside the elevator. We just left Training Division, and we're entering Nourishment Division now. There's a small plaza through the window where kids are hanging out, or heading toward the cafeteria entrance. There are adults among them too. Mothers holding the hands of their little girls. Fathers frowning at their sons.

Families.

"Do you ever dream about your parents?" Oliver asks. "Do you wonder if they're still alive?"

I run my teeth over my bottom lip. It feels strange to think about them. I know they must be real; I know I came from somewhere, but I've never seen them before and I'm never going to. The parents of child workers are usually replaced once they fulfill their birthing quota, and if an exception is made for them, they continue working in the outer sectors but don't meet their children. As far as I can tell, they don't want to.

"I have once or twice," Ariadne says, twisting her hands as the elevator slows to a stop. "But not really."

Ding.

"Do you?" I ask Oliver.

The doors slide open. We step out into the plaza. The cafeteria entrance lies on the far side.

Oliver's mouth lifts into a soft smile. "I like to think Dad's a Surface pilot, and Mom was this nice lady who worked in the security hub back in Crust. It's probably not true, but sometimes it's nice to pretend."

As we walk, I glance at a mother we're passing. Her daughter is a few steps ahead of her, maybe three or four years old, walking with her legs wobbly and a thumb in her mouth. The mother scoops her up in her arms, laughing. "Ellie, you're such a big girl!"

A dull pain shoots through my chest, and I look away. Maybe it's nice to pretend, but it's not smart. We won't ever have that. We won't ever feel like someone is our mother or father, whether or not we learn our parents are still alive and well.

The Developers stole that kind of life from us the day we were born.

After Oliver grabs a snack in the cafeteria, we meet Beechy. He leans against the wall in the hallway where I met him before. Pipeline lights flash behind him through the glass.

"What is it you wanted to show us?" I ask.

He doesn't answer, just pushes off the wall and smiles as he passes. I glance at Ariadne and Oliver before following him.

He leads us to an upper floor in Invention Division, to a hall-way with a lone silver door. He presses his thumbprint into a lock pad, and the door opens. Dim red lights flicker on inside, one by one.

The room is small with another door at its back. A cylindrical pit sits at the room's center, with a ladder on its side. I move to it slowly. On my tiptoes, I hold my breath and peek over the top. Clear water fills the pit. It darkens farther down; it must be a deep pool.

"What's it for?" I ask, my heart beating fast. If he brought us here to go inside this, I don't know if I want to. I can't even swim.

"You've heard that some scientists explore the world outside the Surface settlement, yes?" Beechy says, gesturing for us to fol-low him to the other door.

"Of course," I say, stepping after him and Ariadne into the smaller room beyond. Inside, there are several black cabinets, a bench, and another door.

Beechy opens one of the cabinets, revealing black suits similar to the ones we're wearing. Each has a mask and a small black box attached to it.

"I'm a pilot, like I told you," he says, picking up one of the suits. "And I've been privileged enough to be the pilot for a few Surface explorations. Part of what we do is explore the oceans up there, sometimes to test the water or minerals, other times to col-lect artifacts."

He tosses the suit to me. The fabric is soft and squishy.

"We also observe animals," Beechy says. "It's kind of a special project for Commander Charlie. We've captured a few oceanic life forms on these expeditions and brought them here."

"Inside the pit?" Ariadne asks, hesitantly taking the suit he hands her.

"Exactly. I thought you might like to see them."

I twist my mouth. That means we'll have to swim.

"That's allowed?" Oliver asks, his brows furrowing.

"You'll be perfectly safe," Beechy says, shutting the cabinet and turning to one of the others. "You don't need to concern yourself with anything else."

I study his eyes for some hint of explanation, but he keeps his face carefully controlled. His fingers skim the bigger suits on the shelves until he finds the one he's looking for. "You can change in one of the stalls through the door," he says. "When you're finished, I'll show you how to use the respirator."

"I don't think I should swim," Oliver says, holding up his wounded arm in the sling.

"Oh, I'm sorry." Beechy shuts the second cabinet. "I didn't think of that."

"It's okay. I'll just wait here." Oliver drops onto the bench.

"Are you sure?" I ask. He doesn't seem happy about it.

"Mhm."

Beechy glances at me. His eyes shouldn't pierce me like that. They shouldn't set my stomach fluttering. I force myself to look away from him.

I follow Ariadne through the door into a short hallway with a set of bathroom stalls.

"I don't know how to swim," Ariadne says.

"Neither do I." I push open a stall and hurry inside. If there's any nervousness in my face, I don't want her to see it. "It's probably not that hard, though," I say.

"I hope not," she says.

I slip out of my clothes and into the special suit. It stretches easily to fit my form. The small black box attached to its back must be the respirator Beechy mentioned, which holds oxygen. It's connected by a tube to the mask that will go over my mouth and nose, allowing me to breathe underwater.

A shiver of fear and excitement trails down my spine. I've never been underwater.

We wait outside by the pit while Beechy changes. I tie my curls up so they won't block my vision while I swim. Ariadne trails her fingers through the water, while Oliver eyes it with mild suspicion.

"I hope the animals aren't loose down there," he says.

"Why wouldn't they be loose?" Ariadne asks.

"They might be dangerous."

I take a step closer to the pit and squint, but it doesn't help me see what's down there in the darkness.

We didn't learn much about the two oceans on the Surface in school. We knew a filtration system made their saltwater drinkable, and pipes transported the filtered water to the Surface city and to the lower sectors. We knew that some of the food adults ate came from the ocean, but that was all. It was too far away.

"Ready?" Beechy asks, walking through the door and joining us by the pit.

"Ready," Ariadne says.

"Let's turn your respirators on," he says, moving to me first. He helps me pull the oxygen mask over my head, and fits it over my mouth and nose. A strap and suction hold it in place.

His fingers brush my earlobe. I bite hard on my lip. He takes my hand and guides it to a small red button on the side of the mask. "As soon as we're under, hold your breath and press this for five seconds," he says. "That'll release the oxygen from the respirator, and then you'll be able to breathe."

"Okay." The mask gives my voice an echoey quality.

"You can get in now, if you like. Relax in the water, and you should float with no trouble." He moves to help Ariadne with her respirator.

I climb the ladder, focusing on my breath. This won't be scary—it'll be fun, I tell myself.

I sit on the top of the ladder and dip my toes into the water. It's cold, but not icy. The suit will keep me warm, I think. I hope.

I take a breath and push off the ledge.

Water envelops my body, not cold or warm, but somewhere in between. My head submerges without me wanting it to, and for a moment I panic like I did in the gravity capsule.

Squeezing my eyes shut, I jam the red button down.

One, two, three, four, five.

I gasp for air. Oxygen fills my mask and throat, relieving the pressure in my lungs.

My eyes open, and I see that I've sunk a little in the water, but not much. The darker water is still below me.

Above me, Beechy helps Ariadne into the water. He holds her hand to keep her near the surface.

I focus on the movement of Beechy's arms and legs and mimic it, kicking and using my hands to push me higher. I smile to myself. I don't know why I was scared of this. It feels like I'm floating in the zero gravity capsule, except thicker. Heavier.

"We go down." Beechy's voice, muffled by the mask, is clearer than I expected.

I touch a hand to the strap above my ear. There must be something inside it that helps me hear him.

Ariadne kicks hard, while Beechy pulls her down. He grins at me. I glimpse a wide-eyed Oliver peering at us from the ladder before I turn away, toward the depths of the pit. It's so dark down there. But I won't be alone. So I take a deep breath and swim down.

The width of the pit expands as the water darkens. I swim close to Ariadne, whose cheeks are pale. Soon she fades into the dark, and so does Beechy. I can barely see them at all.

Panic rushes over me. What if I get lost down here? I can't tell how far the pit goes. It might go on forever.

"Will there be light?" I ask, trying to keep my voice steady. "So we can see the animals?"

"Yeah," Beechy says. "We're almost there."

I kick harder. There's pressure in my ears and against my legs, making my movements sluggish. I don't like not being able to see anything. I don't like it at all.

"Take my hand," Beechy says somewhere to my left.

"I can't *see* your hand."

I feel a change in the water. A moment later, his fingers brush my skin. They slide between mine, warm and firm.

"I'm not afraid," I tell him, but it's more to convince myself.

"I know," he says.

We swim deeper. Hollow, eerie bubbling sounds fill my ears. I stare into the darkness, my eyes wide, searching for the source of the noise.

Something touches my face, and I gasp aloud, wrenching back.

Beechy tightens his hold on my hand. "It's seaweed."

Whatever it is, there's a lot of it. The strands wrap around my legs when I move so they're below me. I kick them away and slap them out of my face. Beechy chuckles. I shoot him a glare he can't see.

"Both of you stay here," he says, and lets go of me.

"Where are you going?" Ariadne sounds nervous.

"I have to turn on the lights."

The water shifts as he swims away. I float above the seaweed, slowly kicking my legs, while the water presses on my body. I close my eyes. I focus on the oxygen flowing from the mask into my mouth.

In and out.

In and out.

I open my eyes. One by one, faint green lights flicker on somewhere above me. I blink to adjust my eyes. Now I see the thin, green-and-brownish plant growing in strands in a forest below my feet. Seaweed, Beechy called it. It looks slimy. Disgusting. Beechy sticks his face out of the forest, grinning.

"Look up," he says.

I look up. The green lights are brighter now, lining silver cages on either side of me and above. Some of the cages are giant, while others are small. They float throughout the pit, some so near, we must've swam right past them. My heart beats in my fingertips.

Inside the cages are the animals of the sea.

The fish are easiest to recognize, since I've seen pictures of ones like them before. In the smaller cages, they're only as big as my fist, but fatter. One has eyes that change color and stringy tentacles like whiskers. Another has something like wings, the color of lead, but they're floppier than krail wings and not made of feathers. The fish makes a screeching sound when it opens its mouth.

I smile to myself.

"The most interesting ones are over here." Beechy swims past the smaller cages. I follow him.

Beyond the last small cage sits a giant one. The creature inside seems almost human. It has two legs, two arms, and one head, but its skin is a clear color, looking like the consistency of gel. Where it should have ears, it has gills, and its eyes are fiery red with no irises or eyelids. It curls the only three long fingers of each hand around the steel bars of its cage and watches us, unblinking.

My eyes widen.

"What is this?" Ariadne asks.

"We call it a 'vool,' v-u-l, after the explorer who discovered it." Beechy reaches into his pocket and removes a small, round tin. He swims closer to the creature. I bite back my instinct to tell him to stop.

The vul reaches through the bars and takes the tin from him. It doesn't seem frightened.

"This one's the last of his kind," Beechy says, swimming back a few feet until he's beside me. "But he's been alive for decades."

I stare at the vul, my heart beating unsteadily. The creature lets go of the cage bars and unlatches the tin's lid. Inside are a number of tiny, squished fish the size of my pinkie. He picks one up and chews it with teeth sharp and yellow.

"He's so . . . human," I say.

Beechy nods. "Sometimes I wish we hadn't enslaved him."

"How did the others die?"

He grimaces. "I'm afraid it was our fault. When they were first discovered, there were only a few left. We scared them, so they attacked. We had better weapons."

"That's awful," Ariadne whispers.

I press my lips together. Murder is too common on our planet.

"He has language," Beechy says "It's different from ours, and he doesn't use it much, but he can talk."

"Can he understand us?"

"I don't know."

The vul swallows the last fish in the tin and licks his fingers. He kicks his legs—his feet are webbed—and swims to the lowest part of his cage, where he tucks the empty tin into a box attached to the bars.

I wish he could understand me. There's so much I would ask him.

Beechy's arm presses against mine, and our fingers brush. If we weren't underwater, my palms would feel clammy.

Worry whitens Ariadne's cheeks as she stares at the vul. A small part of me wishes she wasn't here, that Beechy and I were alone in the water. It's a silly thought. A wrong thought. I push it away and focus on the vul to clear my mind.

He swims up, nearing us again, but this time he doesn't touch the cage bars. He presses his fingers together, and they emit a soft red glow. He opens his mouth, and a string of garbled words reaches my ears. They're unfamiliar. But I think they might be important. I think he's trying to tell us something, if only we could understand.

We watch him for a while, and then swim back up to the pit ladder.

"How was it?" Oliver asks.

"Incredible," Ariadne says.

We tell him about the vul, and he says, "Wish I could've seen it."

"I'm sorry," I say. I wish he could've seen it too. "We should've waited until some other time, when you were better."

"It's okay," he says, but he stares at the water like it isn't.

Beechy's arm brushes mine again when he hands me a towel. I ignore the shiver that runs across my skin, and head into the bathroom to dry off and change back into my normal clothes. I don't want to think about Beechy . . . not like that. It doesn't make sense to.

I force my thoughts away from him and think of the vul again, of it living down there all alone in its cage underwater.

I can't believe creatures like that once existed on the Surface—creatures so similar to us, yet so different. Creatures that swam and talked and maybe even walked. Maybe they existed before us humans. Maybe this was their world before it was ours.

Now they're gone. We slaughtered all but one.

But as I slip my boots back on, I wonder if there might be others. Not other vul, but other creatures like them up there, maybe hiding someplace the scientists haven't visited yet. Or maybe the Developers already found them, and they're just keeping it a secret.

Because the Developers kept the vul a secret. They only told the scientists. And that makes sense, I suppose, because scientists are the ones who would care the most. Commander Charlie doesn't tell most of us anything, anyway. What we learn in school has to be approved by him, but there are bits of history glossed over in our lessons, theories of science not explored in depth, and things related to medicine that we aren't allowed to know about, like how certain medicines work to fix people's bodies.

The Developers have lots of secrets, I'm sure. I wish I knew what they were.

17

"Welcome to your intelligence training session," Cadet Waller says.

We stand in one of the higher floors in Training Division, in a room filled with glowing blue, see-through capsules that hum. Intelligence machines. It looks like there are enough for all twenty-eight of us Extractions. The other twenty-eight of us went to train with Colonel Parker today.

"You will be tested on a wide array of material, everything from the principles of gravity to the action potential of cells, to the dates of key events in the Great Rebellion."

I can't help smiling to myself. Today's session should be easy.

Cadet Waller walks up to the nearest capsule, her boots tapping on the floor, and pats it. "You'll each enter one of these. The purpose of this session isn't just to test you, but also to fill in gaps in your knowledge. These hubs are quite special. They're teachers, if you will."

I remember what I learned about intelligence machines: They

interact with their passengers, feeding knowledge straight into their brains like they're injecting a smart gene.

"Each of you, pick a hub," Cadet Waller says. "They'll open for you in a moment."

I stuff the last of my breakfast bar into my mouth and chew fast as I move after Oliver and Ariadne. Everyone else is in a hurry, too. Excited chatter fills the room. This is the kind of session most of us will do well in.

"Over there?" Ariadne asks, pointing to three hubs near the back of the room.

Oliver nods and moves ahead to claim them, pushing his glasses up the bridge of his nose. He doesn't have his sling anymore. Early this morning, he got called down to the health ward for a checkup, and a doctor said his arm is already almost healed, thanks to that shot they gave him two days ago.

I slip in front of the hub between Ariadne's and Oliver's. The machine is about two feet taller than me, with a seat inside, straps, and a steel helmet hanging from the ceiling. The Core's small insignia is etched into the hub's plastic door: a full moon embossed in bronze.

"This is your second-to-last training session," Cadet Waller says, walking down the rows. "One today and one tomorrow. Your time spent in these final sessions will raise your Promise to a score of at least eighty, which, as I said before, is a requirement for Core citizenship."

My stomach jumps. I forgot about the scoring.

There's a loud sound of suction, and the door in front of me slides open.

Everyone immediately climbs into the hubs, including Oliver and Ariadne. I shrug off the Promise score thing and climb into my own. Cadet Waller said these sessions *will* raise our Promise to eighty, anyway. So why should I worry?

I turn around and slip into the hub seat. Cadet Waller and the two science instructors are coming around, helping everyone put their helmets on and strap in properly. I reach and unhook the helmet from the ceiling and slip it on over my head. It's a bit heavy. Thick tubes run off its sides, attaching it to the black machine system at the top of the capsule.

"Figured it out?" one of the science instructors says, climbing into the small space still available in my hub.

"I think so," I say.

He twists one of the tubes to check that it's secure. "Let's just get your seat straps on." He reaches behind me and slips the straps over my shoulders, clicking them into the locks on the side of my seat.

"Why do we need to be strapped in?" I ask.

"Just a safety precaution." He smiles, and steps out of my hub. "Good luck." He presses a small button on the side of the capsule, and the door slides shut, drowning out the noise in the room.

My heart beats fast in the silence. Which is strange because I'm not nervous, really. Or maybe I am. My fingers grip the sides of my chair.

A soft whir fills my ears. A thin visor slides out of my helmet, covering my eyes. Now I can't see anything but black.

"Welcome to your Intelligence Session," a computerized voice echoes through my ears. "Say 'begin' when you are ready to start."

I take a breath. "Begin."

"Solve the following equation," the voice says. Small, translucent blue letters appear:

$^2/_3 = 2873$я

A touch of relief washes over me. Blip mathematics. Carry the numbers, solve for я. It takes me about five seconds to calculate.

"7,452," I say.

The numbers disappear.

"What is the square root of 2,396,304?" the computer says.

"1,548."

The computer asks me another question. Then another and another. I assume I must be getting them all right, since it doesn't correct me.

"Are any nearby planets inhabited?"

"No, we're the only planet in the Ranim Galaxy that supports life."

"What is the rate at which bone density decreases in low g-force?"

"Bone density decreases by five percent per month without exercise, and one percent per month with exercise."

"How long does it take for death to occur by acid corrosion?"

"Ten minutes."

There's a pause, and I panic. I'm sure that's correct—instructors have always said it takes ten minutes for a person to die once they've been exposed to high levels of moonshine.

"Test complete," the computer says.

I let out my breath.

"Final score: one hundred percent."

My lips stretch into a grin.

The *whirwhirwhir* of the machine rises in my ears. "Calculating approximate Promise level."

I stare at the darkness before my eyes, waiting for the number. They've never told me my score before. It could be anything—but it has to be somewhat high, right? Or Commander Charlie wouldn't have let me come here.

A small, translucent blue number appears:

84

Every muscle in my body sags with relief. I already hit eighty. Of course I did. They picked me for this, and I've done well in every session so far. I beat the obstacle course, after all. I must be meant for citizenship.

Something cool touches the skin above my ears. A soft flow of air coming through the tubes attached to my helmet.

I lift a hand to touch one of the tubes. It's made of plastic that feels smooth and cold. I wait for the computer to explain what's happening, but it doesn't.

The number 84 flashes and disappears on the visor screen.

My lips twist into a frown.

The cool air slowly fills my helmet. A tingly feeling rushes through my head after a few breaths. It starts in my ears and trickles down to my neck, and further. The air, I realize, is gas. And it's filling my hub.

My vision blurs.

What . . . What's going . . . ?

My eyelids droop.

I'm floating. Gentle and light, at ease with everything in existence.

The Developers are perfect; they are everything. They give me everything, and I am perfect because of them.

Only because of them.

A rush of burn hits my head, exploding through my temple.

I gag and kick and scream and fumble for the helmet.

Choking; can't breathe.

On fire.

Got to get this *off me*.

But it won't budge. No no no no no no no no.

The computer's talking again. It's saying something, but I can't tell what because I'm trying to breathe and tears are streaming down my face and I'm shaking uncontrollably. Fire still rushes through my head, getting worse, and it needs to *stop*.

"Who would you save?" the computer says. I think it's repeating itself.

I see there's something in front of me that isn't a visor screen. Some other part of the test—holograms of people, but they look sort of real.

I close my eyes and try to stop shaking. It feels like someone's smashing my head in with a hammer, but I have to focus. I have to finish the test.

When I open my eyes again, wetness trickles down my cheeks. I stare at the two figures standing in front of me. Girls, both of them. Their eyes are wide, and they're both thin. Hungry. Terrified. The one on the right wears the leather suit of a Core citizen. The girl on the left clutches her faded, torn dress to her chest. She's from the Surface or one of the outer sectors. Her hair is blond and shoulder-length, and her eyes are green. She looks so much like Laila, I must be dreaming. Laila's dead. She can't be here. She's gone.

"Who would you save?" the voice repeats.

"F-from what?"

"Death."

I look from the Core girl to the girl who looks like Laila. How could I pick anyone but her? Core kids don't need saving, anyway. They're safe here.

"The S-Surface girl," I say.

"Are you sure?" the computer says.

Breathe, swallow, breathe.

"Yes."

There's a pause. The hammer keeps pounding against my temple. Tears won't stop trickling down my cheeks, and I'm gripping the sides of my seat so hard I'm going to break all my nails. Stop, stop, stop, I plead.

"Calculating final Promise score," the voice says.

A number pops up on the visor:

84

I feel relief again, somewhere far in the back of my mind.

Then the number starts dropping. Beep, beep, beep. 76, 75, 74, 73—

No. No. No.

72, 71—

Please.

70, 69—

No, no, no, this is not okay.

63, 62, 61, 60, 59.

The beeping stops.

59.

My heart pounds all sorts of crazy rhythms, in my chest and in my fingertips and everywhere else in my body. It said to pick a person, but I chose wrong. I saved the Surface girl from home. I'm supposed to forget home because it's not home anymore. I'm supposed to show loyalty to the Core, to Commander Charlie.

There's a whir, and the helmet eases off my head. I shove it off the rest of the way with trembling hands, and unlatch the straps holding me down.

I don't know what to do. I don't know what's wrong with me. I can't think clearly when my head's like this.

It hits me that my hub is see-through; I can see into the other hubs in this aisle, the ones with Oliver and Ariadne inside. And someone could've seen me. *Please, please, no.*

The door slides open, and I hear voices out in the room. Cadet Waller and the science instructors are making their way down the aisles. Other Extractions are climbing out of their machines. They don't look like their heads are on fire. They're smiling; they look like their tests went fine.

Their voices make my head throb even harder.

"Intelligence Session complete," another voice says, echoing across the deck. "Average Promise Score: eighty-seven."

I squeeze my eyes shut. I must have the lowest score. With an average like that, only one person could've gotten that low.

"Clementine," Oliver says.

I open my eyes, breathing fast. He's standing just outside, staring at me with a crooked smile and an odd look in his eyes.

"Are you gonna come out?" he asks

I quickly wipe my eyes. "Yeah." I push off my seat and grab the door frame to keep my legs from wobbling. Spots speckle my vision, and my face is so hot I'm sure I'm feverish. But I have to pretend I'm okay. I have to pretend everything was fine, that I didn't mess up.

Even though someone's going to find out eventually, if Cadet Waller doesn't know already.

I swallow hard. "How'd you do?" I ask Oliver. He's still standing there with that odd smile. Maybe it's just because my head's screwing up my sight, but his eyes seem hazier than usual. Like they're looking right through me. Like they're not seeing anything at all.

"I did well," Oliver says.

He doesn't stop smiling. My brows furrow—which makes my head hurt more. I clench my teeth to keep my eyes from watering.

"Hello," Ariadne says, appearing beside me. There's a layer of film over her eyes, and her gaze is unseeing. Just like Oliver's.

"How did you do?" he asks her.

"Very well," she replies, and smiles. "My Promise is seventy-eight. What's yours?"

"Eighty-five."

85. 59. My breath is shaky.

The two of them won't stop smiling and staring at nothing.

I open my mouth to ask, *What's wrong with you?* A cough comes out instead, then another. I double over.

The world spins. I lean on the hub so I won't fall over, but I miss it somehow and land on my knees anyway—hard. Pain slices through my temples, and it takes everything in me not to cry out.

I hear the tap of boots on the ground. Cadet Waller or one of the other instructors might be coming over. I try to compose myself; I try to get back up on my own but it's difficult when I'm shaking.

Ariadne and Oliver don't help me. But Cadet Waller does.

"What happened?" she asks, lifting me back up to my feet. Her eyes are slightly narrowed.

"I'm fine," I say. "I just slipped. Stupid shoes."

"Your hand's bleeding."

I look down, and sure enough, it is. I must've cut it on the door frame of the hub, or maybe when I was inside trying to get my helmet off.

Cadet Waller touches my forehead and frowns. "You feel warm. I think you should go see a doctor. You might be getting sick."

"Maybe," I say, even though I don't think that's what this is. If anything, the gas inside the hub made me sick.

But Cadet Waller must not know my score yet.

"Here, Oliver, why don't you take Clementine to the health ward," she says, moving my hand and placing it in his.

"Okay," he says automatically, stepping forward like he's a robot. I don't like him like this. It makes no sense, but I can't figure it out right now. I can't handle it.

"It's all right," I say, tugging my hand out of his grasp. "I know where it is; I can walk there myself."

"Are you sure?" Cadet Waller says, frowning again.

I nod. "Really, I'm okay. I can walk. I just need to see a doctor, like you said."

Cadet Waller observes me for a moment, searching my face for something. The shape of her eyes reminds me vaguely of the birds of prey I used to see pictures of in my science class back on the Surface.

I try to keep my muscles normal. I try to keep the pain out of my eyes.

"Go on, then," she says.

I glance at Oliver and Ariadne again. They're still standing in the exact same spot, still smiling. Like they're waiting for instructions. What's *wrong* with them? I want to snap them out of whatever trance they're stuck in, but Cadet Waller is right here. And I'm supposed to pretend everything's okay.

So I turn and walk away. I clench my fists and suck oxygen into my lungs as best I can.

I wait until I reach the hallway to let the tears fall uncontrollably.

18

In an empty elevator, I jab the button on the Core map for the health ward. The door slides shut, and the elevator speeds along to the left. I lean against the glass with my face in my hands, breathing too fast.

There's definitely something wrong with me.

Maybe Cadet Waller is right—I just need to see a doctor, and she'll give me medicine and my head will stop hurting and my body will return to its normal temperature. I'll go back to normal.

But that doesn't explain Ariadne and Oliver. Their emotionless eyes; the way their smiles didn't go away. The fog did something to them too, just something different.

The elevator switches to a vertical track and zooms down. I drop to the floor and clutch my knees to my chest.

Visiting a doctor won't do anything to fix my Promise score. That's the worst part. Cadet Waller said we have to have a score of eighty by our last training session, which is tomorrow. If I don't reach that—and how will I reach that if the last session is anything like this?—I don't know what they'll do to me. I don't want to think about it.

The elevator slows to a stop.

Ding.

The doors slide open. I pull myself to my feet. The main lobby of the health ward is ahead, and there's a receptionist helping someone at the counter.

I don't know if I want to be here anymore.

"Can I help you?" the receptionist asks.

She's staring at me. She finished helping the other person, and I didn't even notice.

I clench my hands and step out of the elevator. I have to pretend this has nothing to do with my training session. I have to pretend this is just something I woke up with.

"Sorry, I'm not feeling very well," I say, touching a hand to my sweaty forehead. "I woke up with a fever this morning. Cadet Waller said you might be able to help."

"Oh, honey." The receptionist beckons me over. "Yes, of course we can help. I'll call a nurse. You can take a seat."

I slip into one of the empty chairs, avoiding the eyes of the female patient sitting in the one across from me.

A nurse arrives barely a minute later. She slips a hand around my wrist and pulls me down the hallway. I think she's saying something and scanning the tablet she's holding, but I don't really hear her. I can't really tell where I'm going.

Inside a small examination room, she tells me to sit on the patient table. I do, my fingers crinkling the paper sheet beneath me. The lights hurt my head. Her voice hurts my head.

"Open up," she says. She sticks something small and thin into my mouth that tastes like metal. The word pops up from an old school lesson: *thermometer.*

She pulls it out after thirty seconds and checks my temperature. "Hmm . . . 103.8 degrees. You've got a high one, dear. When did you start feeling poorly?"

I swallow the remnants of the metallic taste. "This morning."

"Did you start feeling worse after your training session?"

Yes. Yes, I did. I shake my head.

"Well, I'll make a note of this. We keep careful records of all patient illnesses, so we can do our best to prevent them in the future." She drops the thermometer in a plastic tin and taps the keypad on her tablet.

"Can you make it better?" I ask. My body won't stop shaking. I'm shivering and it isn't even cold; this room is a furnace.

"Of course! We always can." The nurse sets her tablet down and snaps on a fresh pair of gloves. She moves over by the sink and opens one of the drawers beneath it.

I hope she's not getting a syringe. Please, no more shots.

She turns around and rips off the plastic covering of a small, square patch. I exhale in relief.

"This is a cooling patch," she says. "It should restore your body to its normal temperature in a few minutes."

She lifts the hair off the back of my neck and presses the patch against my skin. It feels like ice. It feels wonderful.

"Thank you," I say.

"If you start feeling worse, come back here right away."

I nod and slide off the table.

"Good luck with your final training session!" She waves me out the door.

The door zips shut behind me. I stand there for a moment, my stomach twisting again because she's right, there's still one more training session.

But it's going to be okay. Of course it is.

I hurry down the corridor, stumbling a little. I touch the wall to steady myself.

On the ceiling, sheets of black and silver metal form what look like fake windows. If I were a million miles away, those windows would open and I'd be able to see the stars. And Logan. He'd know what's wrong with me, maybe. He'd make all of this better.

But there is no real sky here, and there are no easy paths to the stars. Or to him.

I tear my eyes away. I walk faster down the hallway.

The throbbing in my head gradually dulls. When I blink, I don't see as many dots.

I touch a hand to my forehead and relief runs through me. I'm still shaking, but I don't think I'm burning up anymore. I think the patch is working.

I move into the lobby and immediately realize I went the wrong way.

This isn't the main lobby. A sign on the wall reads MATERNITY WARD. Straight ahead, the wall is made of glass. Through it is a waiting area with soft, mostly empty chairs. In the chairs, a couple females sit reading on tablets or twiddling their thumbs. They aren't much older than me.

I turn away from the waiting room, wringing my hands. I don't know how I ended up here, of all places.

But . . . part of me doesn't want to leave right away. Part of me is curious to see what it's like.

Down the hallway to my left, glass lines another, longer stretch of wall. Behind the glass, nurses roam between rows of incubators with tiny bundles of blue inside. Drip bags stand among the incubators with clear and orange fluids connected to tiny tubes attached to the bundles of blue.

A door opens at the back of the room, and a woman enters wearing a pale gown like the one I wore during my beautifying operation. Her hair is matted with sweat, and her eyes shift nervously. A nurse leads her to an incubator near where I stand, where the nurse reaches inside and removes the bundle of blue, then places it with care into the woman's arms. The woman pushes the blue blanket back a little, and tiny hands with tiny fingers grasp the air.

I press my sweaty palm to the glass, holding my breath. I've seen pictures of babies before, but never ones this small. Never in the arms of their mothers.

Birth mothers in the outer sectors don't get to hold their babies. They deliver them while under general anesthesia, and their children have already been taken away when they wake up. This way, the mothers don't have time to get attached.

"Clementine?"

Beechy stands frozen at the end of the hallway, the door beside him half closed. I blink in surprise, then wince because it hurts my head.

"What are you doing here?" he asks.

"Nothing," I say, swallowing. "I was . . . uh . . . wandering."

He smiles a little and shuts the door the rest of the way. "That's a pretty lame excuse." He sticks his hands in his pockets and walks over to me.

"Well, what's yours?" I ask.

"That's confidential."

"That's worse than mine."

He pulls a hand out of his pocket and presses a finger against my lips, stunning me into silence. "Shh, this is a quiet area," he says.

"I don't care." I speak against his finger.

"You should." He pulls his hand away. His eyes trail from my forehead to my cheeks to the bruise on my upper lip.

I turn away to look back at the bundles of blue through the

glass. My stomach flutters. It might be nausea that the patch hasn't relieved yet, but maybe it's not. I think it's because there's space between me and Beechy, and a foolish part of me is afraid, or wants, to make it smaller.

"How was your training session?" he asks.

I press my lips together. Way to kill the mood, Beechy. "Fine."

"Fine?"

"That's what I said."

"I don't believe you."

I twist my hands, staring at our reflections in the glass. My heartbeat feels clunky against my ribs, and my head still throbs a little.

I almost want to tell him what happened earlier. I messed up, Beechy. I messed up and now I might fail training, but I can't fail because I don't think Commander Charlie will give me another chance. I think he'll kill me and get it over with.

But I don't know how Beechy would react.

"Clem . . ." he says softly. His hand brushes mine.

Something cracks inside me, making it hard to breathe. Logan is the only person who calls me that.

"Beechy!" An unfamiliar voice makes me jump.

The door at the end of the hall flies open, and a young woman with spiky black hair rushes into view. Her laughter peals through the air. "I was right! I was right!"

Beechy breaks away from me. "Really?" I hear the smile in his voice.

"Yes!" She squeals and runs to him, flinging her arms around him when she reaches him. She presses her lips against Beechy's. He meets hers with as much enthusiasm.

A sour taste fills my mouth, and I try to swallow it, but it doesn't go away. I touch a hand to my forehead to steady myself.

This doesn't matter. This shouldn't matter.

They teeter in their embrace for several moments. When they pull apart, she casts her shining eyes to me. "Who's this?"

A metal stud gleams in her nose. I think she's the female instructor who handed me my gun the first night I was here, when I had to shoot the Unstable in the glass cage. Her cheeks are full of color.

"Sandy, this is Clementine," Beechy says. He looks at me, then away. "Clementine, this is my wife, Sandy."

The words hit me like a knife to the throat.

"Ah, *this* is Clementine." Sandy's smile widens, and she offers a hand. "Hi."

He's married. He'll grow old with her, because that's what people do here.

I force my lips to smile. "Hi."

"Sorry, she's excited because we just found out we're going to have a baby." Beechy chuckles.

"He's wrong. I'm usually excited." Sandy bumps him with her shoulder and squishes her nose a little. "But yes, today I'm more excited than usual."

Beside me, muffled crying seeps through the glass. Frowning, the nurse snaps on gloves and fumbles with a syringe, while another hurries over carrying a small silver monitor.

"Oh." I pause. "Congratulations." I think that's what people say in situations like this, since pregnancy is a good thing here, not something people are forced into.

"Aw, thanks." Sandy squeezes my shoulder. "You're a sweetie. And a brave one, from what Beechy's told me."

Beechy trains his eyes on me.

I look away, focusing on my breathing. No, I don't care that he's with someone. I don't care that he told Sandy about me.

But I want to run. I don't want to be here with the two of them.

Through the glass, a third nurse takes the bundle of blue away from its mother, while the first flicks the syringe and the second attaches tiny round strips of something like gauze to the child's forehead. The mother holds her hands near her mouth, shaking her head fast.

Sandy pulls away from Beechy to move closer to the glass.

My forehead creases. Was the child born sickly? If it was, thank the stars it's here in the Core. The doctors will be able to fix it.

"What happened?" Beechy says to me, softly.

"Hmm?"

"What happened in training earlier?"

The child's cries grow louder and sound more like coughs. The first nurse eases the needle into its chest, and my stomach flips even though I'm not the one getting the shot. Sandy grips her arm with her hand.

"Please tell me," Beechy says.

I shake my head. "I don't know if I can trust you."

He's been kind to me, yes, but finding out about Sandy makes me think he hasn't told me other things that are important. And what am I supposed to say, anyway? I might fail training; Commander Charlie might kill me tomorrow. Can you help me?

He takes a step back, looking hurt. "I saved you from Sam. You don't think you can trust me?"

"No."

"Well, you can." He sets his jaw. "And you know why?"

"No." And I don't know why he cares so much, either.

"Because I was like you, but I had no one." He puts his hand on my shoulder, and presses harder when I flinch. "Did you hear me? I was exactly like you." His eyes cling to mine, like he's trying to tell me something.

But I don't get what he means.

"In training, I mean," he says slowly, as if prodding me to think. "I came here five years ago an Extraction. I did well in most of the training modules until . . ."

I stare at him. He must mean the intelligence machines—he messed up while he was inside them too.

I open my mouth to ask him how he fixed everything, how he kept from failing his training, but a muffled scream from the mother snaps my attention to the glass. The child seizes in the arms of the nurse, no longer crying. Like it's been electrocuted, and its whole body is heaving from too much energy.

My eyes widen.

Another nurse streams into the room, then another and another. A doctor arrives and waves his hands, giving directions. A nurse shoos us away through the glass. Another grabs the mother's arms and pulls her away from her baby. The mother's still screaming. "No, you can't!" I hear her say, though her words are muffled. "You can't kill her! She'll get better!"

The child goes limp in the nurse's arms.

This can't be happening.

Beechy slips his hand around Sandy's arm. She is stricken, wide-eyed. "Come on, we should go," he says.

She doesn't move at first.

I stare at the tiny hands poking out of the bundle of blue, no longer grasping the air.

No, no, no, they didn't kill it. It's sleeping. They'll fix it. They'll make it better.

"Sandy," Beechy says.

She moves away from the glass and into his arms, her face pale. He leads her down the corridor.

"Come on, Clementine," he says.

I'm frozen, my hand stuck to the glass though I can't remember putting it there. My fingers shake. A nurse screams at me to go away, but I have to see the doctor revive the child. They do that here, don't they? They have nurses and doctors and medicine, not just mud and water, like we had. They can save anyone, if they want to.

But they don't seem to be trying. People are dragging the mother out the back doorway.

A nurse arrives with a small black bag, which she unzips and sets on top of the capsule where the child once laid.

It hits me like a knife: They're going to put the baby inside, and take it away to a morgue and burn it in a furnace. Or do whatever they do with the dead here.

Beechy grabs my arm. I let him pull me away.

But I can't breathe, and I can't stop shaking again because everyone lied. My instructors said children don't die here; Commander Charlie said everyone would be safe here.

They lied. Safety isn't a guarantee for people anywhere, no matter what anyone says.

Even in the Core, they kill children.

19

I run a hand down my arm in the elevator.

"That doesn't happen often," Beechy says. "They only put down the babies they can't cure no matter what they do."

I don't say anything. What does that even *mean*? I thought they could cure anyone. That's what everyone always said.

"And it won't happen to us," he says to Sandy, quieter.

"Daddy won't let it," she whispers, and laughs at the strange hardness that seeps into Beechy's face. Her fingers intertwine with his.

I stare at their hands. Beechy runs his thumb in a slow circle over the back of Sandy's palm. Logan used to do the same thing on my palm. It was meant to be a calming gesture, but sometimes it made me more agitated.

"I'm tired," I say. "I think I'll head to bed early."

Beechy's eyes meet mine, and a flicker of regret runs across his face. But all he says is, "Okay. I'm sure you'll do well tomorrow."

"Thank you."

He nods. He presses his lips together.

When I get off the elevator and the door has shut behind me, I remember I didn't get to ask him about his training. I didn't get to ask how he didn't fail.

I try to forget about it. I realize I'm hungry, so I take the stairs to the cafeteria. I count the steps to focus my mind. I count ninety-five steps, until I reach the proper floor level and move into a corridor near the edge of Slumber Division, near Nourishment Division and the cafeteria.

It's quiet here. I pass doors with lock-pads that lead to bedrooms where people sleep at night, some with roommates and others with their families. But it's too early for people to be sleeping. Right now, most everyone is finishing their day's work or relaxing somewhere. Ariadne and Oliver will be in Recreation Division. I wonder if they're still not themselves, or if they're better now.

I hope they're better.

I'm near an elevator landing when I hear voices.

"The planet Marden has ships," a man is saying. "High-tech ones."

"They haven't come for us yet. So why flee?"

The two men wait for an elevator. I hesitate, unsure whether I want to be seen.

"The moonshine is an integral part," the first man says. "A related problem, along with the problem of the outer sectors. This is the right step to take; we can fix all three."

"When will it happen?"

The elevator dings, and the door opens.

"As soon as the injections have been administered."

They move inside, and the door closes behind them.

I frown a little, and wonder what they were talking about as I move ahead to Nourishment Division.

The cafeteria is almost empty at this hour. Lunch was earlier and dinner will be later. Four girls sit giggling at a table in the corner, but they're the only ones here, except for me.

Tray in hand, I sit at one of the tables far from the girls. My hands tremble a little as I pick up my raerburger. Maybe it's a remnant of the fever that still makes my face warm, but I'm also starving. I take a bite and chew slowly, savoring the taste. Cheesy sauce dribbles down my chin, and I wipe it away with a napkin.

Thoughts play on the edge of my mind. Worries about the baby I saw die down in the maternity ward. Worries about tomorrow and my last training session.

I don't know what they're going to make me do. I hope it'll be easy; I hope I'll be able to raise my Promise to 80 with no trouble, but I can't count on that. I was sure I'd done well during the test earlier, and then I screwed everything up.

I clench my teeth, hard. I can't screw things up anymore. I can't fail. I have to raise my Promise, so I'll be safe, or as safe as I'll ever be. So I can pick a career that will get me close to Commander Charlie, so I can get on his good side and convince him to bring Logan here. So I can feel Logan's fingers on my cheek again. So he can run his thumb over my hand somewhere other than in my memory.

So we can grow old together.

I take a deep breath to steady my heartbeat.

I'm bringing my raerburger back up to my mouth when I notice, out of the corner of my eye, someone step into the cafeteria. A blond-haired boy in a gray suit with a gun in the holster attached to his belt.

Sam freezes, noticing me.

Maybe he'll walk away. Maybe he doesn't care anymore;

maybe he already forgot his promise to make my life hell, and his anger with me for beating his score in Phantom and beating the obstacle course.

A cruel smirk touches Sam's lips. He strides toward me.

I'm on my feet before I know what I'm doing, moving to the trash slot. A detail clings to me: Sam has a gun. He's armed, and I'm not. So I don't throw away my knife or my fork; I clench both of them inside my fists.

Sam is halfway across the cafeteria.

There are two exits. I hurry through the one that isn't blocked, into the plaza outside. It's empty. I break into a run.

I reach the elevator on the far side and slam my palm against the call button. Come on, come on, come on. Sam knows I went this way, and he'll be able to catch up if the elevator doesn't get here fast enough.

Ding. The door opens, and I slip inside. I jab the button for the floor where my bedroom is. Sam doesn't know where it is, and even if he did, he can't break inside my room without my or Ariadne's thumbprint.

But he's coming. He sprints through the cafeteria entrance as I jab the button again.

"Come on, close!" I yell at the doors.

They start to slide shut, and I press back against the glass, sure I'm safe now. Sure he won't make it in time.

His arm blocks it from closing.

Sam pushes the door open and steps inside with me, his face devoid of emotion. The door closes. I want to slip out. I want to scramble away, but there's nowhere to run. He pulls the emergency break knob so we won't go anywhere.

My heart races. I clasp my hands behind my back, hiding the fork and knife between them.

"Get out." I won't let him touch me.

"You think you're clever, don't you? Trying to run." He steps toward me with that smirk still on his face. I press harder against the glass, wishing it would disappear.

"Well, I *am* smarter than you," I say. "I got a hundred on the intelligence test earlier."

"That's funny. You got the same score I did." He moves even closer, slipping his arms around my waist.

Every inch of my body turns rock solid. "What are you doing?"

"I'm starting to wonder if I was wrong about you," he says. "We're both smart. We both got excellent times on the CODA. We both like to throw knives."

"Excuse me?"

"Colonel Sam and Colonel Clementine, leaders of the army, and lovers. Don't you think that sounds nice?

"I think you're vruxing stupid."

He laughs, leaning in toward my lips.

He's trying to mess with me, I can read it in his eyes. I don't know what his game is, but it's a thousand times worse than him threatening murder.

I grit my teeth, pull the fork out from behind my back, and stab at his side.

He blocks it easily and places his other hand on my shoulder, pushing me back against the glass. He smiles and presses the fork into his thumb. "Did you really think you could stop me with this?"

"Get *off* me," I say through clenched teeth, aware that I'm still gripping the knife in my other hand. I can still use it. But I have to wait for the right moment.

"Make me," he whispers.

And then his mouth is on mine.

I want to shove him off, but he traps me with his hands, his body. My eyes burn. This isn't fair. I don't want to kiss him—I want to kiss Logan. It should be *him*, not Sam. I hate Sam. I *hate* him.

But there's something besides anger inside me too. There's a curiosity I'm embarrassed about, and an anxious feeling in my chest as he molds his lips against mine and forces his tongue into my mouth. He tastes like salt and something smoky. His hands clutch my face.

Disgusting, disgusting. I have to make him stop.

I slide down the glass of the elevator, dragging him with me. I tangle five fingers in his hair, pulling him closer.

The other five tighten around the hilt of the knife.

I lash it at his leg. The sound it makes coupled with his cry tell me I did some damage.

He lets go of me. I rise and push past him, and slam a button on the elevator panel. The door opens. Sam reaches for me, but I slip away from his grasp, out into the corridor.

I scramble into the nearest stairwell and down the steps. Sam's shouts echo behind and above me. The stairwell door opens and closes again. His boots pound on the stairs. I wipe his saliva off my mouth with the back of my hand, and hope I won't get in too much trouble for this.

Seven flights down, I burst through another door and race down the hallway toward Slumber Division.

"Clementine!" he shouts.

I glance over my shoulder. His leg seems fine—I must've only scraped it—and he's catching up. He has a gun. He could shoot me if he wanted, but he must not want to, because he doesn't touch it. Or maybe he's afraid someone will hear.

Around a corner, my room lies at the end of the hall. I grit my teeth and force my legs to move faster.

"You wait until I get you!" he yells. "I'm gonna report you for this."

The way he says it, I'm not sure I believe him. Making a big deal over a scrape like that might damage his reputation, after all.

I jam my thumb into the lock-pad, and the door slides open.

Inside, I push the other pad, and the door shuts and locks, leaving Sam out in the hallway, pounding on the wall and snarling. "Open up. I said *open up.*"

I move into the bathroom and lock the door behind me. Inside, I strip off my clothes and climb into the steam-clean capsule. I turn it on the highest setting, and the spew of steam and water from the ceiling faucets drowns out Sam's voice and pounding fists.

I let out my breath. I'm safe now. But he touched me again, worse this time.

Dropping down onto the tile, I pull my trembling legs to my chest and spread my lips apart so water gets inside them, to clean the taste of him out of my mouth.

At least I stabbed him today. That makes me smile a little.

But he kissed me, and it was *wrong.* It should've been Logan. It should've been his hands on my face, his fingers in my hair, his breath on my neck, his taste in my mouth.

I curl up in a ball on the shower floor, wishing I could hear his voice tell me that I'll be okay. That this is another nightmare, and I'll wake up in one more minute.

He's too far away.

I clench my teeth and blink until the tears stop trying to form in my eyes. I have to do well tomorrow. Better than everyone, no matter what. Because I have to convince Commander Charlie of my loyalty, so I can see Logan again.

So I can make Sam pay.

✂

Ariadne finds me a couple hours later, sitting on the floor at the foot of my bed. I tried to fall asleep, but it didn't work. So I sank into the carpet, pulled my knees to my chest, and waited. For what, I don't know.

"Clementine?" Ariadne whispers.

I tense a little. If she's still emotionless, if there's still something wrong with her, I don't want to see her.

But her eyes are wide, and color fills her cheeks. She hesitates when I don't say anything, then drops to the floor beside me, her shoulder against mine.

She fiddles with her hands in her lap.

"What did he do?" she says quietly.

"What did who do?"

"Sam."

I press my lips against my knobby knees. "How can you tell?"

Her eyes move this way and that, not stopping anywhere. When she speaks, her words are no more than a breath. "It's something I was familiar with back on the Surface."

A shiver runs through me, though it's warm in here. I don't want to be right about what I think she means.

"At five," she says, and I'm surprised at how steady her voice is, "a boy built me a small shack beside his, where I could sleep. He was kind to me, at first." She gives me a strangled look.

I nod, understanding. But I know that even if he wasn't kind, she wouldn't have refused his help. Children on the Surface should never refuse help.

"At first, he was kind," Ariadne repeats. She pulls her hair over her shoulder and braids it with shaky fingers. "But soon he wanted something in return. I wanted to run"—her voice cracks—"but I had nowhere to go. Until I was picked for Extraction."

She pauses to take a breath. "The night after the test," she says, "I didn't go back to my shack. I slept in the sewer because I knew if I went back, he'd sneak into my bed, and he wouldn't let me leave for the ceremony. I didn't know if I'd get picked, but I knew I had to run." She brushes tears out of her eyes. "So, I ran. Finally."

"I'm glad," I whisper.

Her hand falls away from her hair and settles in her lap. I reach for it and give it a squeeze. It trembles in my grasp.

We sit like that for a long time, huddled together, not speaking.

And I understand what she said before, about how fear isn't a bad thing. Fear made Ariadne brave enough to run. Fear made me brave enough to leave Logan behind, which was the only way I'd ever be able to save him. And it made me brave enough to shoot that Unstable, and take a risk in Phantom, and fight Sam when he tried to hurt me.

Fear makes me feel weak, but facing it makes me strong.

Over and over, I remind myself of this as we sit there in the silence. Soon, we stand and climb into our separate beds. I pull the sheets up over my head.

I fall asleep with a whisper on my lips, telling myself to be brave.

20

"lementine," Ariadne whispers. She squeezes my shoulder. I stir, stuck halfway between my sheets and a dream of Logan.

"Clem."

"Hmm?"

"We have to go."

With a groan, I open my eyes. It's not morning yet. It's the middle of the night. "What?"

Ariadne bites her lip and turns her head to the doorway, where Cadet Waller is standing.

"Your final training session starts in thirty minutes," she says, her voice tight and clipped. "I'll be back in five minutes. You'd better have clothes on." She turns, and the door slides shut behind her.

I sit up, fully awake now. "Wait, *what*? It's tonight?"

"I guess so," Ariadne says, slipping out of her nightclothes.

My heart races.

I don't even get until the morning.

With a swallow, I push the covers back, stand, and move to get dressed. My fingers shake zipping up Ariadne's suit and knotting the laces of my boots.

Ariadne offers me an elastic to tie up my curls. "One more session and we'll be citizens. Can you believe it?" Her voice is strangled.

I hold my breath as my hands fall away from my bun. I shake my head.

"No, I can't."

Lights flash in the darkness outside Phantom, where Cadet Waller leads those of us who slept on the same floor. Many Extractions are already here, yawning and trying to wake up. No one looks as though they have any idea what we're doing.

"We'll wait for the last few stragglers," Cadet Waller says, "and then I'll explain the session."

Oliver comes over to Ariadne and me. He looks a bit shaky. For a second I freeze up, afraid he isn't better, afraid he's still emotionless, even though Ariadne is normal again. But when his eyes meet mine, they're wide and blue behind his glasses. "Did you sleep well?" he asks.

Ariadne shakes her head.

"Not really," I say.

He looks at his feet, his hand moving automatically to the arm he hurt two days ago. "Me neither," he says.

I want to ask him and Ariadne about what happened earlier, to see if they remember how the hub gas screwed them up. But I'm afraid to say anything here, in front of everyone. People are talking, but someone might hear.

I glance at Ariadne. Her wide eyes are fixed on a spot in the sky.

"Hey, can I talk to you guys for a second?" I ask quietly. "Alone?"

"Um, sure," Oliver says.

Ariadne frowns. "About what?"

"Just come on." I grab her hand and Oliver's, and pull them with me a few feet away, over to a machine with fake guns and a screen for shooting lasers. We can still see the other Extractions, the instructors, and Cadet Waller, but they shouldn't be able to hear us.

"Do you two remember what happened earlier?" I ask.

"What happened earlier?" Ariadne asks.

Red lights flash on Oliver's pale face. "You mean after the intelligence session?" he says.

I nod.

"I do. . . ." He swallows. "I mean, I *don't* remember, and that's the problem. I remember going into the hub and taking the test, and scoring a ninety-eight, but everything's hazy after that. I thought it must've just been me, though. Everyone else seemed normal."

"No one was normal," I say. "Your eyes were glazed over. You were all acting like robots."

"But you weren't?" he asks.

"I was sick, or something. I don't know. I was messed up too, but it was different."

Ariadne's looking at us like we're crazy.

"Do you remember anything?" I ask her.

"I took the test, same as you," she says. "Got a ninety-six. My Promise was seventy-five. What else is there?"

"So they did something to all of us." Oliver's voice cracks. "It just affected us each differently."

"Seems like it," I say.

"What do we do?" he asks. "What if it happens again?"

Cadet Waller blows a whistle over by the Phantom entrance. "All right, Extractions, let's pay attention now."

"Come on, we'd better go," Ariadne says.

"If it happens again, we'll fight it," I say, grabbing Oliver's hand and following Ariadne. "We'll be fine."

He doesn't say anything. But the creases around his eyes tell me he doesn't believe me.

All of the Extractions are here outside Phantom now, and more adults have come too. They form a perimeter around the group of us sixteen-year-olds. I've never seen most of the adults before, but I recognize Colonel Parker and a few of his lieutenants.

"Welcome to your final training module," Cadet Waller says, her eyes sweeping the crowd of us with purpose. "You've all increased your intelligence and physical strength since you arrived in the Core, and it has done wonders for your Promise. Tonight, your training will focus on one final quality that is necessary for all citizens to exude: obedience. In other words, trust and loyalty. This exercise will focus, specifically, on trusting a Developer to help you find safety from danger. Notice the dome behind me." Cadet Waller gestures to Phantom.

She starts to explain how it works, for the benefit of the kids who haven't been inside, which is most of them.

My pulse hammers. This isn't so bad. Working with a team, this will require strategy, but that's something I'm good at.

I might actually have a shot.

Cadet Waller's words snap me back to the present, and all my relief fades. The rules have changed.

"You will each enter Phantom on your own, and you can't carry any weapons with you," she says. "Whatever or whoever you meet inside Phantom won't be entirely pretend; they will be linked to real life forms. In other words, whatever injury you cause them, they will feel it. I must warn you, we've also set Phantom on a very high level of play, which could kill you if you aren't careful."

My eyes are wide, and my heart's beating 140 beats per minute. The last time I was in Phantom, I met Unstables I was stupid enough to think might actually feel my gunfire, even though they were fake, nothing but an illusion.

This time, whatever is in there will feel everything. I will still have to kill.

"As I've mentioned before," Cadet Waller continues, "eighty is the Promise score you must obtain. That is a requirement for Core citizenship. Fortunately, most of you have already reached that score or are very close to reaching it. There are, however, one or two of you who need to show exceptional Promise in this final module to raise your score that high."

Cadet Waller's standing a ways away, but her eyes focus on me. I swear Colonel Parker looks at me too.

Of course, they would've seen my test results by now.

"Those who don't reach eighty," Cadet Waller says slowly, her eyes still locked on mine with not a hint of kindness, "will face permanent removal. We regret that this is necessary, but there is no alternative."

She didn't say removal from the Core; she said *permanent* removal.

Death.

I clasp my hands behind my back so, hopefully, no one will notice how much they're trembling.

"You will each enter the game in a random order," Cadet Waller says, finally looking away from me. "You will receive further instructions once inside." Behind her, the entrance to the dome opens. She steps aside so we'll be able to walk past her.

Closing my eyes, I concentrate on the air flowing in and out of my nose. This is a test, just something I have to do to stay alive. I can do this. I can do this.

She lifts her tablet. "First up is Clementine."

I don't know if I can do this.

Ariadne's eyes meet mine, wide as ever. "Be careful," she whispers.

Oliver glances at me and gives me a pained smile.

I close my eyes and squeeze my hands into balls. This isn't just for me; it's for Logan. He is everything. He's always said I'm clever and fierce and brave, that I deserve a place in the Core. Now I have to make Commander Charlie and everyone else believe it too. So they'll listen to me. So I'll get what I want.

Raising my chin, I clench my fists at my sides and walk past the eyes that are burning holes in my skin into the dome, where my future waits.

Two people stand on the Preparation Deck beneath the flickering fluorescent lights. One is unfamiliar, but I recognize the second, with her nose stud and her hair spiky black. I taste something sour in my mouth again. This time, I swallow, and it goes down.

Sandy breaks into a smile. "How you doing, sweetie?" she says.

"Okay," I lie. "What are you doing here?"

"We're here to give you the rundown before you get in there," she says.

"What's your job?" I ask her, because I don't even know. She seems to pop up everywhere.

Her brows furrow a little. "I'm a weapons instructor, among other things. It's not important right now."

"This is a trust exercise," the other instructor says. "There will be a Developer in a control dock overhead telling you exactly how to combat the danger."

"Understand?" Sandy holds my gaze, like there's something she's trying to tell me but can't say in front of the instructor. "All you have to do is listen and follow his instructions. This is an evaluation of your level of trust."

I nod. My memory replays the sounds of gunfire and screaming Unstables from the last time I was in here. The memories play over and over, reminding me of what I've done and am capable of doing.

Sandy glances at the other instructor before stepping forward and pulling me into a hug. I stiffen at first, then force my body to relax. I close my eyes and pretend I never have to leave her warmth.

"Good luck," she whispers in my ear. "Trust, and *obey*."

The door to the arena slides open, revealing darkness.

I want to ask her if she knows how they kill people who fail citizenship training. In case I—

Stop it, I tell myself. I won't die. I won't. I'll do anything.

Sandy gives me a light push, and I force my legs forward. The door slides shut behind me, and I'm alone.

Darkness presses in on me. Silence.

When I was in here last time, red lettering appeared overhead in a couple seconds. The rules have changed, but what's taking them so long? I want to get this over with.

I turn in a slow circle and flex my fingers. I'd feel so much safer with a copper in them.

There's a zap, and I jump. A speaker comes on.

"Clementine, can you hear me?" It is a hoarse, cracking voice, one I've heard before. A shiver slides down my spine.

Commander Charlie is the one I have to trust. He'll tell me to do something, and I'll have to do it, no matter what.

"Y-yes."

"Excellent. We will begin in a moment."

I squeeze my eyes shut. I need to prove my loyalty to him anyway. What better time than now?

"I will guide you," Commander Charlie says. "Listen to me and do exactly as I say."

My heart races. I start to imagine what I'm going to be up against, then force those thoughts deep down, tuck them somewhere far away. I have to pretend this is only a game, that it's all in my head. Because if I don't get through this, Commander Charlie is going to kill me.

I clench my fists and grit my teeth, as if that'll calm me down.

"Are you ready, Clementine?"

I nod. No point in prolonging the inevitable.

There's a hollow, whining electrical noise like a machine powering up.

Dust fills my lungs. I cough and choke, waving it away with a hand until my eyes clear.

I stand in a desert beside a chain-link fence. The sky is dark, filled with storm clouds. The fence stretches on and on, and I can't see where it ends, or what it separates me from.

I take a step toward it, listening for the low hum of electricity. But the fence is quiet. I turn around, press my back against it, and slip my fingers through the holes.

Tumbleweeds sit half rotting between cacti and rocks. Wind rustles my curls, but it doesn't rustle the plants. There's no movement here. Not a bird in the sky, not a song to be heard. Like the world ended and I'm the only one left.

I squint into the clouds to where I imagine Commander Charlie sits in some game control room, observing me.

"What am I waiting for?" I shout.

Thunder rumbles in the distance, but he doesn't answer. My heart skips a beat. Maybe he lied. Maybe he abandoned me in here and will leave me stuck forever until I go mad or drop dead.

Or maybe that's how I get my Promise up—I find a way out.

I release the fence and walk forward, still scanning the horizon. The whole world is a desert. I wonder how far it goes. I'm in a dome, after all. If I keep walking, will I slam into the wall, or walk in circles and never find anything?

Thunder rumbles, louder this time.

I notice something new: two tiny dots in the distance. People.

A krail caws in my ear, so loud I spin around and bring my fists up to defend myself. I'm not sure what I expect, some giant bird with black feathers staring at me with beady eyes. Some devilish device of the Developers ready to claw me to bits.

But it's not a bird, not a krail.

It's Logan.

21

Logan with his hair scraggly, his lips cracked, and his skin stained with dust. His eyes widen as they take in my face, like he can't believe it's really me.

"Clementine?"

My heart slams against my rib cage. A drop of rainwater hits my nose.

He's not really here. He's a fake, simulated body. But he's connected to a life force that can feel pain and knows he's in here, and I can't breathe because that means they have him. They have Logan, and I might never see him again because what if he gets hurt in here? What if he doesn't make it?

I swallow. "What are you doing here?"

He takes a step toward me, and his fingers brush my jawline where my scar used to be. "I didn't think I'd see you again," he whispers.

Another drop of water hits my hand. A krail caws behind me.

I glance over my shoulder to check on the other figures. They're much closer.

I turn back to Logan and clench my fists tighter. "You have to get out."

"I missed you." His fingers skim my clavicle, leaving tingles of fire on my skin. Lightning flashes in the sky.

"Who are they?" he says softly, and cocks his head at something behind me.

They're men, I see now. They wear the black armor of Surface officials, and each of them holds a thin staff with a sharp, curved blade at its end. They move toward us, closing the distance at a much quicker pace than I reckoned.

They must be the danger.

"Come on, let's go." I take Logan by the hand, but he pulls away.

"Go where?"

Rain drips on me and wind tugs at my hair as I take in the desert again. There's nothing for miles and miles but tumbleweeds, cacti, and the chain-link fence.

The fence. On the other side of it, we wouldn't be completely safe, but I'd feel safer. That's better than nothing.

"Clem," Logan says.

I turn to see the men break into a run. Their boots pound, leaving a trail of dust. The distance between them and us is closing fast. When they reach us, they're going to slice those blades through our necks—they're going to kill us. Cadet Waller said we could die in here.

I shove Logan toward the fence.

"Don't climb the fence." Commander Charlie's hoarse voice rings through the dome, echoing off walls I can't see.

Thunder roars, and rain lashes against my face.

I want to scream and punch something and cower all at once. The officials are close now, so close. And I won't stop moving, but I hear the voice and can't move an inch.

This is a test, and I have to follow orders.

But the men will kill me.

But I have to pass this.

But Logan will die.

But Sandy said to trust and *obey*.

"Don't climb the fence," Commander Charlie repeats.

The men come closer.

"Logan, climb it!" I ram into him.

His brows furrow. He doesn't move. He doesn't say anything.

What's *wrong* with him?

"Use your friend," Commander Charlie says. I swear I can hear the smile in his voice.

"What?"

"Use your friend as a shield."

Logan's lips part, and even though he doesn't touch me, I feel his fingers brush my skin again, in their perfect way.

Still, he says nothing. The real Logan would say something. He would help me figure out what to do instead of just standing there, not doing anything.

I shake my head and blink rain out of my eyes. "No."

"Do it."

"Logan, climb the fence."

"Do it, or you fail."

I can't think, can't breathe, can't do anything, but I have to do something. The men are mere feet away now—mere *feet* and they're going to beat me, they're going to kill me if I don't follow orders.

Whoever this fake Logan is connected to, it's not the real Logan, so I can do what Commander Charlie wants—

But what if he's real?

He's *not* real—

What if I'm wrong?

He stands beside me and does nothing. His eyes don't even water.

Boots splash in mud. Blades glint in the torrent as the men raise their staffs over their heads to slice through my skin. To end my life.

A strangled cry bursts from my throat. Logan is *not real*.

I grab him, and he doesn't fight me. He lets me grab hold of him. I want to keep holding on to him and never let go, but I don't. I throw him into the path of the men and their weapons. The slice and crunch and crack echo through the dome. They don't slice his neck—they slice into his arms and legs and hands, reducing him to bloody limbs.

Logan screams, and my heart shatters. Glass fragments in the dirt and dust.

Rain pelts my body, making puddles in the dirt at my feet. I shove my fingers into my ears and squeeze my eyes shut, but it does no good. I can't stop hearing him. I can't stop seeing him collapsing in his blood. The tears won't stop streaming down my cheeks.

It's not him—not really—no way—they're just pretending—they won't hurt him—

It's only a test, only a simulation, and he's fake—I *hope*—but I can't stop sobbing. Because all of this could be real as life, real as moonshine, and I might have killed the boy I love.

When I open my eyes, I'm ready to scream and claw my nails into Commander Charlie's face, or maybe collapse and never get up, but it's not over.

I stand on the edge of a cliff, and night has fallen. The rain has stopped, but I'm drenched in water. Far below me, so small I have to squint to see them, waves froth on a sandy shore. The moon hangs over me in the sky, giant and terrible, shimmering pink through the shield.

My hands tremble as I run them along my arms. My teeth chatter from the cold. I wonder what they're going to make me do next.

pew-pew

p-p-p-p-p

Black and white lines flicker across the sky.

I stop breathing.

ZAP

A flash, and the acid shield wipes out across the sky. There's no barrier between me and the moon's poison.

There's no way. There's no way.

I want to turn and run as far as I can, and I'd do it right this second if my legs weren't shaking so badly. They said I could die in here. That acid can really kill me. So why include it in this test, unless they want me dead?

My heart pounds so fast I can't think straight.

This is still a test. Sandy said to follow orders.

"What should I do?" I try to steady my voice. It doesn't work at all.

"Do nothing," Commander Charlie says, calm and collected.

Adrenaline pumps through my veins. I'm angry and I will not stand here and *do nothing*. The second the acid reaches me, I'm done for. It'll take me ten minutes to die. Ten minutes of heart palpitations and screaming and lungs constricting and my skin charring black.

The acid will reach me soon.

I turn my head around wildly. A rock would do the trick. I

could bash my head in, quick and painless. At least more painless than acid corrosion.

But there aren't any rocks. I'm standing on a cliff, yet all the rocks are either too big or too small. I snatch a jagged one from the ground that'd leave a bloody scratch in my head, but that's not good enough.

With a snarl, I launch it into the air. It cascades in a high arc before dropping over the side of the cliff, careening toward the ocean.

The ocean.

I take a step and set my feet upon the cliff's edge. Loose rocks slide beneath my feet. They tumble to the waves below. No doubt there are rocks down there too. Jumping into that water would feel like slamming into a brick wall, and the boulders would smash me to bits. But it'd be less painful than moonshine.

My uneven heartbeat pounds through my ears, the last reminder of my mortality. My limbs still shake, and *Logan, Logan, Logan* is all I'm thinking. I shouldn't have let Commander Charlie hurt him. I shouldn't have done it.

"Don't jump," Commander Charlie's voice softens and echoes through the simulation. "Stay where you are."

I grab another rock from the ground and fling it into the sky, screaming. "You're supposed to protect me!"

"Trust me."

I drop to my knees and jam my face into my palms. Choking sounds bubble up from my throat. I don't want to die. I don't want to die.

Please don't let me die.

I lift my head and stare at the sky, where moonshine rushes toward me in a cloud of pink mist. Tears fill my eyes.

If I don't follow his orders, Charlie will kill me even if I get out alive—

But I'll die in here—

But it's not real—

But Cadet Waller said I will—

A sob shakes out of my throat and I wrap my arms around my body, squeezing myself and closing my eyes. I breathe in and out again, trying to forget where I am and what I've done. Trying to ready myself for the sting of the moonshine and the horrible wrenching feeling I know is coming.

It is the feeling of death.

22

"Great job, Clementine. You will make a fine citizen."

When I open my eyes, the midnight moon and moonshine are gone. I'm alone in the darkness of the dome.

The door slides open to my left, letting a fierce stream of light in. Sandy moves through the door and then she is beside me, pulling me to my feet, into the warmth of her arms.

"Sweetie, you did it."

"They . . . you mean . . ." I try to say the words, but they don't get out.

"Your Promise is eighty-two."

When I breathe, it's so shaky it's more like a sob.

I'm safe. I'm not going to die.

But my temple throbs, and I touch a hand to it. I still hear Logan's scream in my head.

"Please tell me he's okay," I whisper.

Sandy's brows furrow. "Who?"

"My friend. Th-the one they made me use as a shield."

When she speaks, her words are careful and slow. "Clemen-tine, no one in there was real. It was a simulation."

"But Cadet Waller said—"

"I promise, it wasn't real. They just wanted you to believe it was."

She gives my arm a light tug, and I make my feet move. Through a doorway, I enter a steam-clean capsule that dries the rainwater from my suit and body. Outside the capsule, Sandy guides me through another door into a back area of Recreation Division, and then into a hallway.

"You . . . you mean it?" I say.

"I promise," she says again, and squeezes my arm tighter.

I close my eyes and take a shuddering breath.

Logan isn't dead. I didn't kill him.

Beechy waits for me at the end of the corridor. He must've been in the crowd on the main deck. Sandy waves to him from a distance, but I go the rest of the way to him alone because she has to hurry back inside Phantom to guide the next Extraction. My heart still beats too fast in my chest, and I breathe deeply to try to slow it down.

"Congratulations." Beechy's eyes are warm, deep, and golden brown. "They announced that you passed."

"Thank you," I say, and run a palm over my arm.

"Rough time in there?"

I give him a tight nod and lean against the wall.

"Come on." He holds out his hand. A smile tugs at his mouth. "I want to show you something."

In a corridor in Invention Division, Beechy presses his thumb into a lock-pad in the wall. A black door slides open, and we step onto a metal ramp.

To my left and to my right, beyond the railing and far below, fog clouds a deck where lights flash on dark shapes I can't make out.

"What are they?" I ask.

"Spaceships."

I touch the railing to peer over it better. That must be the flight port.

"They're not why I brought you." Beechy tugs on my hand to pull me along. His palm is strong and warm in mine.

Up the ramp, a flight pod sits shrouded in shadow, close to the ceiling. I frown and wonder what it's doing here. Beechy uses his thumbprint again, and yellow bulbs light up one by one along the pod's silver rim. The door slides open, revealing a comfy space with two pilot seats, a control panel, and a visor over a screen like a window.

"This is our flight simulator," Beechy says, leading me inside. "I've spent quite a lot of time here, what with the learning how to fly and then the teaching."

He settles into one of the seats and flips switches on the ceiling. The door slides shut behind me. I slip into the other seat and pull my legs onto the chair, scanning the dash with its levers and buttons and screens. "Why'd you bring me here?"

Beechy looks at me and smiles. "For this." He fiddles with something on a monitor, and the silver visor slides down, revealing starlight.

My lips part. This is *real* starlight. Real yellows and purples and greens and blues through the moonshine shield. A billion stars in front of me, spreading vast to the farthest reaches of the universe, where maybe there's someplace safer than here. Someplace better.

Beechy fiddles with a knob, and the image slides to the left even though the pod isn't moving. A sliver of the moon appears. A quarter moon, much of it in black shadow, but it's still giant. It looks so real, so easy to reach if only this pod could really fly, that I can't speak.

It's been mere days since I left. But now that I'm trapped a million miles underground, the sky means freedom.

"It's an image of the real sky." Beechy's voice is a soft breath. "What it looks like over the Surface tonight. We keep a running video feed for observation purposes and flight practice."

My heart flutters. This is Logan's sky. I wonder if he's up there seeing it now. If he pulled himself onto a roof, if he's lying there watching clouds and stars drift by.

I wonder if he's forgotten me already, or if he thinks I've forgotten him. If he knows I killed a fake version of him tonight, even though I didn't want to.

An ache fills my lungs, burning my throat. I hug my knees to my chest.

Beechy watches me out of the corner of his eye. "Which friend did you meet in Phantom?" he asks.

I bite hard on my lip. So hard, I taste blood.

"Someone I still have to save," I whisper.

"How long does he have?"

I play with my bootlaces. "Three years, if he's lucky."

He taps something into a monitor. "Three years is a long time."

I shake my head. "Not long enough. And with the moon and everything . . . he might have less than that."

"You don't think I know?" Beechy stares straight ahead at something I can't see, or maybe at nothing. "Mantle is just as bad as the Surface."

I watch him, curious. I saw the main production facility for that sector on our way down here. I know Mantle is the place responsible for manufacturing weapons and other machinery. I know it lies underground, between Lower and Crust. I know children die there as often as they do anywhere, but I don't know much more than that.

"Could you tell me about it?" I ask, then hesitate. "I understand if you don't want to. . . ."

"It's a smoke-filled cage," Beechy says bitterly. "The factories take up so much of the sector, the work camp isn't much of anything at all. It's just two skinny rooms with compartments in the steel walls, sort of like bunk beds except they're smaller and completely enclosed. Officials lock you inside at night. You're stuck in a box all by yourself, and you can't breathe. You can't sleep. If you cry too loud, they open the box and make you run the furnaces all night instead. You're always covered in soot and grease, and they never let you wash. They give you three cups of water per day and one bowl of this disgusting meal mixed with protein. Kids try to get their bodies caught in the machines to kill themselves. Half the time, it doesn't work or someone catches them."

He sighs and runs his fingers through his hair. "I'm sorry," he says. "I doubt you wanted to hear all that."

"I don't mind." I fiddle with my hands in my lap. I've been so preoccupied by my troubles down here that I forgot how much worse it is up there.

"You remind me so much of someone I knew when I was younger," Beechy says. His eyes flicker with emotion, watching me.

A strange tightness tugs at my chest. He said that before, the first time he saw me.

"Really?"

He nods. His voice quiets when he talks again: "I think I was seven, and she was maybe fourteen. She protected me for a little while, when things got bad. She was brave like you. And she had your hair." He runs his fingers through his own hair, and sighs. "She became pregnant—maybe from one of the other kids, maybe from an official. I don't know. She kept it hidden for a long time. I think she persuaded some people to keep it quiet . . . but I found her dead one night, shoved halfway inside a trash chute."

Sorrow flickers across his face. "Her baby was in the chute with her, already born, and still alive, but barely. There was an older boy with me when I found her, and he saved the baby. I think he snuck her into the sanitarium somehow."

I know what he's thinking—that her baby was me. Babies are transferred from one outer sector to another sometimes, after all. Whenever they're born, they're taken to where they're needed.

I can't breathe right, but I manage to swallow. "Beechy, that doesn't . . . Just because you knew some girl who had hair like mine and she had a baby doesn't mean the baby grew up to be me."

"I know," he says. "That's why I, uh . . ." He averts his gaze, and his cheeks flush red. "I checked your records. I have access to the citizen registrar system, and I found out your birth history and the names of your parents."

I stare at him. "You *what*?"

"I know, I'm sorry. I should've asked for your permission. But I had to know if I was right." His hand finds mine. "I'm sorry," he says again.

But it's not that he did it without my permission. It's not even that he found out the names of my parents.

It's that they have names. They're real people. I've always known that, of course, but it never felt true until now.

"And . . ." I swallow. "What did you find out?"

Beechy waits a moment to answer. "I was right. Your mom gave birth to you in Mantle."

I nod. But my throat thickens as I remember Beechy's story. I've never imagined my mother's death before, but if I had, I wouldn't have imagined one like that. I blink several times because my eyes start to water. It's silly, really. She's been dead for a long time. But I can't help it.

I swallow again, harder this time. "What was her name?" I ask.

"Are you sure you want to know?"

"I think so."

"It was Mae."

"Mae." I try the word out on my tongue. I can't tell if it feels right or not. I have no picture of her to match the name with. "What's my father's name?"

"It wasn't in your records," Beechy says. "They could've done a DNA match to figure out who it was, but it looks like they didn't. Or if they did, it's in some other area of the records I don't have access to."

A horrible thought rushes through me: What if my father is one of the officials in the Surface camp? Beechy said it could've been an official, if it wasn't one of the boys in Mantle. And he might've been transferred to a different sector. He might even be here in the Core.

"Listen, it doesn't matter who your father is or was," Beechy says, slipping his fingers into the spaces between mine. "Your mother was wonderful, I can assure you. And *you* are wonderful."

I laugh a little.

"I mean it." He reaches out and touches my cheek, and lifts my head so it's no longer resting against my knee. I have no choice but to look at him. "You're alive, and that's all that matters," he says. "I'm going to keep you safe for her. I promise."

I breathe in and out, focusing on the warmth of his hand against my skin. He's right; there are things to be happy about. I'm alive and safe. Logan isn't dead.

But I think of him again, and of what happened inside Phantom, and I can't stop my heart from tightening in my chest. The Logan I met during the test wasn't real, but what if he had been?

Would I have killed him to save myself?

23

The New Citizen Ceremony begins after breakfast the next morning.

We stand in a gray room connected to the Pavilion where I shot an Unstable my first night here. I glimpse the viewing pods through a doorway at the back of the room, but Commander Charlie stands there, blocking it. Two Developers stand on either side of him. To their left and right, Colonel Parker and six other colonels are present. They wear full black armor and carry their helmets under their arms.

The gray walls are mostly bare, but the Core flag covers half of one. My eyes go to the words in the silver circle between the blue and black stripes: INVENTION. PEACE. PROSPERITY.

Oliver stands on my left, and Ariadne stands on my right. They both passed the test. Everyone passed.

My palms sweat, even though I have nothing to be afraid of anymore. Because my work isn't finished yet. I still have to gain an audience with Commander Charlie. I still have to convince him to save Logan.

"Congratulations, new citizens," he says as we stand before him. "We thank you for your hard work in training, and for your continued devotion to our cause. Please come forward."

We form a line and approach him. I try to keep my face normal. I watch him and the other Developers greet each person ahead of me, one at a time.

Then it's my turn.

I shake hands with the first Developer, the only female. The skin is tight around her eyes. "Congratulations," she says, touching my hand only lightly.

I shake hands with the second Developer, the youngest, though he's still much older than me. A dark-skinned male with a subtle trembling in his fingers. "Congratulations," he says.

I step past him, my heart thudding. Commander Charlie's eyes look into mine, and his thin lips stretch into a wide smile. "Ah, here she is," he says. "Ms. Clementine. Congratulations on your citizenship."

He offers a gloved hand. I take it, noticing he wears a small golden lapel pin of a moon on his suit jacket. "Thank you, sir." I manage to smile back.

"I look forward to your career decision," he says, and pulls his hand away.

He's already looking to the next Extraction, but I can't help the relief that runs through me, untwisting the knots in my stomach. He knows who I am. He looks forward to my career choice.

Maybe getting the chance to work with him won't be so hard.

Cadet Waller says there's one other part to the ceremony. She leads us to a room in Training Division with soft blue benches and a silver door at the back.

"Have a seat," she says. "We'll call you through the door in the order in which you passed the test, starting with the last person and moving backward to the first."

She calls the first name.

Ariadne slips her arm through mine and rests her head on my shoulder. Oliver sits to my right, twisting his hands in his lap. His glasses are a bit more cracked after last night, after whatever he did to survive in Phantom.

"What if they do something to us?" he says. "Give us drugs, or something? I'm scared they're going to mess everyone up again, like they did in the intelligence hubs."

"They're not," Ariadne says. "They didn't do anything in the first place."

"You don't even remember," Oliver says.

"Exactly. So it never happened."

"Because that's the logical conclusion—"

"Don't." I reach for Oliver's hand. "Please don't argue. We're safe now, remember? We passed the test." I tell him that, but I feel a bit queasy. We still don't know why they gave us the hub gas, after all. Or even what it was.

"I hope you're right," he says, pulling his hand away.

He's the next one called through the silver door.

Ariadne is called soon after. She slips her arm out of mine. "See you soon," she says with a smile.

I smile back. "See you."

I was the first to pass the test, so I'm soon left waiting alone. I cross my legs on the bench, close my eyes, and listen to the room around me. There is silence, except for the low hum of the lights. No screams outside, no buzzing cam-bots, no pounding feet.

I think I could get used to this, while I work to befriend Charlie and convince him to transfer Logan here. I'll find a way, but it's like Beechy said, there's time for that. I'm ready to live without worrying every day.

The silver door opens, and Cadet Waller appears. She gives me a curt smile. "We're ready for you," she says.

I slide off the bench and follow her. Through the door, she points me into a small room with hooks on the walls and a clothing slot like the one in my bedroom.

"If you'll please change out of your suit and into the outfit that comes out of the slot. As soon as you do, the next door will open." She glides out of the room, her smile looking like she had it cosmetically plastered to her face.

I unzip my leather suit. The fabric is soft and stretchy, and I slip out of it easily. I press the button on the slot and change into the clothes that slide out of it: a plain tank top and a pair of shorts more like underwear. They don't cover much of me, but the air is warm.

I take a deep breath and stand in front of the next silver door.

After a moment, it slides open. I step forward.

Two figures block my path. Two women with the same blue eyes and black curls, wearing surgeon coats and caps.

My stomach clenches—

squeezes—

drops two stories.

"Hello there! It's good to see you again." Nurse One smiles at me, while Nurse Two slips her fingers around my wrist and pulls me into the room. It's a round examination room with blue lights and a white reclining chair.

I must be dreaming, because this can't be happening again. I'm supposed to be finished with metal hubs, Unstables, and examination rooms.

But I notice one good thing: There aren't any metal tables or drip bags with blood and clear liquids. Still, I can't help saying, "Could you please tell me what I'm doing here?"

"You're here for a quick and easy examination," Nurse One says. "It's a standard procedure for all citizens, designed to check you once a month and make sure you're safe, happy, and healthy."

"The doctor will be here in a minute," Nurse Two says, guiding me into the chair.

I lean into the mesh and press a palm to my flip-flopping stomach. This isn't anything to worry about. This is standard, an examination, not another operation.

"Good morning." The doctor whistles as he enters the room, making four taps on his tablet before handing it to Nurse Two. He flashes a smile. "How are you today, Clementine? Promising, eh?" He laughs. "This is nothing to worry about, I assure you. First, I'm going to do some quick checks to make sure you're healthy." He rolls up his coat sleeves to sanitize his hands in the sink. "Nothing to worry about, like I said."

"I'm not worried." I'm afraid I say it a tad fast.

"Well, of course not. That would be silly." Nurse One hands him a stethoscope from a hook on the wall. He sticks the ear tips into his ears, and presses the silver disk to my chest. "If you'll take a deep breath for me."

Breathe in, breathe out.

"Perfect."

Nurse Two taps on the tablet keypad. Nurse One takes the stethoscope from the doctor and hands him a small monitor, from which he pulls three multicolored wires with small cups on the ends. "I'm going to take a reading of your brain waves, Clementine. It's quick and easy. Nothing to worry about."

I wish he'd stop saying that.

I fold my hands in my lap. He dabs dots of a sticky material onto my forehead, then presses the electrodes to my skin. His fingers fiddle with the knobs on the monitor.

There's silence in the room, apart from a soft whir from the monitor.

"Perfect." He pulls off the electrodes, and Nurse One puts the monitor away. I wonder what sort of reading I gave him, and why he needs it.

He claps his hands together. "That's all for today, except for your injection, which the nurses will administer before you move through the next door to learn about your career choices. Quick and easy, eh? Do you have any questions for me?"

"An injection?" I repeat, digging my nails into my legs.

"The nurses will explain. Okay? Great. I'll be off, then." He gives me one more smile, then leaves me alone with the nurses.

Nurse Two sets her tablet aside and begins sanitizing her hands.

"This will be quick," Nurse One assures me, wrapping a tight strip of latex around my upper arm.

"What is it?" I say.

"A little injection all citizens of the Core receive once a month."

Nurse Two scrubs with foam for what must be a full minute until she's satisfied. After snapping on gloves, she reaches for an object sitting in a rectangular tin on the counter, beside jars of cotton balls.

She turns enough so I can see what she's holding.

The needle is long and thick, protruding from an orange syringe. This must be the injection Cadet Waller showed me on the day of the Extraction test.

My sweaty palms grip the armrests. Nurse Two touches the needle tip to my shoulder, and I flinch. Her lips form a small frown, but she doesn't stop. She pushes the needle through my skin. There's a sharp jab of pain.

"I'm sorry, what's this for?" I ask.

"We live in close quarters in this sector," Nurse One says, setting a hand on my other shoulder. "There's a high risk for spreading disease, so inventors developed a serum to protect against it. Everyone receives this once a month."

Nurse Two presses the plunger, sending a stream of orange liquid into my arm. It rushes through my veins, up my shoulder, toward my pounding heart.

She removes the needle. Nurse One places a small, round piece of gauze over the spot.

"Quick and easy," she repeats.

I smile vaguely. My hands shake. I swear I can feel the liquid trickling through my temple but that's impossible. I must be imagining it.

Overhead, the fluorescent lights seem stronger, a brighter shade of yellow. I squint to see what Nurse Two is doing. She sets the needle back in its metal tin and strips the gloves from her hands.

A nauseous feeling sinks into my stomach like a heavy weight. I press a palm to my stomach and squeeze my eyes shut.

"Is it normal to feel sick?" I ask.

"That is a potential, mild side effect. It should pass shortly." Nurse One gestures to the exit door. "Head through there, and instructors will meet you for the final part of your ceremony."

I nod, wondering what was inside the injection. Are they *trying* to make me sick? Gritting my teeth, I ignore that thought and force myself to rise from my chair and walk. I clench my fists at my sides and take deep breaths to steady myself.

"Have fun!" Nurse One waves me out the door.

I see spots as I walk through the hallway, and my vision blurs. "In here," Cadet Waller says.

The doorway tilts, and I lean against the wall for a split second, breathing too fast. My eyes are wide. They did something to me. Just like Oliver was afraid they'd do. They lied when they said I'd be safer.

Gritting my teeth harder, I use the wall to heave myself into the next room.

Cadet Waller stands next to an instructor I don't recognize, and another whom I might, but her face is too blurry. I can't tell where I am.

"Congratulations, Clementine," a familiar voice says. The face is *Sandy*.

I swallow. What's she doing here? She's an instructor, I think, but still . . .

"It's time for your career assignment," Cadet Waller says. "Afterward, you'll receive new civilian attire to change into."

I nod, hoping they can't tell how much I'm trembling. They did this to me, so I have to pretend it didn't work. I don't want them to know.

Cadet Waller glances at her tablet screen. "Your preliminary career assignment is mathematics: data sampling. You will report to Training Division Room 54B this evening for further instructions—"

"Wait." I cut her off, squinting and shielding my face because the light is way too bright. "Wait. I thought we get to pick careers."

Cadet Waller frowns. "I don't know where you heard that. We assign careers based on our observation of your skills—"

"No, you're wrong." I raise my voice more than I intend to. "I need to pick—I need to work for Commander Charlie."

"Clementine, it doesn't work like that," Sandy says. She seems really nervous, but I might be imagining that. "You might be able to work your way up to a position with Commander Charlie, but you can't start with one right away."

"That's not good enough!" Again, I yell too loud. My voice makes me wince.

But this isn't okay. It's not supposed to work like this.

My head isn't supposed to hurt this bad.

"The injection didn't work. She's not being submissive," I hear Cadet Waller whisper as she reaches to turn on her earpiece. "I'll call the commander to find out what he wants done with her."

"No, he's busy. I'll take care of this." Sandy moves toward me. "Do you feel all right, Clementine?" Her face blurs again. Her hand touches my burning forehead, while her other steadies my arm.

I think she mouths something, but I can't tell what. A fierce ache slips through my body, like a thousand blades slicing through my skin. It takes everything in me not to cry.

"I think she's just tired from last night," Sandy says, turning away. "I'll have her sit down and keep an eye on her."

"You're sure?" Cadet Waller says.

"Yes. Come on, sweetie." Sandy puts her hands on my shoulders and guides me through a door. "You can change into your new clothes."

The door closes behind us. She helps me onto a soft bench. "The red suit right there is for you." She points at a blotchy shape on a wall hook. "Get changed, and then I want you to stay here, Clementine." She grips my shoulders. "You hear me? Stay here. I'll be back to check on you in ten minutes."

I can't tell if she's trying to help me, or if she's working with the doctors and Cadet Waller. I don't know if I should trust her or run away. But I have to lie down; my head hurts too much. Tears slip out of the corners of my eyes.

Maybe I say, "Okay." Maybe I stand and put the suit on.

Somehow, I end up on the bench wearing red, curled up in a ball. My breaths are uneven. My body shakes and sweats uncontrollably.

I have to know—I have to figure out what was inside that injection—but my head's on fire and my heart is pounding too hard and I can't think and it needs to *stop*. Why can't they just leave me alone? Why can't things be okay?

A soft buzzing reaches my ears. Through the haze of tears, I notice a tiny black blur rests in the edge of the ceiling, with a flashing red light.

A camera.

They're watching me. Someone is monitoring the effect of my monthly injection.

Whoever's watching has no right to see me weak like this. Especially if they did this to me. Especially if they want to make me weak.

I push myself up with my elbows and throw my legs over the side of the bench. I can barely see, and I want to rip out the knives in my arms and legs and hands, but there aren't any. Tears still streaming down my cheeks, I grope for the wall.

Sweat makes my palm fumble on the door handle. I get it open and stumble into the corridor before anyone can stop me.

24

I don't know where I'm going.

There are doors and more doors, and branching corridors. I run, crashing into the walls and dragging myself around corners. My stomach heaves, and I try to stop it, but it's no good. Remnants of my breakfast end up on the floor.

I wipe bile off my mouth with the back of my palm. An elevator appears, and I stagger into it. My fingers slip on the emergency brake knob, then pull it so the whining of the shaft breaks off.

In the corner, I curl up in a ball, drenched in sweat and crying and shivering.

I'll be okay.

I cough up something that tastes like blood.

Why am I not okay?

Whatever's inside the monthly injection did something to me, the same way the intelligence hub did something to me. But the hub did something to everyone else, so maybe that's happening now too. Maybe the other Extractions are fine—or as fine as vacant, expressionless people can be.

I have to focus. I solve Yate's Equation—the longest and hardest equation a person can solve—in my head to help myself calm down.

I try to think. I think back to yesterday, to the helmet over my head, and the cold gas seeping out of the tubes, and me breathing it in. At first it made me feel like I was floating, content with everything, trusting the Developers. And then it didn't—then it made me hurt almost as bad as my body hurts now.

The gas and the injection must be made from the same chemical.

But the gas didn't hurt Oliver, Ariadne, or the other Extractions. It made them more like robots.

The injection didn't work, Cadet Waller said. *She's not being submissive.*

It hits me. I know what the chemical is. That time in the hub wasn't the first time I've been this sick—this happened to me before.

It was wintertime, and I had just turned eight. A slick layer of ice covered the ground. Since the crop fields were dead, everyone had to work in either the packaging warehouse or the greenhouses, where plants continued to grow hydroponically under special lights.

Logan, Laila, and I were following the train tracks home one night, running so we wouldn't catch frostbite, when the hovercraft passed by overhead. It looked like it had come from the city and was on its way outside the settlement, for whatever reason. It was flying too low, and there was an opening at the back. When the ship tilted toward the sky to gain altitude, a couple bundles fell out and nearly landed on top of us. I screamed as Logan pulled me out of the way, tripped over a track, and skinned my knees.

While I wiped the ice off my trousers and tried to make my teeth stop chattering, Laila took a hesitant step closer to one of the bundles. Its drawstring was already loose. A simple touch made its contents spill onto the ice: delicate green stems with silver petals.

Laila's laughter pealed through the air. "Look at these!" She pulled a heap of them into her arms. "Real flowers!"

Logan picked up one of the asters. He turned to me with a radiant smile. "I bet they'd look pretty in your hair," he said, and tucked the stem behind my ear.

A cold wave of air washes over me in the elevator, making my teeth chatter. I feel like I did then, once the aster pollen seeped through my skin into my bloodstream. But I was tough, and the fever broke after a couple days. It wasn't until later that I heard the story about the Core scientist who genetically modified aster flowers to make them useful as stress or pain relievers for sick patients.

But when we learned about the asters in school, there was no mention of their pollen being used in great amounts, even in the sanitarium. Yet silver asters were on the Surface in the back of the hovercraft that day when I was eight, for one reason or another. And their calming effect didn't work on me. My body attacked the serum instead of accepting it.

I stare at my shaking hands.

I'm allergic to silver asters. I'm having the same allergic reaction to whatever injection they gave me.

They must have used pollen in the monthly injections.

A knock on the elevator door snaps me out of my head.

"Hello?" The voice is muffled through the wall, but firm like an official's. "Is someone in there?"

Oh no. I pressed the emergency brake knob—it must have alerted security. Sam did that before, and security didn't come, but he's an army lieutenant. The army *is* security.

I get to my feet, breathing fast, and use the wall for support. I hold down the button that keeps the door shut, release the emergency knob, and press the first floor number I find. Twelve. Good, someplace far away.

The elevator rumbles as it starts to rise, leaving behind the official pounding his fist on the wall. I drop to my knees and hold my head in my hands. My stomach churns again, and I clamp a palm over my mouth so I won't vomit.

Silver aster pollen can't be for disease prevention or Promise elevation, it doesn't work like that. The pollen releases two hormones: serotonin and GABA. Serotonin calms and relieves stress; GABA slows overall brain activity. My school instructors always focused on the fact that pollen could be a pain and stress reliever, but if GABA slows the brain, it also inhibits reason. It could make it easy for a person to be influenced by someone else.

It could make people submissive.

Maybe the flowers were in the back of the hovercraft that day when I was younger because the ship was headed to the Karum treatment facility, where Unstables are kept. Maybe the Developers use the pollen to make Unstables submissive, to try to cure their craziness.

But they use the pollen on civilians too. They administer the injection once a month, probably in a subtle dose that keeps everyone docile. It makes them easy to influence.

No wonder no one has any issue with the murder of child

workers in the outer sectors. Commander Charlie is controlling all of his citizens.

Wheezing, I lift my head and scan the buttons for the decks. I need to find Beechy. He said he was like me before—he said he had trouble during the last part of his citizenship training, and he must've meant the intelligence machines.

Maybe the pollen didn't affect him, either. Maybe it still doesn't. Maybe he can help me.

But I don't know where he is. The elevator jolts to a stop before I can figure out which floor to try.

Nausea overtakes me again. I stumble out of the elevator, open the first door I find, and stick my head into a trash chute in the wall.

A snapping sound comes from a ceiling speaker. "Attention."

I freeze, still leaning over the chute, my mouth dripping and a putrid smell filling my nostrils. The voice is hoarse, cracking in places. Commander Charlie.

"All citizens of the Core, please report to the Pavilion."

Another snapping sound.

Silence.

I stare at the white tiles on the floor. I blink to clear my vision, but it remains blurry.

Footsteps echo in the hall outside. A woman's voice: "—she came up here on one of the elevators. Cadet Waller said her injection went wrong, and Commander Charlie wants her found and subdued."

My heart skips a beat. Is she looking for me?

"I don't get why it's so important we have to find her right this second," a man's voice says.

"She's an Extraction. The commander handpicked her himself."

I have to get out of here.

"Check that classroom, will you?" the woman says.

Gritting my teeth, I heave my body toward the room's back door. It opens into another corridor. I hold my breath and try to shut the door softly behind me.

My fingers slip. The clang is loud.

There's a shout.

My feet move of their own accord, and I run, adrenaline and poison coursing through my veins. They know the injection didn't work. They want to catch me so they can try again. I can't let them.

I round a corner and crash into the stairwell banister.

Their footsteps pound on the landing above.

There's no time. I careen down the stairs, praying I won't fall and break my neck. But if I did, I'm not sure I'd even notice.

Vaguely, I'm aware of Charlie's voice over the loudspeaker. He demands, again, that all citizens report to the Pavilion. It could be dangerous, if that's where he wants me. But in a room filled with ten thousand people, it'd be much easier to blend in.

I throw up twice more before I get there, leaving a trail of vomit for whoever is chasing me to follow. Through a Pavilion door, I squeeze into the crowd slowly filling up the viewing pods, keeping my head low so no one will see my face. There are way too many people. Their body heat makes me sweat even more.

"Clementine?" someone says.

I jump, looking frantically around to see who spoke. Not an official—not the people who are looking for me—please.

It's Oliver. He waves at me, and slips through the crowd to join me. Even from a distance, I can tell he's not himself anymore. His smile is too fake; his eyes too unfocused.

I feel like throwing up again. I was afraid this would happen.

"May I join you?" he asks.

"Sure," I say. We follow some people up the stairs into one of the viewing pods close to the wall. I glance at the crowd still below to make sure no one is following me. Hopefully, I lost that woman and the official. *Please.*

We settle into the seats in the pod. They're soft, made of leather. We have a clear view of the Developers' pod at the far end of the Pavilion. It's empty right now. The screen above it shows the insignia of the Core.

"Are you excited?" Oliver asks, still smiling. There's a film or glaze over his blue eyes.

My throat tightens. If I squeezed his hand, if I shook him, would that wake him up? I don't think so. Silver aster pollen isn't venom; there isn't a cure for it.

I swallow, pressing my hands into my lap to still them. "For what?" I ask.

He gestures to the noisy crowd. "The instructors said something important was happening today."

They must've said that after I ran away. My head won't stop pounding. I want to curl up into a ball. I want to collapse. I want to be done with this.

I draw tangent and cotangent graphs in my head until the crowd quiets. In the Developers' pod, people step into view, including Commander Charlie. A spotlight shines on him as he moves front and center.

"Here we go." Oliver's shoulder brushes against mine.

I want to make him better, but I don't know how. Tears trickle out of my eyes again, and I feverishly wipe them away.

Commander Charlie's face fills the video screen. There's a harsh crease in his brow. "Good evening, civilians. I come to you tonight with news I didn't wish to share until we were certain it was true." He pauses, and his eyes sweep the crowd. "You are all aware that our planet is neighbor to a treacherous moon. A long time ago, Kiel's atmosphere kept us safe from it, but pollution ripped the ozone layer apart. Then came the age of death and terror, and the need for an artificial shield. That shield has managed to keep its full terror at bay for several decades now, with some small exceptions."

I remember the stories I used to hear about on the Surface: the random deaths of both children and adults from acid corrosion. The signs that the shield particles weakened over time and needed to be replaced to keep us safe.

"I regret to announce that moonshine levels are rising," Charlie says.

Muttering courses through the crowd.

"Our most skilled scientists have discovered large breaks in the shield where the particles are severely damaged and some of the acid is getting through, affecting more citizens on the Surface than ever before. Hundreds of people."

I gape at his blurry face in my vision. He must be joking. I was there, what, six days ago?

"Let me show you what I mean," Charlie says.

His face fades away on the screen. In its place, there's a dark, rainy street. Moonlight glints on the wall of a skyscraper. Kids huddle together on the pavement, their eyes wide and their bodies shaking.

My heart is pounding.

I hear muffled screams through the screen speakers. Officials haul bodies onto stretchers—some bloody and bruised, others blackened and charred.

The image slowly fades.

"They're dying up there," Commander Charlie says softly.

"Our scientists have been trying to replace the damaged shield particles, but even the new ones are still allowing leaks. Our technology is no longer keeping the acid at bay, and it has become clear that our planet and people will not last long if we continue to reside beside the moon."

Blood pounds in my ears, echoing, drowning out the Pavilion. But there's nothing to drown out. No one speaks.

If we continue to reside beside the moon.

A strained smile touches Charlie's lips. "Now, please don't panic. We've sorted out a most efficient way to deal with this problem. I will let one of our evolutionary scientists explain."

He steps back, and a new person steps into the spotlight. A man wearing a lab coat, whose cheeks are a bit green.

Beside me, Oliver stares with a muddled smile.

The scientist clears his throat. "Our tests have confirmed that acid levels beyond the shield have risen nearly fifty-eight percent since the time of the shield's construction. The materials we used to build the shield are no longer strong enough to keep the acid out. We've tried replacing them, we've tried using different materials . . . nothing is working. And, as you saw on the video, it's already affecting the population up there. Death has become rampant again. Last week alone, there were forty-two deaths in the work camp confirmed to be caused by acid, and in the past week there were fifty-six. It's only going to get worse. By our estimates, the Surface population will be completely destroyed within the next five to six weeks. The acid will begin seeping into the lower sectors even sooner than that."

I can't breathe.

"There is a solution," the scientist says, "and we have the original Developers to thank for it. They made a smart decision during the construction of the underground sectors: They built the

Core as an actual space station. It has powerful ion engines and hyperdrive field generators, with a control room centered in Restricted Division. The engines are strong enough to break us free of the sun's gravitational pull. In other words, we can fly away from the moon."

More buzzing in the crowd—a buzz of excitement this time.

But this doesn't make any sense. Maybe the Core is a space station, maybe we can fly away, but the numbers the scientist mentioned can't be correct—forty-two deaths caused by acid *last week*? I was still on the Surface. I would've heard about this. I'd have known something was wrong with the shield.

I play through the shots from the video in my head again: the bodies on stretchers; the officials carrying them; the kids watching. They weren't in the work camp. They were in the Surface city.

Kids from the camp are only allowed in the city one day of the year—the night of the Extraction ceremony. It was raining that night too, I remember. The night of the riot.

I wouldn't be surprised if forty-two kids were killed by officials that night, but I know the moon didn't kill them.

"However, the engines aren't strong enough to move the entire planet," the scientist continues. "Only the Core can fly away. The engineers who built the lower sectors knew this, and left a gap of lighter steel between the Core and Lower that could potentially be blasted apart.

"Thanks to recent technological developments, this is now possible. We've developed a highly concentrated nuclear fission bomb—we call it KIMO—that will send a ripple of energy through the gap. The energy will split the gap and blast the outer sectors away, while at the same time we'll put up a new, stronger shield around the Core—"

"Essentially," Commander Charlie cuts in, stepping back into the spotlight, "we can escape, my dear citizens. We will, at last, be free of the moon's poison. It is a sad reality that we will lose many valuable people in the outer sectors. But this is the only way."

Murmurs of agreement slide though the crowd.

No, no, no. He'll kill everyone up there. He must be lying about part of this, at least, but no one except me seems to be questioning him—not even Ariadne or the other Extractions who came from the Surface and know the acid isn't killing people up there. They're all subdued.

"We'll be able to launch KIMO very soon," Commander Charlie says, clasping his gloved hands against his stomach. "We're in the midst of final preparations to ensure that the Core's engines are in pristine condition, and that we're capable of producing our own food and water and clean air from space matter, so we won't die without the assistance of the outer sectors."

I'm shaking my head and making fists with my hands, and everyone can see, but I don't even care. I want to scream at Charlie. He'll kill them all. He'll kill Logan, and all the babies who never get to meet their parents, and all the kids who have only one shot at escape, but are still holding on to hope regardless.

He has a reason, but I don't believe it.

"We're going to need your help, your cooperation, and your trust," he says. "But we will accomplish this soon—within two weeks at the most if all goes according to plan. We will save ourselves. We will prosper."

Oliver's smile widens beside me. The first citizen claps. Then another, then more and more rise, until the room fills with the noise, their controlled, rhythmic offering of thanks to the man who will save them from a terrible fate, but leave thousands of people to die. Their bodies press against me, so close I can't breathe. They suffocate me.

Tears. My vision is still blurred, and I'm still shaking and trembling from fever. I don't care if these people are subdued, if they can't think for themselves. I'm sure at least a few of them still have some strength of mind. And I can't believe them. I can't believe any of them.

I stumble my way out of the pod. Oliver doesn't stop me. I wish he would. I wish he would wake up and run after me, so I wouldn't feel so alone.

25

I go to my bedroom and lock the door. It's not smart—Cadet Waller probably still has people looking for me, since I ran after the injection—but I have to take a minute. I have to think, and I don't know where else to go.

I throw up in the toilet. My stomach is empty now, so I dry-heave. Mucus and saliva in the water.

I want to find Beechy or Ariadne and ask them to help me stop Charlie, but I'm scared. Ariadne is definitely subdued, and Beechy probably is too. The monthly injection may have changed them, and they'll think I'm crazy and tell everyone, and I'll end up marked Unstable.

I'm scared because Logan is going to die if I don't do something. *Everyone* up there is going to die. It makes me want to scream and rip my hair out, or curl up in a ball and sob until I have no more tears.

I switch off the lights and drop onto the floor on the other side of my bed, so I'm hidden from anyone who might stand in the doorway. Hopefully no one will think I'm here if they check. I pull a blanket off the bed and wrap it around my body, curling up on my side in the carpet. Every breath sends shivers through my body.

I clench my teeth so hard it hurts. There must be other Core citizens who came from the outer sector camps, who would care about the people up there if they weren't subdued. Instead, they'll take the word of Charlie and the scientist as fact and ignore how their reasoning for KIMO and their whole plan doesn't make sense. The Surface death rate from acid can't be that high. The shield can't be that far gone, not in six days.

Yes, the shield's been responsible for deaths in the past when acid leaked through, but never that many. Even if the acid levels are rising, the shield particles couldn't corrode that fast. The death rate wouldn't jump so high.

If Charlie's lying about the shield not working—and he must be—this is an excuse. He wants to fly the Core away for some other reason. He just wants to keep his citizens from knowing.

I dig my nails into my cheeks, choking back a sob. I can't let him kill them all. He said everything will be ready in a few days. I have to stop this. But how? KIMO will blast the outer sectors away. It'll destroy Logan and everyone up there, all those children who are not worthless.

I could pretend to be subdued, that I was okay with all of this until I learned exactly what's going on here and how to stop it, except Charlie said we only have a few days. And I don't think I can pretend. When they find me again, they'll give me another injection. Probably a stronger dose, since the first one didn't work.

A stronger dose might kill me. It would definitely make it impossible for me to think clearly and figure out what to do and pretend I'm okay.

But maybe if I could find KIMO before they catch me, I could mess with the mechanism somehow, to at least slow down Charlie's plan until I figure out exactly what's going on. Beechy's a mechanical engineer—he might help me.

The sound of the bedroom door zipping open makes my body freeze. It was locked, so only Ariadne or security could unlock it.

There are still people looking for me.

Giggles. Fast breathing. Two bodies fall onto the other bed.

I'm a statue.

"I don't know why I didn't want you before," Ariadne whispers.

It's not security.

"She's poison." Sam's voice. "You needed a cure."

Sam is in my bedroom.

"The injection?" Ariadne giggles again. "It made me feel funny."

"Shh. Stop talking."

Sam is in my bedroom with Ariadne, tangling in her sheets. My heartbeat is so loud under the blanket, I'm sure they can hear it. This must be a nightmare.

"Be careful," Ariadne squeals.

Sam doesn't answer.

I want to drown in the carpet. I want to die. I want to run.

A speaker crackles on in the ceiling. "Attention," a voice says. "All citizens, please report to your rooms for a mandatory security check. Again, all citizens, please report to your rooms. . . ."

Sam whispers something I can't hear. The bed creaks, and laughter follows their feet into the bathroom. Water turns on in the shower.

I throw the blanket off, stand, and get to the door, shaking. Ariadne shouldn't be with him. He's just as bad as the boy she ran from on the Surface, if not worse. But it's not her fault—I bet it's the injection. I bet Sam tricked her once she was subdued.

I'd help her get away from him, but I don't think she'd listen to me.

In the hallway, the sound of boots clunking and people chattering reaches my ears. Citizens returning to their rooms because of the message over the speakers.

I have to find somewhere to hide. If they're doing a mandatory security check and they find me, they'll find out the injection didn't work. I can't let them give me another.

I'm staggering down the corridor when I hear someone shout behind me. "Hey!"

I glance over my shoulder. Sam pushes through my bedroom door with nothing but a towel wrapped around his waist. Even from a distance, it's hard to miss the smirk on his face. *Vrux.* He must've heard me leave.

"She's here!" he yells, turning his head away from me. "The girl you want is over here!"

Citizens round the corner, and officials in gray suits and knee-high boots push past them. I see who's leading them, and I can't stop my feet from faltering. It's Beechy. What's he doing with them? Please don't be helping them. Please be yourself. Please make everything okay now.

He sees me and slows, staring at me.

Please don't be subdued.

"Help me," I plead.

He narrows his eyes. I can't see them clearly from this far away, but I bet they're covered in film.

"Is that her?" an official says.

Beechy nods. "Get her."

I flee.

There's nowhere safe in the Core, now that I'm alone. There's nowhere to hide.

I take the stairs and follow them down, as far as they go. They're empty, though I hear voices through the doors on the stairwell landings. Everyone still has to report to their bedrooms for the security check. I guess I'm the only one who ignored the announcement.

I trip and fall; I pick myself up, ignoring the fever raging inside me and the sounds of the officials' boots pounding on the steps above. If only there were a building, then maybe I could climb high enough to escape them. But I'm not on the Surface anymore.

I go to the lowest point instead: Restricted Division. It's the most dangerous too, but maybe they won't expect me to go there.

The stairs end at the lowest deck accessible to the average Core civilian. I hesitate in the stairwell, wedging my hand into the door frame to open it a crack. Two men in lab coats hurry down the corridor outside, talking fast. I can't understand them.

For a second I think they're coming right at me, and panic rushes through my body. But they turn a corner, and I breathe out in relief.

I count ten seconds. I wait to make sure the corridor's empty. My heart hammers in my chest.

Nine, Ten.

I stumble out of the stairwell. Blue lights dot the ceiling, along with blurry white dots, though those might be in my head.

I don't know where I'm going, so I just keep moving.

I pass a few branches into other corridors—glancing quickly to make sure they're empty—and reach the end of one. The hall breaks off and turns to my left and to my right. In front of me stands a pair of double doors. They're black, each with a dark blue

X over circles of white that could be window holes. But they're not windows; there's no way to see inside. Somewhere beyond them, the Developers reside in safety and comfort. Beyond these doors, they control everything.

About five feet down the corridor to my left, another door leads into the same side of the wall. There's no X on that door, but there's small red lettering: RESTRICTED PERSONNEL ONLY.

KIMO must be somewhere near here. This division is the only place no one's allowed to go without Commander Charlie's permission.

Possibly I could trick the security system and get in. I could find KIMO and its blueprints and see if I recognize any of the mechanisms. It sounds impossible—I don't have much skill with mechanics, after all—but they're going to catch me soon anyway. I can't hide down here forever.

What else do I have to lose? I might as well discover what I can.

My heart beats fast. I pull my arm back into the sleeve of my suit, as if I'm taking it off, and cover my thumb with the fabric. I touch the lock-pad in the wall—

All the lights in the hallway turn red.

"Unidentified human," a voice blares from the walls. "Unidentified human."

I stumble back.

"Unidentified human."

A metal door clangs shut. Shouts and footsteps come from the corridor behind me. The officials must've realized I went all the way down the stairwell.

"Unidentified human."

I run down the left-hand corridor.

"Unidentified human."

There's a drain hole in the floor that might be big enough for me, but there's a metal cover over it.

"Unidentified human."

I grit my teeth, grab the bars, and tear the drain cover loose. It loosens easily. I stumble back and nearly hit the wall.

"Unidentified human."

The officials are close now, too close. I check that the drain hole will work—there's a horizontal passageway a few feet down, which will be wet but should hide me. I drop down until my feet hit the floor, slick with water, dragging the cover with me and securing it in place. The fever makes me disoriented and clumsy.

"Unidentified human."

Crouching to fit, I crawl farther into the passageway so I'm no longer visible through the drain cover. The scent of rusty metal tickles my nose. I plug it to keep myself from sneezing.

"Uniden—"

The alarm stops blaring.

"Where'd she go?" someone yells.

"Check everywhere," I can hear Beechy say.

Even Beechy is subdued. Even he abandoned me.

Please don't look in here, I beg.

"She can't have *disappeared*."

"I don't think she's down here," Beechy says. "I think she set up a divergence."

"How the vrux—"

"She's smart," he says. "She's the smartest girl you'll find here. Trust me on that. Come on, let's check somewhere else."

The clunking boots fade away, along with the voices. Part of me wonders if he knew I was still down here, and pretended I'm not because he's still trying to protect me.

It's a nice thought, but I don't think it's true. I'm sure they'll come back if they don't find me elsewhere. They'll check the security cameras and realize I crawled inside here.

If I want to do anything about KIMO, I'll have to find out where it is tonight.

But I can't fight sleep anymore, so I let my body slump on the wet ground. If I close my eyes, I can pretend I'm not in a hole in the floor or even in the Core. Not stuck underground, while Logan and all the other people far above me unknowingly await destruction. I can pretend I'm safe and they are too.

I shiver as the sweat of fever overtakes me. I stop fighting.

26

I wake to a drop of water hitting my nose. The darkness disorients me. I have to blink many times before I have some sense of where I am.

This isn't the first time I've woken this way. When I was younger, some bullies threw me into the muck of a sewer one night. I woke the next morning and wandered until I found my way into the sunlight.

Wincing, I rise until I'm sitting as best I can, with the walls narrow and close over my head. My head feels clearer, but my body aches with every movement. I try to ignore it. I set my palms on the wet steel of the drain floor and crawl to the opening.

Through the bars, I don't see anyone or hear anything. It feels late at night, or very early in the morning, though of course I have no way of knowing. There must still be people looking for me.

I'll pretend they don't exist. That'll make this easier.

Still, I'm slow and careful as I remove the drain cover. I start to climb out, then stop, thinking better of it. I untie my laces and tuck my shoes and socks behind me in the passageway. I flex my toes and sigh in relief. I missed the freedom of bare feet.

The corridor lights flicker overhead as I climb out of the drain and replace the cover. I stand and take soft, shaky steps, and peer around the corner to the elevators. The place is empty.

There's a creak. I slam back against the wall. Out of the corner of my eye I see the lone silver door to the left of the main Restricted Division entrance.

It's open.

I stare, my heart thrumming in every part of my body. A door like that could only be open on purpose. This must be a trap.

If I were smart, I'd run. I'd find somewhere to hide. But this might be my only chance to get inside and find KIMO's blueprints. I might be crazy, but I have to take it, even though it's dangerous. They're going to catch me, anyway. There's nowhere to hide.

The door's metal edge is cold as ice. There's only darkness beyond it. I pull the door open another inch and take a step.

A spotlight turns on.

Instinct screams at me to run. There are security cameras in here. Someone must've heard that or seen it.

But I won't be a coward.

I clench my fists at my sides and step into the room. Thick smoke shrouds the place, full of darker spots the light doesn't hit. It smells clean and crisp, like wet metal, or the fog that collects over the Surface camp when the clouds are low. I step through the haze, and it parts for me, giving me passage to what the spotlight shines on. My eyes widen.

It's a spaceship. It's massive, even bigger than the hovercrafts I used to travel in on the Surface. It's shaped like an oblong disk. The cockpit window faces me. Above the cockpit, farther back on the roof of the craft, sits an enormous steel ball. It looks like an escape pod that could be jettisoned.

I walk slowly forward, squinting so I can see the pod better. There are blue letters on the side of the escape pod. They spell out K-I-M-O.

This is the transport ship. The bomb must be on it.

I take a step back.

This was way too easy to find. Someone's here. Someone's watching.

I want to turn and run and get the vrux out of here before they come for me, but I can't. I found their bomb. I have to see if there's anything I can do to slow it down or disable it.

Pale lights flicker off to my left through the fog. I catch sight of an edge where the floor drops away between me and the lights. It looks like the Pipeline, or a passage connected to it for launching. As soon as the Core can survive without the other sectors, all the Developers have to do to set off the bomb is fly this transport ship to the gap between Lower and Core and start the countdown.

A simple click of a few buttons, and they will destroy most of the world.

There are footsteps through the door behind me. Voices too.

I tense, looking wildly around for a hiding place. I don't have many options. Stumbling forward, I hurry around the ship to a luggage bin against the far wall. I squeeze into the space behind it and crouch low, wrapping my arms around my legs. My heart beats so fast, I'm sure whoever's coming will be able to hear it.

The footsteps stop abruptly. "Who left that door open?" a man says.

"My apologies, sir," says a voice I recognize. Sam. "That may have been me. I was just in there checking that the bomb is still secure."

My brows furrow. *Sam* left the door open?

The first man sighs. "Lieutenant, please be more careful next time."

The lights turn off in the room, drowning me in darkness. Sam's response fades away as the door closes.

I'm too frightened to move for a long time. This could still be a setup.

Finally, I slip out from behind the luggage bin and take careful steps toward where the ship was before. I can barely see a thing. The only lights left on are tiny blue ones dotting the ship's rim.

I feel my way to a set of ladder rungs on this side of the ship. I squint to see where they lead. I'm pretty sure it's to the roof, and the escape pod. I might as well learn what's up there, since the pod is the part of the ship with K-I-M-O on its side.

I find a foothold and pull myself off the ground, then reach for the first rung.

If I had the bomb blueprints, I could study them and figure out exactly where the missile is being kept on the ship. I could find the right wires to switch off the system, but there's no time for that. Instead, I run on pure adrenaline, hoping luck is on my side for once. It's a horrible, helpless feeling when I think about it too hard.

So, I don't think. I climb.

When I reach the sloping roof, the ladder continues up a few more rungs, close to the steel ball. It's clearly attached to the ship by a short tunnel rising from the bridge, so it must be an escape pod. A tiny red light blinks on the pod's control panel, through the window.

The K-I-M-O imprint is on the other side of the pod. There's something odd on this side of it, jutting out of a circular space in the hull: the tip of a rounded cylinder, like a torpedo.

I suck in my breath. The tip is even bigger than I expected; at least half the size of my whole body. It does look a lot like the missile heads I've seen pictures of before. But could this really be it? It seems like a strange choice to embed a missile this size in an escape pod. Unless the pod plays a key role in the detonation. Unless the pod was designed specifically for this mission.

I adjust my hold on the last ladder rung, breathing hard. There might be a disabling key on the pod's control panel. I need to get inside the escape pod, but how? There's no exterior door. I'd have to enter the bigger transport ship first, but I have no idea how. It seems like a surefire way to get caught.

I don't feel the official's fingers touch my ankle until they squeeze and drag me down. My hand slips from the ladder. A scream escapes my throat.

I grab hold of a rung and kick as hard as I can at my attacker. It must be an official—someone who knew I'd come in here, who was waiting for me.

His fingers squeeze my ankle again. His nails dig into my skin and wrench my leg. My palms grasp at nothing, and I fall.

The ground slams into me, and my body slumps.

I come to, coughing. The boy drops beside me and reaches for my face. Snarling, I aim a kick at his abdomen, but of course he is too tall. I still can't make out his face.

He kneels on top of me, pinning me. He shoves a gag into my mouth.

Tears of weariness gather in the creases of my eyes, and my chest heaves as I draw a breath. My attacker slams his fist into my neck, and forces me onto my stomach. I cough and cry. The gag wedges firmly between my teeth.

The spotlight in the room comes back on, and my attacker forces my head back. I see the knee-high boots of another official marching toward me. I see legs, a torso, arms, and a face.

27

It's Sam. Of course it's Sam.

A grin is etched into his face, and I want to rip it off with my nails. My attacker pushes me harder into the ground, pressing my lungs against the floor.

I can't breathe. I can't breathe.

"Thank you for your help, Justin," Sam says. He makes a clicking noise with his tongue and shakes his head at me, crouching with his hands on his knees. "Did you really think I left that door open by accident? You should've listened. You should've treated me well yesterday, like Ariadne treated me well earlier tonight. What good has this act of rebellion done you? Did you break the machine? Will your boyfriend be safe and happy on the Surface now?" The smirk folds easily into Sam's face. "Funny, it doesn't look like that to me. It looks like you are in some deep krite."

I want to know what he did before he came here, when he lived in a work camp in an outer sector. I want to know why Charlie would Extract him early and give him a special rank in the military.

I want to know before he kills me.

He laughs and prods my jaw with a finger. "I could do you a favor, I guess, and help you get your scar back." He stands and bounces on the balls of his feet.

I choke through my gag and thrash against the boy holding me. Let me *go*—let me *go*—

Sam grins. "Good, good, nice to see you've still got some fight in you."

"What's going on?" Cadet Waller's voice comes from somewhere in the fog.

"Get her up," Sam snaps.

The pressure lifts off my body, and a hand drags me to my feet. I try to break free of its grip so I can run.

Sam slaps my face, and his nails cut my skin.

Raw, raw, raw, and stinging.

Cadet Waller freezes when she sees us. Two officials flank her. She purses her lips, straightening. "Hello, Clementine. Sam, did you find her here?"

"Yes, ma'am. She was trying to mess with KIMO, but I stopped her," Sam says.

She gives me a small, rueful smile.

"You caused quite a mess today. But it won't happen again."

She turns. "Sam, bring her along. I hate to rouse Commander Charlie at such an hour, but this is necessary."

Sam and one of Cadet Waller's officials grab my shoulders.

In the main corridor of Restricted Division, I keep my eyes on the ground and try to control my breathing. My heart pounds in my chest, in my throat, and in my ears. But I won't give Sam or Cadet Waller or anyone the satisfaction of knowing my fear.

We stop outside the pair of double doors with dark blue Xs

over circles of white. Cadet Waller taps a command into a security pad in the wall. There's a snap, and a voice comes on: "Who is it?"

"Waller. I have the girl."

The door slides open. "Enter," the voice says.

A hand clamps over my eyes. Sam shoves me forward, and my feet stumble. Pain shoots up my side and through my temple.

I'm disoriented when the hand and gag fall away. A bright white light blinds my eyes. I start to raise my hands to shield my face, but they're still tied. Blinking doesn't clear the sparkles of light and distorted shapes.

A figure steps into the light. The silhouette of someone with the power to kill me or let me go.

I don't think Commander Charlie will let me go.

"Hello, Clementine." He says it like I'm an old friend instead of a traitor. Like we're meeting for a chat instead of an exile sentence.

"Just shoot me and get it over with," I say, half choking the words. "I know you have others to kill."

The white light dims. "I have no intention of shooting you," Charlie says. "Not tonight."

"Then what—"

"Your survival is very important to me," he says. "Why do you think I've overlooked your mishaps thus far? As you were one of the last transfers from the outer sectors, we picked you carefully, with a certain career position already in mind. I'd intended you to become one of our intelligence agents for the military. Sam here even suggested you'd make an excellent lieutenant."

I gape at him. "*Sam* suggested that? Why?"

"You have excellent skills in the sciences, and you've already passed CODA. You would make an excellent addition to the leadership of the Core security team, there's no denying that. However"—Charlie's frown deepens—"you caused an inordinate amount of trouble tonight, and I can't have that. Obedience is the one area where your skills are not up to par. Is there a particular reason you won't respect me, Clementine?"

"Why should I? You lie about everything."

"Do I? Please, enlighten me."

My whole body is shaking, and I'm seeing stars when I blink again. "That speech you gave tonight. You said people on the Surface are dying from the acid. But that video footage you showed was from the riot the other day."

His eyes study me with mild amusement. "I assure you, I didn't lie about the acid."

"Yes, you did." My voice rises in panic. He's lying again. He has to be. "I was up there last week. There weren't forty-two deaths from acid. You think no one would notice?"

"We do have the ability to keep things quiet."

"I'm not stupid." My head throbs harder from my anger. "And I'm not subdued, either."

His face stirs with some emotion I can't read.

"Yes, I know you subdue everyone," I say. "I know that's what the monthly injections are for."

"I can see that," Charlie says. He looks over to Sam or someone else behind me, then back to me. "Care to explain why yours didn't work?"

"I wouldn't tell you if I knew."

"No matter. It can take time for the injections to work properly on new Core citizens. We have time."

I shake my head. "It won't work. I'll fight you every time."

"I'm offering you a chance to remain here, Clementine. Don't you want a happy life?"

"No one here is happy. They don't know any better."

"They are happy. The injection doesn't change their emotions; it makes their brains more malleable, easier to train. I keep them subdued because it makes life easier for them. The troubles facing Kiel are far bigger than you or they can possibly understand."

"Because you hide things from us." My voice is hollow.

He nods, quite calmly. "I hide what is necessary to ensure my people's survival. I do what's best for those who are most likely to survive the danger we're in; I protect the Promising. You must understand, if I could save everyone, I would. But I can't. So I pick the ones who can do the most to help our society. The loss of those in the outer sectors is a regretful one, but it can't be helped. If you realized they're weaker, and therefore less useful, their loss would be easier for you to accept."

Hatred ignites my muscles. I lunge for his throat.

Sam pulls me back before I can touch him. I try to force him off me, but it's no good. My legs give out from lack of energy. He lifts me back up. His hot breath touches my neck. The other official works the gag back into my mouth.

Charlie adjusts his collar and straightens.

"Daddy?" A voice emerges from the shadows behind him. A woman steps through a doorway, and my heart stops. "Daddy, what's going on?"

Sandy stands in a silk nightgown. She sees me and frowns.

"Nothing to worry about, child," Charlie says. "You can go back to bed if you don't want to see this."

She's his *daughter*?

"No." She smiles, and not in a warm or a kind way. "I want to see this."

If she's his daughter, I don't think Charlie would subdue her. She must've only been pretending to be kind.

Another shadow steps into the light. And I break inside.

Beechy doesn't say anything at all. He slips his fingers through Sandy's, and he looks at me with an unfeeling gaze. But his eyes aren't glossy; they aren't covered with film. Whatever he's doing right now, it's his choice.

Water fills my eyes, and I clench my teeth behind my gag. He is a liar, after all.

Charlie's lips spread apart, slowly. "I tried to reason with you, Clementine, but I can see you're too far gone. Those who are no longer stable can't be reasoned with. You can no longer be a citizen of the Core."

I stopped being a Core citizen when I realized they're all brainwashed.

"Your lack of obedience and understanding is a shame, really. Your skill set would have been useful after we set off KIMO, particularly in the coming war." He smiles at me, his eyes glinting with a secret.

Memories flash back at me: standing in line for the officials' obstacle course and Ariadne saying, *Maybe they're trying to turn us into soldiers*; Sam wrenching me from the ground in Phantom, saying the game isn't just a game, it's a training module to help people practice strategizing—*in case there's ever another rebellion in the outer sectors and we have to fight them.*

But Charlie's plan with KIMO will destroy the outer sectors. There won't be any rebellion to stop.

So who would we be fighting?

"What war?" I try to ask, but the gag doesn't let me say the words right.

Charlie ignores me, though I'm sure he knows what I said, and turns away. He presses his hand to a spot above his ear, where some comm device must be hiding in his hair. He says something softly, then lowers his hand and turns back to me. "You won't be returning to your room tonight. You, my dear, are going to the Surface."

Fear and then relief slide through my bones. I'll be with Logan. Nothing else will matter for a little while because I won't let anyone separate us again. Our world will end together when the bomb goes off.

Charlie must read something in my face, because he shakes his head. "No, not back to your friend. You are going to the Karum treatment facility."

His words drain every last bit of warmth from my cheeks.

"The doctors there believe they may be able to make you better before we're ready to set the bomb off," Charlie says. "I do hope they're right, for your sake as well as mine."

A door opens, and a nurse in white attire enters with a metal tray and an injection syringe. She doesn't know I'm allergic, and she wouldn't care anyway.

"No," I cry through the gag.

I rip my arms free—

I kick and struggle and fight—

I won't let them break me—

In two seconds, Sam and the other official have me in a binding hold.

I'm a glass cage. I'm a glass cage with a heart screaming to escape, but it can't get out. I can't escape.

Sam rolls up my sleeve to expose my shoulder. I jerk away. I shake. I tremble.

In my head, I see Rebecca, wild-eyed as the officials dragged her from the hov-pod on the Surface. I see the woman I shot in the bloody glass cage in order to enter Core society. The ones in Phantom who reached for my ankles, whispering "Help" over and over and over again.

The point of the needle touches my skin, and I shatter.

I am Unstable.

28

Blue lights flicker. I blink and they turn to dots. Crystalline. I know they're lights because there was only darkness before. And there's a putrid smell in my nose. Whatever hard thing I lie on feels like ice against my back.

"She's waking."

A blurry face leans over me, blocking the blue lights. Lips part at the face's center, and bright white squares appear. The doctor smiles. "Can you see me, Clementine? I'm Dr. Tennant. I'm here to help you."

His voice makes my head hurt. I squeeze my eyes shut.

He is lying. But I don't know why. I don't know where I am, or what I'm doing here. When I try to remember anything before the darkness, there's nothing.

I feel a prick in my leg, sharp and piercing. I suck in my breath. "Stop," I try to say, but my throat is blocked. There's something inside it.

"It's okay," the doctor says.

I feel something hot spread through my thigh—blazing hot, like fire.

"Stop!"

"It's okay," he repeats.

It's *not* okay. The thing inside my mouth makes it hard to breathe, and my arms won't budge because my wrists are shackled.

The fire spreads to my toes.

I heave my body up as high as I can, screaming through the tube they shoved down my throat. I smash my back into the table. Glass shatters behind my head. A hand presses on my arm.

"Calm down." The voice is firm, steady.

I scream again as the fire cuts into my torso. I kick at Dr. Tennant. He made a mistake; he didn't tie my legs down.

Salty tears blot my vision worse than before. A door opens, and I hear shouts. Hazy figures lean over me and clamp iron cuffs onto my ankles, while I keep screaming.

I feel another prick, this time in my neck.

I'm lost again.

29

Again, I awaken on a metal examination table. The lights are blue, round this time, set inside metal disks like small satellites.

My head throbs, even though the fire's gone. My throat feels sore where the tube used to be, and sweat drenches my body. I must be running a fever.

My heart flutters a little, but my chest rises and falls slowly. There's a light, sweet scent to the air that calms me. Like an aster flower not covered in grime.

I don't know where I am, or why I'm here, or how long it's been since I arrived.

A door latch unlocks somewhere behind me. The white-coated doctor who enters the room is handsome. Dark hair flows in a soft wave over his head. When he smiles, his unspoiled teeth shine like diamonds.

"Good evening, Clementine," he says.

Is it evening? I have no sense of time. The least they could do is put a window in my room that lets me watch the moon rise.

"How do you feel?" he asks.

"Better." The word sticks on my tongue. I swallow to fix it, but it makes my throat sore.

"That's wonderful." He taps something into his tablet. "Can you tell me who you are? Basic facts?"

I nod. He already knows, I'm sure, but he wants to check how much the fever screwed up my memory.

"Clementine, S68477." Again I slip over the vowels, but I push through. "Sixteen. Surface civilian."

"Any family?"

"None."

"And what do you think of Commander Charlie?"

I open my mouth to respond, but something keeps my voice from working. Like I'm not sure what to say, only I thought I was, a second ago.

My brows furrow.

"It's all right," the doctor says. "Take your time."

I try again, but find myself pressing my tongue to the roof of my mouth, so hard it might form welts.

"Nothing?"

I shake my head. "Sorry."

"Hmm." He makes another tap on his tablet. The crease in his brow tells me I displeased him, but he's trying to hide it.

"Is that bad?" I say.

"It's unfortunate," he says. "But not to worry. It will come with time."

I nod and lick my chapped lips. "Anything else?"

"Not from me. I'm going to call the nurse in to give you a little shot. Nothing to fret about." He smiles and shows me his pearly white teeth.

The nurse enters after he leaves. She doesn't speak to me,

but she hums as she snaps on plastic gloves and moves to a metal tin.

I bite my lip. "You'll have to prick me again?"

"I'll insert it into your drip bag this time."

I lean my head back and tilt it to the side, ignoring the ache. A thin black tube connects a vein in my shoulder to a bag half full with clear fluid. The nurse turns to it, still humming, and the injection syringe comes into view. She prods the needle into a tiny hole on the side of the bag and presses the plunger. Silver-colored liquid mixes with the clear like small, expanding clouds.

I sigh and turn my head to the ceiling again. The aster smell thickens in my nostrils. In small amounts it's light and fresh; now it's tangy and putrid, and it makes me nauseous. Why anyone would keep a scent like this in a room, I don't know. It's horrid. Don't they know I'm allergic?

My limbs freeze. My eyes widen.

Memories flood my brain:

Allergy—

Pollen—

Injection syringe—

Logan—

Moonshine—

Charlie—

I came from the Core. Charlie sent me.

"You all right, dear?" the nurse says.

My heart races to the speed of a ticking time bomb.

She takes a step toward me, her face lined with creases of concern. "Honey?"

My wrists and ankles are clamped in irons. I have no use of my hands.

She touches my side lightly and smiles. "Dear, it's all right."

I slam my head sideways, lift my upper body, and rip the tube from my shoulder with my teeth. It's not as clean as I'd like it to be; my teeth catch my skin and set it stinging.

The nurse screams for help.

They're on me in ten seconds, three guards and my doctor. I'm surprised they think they need that many, since I'm already tied down.

I gnash my teeth at their hands and shriek to give them trouble, but it doesn't do any good. They shove a tube back down my throat, choking me. Their hands mask my eyes, and the blue lights disappear.

I know where I am now.

30

The world is dark when I open my eyes.

I'm curled up on my side against something hard and damp. My body trembles, and an aching dryness fills my throat, so much it hurts to breathe. One second, I'm ice, shivering in almost no clothes. The next I'm on fire, sweat trickling down my forehead. I'm a star burning up before it dies.

The darkness is hollow, without the tiniest speck of light. My eyes could still be closed, for all I know. The world could stretch on forever, or end, and I wouldn't know it. Logan could die, and I wouldn't know it.

I curl into a tighter ball. I wish he were here. I long for his face, his arms, his hands. His lips. The last time our lips touched, it didn't last long enough.

I wish he were here, or Beechy or Oliver or Ariadne—the way they were before they abandoned me—or *someone*. Anyone.

Charlie has stolen everyone.

Tears threaten my eyes, and the hollowness sinks into my

stomach. I clench my fists and try to ignore it. I wipe my eyes and try to stand, so I can find out where the world ends.

My hand finds a hard wall to my right. Wet and slimy, it leaves residue on my fingers. When I reach to my left and in front of me, all I feel is air.

Palm on the wall, I heave my body up, but my legs are shaky. They wobble, and weariness drenches my limbs.

My knees knock into the ground. I lie on my side, wishing I weren't so weak.

My eyes must close without my knowing it.

I dream I'm a bird with silver feathers, perched on the high branch of a tree, casting beady eyes at the moon. A fierce gale knocks me off my branch. The wind throws me about, wrenching my wings this way and that. I plummet to the ground in a mess of fraying feathers.

In a deep, dark trench, I land in human form, my body trembling. Bony arms reach for me, their muddy fingers tugging on my dress. "Help," they cry. "Please help us."

Before I can do anything, they sprout slick navy suits. They morph into Developers who point guns at my temple.

"There is nowhere to hide," they whisper.

I wake shaking on the hard, damp floor of my Karum cell, drenched in sweat and darkness. Go away, I tell my dreams.

My fingers fumble to touch the wall again. It's a little easier to stand today, tonight, whatever time it is. In the dark, time is a trap for insanity.

My legs still wobble. Every step, I grit my teeth and push through the ache, the fire, the glass shards ripping through my body. My cell seems to be small. I find no cracks in the cement. No door. It's like they threw me into a hole in the ground and built a ceiling over it.

I drop to my knees and press my palms into my forehead, breathing hard. I'm afraid they'll never let me go. That the moon or KIMO will kill us all and I'll never see Logan again.

I'm about to let a river of tears down my cheeks when a loud, echoing clang startles me, coming from inside the wall. I hold my breath.

In the silence, I hear another sound: a slow, shaky sob, somewhere beyond the cement. My heart flutters. There's someone there.

"Hello?" I say, crawling and pressing my ear to the slimy wall.

I don't hear anything at first. Then it's there again: the quiet sobbing that isn't coming from me. Relief floods my body.

It doesn't matter that whoever it is doesn't say a word. It's enough to hear them and know I'm not alone in Karum.

I'm not alone.

A creak overhead jolts me awake. The roof makes a great scraping noise, and a ray of white light seeps through a crack in the ceiling.

I scramble to my feet as the light blinds me and envelops my cell. I throw my hands over my eyes and press my body against the wall.

Go away, I think. Not yet. I'm too weak to fight, if they've come to take me back to the metal table and the injection syringes, or to kill me. But I have to fight.

I spread my fingers apart and glimpse a metal ladder lowering into the hole. A guard climbs down, followed by an adult in a skirt, a blouse, and red high heels. I try to ignore the soreness in my legs that makes it hard to stand.

The woman steps onto the ground. Her eyes look almost yellow in the light. They trail over my figure, and she purses her lips. "Hello, Clementine." She hates me. I can hear it in her voice.

Good, I think. I hate you more.

"I'm here to discuss some things the staff finds intriguing about you." She crosses her arms and taps her foot. "Let's cooperate, shall we? I'd like you to explain why our calming injections don't work on you."

I bet she already knows the answer. She's trying to see if I'll be honest. "I don't know," I say. "Doctors said they'd figure it out."

"And they will. At first it was thought that you're merely strong-minded, but . . ." Her eyes trail over my petite figure. "I don't believe that's the correct reason."

She thinks because my body is weak, my mind is weak. She knows nothing. I want to strangle her, but instead I latch on to what might help me more than that—weakness.

"It—it's not the reason." I curl into myself against the wall. "I can't . . . I'm not . . ." I force a whimper.

Confused concern forms a crease in her brow. "Yes?"

I shake my head and clutch my knees to my chest. "I didn't mean to cause so much trouble. I just want to go home. . . ."

She studies my face and taps her chin with a fingernail. "You know, Clementine, the only reason you're still here is because you keep refusing to set your faith in Commander Charlie. If you were to change your mind and not give us any more trouble . . . a return to the Core would not be difficult to arrange."

I stare at my knees. In the light I see how dirty they are, how bony. I could do it. I could keep up an act, looking like this. My body is frail, and they'd believe me if I cried. I could convince them I've had a change of heart and agree to never again question Charlie. I could do it, and they would send me to the Core.

But KIMO would still go off. The preparations must be almost ready—Charlie said it would take only a week or two, at the most. Logan and everyone else in the outer sectors would be destroyed. If I went back to the Core, I'd be safe, but they'd be dead.

Maybe that's better for me than this, but it's not good enough.

I lift my head to the woman.

She observes me with her yellow eyes. "Well?" she says.

I lunge at her, and she gasps. Pain cuts through my legs, my arms, my hands, but my fingers grab her throat and squeeze. I press red welts into her skin.

I grit my teeth—gasping—

The woman falls to her knees, choking for breath and clutching her throat. Go on, squeeze, I urge her. Finish what I started.

The guard binds my wrists with rope.

Yellow Eyes collects herself and stares me down, her teeth clenched. "I didn't think she'd cooperate. Throw her in with the others." She grabs a ladder rung and heaves herself back up with trembling hands. The guard shoves me after her.

I scare her, I really do. I scare all of them, and that's why they seek to control me. I'm not weak.

I am powerful.

31

They haul me through tunnels of cement and stone. My heart beats too fast in my chest, threatening to shatter if my body doesn't stop aching. If the Karum guard doesn't stop digging his hands, fingers, and nails into my body.

Here and there, I glimpse a high window where a speck of red sunlight blooms. It must be daytime in the world outside. It feels like I've been trapped in night.

We come to a round metal door. The woman taps a code into a lock-pad—only three digits long, I notice. With six numbers on the lock-pad, that's two hundred and sixteen possible combinations to get it open.

The hinges swing to let us in. Beyond the doorway, the walls are jagged rock. Icy air drifts through the cave, and muffled, hollow sounds like voices emerge from the three tunnels that branch off. Whispers.

The woman and the guard take me down the left-hand tunnel. The ground slopes, and we turn a corner. The end lies ahead.

Relief floods me. My arms hurt from the guard wrenching them. My legs hurt from dragging on the floor. I grit my teeth to keep from crying.

We come to a wide circular space. Doors formed by iron bars lead to six separate cell compartments. I can't tell which ones are already filled. The dim bulb hanging from the ceiling in the circular space doesn't cast much light.

The guard takes me to the middle cell. Keys jangle in his pocket, and there's a click as the key goes into the lock. The barred door opens. He throws me inside. My knees scrape on rough floor. A damp, rotten smell bleeds into my nostrils.

"Welcome to your new home, Clementine," the woman says. The bulb light glints on the pale pink shade of her cheeks. "Try not to rot too quickly."

The lock clicks, and she is gone.

I swallow, shivering in my thin rags. My eyes flit to the other cell doors. I can only see two from here—the two on the edges of the circle. The others sit too close to mine. But I can tell some of the cells are occupied. I can hear people breathing.

Dangerous. That's what the instructors always called Unstables. Adults said they're dangerous, brutal people consumed by insanity. That they would kill everyone if they were allowed to escape.

But Charlie said that too. I don't believe anything he says anymore.

Still, it takes me at least a minute to work up the courage to speak. "Hello?"

There's nothing at first. Just that soft, slow breathing.

Then a bony hand wraps around a bar of the farthest cell to my right. A face comes into view. A woman covered in blotches of bruises. Gray hair grows in uneven patches on her otherwise bald head. Her eyes are dead, dark as my old cell. She's an old one—a strong one, to have survived in Karum for so long.

She smiles at me. The wrinkles deepen around her mouth and her eyes. "What's your name?" she asks.

I try to speak, but it's hard when my lips are numb. The air is a block of snow. "C-Clementine," I manage.

"What did they get you for?" another, hollower voice says. A second Unstable wraps his hands around the bars of the farthest cell to my left. An old man with dark skin and a scar on his forehead so jagged it must've been done on purpose.

"Their injection," I say. "The one that makes everyone submissive. It didn't work on me."

The old woman smiles. "That's a good one. Easy to prove."

I nod and pull my legs against my chest, thinking of warm things. Of sunlight and blankets and fire. Hollowness fills my stomach, and I latch on to it. Anything but the cold.

"Do they ever give us food?" I ask.

"In the morning," the old woman says. "Barley bread, cheese, and a water skin."

My hands tremble from hunger. I'm not sure I can last until morning. But I'll have to.

"H-how long have you been here?" I ask.

The old woman laughs, soft and light. "Who knows? A long time for some, even longer for others. I was young when they brought me."

"My age?"

"A bit older."

"How . . ." I bite back what I was about to say: *How are you still alive?* "What do they do with us? They could just kill us."

"They call us Unstable, as I'm sure you know," she says, smiling.

"It means 'prone to psychiatric problems.' Got any ideas what we really are?"

My teeth catch on my bottom lip. Well, if they're both like me . . .

"They can't subdue us," the dark-skinned man says. The light glints on his scarred forehead, and his dead eyes stare at me. "Sometimes we know too much, or we ask too many questions. They try to make us conform, but we fight them and don't give in."

"Are you allergic to their injections too?"

"Is that what you are?" He frowns. "Don't let them hear it."

"S-sorry," I say. My stomach feels sick. I wrap an arm around it, bending my head and breathing slow. "You still didn't say why they keep us alive."

"We have the strongest minds out of all the citizens," the dark-skinned man says, moving away from his cell door so I can't see him anymore. "They observe us and do experiments. They keep us alive as long as they think we're useful."

"They don't like us very much, though." The old woman's lips stretch apart, showing me teeth that appear black from a distance. "We can see straight through their lies."

"I thought they were scared of me," I say.

"Of course they are."

I can't help smiling a little. How silly I was to think these people were dangerous.

They are dangerous, but for Charlie. Not for me.

A thought stirs inside me. A hope. If some of them were locked in here for knowing too much . . . maybe they know things about Charlie.

Maybe they know something about his war.

Whistling reaches my ears from somewhere past the cells, in the tunnel. I stiffen, bottling my breaths. Two guards strut into view.

"Ella, time to go," one says, walking to the old woman's cell. He sticks his key into the lock.

She sighs. "See you soon," she says to me and my cell mates. "Hopefully."

Her laughter echoes through the cave. The guards drag her away, while my eyes widen and my hands tremble.

32

The narrow table is cold and hard against my back.

I lie inside a machine in the wall that feels like a tight box. My hands are clenched at my sides, trembling though Dr. Tennant said I need to be still. I can't be still. There's a whir in my ears and too-bright blue lights on the ceiling two inches from my face.

"Don't worry," Ella said. "What they do here isn't as bad as you think it will be."

Yesterday, she came back with a thin, metallic tube attached to her belly. An experiment. Inside the tube, a tiny animal like a miniature muckrat scuffled around, trying to escape. When it couldn't break through the metal, it tried to break through her skin, instead. Sobs came from her cell all night. It's hard to believe someone who cries.

I can't breathe inside this box.

Fred, the dark-skinned man, didn't lie to me. He didn't speak when the guards came for me, but his eyes told me I'm right to be afraid. I'm right because fear is what they do here; fear is the weapon they use to make us weak.

Let me out, let me out, I want to scream.

The whir stops. The table I'm lying on slides out of the hole in the wall, out of the box, and I suck air into my body. It tastes stale, but good to my lungs.

Dr. Tennant snaps on white gloves. "It looks like you're allergic to bavix, a protein in the aster pollen inside those injections we've been giving you. Thank goodness we caught it. We'll have to try something different." He smiles, showing me his polished rows of teeth.

A boulder the size of a planet wedges inside my throat. I swallow, but it won't budge.

✕.

Again I awaken atop a metal table with a tube in my arm. The drip bag is full of viscous purple liquid. This time I know where I am and what happened. I don't know what the purple is.

Back in my cell, sometime during the night, I wake and vomit the bread and cheese a guard brought me earlier. My stomach heaves again and again, even when it's empty. Sweat trickles down my back. I'm a drenched rag, a body dragged out of an ocean.

I hold my head with shaking fingers.

"It's okay, honey," Ella says from her cell. "It'll be okay. I promise."

Today, she told us, there's a burn mark on her belly. The doctors removed the tube earlier to assess how much damage the muckrat had done. They seared the wound without giving her anything for the pain.

"Be strong, Clementine," she whispers.

"T-tell me something," I say. "Please distract me."

At first she doesn't respond. When she does, her voice is so soft I can barely hear it from my cell. "There isn't much left. My memories . . . they're more like dreams."

"Please."

Another pause. "I remember warmth from sunlight. Wind in my hair. Leaves dipping in color from green to gold. A boy whose smile made the summer rain stop falling. A handsome boy."

Convulsions rack me again, and I dry heave, spitting mucus onto the floor. I press a palm to my stomach. "What happened to him?"

"A handsome boy," she whispers.

She doesn't say anything else.

I count the number of times guards bring us food between my new injections. Three times. Three days.

The pain doesn't go away. The little sleep I get at night is marred by periods of waking when I can't stop coughing and crying. My stomach is a never-ending flood of acid.

"What are you giving me?" I ask the nurses.

They smile sweetly. "Something that will help you."

They're liars.

The doctors keep Ella longer than usual, into the night. I'm trembling alone in the back of my cell, my bony arms clutching my knees to my chest, when I hear Fred's hollow voice in the darkness: "You awake, girl?"

I've never heard him call anyone else that, so he must be talking to me. "Yeah," I say.

"Glad to hear it," he says.

Today, doctors injected him with a high dosage of their aster serum and with some of my blood. They're curious to see if my allergy will spread to him and cripple him, the way some food allergies spread through blood transfusion. We both have type O blood, that's why the doctors picked him as the test subject.

He's been feverish and aching all day, not seeing things clearly. Earlier he kept saying he was going to die. I can't stand knowing my blood did this to him.

"You're doing well, you know," Fred says. "Better than I did when I first came here."

I almost laugh, but it hurts my stomach. "Doubt that."

"It's the truth."

I bet he's lying to make me feel better. "How"—I have to pause to gasp for breath—"how old were you when you got here?"

"No idea," he says. "Age doesn't matter in here. After a while, time is all one big blur."

"Then why stay alive? Couldn't we just starve ourselves?" I ask before a coughing fit overtakes me.

He waits for me to stop before he answers. "You have to stay alive because you're better than them. Don't you forget that. Don't you let them make you believe you aren't gonna get outta here and feel the sun on your face again."

"But I'm not."

"Sure as the stars, you are."

I shake my head even though he can't see it. I don't have the strength to run, or any way out. And where would I run, if I could? Once KIMO goes off, all of this will be gone. There won't be a Surface for a person to stand on to feel the sun.

"You got someone out there?" he says. "You got someone you miss?"

Logan's face comes to mind, and my chest tightens like someone shot a bullet through my ribs. "Of course."

"They got a name?" Fred asks.

I don't know if I want to say it. Saying his name makes me feel like I'm losing him again. But I take a deep breath and manage to say it: "Logan."

"Good, fine name," Fred says. "You stay strong. You get outta here for him."

I lie down on the cold ground and curl up on my side. I want to be strong for Logan. Of course I do.

But what Fred said isn't possible, and he doesn't get it because he doesn't know what's happening outside this prison. He doesn't know the bomb is going to kill Logan before I can get to him, even if I do get out. I have no way to stop it.

I'm alone. There's no one on my side.

By the fifth day of the injections, I can't handle it anymore.

When the nurse tries to administer my shot, I struggle against her. I beg. I plead. "Stop, *please*. You're gonna kill me. What do you want from me? What do you want me to do?"

"Commander Charlie wants your loyalty, Clementine," she says, touching my hand as if she's trying to be gentle. A guard is holding me down. "If you give in to the injections, if you pledge to be obedient to him, this will all be over."

"No, I won't. I won't. Not unless he stops the bomb."

The nurse laughs. "Well, he won't do that. You're not that important."

She reaches for the syringe and jams the needle into my arm. I clench my teeth to keep from crying out.

On the seventh day, I lie on a metal table, staring at the purple liquid dripping into the tube attached to my wrist. The doctor walks in, and I lose it. Crying, choking on air. I open my mouth to say I'm sorry, that I'll do anything Charlie wants if he lets me out of here.

He smiles, showing me teeth that are too white. "Is there something you wanted to say, Clementine?"

I want so badly to give in, to be done with this.

But I can't do it. These doctors and nurses think they're so much better than all the kids in the camps, so much better than *everyone*, and I can't give in to them. How could I even consider it? I can't keep being weak like this.

I don't throw up that night. My stomach flip-flops and tumbles, but I hold back the bile. It's a small feat, but it's something.

On the ninth day, I stop crying.

The doctors increase how much they plunge into my veins at every meeting. They take brain scans to figure out what I'm doing to combat the medicine, but they don't understand. And I don't help them, even when they reason with me.

I don't care what they do or what they give me. I will not be subdued.

So on the tenth night, when they give me something that makes the world fog and darken—

darken—

darken.

I am ready.

33

"Three days," someone whispers. "Four, maybe?"

"Two, I hope."

The world is a blur of blues and whites. My lashes feel like they're crusted with goo. It's hard to open them.

"It's taking too long. Don't they know the moon might—"

I cough.

"Quiet," the nurse snaps. "She's waking."

There are pins in my body. There are needles stuck into a thousand points on my skin, and I need air and water and something to stop the fire, but what were they saying? They were talking about the moon—

The nurse leans over me, pursing her lips and touching a gloved palm to my forehead.

"Please." I try to speak. "Please tell me—"

"I won't give you anything for the pain," she says. "You agreed to this the moment you stopped cooperating."

"Please—"

Her fingers spread my lips apart and jam a tube down my throat.

I gag and retch and flail, but the pain is so bad I have to stop. I have to stop, and I feel cold trickling down my throat. Something like water, but not water.

The tube comes out with phlegm and mucus, and I want to clutch my throat, but my wrists are tied down.

"You won't be able to eat anything tonight," the nurse says. "So don't even try."

"What did you do?" I gasp.

"Dr. Tennant harvested some of your eggs and brain cells." The nurse smiles. "No one can deny that you're intelligent, Clementine. There's hope that your offspring may prove more obedient and helpful in future generations, once the Core is far away. Don't worry, dear. We're almost done with you."

Her heels tap on the linoleum as she walks away.

I can't breathe. They stole what is *mine*; they stole my children. I thought they'd already stolen everything, but I was wrong.

And Charlie is going to set off the bomb—that must be what she was talking about before she saw I was awake. Four days, three days, two days.

She said they're almost done with me.

Back in the cell, the guards leave me in a huddle on the floor, a tangle of clammy hands and trembling legs.

Ella stares at me, wide-eyed, both of her hands on the bars of her cell door. A clang echoes in the hallway past our cells. The guards are gone.

"What did they do?" Ella asks.

"Doesn't matter," I say, wrapping my arms around my body. I can feel crusted blood on my rags when I move. The nurses didn't give me fresh clothes.

"Clementine, sweetie . . . it matters a lot," Ella says.

She's right, but other things matter more. When Charlie sets off the bomb—and it'll be soon, I'm sure—she and Fred and every other Unstable in here will die. We'll all die, and they don't even know yet.

I'm afraid to tell them. But I think I have to.

My eyes flit left and right while I try to figure out where to begin. I flatten my sweaty curls with my fingers. I take four deep breaths.

"Why did they throw you in here?" I ask.

"We already told you why," Fred says from the dark of his cell.

I clench my teeth and scoot forward, wrapping my palms around the iron bars caging me in here. "No, you didn't. You told me why they keep us alive, not what you did, specifically, that led them to lock you up. Please tell me. Maybe it was a long time ago, but I know both of you remember."

Ella's staring at the ground. "I had several incidents," she says. "The final one was when I broke into the Core medical facilities. I destroyed several crates of their monthly injection vials."

I glance at Fred. He sits with his back against his cell door, shivering maybe from the cold, maybe from the remnants of my allergen in his blood.

"I killed someone," he says. "Someone close to Commander Charlie. I was too useful for him to execute."

My eyes widen. I didn't expect that. I swallow hard, and pull my hands away from the bars.

"And you, girl?" Fred asks. His head turns, and his dead eyes stare at me from across the way.

"I . . . tried to sabotage a plan. Charlie's plan." My voice is shaky. "But I didn't have enough time, and it didn't work. I wish it would've. Things might get bad."

There's silence for a moment.

"What do you mean?" Ella says, her brows furrowing.

I take a deep breath.

And I start to talk.

I explain KIMO and Charlie's whole plan, how he's going to destroy the outer sectors and fly the Core away. How he's using moonshine as an excuse, but I don't believe it's a real one. My heart rate speeds up. It's beating faster than a healthy human heart should by the time I finish.

A whole minute passes.

I dig my nails into my ankles. I pull my legs closer to my body. "Please, someone say something."

"Is this the truth, Clementine?" Ella's voice trembles.

"Of course it is. I heard it all from Charlie's mouth."

"I'm sorry." Fred's words are quiet, but I can still hear the sob behind them. "I'm sorry, I'm so sorry."

He's crying. He's holding his head in his hands and rocking back and forth on the ground.

My lips twist into a nervous frown. I don't know why he's doing that. He's going to die, so the crying makes sense. But why is he saying *sorry*?

"Fred, this isn't your fault."

"Yes, it is." He looks up at me. Teeth clenched, eyes streaming tears. "You don't understand. I designed the bomb."

I gape at him. "You *what*?"

"I did, I did." He scrapes his nails over the patches of hair on his scalp. "Didn't know he was gonna vruxing use it for this. Thought I was designing it to blow up the acid generator—bet that idiot's been lying to me all along. Bet he's not even gonna let me outta here like he said."

I blink fast, trying to sort out what he's saying. He designed the bomb. When? While he was here in Karum? But Charlie told him he was making it for something else—an acid generator?

I falter. Can't quite catch my breath.

Did I hear him right?

"The acid generator," I repeat. "What do you mean?"

"Exactly what I said," Fred says. He's rocking back and forth again.

"Fred," Ella says, her eyes wider than mine. Whatever Fred's saying now, he's never told her before. "What do you mean?"

Fred stops moving. Pauses. Lifts his eyes to Ella's. "It's not what they teach people. It's the truth. Hardly anyone knows."

"The truth about what?" I ask, even though I'm afraid to hear his answer.

"Moonshine," he says. "The acid. They teach you that the moon's always bled acid, right?"

"Yes," I say.

"What else do they teach you?"

I swallow. "The moon's always been dangerous, but it didn't harm us until pollution corroded the atmosphere—"

"Wrong," Fred says. "Three hundred years ago, the moon became lethal when an acid generator was built on its surface. What else?"

I glance at Ella. Her wide eyes are locked on Fred.

"They teach us the underground sectors were constructed by scientists to save everyone," I continue, "and the five scientists who headed Project Rebuild were elected as the Developers. They became more dictatorial after the Great Rebellion, when they started the work-camp system."

"Mostly true, except one of the five so-called scientists was actually the leader of the military. Commander Charlie is descended from him, which shouldn't surprise you." Fred waves the thought away with a hand. "But that's not important. What do they teach you about Kiel? What do they say about our planet compared to all the other planets in the galaxy?"

I bite my lip, my mind racing through all the lessons I remember for what he might want me to say. "We're the only planet with life."

Fred's hollow laughter fills the cells. "That's the biggest lie. There's a planet very close by that's inhabited by humanoids."

All the breath drains from my lungs. He's kidding. He must be.

"That's impossible," Ella says.

"Is it?" Fred asks. "Everything you know—everything *anyone* knows is approved by the Developers. Half of it's a lie or warped. You must know that already."

I remember the bits of history glossed over in my school lessons; the theories of science not explored in depth; the vul inside that tank in the Core, the last of a species Commander Charlie let hardly anyone know about.

He is a liar. But would he really take it this far?

"You want more proof?" Fred says.

I look over at him again. He has his hands wrapped around his cell bars now.

"Charlie named the bomb I made KIMO," he says. "That stands for Kiel Intelligence Military Operative. They were a special corps in the military way back when, devoted to a project for taking back the other planet, Marden."

Marden. Something stirs inside me. I've heard that name before.

"Where is Marden?" I ask. "Why would we need to take it back?"

"It's only eight light-minutes away from us at its closest point, about a couple months away by spaceship," Fred says, his eyes growing distant. "Our people came from there a long time ago. We were one of the two major species on that planet, along with the aliens. In Recorded Century 29, I believe, humans came here and established a colony due to severe tensions with the aliens. In RC 32, three centuries ago, the Mardenites flew a ship over and built a generator up there on the moon, a vruxing powerful one. It pumps out enough acid every hour to destroy a piece of land the size of the Surface city."

I press a palm against my clammy forehead. "They want to kill us."

"Sure seems like it."

"Why?" Ella asks.

"We tried to enslave them—our ancestors did, anyway. The original colony sent warships back to Marden in RC 31. The aliens retaliated, but we captured some of them. Left their villages in ruins. We came back here and then went right back again with even more ships some fifteen years later. Captured even more of them. Then they revealed they had secret biological weapons, and they crippled our fleet, so we had to leave again. But they were scared we'd go back. So they brought one of their weapons over here and put it on the moon. Luckily our technology has been able to keep it at bay so far."

Needles, needles, needles all over me.

"Don't they know there are thousands of innocent people here?"

"All contact with Marden was cut off after the Great Rebellion, and that was two centuries ago. There's no way to tell how much their current leaders know or remember."

I swallow, struggling to get air into my lungs. "How do you know all this? No one else does."

Fred's lips form a thin line. "No. They don't."

I wait for him to go on.

"All the army leaders learn the history, and I was an army colonel," Fred says, turning his head away. "I was also the head of Core science and technology. I was training to take over for my father. To become one of the Developers."

I stare at him for so long, the sun might've risen and set in the world beyond these walls.

"You were Charlie's follower," Ella says.

Fred turns back to us with raw pain in his eyes, confirming her thought.

He was Charlie's follower, but it didn't last, I remember. He turned on him just like we did; that's why he's here.

"I'm not proud of it," Fred says. "Especially now. I never would've designed that bomb if I'd known he'd use it for something else."

The bomb. Fred's words jolt me back to the present.

"So Charlie's going to set off KIMO," I say, "but he's not using it to blow up the acid generator—he's using it to destroy the outer sectors."

"That's what you said," Fred says.

I nod. It makes sense, of course. Charlie could care less about the acid, since he's leaving the moon behind. But he does care about Marden. Marden, which probably has a safer atmosphere than Kiel does. Marden, which was our ancestors' home before tensions with the aliens led us to search for a new one.

Marden, which we've tried to conquer twice to no avail because our warships aren't strong enough.

"The Core is a warship," I say slowly, as the realization dawns on me. Charlie and that scientist said it was designed as a spaceship with powerful ion engines and hyperdrive field generators.

Why not weapons too? "He's using KIMO to destroy the outer sectors so he can fly the Core to Marden. So he can go to war."

Fred nods stiffly.

This is the war Charlie meant. A war against Marden, and the people of the Core will be his soldiers. He has ten thousand of them, and they're all subdued. The warship probably can't fit any more than that, so he doesn't need the people in the camps. He needed them only long enough to keep collecting resources until the Core had the full capacity to survive on its own. He said it himself—he said he'd launch the bomb as soon as we're capable of producing our own food and water and clean air from space matter, to ensure we won't die without the assistance of the outer sectors.

He's finished with them. He's going to kill them all. Disabling the bomb is the only way to stop him.

I don't know what to do. I can't disable it. I can't even get out of this prison.

There's a clang down the hallway, and I jump. Boots clunk on the rocky floor. Two shadows slip into view and elongate. I scoot away from the bars and fall back into the darkness.

The guards step into view, stone-faced. They walk straight toward my cell, and I stiffen.

"I'm sorry, girl," Fred whispers.

"Citizen S68477." One of the guards unlocks the door. "You're coming with us."

34

The guards lead me down the passageway, a hand around each of my wrists. My heart pounds. I don't know why they came for me so late. If our cells had surveillance, Fred would've known, so I don't think it's about what I told him. It must be something else.

When we reach the examination room door, one of the guards sets his knuckles on the metal and raps three times. In the silence that follows, a muffled cry comes from behind the door.

I turn to steel.

It's barely any sound at all, but every inch of me reverberates with recognition.

I know that cry, that voice. I know it so well.

The door opens, and I want to run to him, but I can't because the guards have my wrists. He's lying on a steel table. His black hair is untidy, matted with sweat. Wires crisscross his chest, connected to his skin by plastic suction cups. A nurse stands beside the table. She is tight-lipped, but her eyes shine.

Dr. Tennant looks up from his tablet and smiles. "Welcome, Clementine."

I want to rip the wires off Logan's chest and strangle the doctor and nurse. I want to scream his name. They're going to hurt him.

"We brought your friend," Dr. Tennant says. "Aren't you going to say thank you?"

"Why is he here?" I ask. I'm shaking and my breaths are tangled. These doctors shouldn't know he's important to me—he's just a boy on the Surface. Did Charlie tell them, or Cadet Waller?

I told someone he's important only a few days ago. I told Fred.

"We thought you needed some persuasion." Dr. Tennant sets his tablet down and snaps on a pair of gloves. "Logan here seemed like he'd do the trick nicely."

"You can't hurt him."

Dr. Tennant ignores me. "Turn it on," he tells a nurse.

She steps away from the table and moves to a red button on the wall. She presses it.

Logan's body convulses. Screams bubble up from his throat. His chest lifts off the table and slams back down again. His head knocks against the steel. His arms would be flailing if he weren't strapped down.

"No, no, no, no, stop!" I'm crying.

Dr. Tennant holds up a hand, and the nurse releases the button momentarily.

Logan's body falls limp.

"What do you want to say, Clementine?" Dr. Tennant says.

"Stop hurting him!" I wrench against the guards, but they hold me tightly, twisting my arms behind my back. I feel them clamp irons around my wrists.

"Up the amps," Dr. Tennant says.

"No . . ."

The nurse presses the button again.

Again, Logan's body convulses, but he doesn't scream this time. He jolts this way and that, again and again, and I'm sure they're going to kill him, if he's not already dead.

"Stop it!" I yell. "Stop it—stop—*please*."

"What will you do?" Dr. Tennant asks. "What will you do for Commander Charlie?"

I'm a glass statue about to shatter. Logan won't stop convulsing and hitting the table hard—his brain's going to explode—and I have to do something. I will do *anything* to make them stop.

"Clementine," Dr. Tennant says.

"Anything!" I scream. "I'll do anything—I'll say anything—I'll obey—I won't fight Charlie. Just please don't kill him!"

Dr. Tennant gives the signal, and the nurse releases the button. Logan falls limp.

"Very good," Dr. Tennant says, smiling. "You know what this means, Clementine? You're going back to the Core. But if you go back on your word and don't obey, you will be killed."

"What about Logan?" I ask, still trembling.

"We'll see what Commander Charlie wants us to do with him," Dr. Tennant says. "'Take her back to her cell,' he says to the guards.

The guards pull me away, giving me no time to even touch Logan. The door slams shut behind us.

I can't help thinking I shouldn't have given in. I shouldn't have said I'd do anything.

The bomb's still going to go off, and it still might kill him.

Back in my cell, I curl up in a ball and cry into my arms. I don't know what to do. I'm weak and helpless here, and it's not going to change when they let me out. Charlie's going to keep trying to subdue me.

He's still going to murder half the world.

I'm wiping the water off my cheeks and trying to fix my screwed-up breathing when something clatters against the bars of my cell.

I jump. Hold my breath.

After a moment, I cast my eyes to the ground outside my cell. There's a small, flat rock on the floor, about half the size of my palm. Someone must've thrown it.

I look up and see Fred peering through the bars of his cell.

"Did you—" I ask. *Did you throw that? Did you tell the doctors about Logan?*

"Pick that up, girl," he hisses.

I almost shake my head. How do I even know if I can trust him? Everything he said about Marden and Charlie and the moon might be a lie. I don't know whose side he's on.

But my curiosity gets the better of me. I reach through the bars and snatch up the rock. There's something on it—a sketch or words, maybe. Fred must've used another rock to scrape into this one.

The ceiling lamp outside my cell is dim. I tilt the rock and squint to see what's written on it.

It's blip mathematics:

$$\tfrac{1}{2}\And = (87\And\text{-}547) + \ldots$$

I know this equation. It's Yate's Equation. The full thing is five times this long, one of the most complicated equations to solve. But I memorized how to do it a long time ago.

"Can you solve it?" Fred asks.

"Yes," I say.

"Good," he says, and I can hear the relief in his voice.

"Why?" I ask.

"It'll disable the bomb," he says.

I gasp.

"Thought I was being clever, you know," Fred says. "Not many people can solve it."

"It'll turn the bomb off?" I ask. "It'll make it stop?"

Not that this helps me much. I'm still stuck in here. Charlie's not going to let me near the bomb.

"It should," Fred says. "Charlie might've changed the code since I set it up. But it's the best I can give you. Screwed everything up for you, didn't I?"

I clench the rock inside my hand. The sharp edges dig into my skin, but I don't care. "Why'd you do it?" I ask. "You told the doctors about Logan, didn't you?"

"I'm sorry." His voice cracks. He leans his forehead against the bars. "Charlie promised to let me outta here if I helped him break you. I didn't know about his plan for the bomb, or this war of his. . . . I've been in here for ten years. You must understand." His gaze lifts to meet mine again.

I turn my head away. But I do understand. I just promised I'd do anything for Charlie if those doctors would stop hurting Logan, didn't I?

There's a clang down the passageway.

My body tenses. More guards again?

"Hide the rock, girl," Fred hisses. "Throw it away."

I crawl into the back corner of my cell and hide it in the darkness. I turn around, and my heart stops.

Logan's eyes are downcast. His wounded leg and his good one drag on the floor as the guards haul him across the stone.

The lock clicks and the door of my cell opens. They throw him forward. He lands on his hands and knees, breathing heavily.

He is here with me, finally.

The door swings shut. The guards walk away.

I don't know what this means, Charlie throwing Logan in my cell. Is he going to save him? I want to believe that. But more likely, it's a cruel joke. He's giving me what I want so he can rip it away from me again.

Logan's hair flutters with every breath. I focus on that, and the way his lips part. Little things, but I ingrain them in my memory. I won't abandon him again, and I won't forget him. Not ever.

I bite my lip. I reach out and touch my hand to his cheek. "Logan?"

His hand finds mine and grasps it. Tears touch my eyes. I don't fight them.

"Are you okay?" I whisper.

He moves his head so his hair brushes my forehead. A smile tugs at his lips. "I'm all right," he says. "It doesn't hurt anymore."

"Don't say that if it isn't true."

"I don't lie to you."

I press my lips together. He grits his teeth like his eyes are burning and his body is on fire, but he's trying to stay strong for me. Like he's shattering, but he doesn't want me to think he's weak. But I don't think that—I'd never think that. Just because the Developers thought I was Promising and he wasn't doesn't mean he isn't strong. He's the strongest boy I've ever met.

He moves his leg a little and lets out a choking sound he can't keep back. I move a hand to his leg instinctively, but when I touch it, he shakes his head.

The doctors and guards must've hurt him before I even saw him. I want to murder Dr. Tennant. I want to strangle him in his sleep.

I want to hold Logan forever and kiss away his pain. I want to say *I'm sorry for leaving* and *I love you* and *Please don't leave me* and *I won't leave you ever again*.

But I'm such a wreck all of a sudden that when I open my mouth all that comes out are three words. Three vruxing words that aren't good enough, in a whisper that's much too small: "I missed you."

Logan's lips breathe in my ear: "I missed you too."

"I didn't want to leave you."

"I know." His fingers find my collarbone and run along my skin, gently. I guide his hand to my cheek and hold it there. My tears trail onto it.

"Is it worse out there?" I ask, thinking of the acid shield Charlie claims is breaking down. I don't think he was telling the truth— after everything Fred told me, I'm sure he wasn't—but I have to know for sure.

"Officials have been killing a lot more people," Logan says. "They don't even take kids to quarantine anymore; they just burn them in the streets."

A stone cuts into my throat. I try to swallow it down, to no avail. "That's horrible."

"Yeah, it is."

A cough racks Logan's body. He pulls his hand away from my face and wraps an arm around his stomach.

"Water?" I ask Logan, forcing down my worry.

He nods, squeezing his eyes shut.

I turn to the back of my cell. I have a water skin left there from earlier. There are only a few drops left in it, and I'm thirsty myself, but I don't care. I grab the leather skin and press it into Logan's palm.

He sips the drink gratefully. He wipes his mouth with the back of his hand and gives me the skin. "Thank you."

"They'll bring more in the morning. You can have my portion."

"I won't take it from you, Clem." He laughs shakily.

"I'll force it down your throat."

"You haven't changed." His voice is soft as he studies my face. His eyes trail over where the scar on my jaw used to be. He looks away, like it pains him to see something different. "Well, in some ways."

I brush his arms with my fingers. There are bruises on his wrists. Black and blue, darkest where the doctors must've stuck needles into him.

I'll hurt them. I'll murder them.

"Why are you in here, Clem?" Logan asks, his forehead creasing.

I stare at him.

He doesn't know. Not about Charlie's bomb, or his plan, or his moonshine excuse. Or the acid generator.

Of course he doesn't know. No one in the camps knows.

I take a breath and slip my fingers through his. His hand feels cold.

"I have to tell you something," I say.

"Okay," he says.

"It's bad."

"Just tell me."

I open my mouth, but before I can say a word, the gunshots start.

35

The shots reverberate through the walls, blasting through my ears like bullets slamming into my body. Seven times. I clutch Logan and look around frantically, wishing I could see through the walls, because the shots sound close by.

They sound like death is on its way.

"What's going on?" Ella says. The sound must've woken her up. Her voice sounds panicky.

There's another shot. And another.

I don't understand this because the guards are the only ones with weapons. Why would they shoot us after all this time, when the bomb's going to go off anyway?

The door clangs open at the end of the passageway beyond our cells. There are shouts and pounding footsteps. They're headed this way.

I don't have a weapon. I don't have anything.

Logan pulls me hard against his chest, to shield me from whatever's coming. But bullets and lasers can fly through skin.

"Clementine!" someone yells.

The voice knocks the breath out of me.

It sounds like Beechy.

Beechy, who abandoned me. Beechy, who let Commander Charlie throw me in here without saying a word.

He comes running into view. He's wearing the garb of Core officials: gray suit, knee-high boots, belt with weapon holsters. He's carrying a pulse rifle.

What is he doing here?

"She's here!" he yells, making for my cell. He's breathing fast, checking the other cells for their inhabitants too. "So is Colonel Fred!"

Two more people in official garb stumble into view. I don't recognize any of them.

Beechy pulls out a pair of keys and unlocks my cell door. One of the others goes to Fred's, and the last official goes to Ella's. Ella is wide-eyed; Fred looks relieved. He must think they're getting us out and we're going to be safe, but I don't know about that.

"Come on, Clem," Beechy says.

He offers me a hand. I don't know if I want to touch him. I don't know what's going on, but I take it because there's urgency in his eyes and there was a time when I trusted him.

"What are you doing here?" I sputter.

He helps Logan out of our cell. "Breaking everyone out," he says. He pulls a copper out of his belt holster and thrusts it into my hands. "Charlie is transporting the bomb to the explosion site. He sent us to bring you and Colonel Fred back to the Core—don't ask me why, because I don't know—but we're abandoning his orders. We're getting every Unstable out, and we're going to intercept him. We're fighting."

Charlie's transporting the bomb. It's ready.

Fred doesn't look relieved anymore. He's gripping a gun an official has given him, with a trembling hand. Logan has a gun now too, and so does Ella.

But I still don't get this. I have to understand.

"Why would you save us?" I ask Beechy. "You let Charlie throw me in here. You stood by and *watched*. So did your wife, Sandy. His *daughter*."

Beechy runs his fingers through his hair, agitated. "Clementine, I'll explain everything, I promise you. All you need to know right now is that we're running. We're fighting him. Can you fight with me?" He takes a step forward, begging me to believe him with his eyes. "Please."

I want to demand answers, but he's right. Gunshots still ring out in the distance, and Charlie's on his way to set off the bomb.

There isn't time.

"Fine," I say, gripping my copper. "How many of you came here? The guards don't sound happy."

"Eight others. But there are more inmates than guards."

"There are also doctors."

"We outnumber them if you're each carrying a weapon. We can get out of here. Trust me. But we have to hurry." He turns down the passageway.

Fred holds his gun up, ready to fire, and limps after Beechy. One of the officials slips his arm through Ella's to help her walk. She's shaking in her skin, from the cold and whatever the doctors did to her yesterday.

Beechy didn't account for the fact that most of the inmates are weak. Some can't even run; how will they aim a gun?

But there's no time to find a better solution. Gritting my teeth, I slip my fingers through Logan's. "Come on," I say. I hope to the stars I can trust Beechy.

"Clem, what the vrux is going on?" Logan asks me. His jaw is hard. He must be so lost in all this.

I press my lips together. I tell him what I can while we break out of the passageway and run down a corridor with Beechy, the rebels, and the other inmates from the cells near ours. I tell him fast.

※

Beechy shoots the first guard we see.

We're in another corridor now, one I don't recognize. I haven't seen enough of this facility. I have no idea how far off the exit is.

The gunshots sound like they're just ahead. Beechy explained some of the rebels have already released the Unstables from the cells on the other side of Karum, and the guards are trying to stop them from leaving. I don't know if it's working.

Beechy shouts orders from the front of our stumbling, staggering, limping group: "Stay close to each other. Follow Cady"—he points to a woman rebel with long black hair—"and she'll get you to the exit corridor. Shoot anyone who gets in your way. Get out as fast as you can. We'll take care of Karum personnel. We'll rendezvous by the flight pods waiting at the back of the facility."

I'm not ready for this. But I let go of Logan's hand so I can use both hands to hold my copper. "Logan, stay close to me," I say.

"You too," he says, gripping his own weapon. His teeth are clenched, and his cheeks are pale. He knows about the bomb now. He knows Charlie's going to kill everyone in the camps and cities in all the outer sectors unless we stop him.

But I'm not even sure we'll make it out of Karum.

We turn the corner into a wider area, something like a lobby. But smoke clouds my view and I can hardly see anything. There are lights flashing everywhere—reds and blues and purples from the laser guns some of the guards must be carrying. People in white coats and guard uniforms blend together with the people in official uniforms and Unstable rags.

A red laser whizzes past my ear.

I duck, gasping.

Lifting my copper with trembling hands, I fire in the direction the laser came from, at one of the men in guard uniforms. I can't tell if I hit him. I don't think I did.

Another laser whizzes past. Eyes wide, I jump out of the way and trip over a body, landing hard on my knees. Blood pools in the hair of the dead nurse.

I gulp down the urge to vomit. I scramble to my feet.

The *zaps* and *pings* of gunfire ring loud in my ears, drowning out voices. The smoke makes my eyes water, and I blink fast, looking around wildly to tell where I am. I can't see Logan or Beechy or Fred or Ella or anyone anymore.

"Logan!" I scream his name.

There's a *zap* too close to my head, and I duck again and the laser hits the ceiling. There's a loud cracking sound. A light shatters.

Shards of glass rain on my head. I shield myself with my hands and scramble out of the way, but I trip instead. There are so many bodies on the floor—and I can't tell if they're on my side or Charlie's. It matters, but it shouldn't.

A body crashes into me.

Ella stumbles, blood spilling from a hole in her chest.

The copper slips from my hand. I grab on to her to keep her from falling. Her eyes are wide. A strangled sound comes from her throat.

"No!" I cry.

A laser strikes her back. She falls limp in my arms. Smoke sizzles on her rags.

I'm crying and choking and I can't move because I'm holding her. I can't put her down. People will trample her. People will trip and get her blood on their hands, and they won't even care, but they *should* care.

Someone touches my back, and I start to let go of her. I start to whip around to defend myself.

But it's Logan. He says something I can't hear. I can't see him well through my tears and the smoke.

He eases Ella out of my trembling arms and transfers her bleeding body to his.

He's going to carry her.

A laser flashes too close to Logan's shoulder. My fingers fumble to snatch my copper from the ground. I turn and aim a shot into the steam. I don't stop to see where it hits. We're already running.

We scramble through the smoke, the dead bodies, the flashing lights.

There's a hallway ahead. Cady is standing at the entrance firing a pulse rifle, gesturing wildly for us to head down that way, ahead of her.

Something hot grazes my shoulder. Heat trickles like liquid fire across my skin.

I scream and stumble, but I don't stop running. The laser only grazed me. I'll be okay.

Some more steps down the corridor, and there's a doorway, a passage leading out into the night.

It's too quiet out here. The wind bites my skin.

Green grass stretches at our feet, sloping to cliffs over the sea. We're the only ones here so far. We're the first ones out.

I double over, gasping for breath. Trying to focus on something other than the pain in my shoulder. Logan pauses to rest too, but he's still holding Ella's body. He's squinting into the dark toward the sea cliffs.

"Clem, her body," he says softly. "Should we . . ."

I swallow hard and follow his gaze to the sea. The ocean instructors told us about when we were young. The Surface camp and city are somewhere behind us, a hundred miles at least.

I know what Logan's thinking. I don't want to let Ella go, but I know we have to. And I think coming to rest in the sea would make her happy. So I whisper, "Okay."

We walk to the edge of the cliff. Fierce moonlight sparkles on the water below, where waves crash on the rocks, roaring in the night.

Logan glances at me, his lips tight. There's blood on his cheeks that I hope isn't his.

"Should I do it?" he asks.

I glance at her frail, broken body. Red stains her rags. There are bruises around her eyes. I wish she could open them and laugh at me for thinking she's only sleeping. I wish she'd tell me more about the handsome boy whose smile made the rain stop falling.

I wish I could tell her *Thank you for those nights* and *I'm sorry I couldn't save you* and *I'll kill Charlie someday to get back at him for this, I swear,* but I can't.

"Here, I'll help you," I say, wiping my eyes.

I slip my arms under her skinny legs, gritting my teeth to ignore my throbbing shoulder, and Logan carefully holds her head up. We lift her body over the water.

I count: one—two—three.

And we let her go.

I watch her body splash in the water, barely missing the rocks.

Logan wraps his arms around me. I bury my head in his shoulder, blinking tears out of my eyes.

"I'm sorry," he says.

"I'm sorry too. I'm sorry they hurt you. I'm sorry I left."

"It's not your fault, Clem."

"But it is." At least part of it is. If I'd agreed to obey Charlie in the first place, they wouldn't have brought Logan to Karum. They wouldn't have electrocuted him or given him those bruises on his arms.

His arms loosen around me, and I'm sure he's going to agree. I'm sure he's going to say *I hate you for leaving* and *Why didn't you save me?* There are a million "I'm sorrys" but I'm not sure they'll ever be enough.

Instead, he turns me around gently. His hands have Ella's blood on them.

"It's not your fault. I promise," he whispers. His starry-night eyes stare straight into mine, sending a flutter into my stomach. He holds me like I'm a shard of trembling glass. Like he's sure he's going to make a mistake and I'm going to break, but I'm waiting for it. I've wanted it forever.

He leans in, and our lips touch. Brushing, barely touching.

I close my eyes. I breathe in his smell that I know so well, and I lose myself.

His fingers tangle in my curls. Our noses touch, and our cheekbones bump.

Slowly, little by little, we figure out this newness. This mess of beauty that isn't messy at all because there's me and there's Logan. The two of us and the stars flickering over our heads. I know him, and he knows me without saying anything.

And I forget what it means to be afraid.

36

The others come stumbling out of Karum, bruised and blood-ied. Fred is alive. So are Beechy and Cady, and others I don't know the names of. I don't count how many of us are missing.

I try not to think about all the people we killed to get out of there alive.

"We have to hurry," Beechy says, wiping the blood off a cut on his forehead.

Charlie must already be at the detonation site by now. I don't know how we're supposed to stop him from starting the detona-tion timer. But I hope we can make it. I hope we can try.

We scramble into a group of flight pods. They are parked in the grass at the side of the facility, where the rebel pilots land them earlier. Logan and I enter the smallest one with Beechy.

The copilot seat swivels, and Sandy's sitting there. She gives me a nervous smile. There's a small bump on her belly, where her baby grows inside. "Hey," she says.

The last time I saw her, she stood back and watched while Sam held me down and a nurse stuck a needle in my arm. I learned she was the daughter of the man who ruined my life and Logan's.

But I force my lips into a smile and take one of the passenger seats behind hers. She came here with Beechy, I remind myself. And Beechy just broke everyone out of Karum, going against Charlie's wishes.

Unless he lied about that. I wouldn't put it past him.

Logan slips into the seat beside me and fumbles for the seat strap. Beechy takes the pilot chair. He flips a switch on the dashboard and the interior lights dim. The door slides shut. The engine rumbles on.

I pull my seat strap over my waist and click it into the lock. Beechy pushes a lever forward, and our pod lifts off the grass, following the others into the air.

I press a hand to the wound on my throbbing shoulder and look out the window to watch us leave Karum. The massive steel facility looks lonesome. Abandoned. Its hallways used to be filled with the echoes of screams and the pounding boots of the guards.

Now they're quiet.

"Cady, make sure you're behind me when we reach the Pipeline," Beechy says.

I glance at him, confused because Cady isn't in here. But I notice he's wearing an earpiece, so he must be talking to her through that.

He still hasn't told me how he ended up a rebel leader, or why he didn't tell me he was. Why he let Charlie throw me in Karum.

I wait until I'm pretty sure he's finished listening through his earpiece to ask him. "Are you going to explain everything now?" I ask stiffly.

"What do you want to know?" he says.

I want to know a lot of things, but I start with the first thing that pops into my mind: "Sandy is Charlie's daughter. Why didn't you tell me?"

"That was my fault," Sandy says, biting her lip and keeping her hand on her baby bump. "I told him not to. I was afraid you'd think badly of me."

"Well, you did stand by while your father threw me in Karum."

"I'm sorry about that," Beechy says, running his fingers through his hair.

"We couldn't do anything to risk our cover," Sandy says. "He believes we're on his side. That's why we were able to come here and rescue you."

"So, what, it was an act?" I ask. "Beechy pretended to be subdued when he and those guards chased me? You could've done something to help me—"

"I was half subdued." Beechy fiddles with another lever on the dashboard. "I got my monthly injection, same as you."

"What does that mean? *Half* subdued?"

"I was fighting it. It takes time to fight it, though I can fight it, and I do fight it. I'm not the only one, either—a good number of us in the Core just pretend to follow Charlie's orders. He'd mark us as Unstable if he knew. I was going to tell you, but then Charlie announced his plan and . . . things got complicated."

"And then you abandoned me," I finish.

He sighs. "I'm sorry, Clementine. I made a mistake. I should've told you sooner."

"Yes, you should've."

"I'm sorry."

I turn my head away, clenching my teeth, partly because my shoulder still hurts, partly because this isn't fair. I get that Beechy made a mistake, that he had to pretend to follow Charlie's orders in order to survive, but if he'd told me, I might not've ended up in

Karum and had a million needles stuck into my skin. I could've told him about my allergy, and maybe he would've known how to help me not feel like I was dying after the monthly injection.

Maybe we could've come up with a plan to sabotage Charlie's bomb much sooner, instead of waiting until the last second.

"Clementine, please forgive me," Beechy says softly.

I stare out the window, refusing to look at him. We're skimming above the ocean now. Pink moonlight shimmers on the black waves. In the cloudless sky, acid swirls on the surface of the atmospheric shield. It blocks too much of the moon's surface for me to tell if Fred was telling the truth, if there really is a generator up there.

But I think I believe him. I know, at least, that I don't believe Charlie.

"So you don't support Project KIMO," Logan says beside me, to Sandy.

Sandy shakes her head. "My father's not in his right mind. He doesn't know what he's doing."

"He's obviously lying about the acid shield being broken," Beechy says. "We would've corroded the second we stepped outside if things were really as bad as he made them sound. I wish we knew what his real aim is, but we don't."

I frown, glancing at Sandy. "He didn't tell you?"

"He tells me very little," she says. "His policies are strictly between him, the other Developers, and the army colonels."

I chew on my bottom lip. She probably doesn't know about Marden then, or the war, even. Does *anyone* know? Sam knew something about soldier training, but he thought it had to do with preparing for a rebellion in the outer sectors. That's what Charlie told everyone except the Developers and the heads of his military.

I want to expose his lie. However, the bomb is more important right now.

"What's the plan when we reach the explosion site?" I ask.

"Five of our six pods will land at the site." Beechy nods at Sandy, who reaches into an overhead compartment and withdraws a folded piece of paper. She opens it in her lap, turning her chair.

I lean closer to see it, and so does Logan. It's a sketch of the launch site, a flight hangar between Lower and the Core. The sketch shows the ship transporting the missile on the far left side of the platform and the spot where we're going to land on the far right. Red dots show where Charlie's men will likely be in position.

"Our goal is to take over the site and capture my father before he sets the timer on the bomb detonator," she says. "The sixth pod is taking Colonel Fred and the other Unstables who are too old to fight straight back to the Core."

"The other Unstables agreed to this?" I ask.

"They all seemed very eager to attack my father," she says, and I notice there's a slight unsteadiness to her voice. I'm not sure she wants him to die, even though she hates his policies.

"Anyway," she says, "we have a few rebels undercover at the site already. There should be enough of us to overrun his people even if the Unstables don't fight, as long as we get there in time. We've been training to overpower my father for a long time. We hoped it would happen under different circumstances, but there's nothing we can do about that."

She folds up the map and puts it away.

"What's your backup plan?" Logan asks. "Charlie could very well have set the timer before we get there."

He has big circles under his eyes and tension in his jaw. His fingers slip through mine, steady.

"Even if it's been set, we'll have some time before the bomb explodes to try and reverse the detonator," Sandy says. "We just don't know how long."

"That's our problem," Beechy adds, steering our ship to the right to follow the other pods. "We couldn't get our hands on the blueprints, so any attempt to reverse the timer and disable the bomb will be guesswork."

"There is one other thing we could do," Sandy says, her voice quieter. "A last resort. We could fly the ship that's transporting the missile out of the atmosphere, to explode the bomb far enough away from the Surface that it wouldn't cause any damage."

"But there might not be enough time for that," Beechy says. "Which is why our best bet would be to find some way to disable the bomb."

I press my lips together. I have to tell them I know how to disable it. But my stomach flips when I think about it.

Maybe because Fred said there's a possibility Charlie changed the system. Maybe because using Yate's Equation might not work.

"I . . . I might be able to help," I say.

Sandy's head turns. Logan's brows furrow.

"How so?" Sandy asks.

What's wrong with me? *Just say it.*

I swallow. "Colonel Fred . . . he's the one who designed the bomb. He told me things about it, like why he agreed to build it in the first place. He thought it was for something else. And . . . he told me how to disable it."

But it might not work.

"What did he tell you?" Logan asks.

I take a deep breath and do my best to explain. It's clear as soon as I begin that Sandy had no idea her father was keeping something this big from her.

She had no idea Marden exists.

✳

The Pipeline entrance on this side of the Surface sits nestled in the rocky, snow-topped mountains we come to after the ocean ends.

By the time we move into the tunnel to the lower sectors, we have a backup plan, which Beechy has coordinated with Cady and the other rebels through his earpiece. If Charlie detonates the bomb, we'll still try to overpower him. Beechy will help me get inside the ship with the escape pod carrying the missile, and I'll solve Yate's Equation on the control panel. Hopefully, that will switch everything off.

I fiddle with my hands in my lap and stare at the flashing lights on the tunnel walls. They all believed what I said about the moon's acid, how it came from a generator put there by aliens from the planet Marden, who want us dead. Logan looked disgusted, and Sandy kept shaking her head at her father's insanity, but she said she believed me. She trusts Fred because she knew him when she was younger, before he was thrown in Karum. Because she trusts Fred, so does Beechy.

A half hour passes in the Pipeline, maybe more. My palms grow sweaty, and my heart races no matter how many digits of pi I recite to stay calm. We have a plan now, but we don't know if it'll work. We don't even know if we'll have time for it. No one knows what the timer will be set for once it starts.

Even if using Yate's Equation would disable the bomb, the bomb might blow the planet apart before I get to use it.

Finally, finally, the pods ahead of us start slowing. Beechy eases back the flight clutch to match their speed. Ahead of us, three of the pods disappear into a tunnel that branches off perpendicular to the Pipeline. Another pod keeps going, still heading for the Core. Fred is inside that one.

I wonder if I'll ever see him again.

We veer into the tunnel, slowing further and flying close to the ground as we enter the massive flight hangar. There are pods and hovercrafts ahead, and lights dotting the floor. I don't see people, but there must be people there, with so many ships. I wonder if they're here to help Charlie prep the bomb or to make sure no one gets in the way.

I pray there aren't more of them than we can handle.

We hover to a stop. Our engine's whir dies.

Beechy flips a switch and the door slides open. Sandy's already standing, opening the overhead compartment to remove the weapons stored inside.

I unlatch my seat belt, my eyes skimming the deck outside the window. Hovercrafts and smaller ships that must've carried personnel here block most of my view. But the KIMO ship should be on the other side of them, on the far side of the deck. With Charlie.

Sandy tosses me a copper. "You wait three minutes before you leave, okay?"

I nod.

Beechy's talking into his earpiece. He finishes and slips a smaller gun into his belt holster, then glances at me. "Good luck," he says, flashing me a tense smile.

"You too."

He hurries down the ramp. Sandy follows after him, shutting the door behind her.

I slip off my seat and drop to the floor. Logan follows suit, so no one will be able to see us if they look through the window.

Beechy and Sandy are going to pretend they're here to see if Charlie needs help with anything. While they're distracting him, we'll jump out with the other Unstables and the Core rebels, and attack. With any luck, we'll throw Charlie off his game.

On the floor of the pod, Logan pulls me to him and breathes against my forehead. I count the seconds. My heart pummels my ribs.

One hundred seventy-eight, one hundred seventy-nine, one hundred eighty.

Holding my breath, I push off the ground enough to glimpse the deck outside the window. It's empty.

"Clear," I say.

Logan presses a button, and the pod door slides open. We hurry down the ramp. The deck air presses on my skin like ice. My Karum clothes are too thin. My hands are trembling.

The rebels and the other Unstables are already outside. Now I can't help counting how many of us are left: There are seventeen besides me and Logan.

In a hushed voice, Cady directs people in different directions so we can attack from all sides. Unstables disappear around the hovercrafts and pods with guns in their hands.

"You two, come with me," Cady says, beckoning to me and Logan.

I take a breath and follow her. We duck under the wing of a fighter jet and slip around a small hovercraft.

"Get back," Cady hisses.

There are people ahead. Officials in black armor.

Logan grabs my arm and pulls me back. All three of us press against the side of the ship. The one ahead of us blocks the nearest guard from view, so I hope it hides us too.

But my throat clenches tight. There are too many officials—I bet there are more than Sandy and Beechy thought there'd be. There's no way they can distract them all.

"On my signal, we're attacking," Cady says quietly, touching her earpiece so I know she's talking to everyone and not just to us. Her hand drops, and she turns to me. "You know the code to disable the bomb, yes?"

I swallow. "I think so."

"You might need it. Beechy says Charlie's about to set the detonation timer."

"Okay," I say as calmly as I can. Inside I'm screaming *no, no, no, no, no.*

"Three . . ." Cady whispers.

This isn't going to work.

"Two . . ."

The guards don't have any distraction, and neither does Charlie.

"One—"

"Wait!" The word flies out of my mouth before I can stop it, just as Cady is about to yell her signal.

"What?" she snaps.

"Let me go first, please." I don't know what I'm doing. "I think I can distract Charlie's officials." I don't know what I'm saying.

"No," Logan says. "You'll get shot."

I might. It's a very strong possibility.

"Charlie won't let them kill me," I say. "He wants me alive, or he wouldn't have asked Beechy to come for me in Karum." I hope it's the truth, but it doesn't even matter. "Please, let me try. You can attack if it doesn't work, and if it does work I'm sure you'll surprise them."

Cady purses her lips. She's thinking about it. She's wondering if I'm smart enough and quick enough, and if Charlie's officials will find me distracting at all.

If Sam is here, I know he will.

"Fine," she says. "Be careful. We'll stay out of sight."

I pull away from Logan, refusing to look at his face. I don't want to see the pain in his eyes. He must think I'm abandoning him again.

At least it isn't to save myself this time.

I grip the copper in my hands. I take shaky steps away from our hiding spot. It doesn't matter if the officials see me now; I want them to.

There's the one ahead of me, and several more beyond him, patrolling or standing between the ships. I still can't see the KIMO transport ship, but I can see smoke spewing into the air beyond some of the nearest ships. The bomb must be over there.

My heart hammers beneath my ribs. The official's back is turned to me, and no one else has noticed me yet.

I breathe in and out through my nostrils. I lift my copper until it's level with my eyes.

"Where's Commander Charlie?" I ask loudly.

The official spins to face me, lifting a heavy gun. Panic rips through me, and I start to duck.

But he freezes.

It's Joe, the muscular boy who carried the biggest gun in Phantom. There's a layer of film over his eyes, but he still knows who I am. He looks furious.

"What are you doing here?" he asks. "How'd you get here?" He's checking behind me to see if there's anyone else with me. I pray the others are out of sight.

"I stowed away on Beechy's ship," I say. "Answer my question. Where's Charlie? I need you to take me to him."

"Hey, Lieutenant Sam, look who I found!" Joe calls over his shoulder.

One of the officials standing beyond another fighter jet turns. Sam's whole body tenses when he spots me.

An image flashes through my head of me moving my arm a few inches to the left, pulling the trigger, and shooting him through the chest.

But I'm not brave enough. He's already striding toward me with his rifle raised, snapping for others to join him. Five officials. I don't run. I let them surround me.

"What the vrux are you doing here?" Sam yells.

"I snuck onto Beechy's ship," I say, trying to keep my voice steady. "I need to see Commander Charlie. There's something he needs to know before he sets off the bomb."

I'm spewing lies, praying Sam isn't smart enough to see through them.

"Check the perimeter," he says to the men from his squadron. "There might be others."

"No—" I start.

"There's just me," a voice says behind me, and my heart nearly splinters into a million pieces.

I turn. Logan's pointing a gun at Sam.

37

Sam's lip curls. "Is this your boyfriend, Clementine?"

"No," I say quickly. "No, he's—"

Sam flicks a finger, and one of the officials tackles Logan. I cry out. He knocks the gun out of Logan's hand and twists his arms behind his back.

"Stop it!" I aim my copper—to shoot Sam, maybe—but another official wrenches it from my hands before I can blink. The butt of a rifle slams into my back. I stumble.

"You're both under arrest," Sam says. He sticks his gun into its holster and moves behind me, grabbing my wrists and forcing me forward. An ache spreads through my back where the rifle hit me.

Sam's nails dig into my skin as he hauls me across the hangar, while the others bring Logan. I twist, trying to break free of Sam, but he's too strong. I feel his hot, dirty breath on my neck.

I want to spit in his face. I want to put a bullet in his head.

Around a flight pod, I see Charlie. He's talking to some of his men—scientists, maybe. Sandy and Beechy are there.

Behind them and a few more passenger ships, I glimpse the

massive transport craft that I climbed into in Restricted Division, that carries the KIMO missile inside its escape pod. The ship spews steam onto the hangar. I have no idea if Charlie already set the timer, but wouldn't he have left if he had? I don't think he'd stick around to watch the countdown to zero.

Please, please let the timer not be set yet.

"Commander!" Sam calls.

Charlie turns to stone when he sees me.

"The initial system—" a scientist is saying.

"Please excuse me one moment," Charlie says, holding a hand up. He's calm again. Collected. But the vein in his neck stands out.

I wonder what he wants with me and Fred, why he cared enough to save us instead of letting the KIMO missile destroy us.

"Sandy, please explain this," he says. "You said she and Colonel Fred were safely on the other transport vehicle on their way to the Core."

"She was, Father," Sandy says quickly.

"So why is she here?"

"I hid in their transport," I say, snapping the words. "It was almost too easy. You should do a better job training your personnel."

Charlie's eyes narrow.

This is dangerous. This is so, so dangerous; he could kill me right this second if he wanted. Logan too.

He eyes him now, assessing Logan's figure. Realizing this is someone important to me. Noticing, I'm sure, how he puts more weight on his right leg than his left.

"I don't have time for this," Charlie says. "Lieutenant Sam, please escort the prisoners to my ship." He turns away.

I let out my breath. At least he's not going to shoot us yet.

"Actually," he says, haltingly, "I've changed my mind. Shoot the boy."

There's a moment where I don't quite understand, where I think he must be kidding. Then Joe lifts his gun and presses the barrel to Logan's head.

"NO!" I twist away from Sam—wrenching—kicking—

You can't—you can't—

There's a whizzing sound, and a ping.

Another official helps Sam hold me back.

"No . . ."

Did I lose him? I can't. *Don't you dare go.*

Joe drops his gun and stumbles. Blood oozes from his back.

Behind Charlie, Beechy's holding a smoking pulse rifle. He shot Joe.

Charlie realizes this at the same moment I do.

There's the sound of another shot, then of pounding feet as the rebels come running. Sam yells something, and his men whip out their guns.

The air fills with laser beams. I drop to my knees and duck my head. A red laser blasts a lamp in the floor beside me. The bulb shatters, and glass flies everywhere. I scream, blocking my head with an arm. Shards scrape my skin. They set it stinging

It takes me a second to realize Sam has let go of me.

I crawl beneath the lights and smoke until I reach a pod. I move to the other side and press against the metal, hoping it'll shield me. Piercing noises from the guns reverberate in my ears. The flight deck rumbles beneath my feet.

"Logan!" I cry. Smoke from the lasers clouds my vision. I don't know where he is. I don't know if they shot him.

And I don't know where Charlie is, either.

A body thumps as it falls two feet away. A copper slides out of the official's grip, and I snatch it up. As I stand, I peer around the pod corner and aim at the first man in armor I see. The bullet grazes his side, and he almost trips.

His head turns.

Sam snarls and aims his next shot at my head.

I jump aside, and the laser beam hits the pod instead. He fires a second time. I try to shoot back. The copper slips from my sweaty hands and clatters too far away.

Someone—Cady, I think—starts shooting at Sam too, distracting him. I turn to run. I make it past one more pod before I almost crash into Logan.

I blurt out a word that sounds like his name. He grabs my shoulders and drags me behind a ship. He's breathing hard, and there's blood on his shirt.

"I think Charlie sent someone to start the timer," he says.

"I don't know if I can disable it." My panic spills out with my words. "He's gonna kill us, Logan. He's gonna kill us if we don't stop him."

"I won't let him."

"He's stronger than us."

"No, he isn't."

An explosion behind us rocks the hangar, and I cry out, stumbling with Logan. But it wasn't the KIMO bomb. Someone threw a grenade.

The bomb. I have to disable it.

"I can't leave you, Logan."

"I'll be right here. I promise."

"Okay, but if you die—"

He kisses me, roughly.

For a second I'm lost, not here anymore, not breathing.

The force from a nearby laser blast blows us apart. My back slams into the ground.

It takes me a second to recover. I gasp for air.

"Run!" Logan chokes, trying to get up.

To my left, Sam is coming for me again. His gun is aimed and he's pushing past other officials to get to me.

I ignore the ache roaring through my body and scramble to my feet, racing away from Sam. I'm not that far from KIMO. The steam is getting stronger, so it should be just ahead. But the ground is rumbling again—a steady tremor, not from a grenade. It scares me because that probably means Charlie or one of his men already did something. They may have started the bomb's initiation sequence.

A sharp pain from a laser pierces my elbow. I cry out and stumble. My knees hit the metal deck.

I'm trying to stand when Sam's nails dig into my ankles and he wrenches my leg. I kick against him. With a snarl, he forces me onto my back. The cold muzzle of his gun touches the skin between my eyes.

His knee presses into my stomach, pinning me and making it hard to breathe. "Aren't you going to scream?" he asks. His voice is scratchy from all the yelling. The smile he gives me is cold.

"Just shoot me if you're going to."

I don't want to die, not here, not this way, but I won't scream. I won't cry.

But the weight lifts, and air returns to my lungs. Someone heaves Sam off me.

"Go!" It's Sandy. "Beechy needs your help. I'll hold him off!"

I'm gasping and hurting and shaking, but I make myself turn over. Somehow I manage to push off the ground.

A laser beam ricochets off a fighter jet, and I throw an arm over my eyes. It misses me by a foot.

The engine steam is thick now. I can barely see at all. I ram into something hard—a pod, maybe.

"Beechy!" I yell. Sandy said he needs my help, but I can't even find him.

Figures stumble into view through the steam. One of them looks like Charlie. "Get to the transports!" he yells. "Get everyone out of the no-fly zone. Abandon the rebels."

"Charlie!" I scream his name.

He doesn't see me at first, but his face contorts with anger. He looks wildly around.

"You set the timer, didn't you?" I yell.

He spots me. His nostrils flare. "Of course we did," he says, striding toward me. He withdraws a gun from his pocket, and before I can blink, he slams the barrel into my jaw.

Fire—burning—breaking—

I topple over, clutching my jaw.

Charlie staggers away.

The bomb has been activated. Who knows how long the timer is set for? If I can't disable it, we'll be stuck here on this deck when it goes off, when the explosion rockets everything but the Core into space. When the world ends.

I don't see the laser beam that brings Charlie down, but I hear a thud. When my vision clears and I squint through the steam, he is deck-bound. Not dead, not even close, but it looks like the laser went through his left leg. He's screaming. He can't get up.

I turn to see who shot him, and there's a hand helping me up. Beechy's hand. There's a gash in his shoulder. Blood soaks his leather suit.

"Beechy, he—he set it. It's gonna go off."

"Think you can disable it?"

"I can try." Charlie's going to kill me either way. I have to try.

"Good."

"Stop them!" Charlie yells at one of the officials who came back for him.

Beechy takes my hand, and we run across the rest of the hangar and through the steam to the hovercraft. Lasers shoot at us from behind. I duck to avoid them.

The cargo lift is already open. We scramble up the ramp. A laser barely misses my head. Beechy aims a shot over his shoulder. I can't tell if he shoots the man down.

At the top of the ramp, Beechy finds an indoor panel on the wall and slams a button. There's a hiss, and the ramp lifts and seals behind us, hiding the fog and the officials from view.

"Can't they still get in?" I ask.

"It should take them some time. Hopefully, the rebels will stop them before they figure it out."

The ship still rumbles beneath us.

"Where's the bomb?" I ask.

"We can access the control panel from inside. I think it's this way." Beechy grabs my hand and pulls me down the narrow corridor.

There are compartments overhead and on either side of us, and passenger seats here and there attached to the walls. We pass another corridor leading to doors and a bunk room at the end.

We come to a ladder. Beechy goes up first. I follow him, scrambling up the rungs.

We get to our feet in another, shorter passageway. At the end is a door with a window, and a second door beyond it, leading to what looks like an escape pod. The one with the missile inside it.

Beechy presses a button near us on the wall, and the doors zip open one at a time.

There's someone inside the pod, sitting in the cockpit chair with his head bent over. He jumps to his feet and spins to face us, lifting his copper level with his face.

"Drop your weapons," Oliver says.

38

Oliver's eyes are muddled behind his glasses, not the way they should be.

I'm going to be sick. I want to run and find Charlie and vomit bile and mucus on his shiny black boots. He told his other men to get to their ships, but he left Oliver. He was going to leave him here to die.

"Drop it," Oliver says, pointing his copper at Beechy's forehead, "or I'll shoot." The words sound like someone planted them in his head; like he's a machine reciting letters.

Beechy's nostrils flare, but he lets his gun clatter onto the metal. There are two of us, and we can handle Oliver. But I have to try reasoning with him first.

"Oliver, please put the gun down."

He doesn't say anything. But he turns the copper on me, and I flinch.

"Drop your weapon," he says. He's staring at me, but it's like he's staring right through me.

My voice shakes when I tell him, "Charlie left you here, Oliver. You know the bomb's gonna go off, right? He left you to die."

A flicker of worry touches his eyes. Then it's gone. "Drop your weapons" is all he says.

"Clementine, there isn't time," Beechy says.

"I know," I say. We have to overpower him, but I'm not ready yet. Oliver is still here, underneath the injection and all the lies. I can still reach him.

"Oliver, *please*." I want to wrap my arms around him, but I'm afraid he'll try to kill me. "We're not trying to mess things up, I swear. We're trying to save everyone."

Oliver flips a switch on the copper, taking it off stun. "I'm giving you ten seconds to get out of here. Ten, nine, eight—"

Beechy slams his fist into Oliver's hand, knocking the gun away and setting it off at the same time. An orange beam strikes somewhere behind me. I duck and gasp.

Oliver snarls and struggles against Beechy, trying to push us out of the escape pod.

"Help me," Beechy says.

I'm sorry, I'm sorry, I'm so sorry, Oliver.

I ram into him. He loses his balance. We grab his arms and pull him until all three of us are out of the smaller transport, back in the narrow passage of the hovercraft.

"I'll secure him," Beechy says, grabbing both of his arms. I press flat against the wall to let him pull Oliver past me. "Get in there and check out the control panel. I'll be right back."

"Please don't hurt him," I say. Oliver's been hurt too many times because of me.

"I'll try not to."

I swallow hard and move into the escape pod. I hit a button

that shuts the doors behind me, putting one more barrier between me and Charlie. Just in case.

I scan the transport. There's a complicated panel of buttons and a screen before the pilot chair in front of me, and a window on the wall. It's steamed over, but the word K-I-M-O on the top of the panel tells me I'm in the right place. The bomb must be connected to this transport, maybe above me or below me, or jutting out from one of the sides.

I slip into the pilot scat and wipe two fingers across the control screen, hoping it's a touch screen. Words pop up:

PROJECT KIMO

1:38:17

ENTER DEACTIVATION CODE

The 17 drops to 16, and then to 15 and to 14, and all the air goes out of my lungs. It's showing me how much time is left until the bomb goes off. One hour thirty-eight minutes and twelve seconds.

My hands tremble as I touch ENTER DEACTIVATION CODE. A blank bar pops up with a blinking cursor and a keypad with letters and numbers and math symbols below it.

This is it. Either Fred gave me the code that'll turn the bomb off, or I won't be able to stop it.

I tuck the curls behind my ear, trying to ignore how fast my heart is beating. I have to focus.

Fred said to use Yate's Equation. But did he mean type in the problem, or the solution?

I try the solution. I memorized it, but I go through the steps in my head to double-check the answer. When I'm sure it's correct, I type it in:

674837.475

A fierce tremor runs through the ship, shaking the transport. I clutch the arm of my chair with one hand. I touch ENTER on the keypad with the other.

A red bar replaces the blank one:

ACCESS DENIED

No, no, no. It didn't work. This has to work.

The red bar goes away, and I press ENTER DEACTIVATION CODE again. This time I type out Yate's full equation, all sixty characters of it.

ACCESS DENIED

The doors slide open behind me. "Is it working?" Beechy asks.

I shake my head. I try the solution again, my fingers flying across the screen. There's blood on them from the cut on my aching jaw and the one on my shoulder, but I don't care.

ACCESS DENIED

I don't know what to do.

"Charlie must've switched the code," I say. "It's gonna go off. We can't stop it."

I'm fighting back tears again. Grady's going to get blown to bits, and so is that girl, Nellie—I don't like her but she doesn't deserve to die—and so are all the kids in the camps, and the adults up there too; all the people Charlie doesn't think he needs anymore. And the trees and the grass and the shacks and the animals. It's all going to be gone.

And so am I. Charlie isn't going to welcome me back to the Core; he's going to shoot me if I go back there. I'm going to splinter, shatter, explode into dust. So will Logan and Beechy and Oliver and everyone I care about in the entire world.

We are going to run out of time.

"There's still one more option," Beechy says. His voice shakes, and I can't look at his face. "We could fly the hovercraft away. We could get the bomb as far away as possible, so it wouldn't cause as much damage. Hopefully, we'd have enough time to deploy the bomb and fly out of its range before it detonated. But regardless, it would screw up Charlie's plan."

I stare at the timer on the screen. The number is down to 1:32:57.

I run my fingers through my curls. I exhale; I inhale; I exhale.

Beechy's plan would work. We could save everyone. And buy our friends more time to stop Charlie.

But I don't know if we'd have time to deflect the bomb and save ourselves too.

I squeeze my eyes shut. *I'm going to die either way.* This is the best way to go, isn't it? Saving the world.

But oh, how I wish we had more time.

I open my eyes and wipe my nose with the back of my hand. "Okay."

"Are you sure?"

"Mhm."

Beechy places a hand on my shoulder. "You know we can't tell the others, right?" he says, and I can tell he's trying hard to keep his voice steady. "They'd try to stop us or come with us. We can't do that to them."

I nod, tight-lipped. The thought of leaving Logan without saying good-bye and never seeing him again, not even for a moment, makes my chest and my heart hurt so bad I might explode and shatter into a billion shards of glass.

But this is the only way to save him.

Back in the corridor near the cargo lift, Oliver's thrashing in one of the passenger seats. Beechy tied him down with wires he must've found in some compartment, but they don't look like they'll hold him much longer.

"Can you try to secure him better?" Beechy asks, ducking his head to hurry down the passage to the main cockpit. "I'm gonna get us out of here."

I nod, glancing at the sealed door to the cargo lift. I don't like that we're taking Oliver with us, but we can't open that door without risking getting shot by someone still outside, or letting Logan and Sandy find out what we're doing. I have to be okay with it.

But I hate it. I hate it.

Oliver's spewing words in his seat, though I don't really hear what he's saying. His voice grates in my brain. There's no way I can listen to it.

I move to the wall of compartments beside him, not looking at him. It's full of cubbies with wires and tools and kits inside. I open another compartment and find folded blankets. Grabbing one, I rip off a strip I hope will be thick enough.

When I turn to him, Oliver's eyes shoot daggers at me. "I knew they were right about you," he mutters. "Completely Unstable."

I jam the gag into his mouth. My hands shake as I work the fabric between his teeth.

The gag goes too far back. He chokes.

"I'm sorry." I gasp, fumbling to loosen it.

Oliver's teeth snap and cut my finger.

"Ouch!" A dot of blood appears on my pinky. Beneath my feet, the ship's rumbling picks up, and an engine whir starts.

"Might want to buckle in, Clementine!" Beechy shouts from the cockpit.

Oliver thrashes in his wires, trying to spit the fabric out of his mouth. I reach to tie it off, but he shakes his head so fast I can't catch it. He isn't going to cooperate.

I scan the blue cubbies for something that might help me. The rumbling makes me lose my balance; I clutch the wall.

My eyes fall on a small, clear kit in one of the compartments with bandages and tiny red bottles inside it. A medikit. I get the compartment and then the kit open, and fumble through the medicine bottles. Sleeping pills might do the trick. But there are none. There are painkillers for mild to severe injuries, and tiny bots for reading blood pressure, but no sleeping pills.

I'm about to scream in agitation when I notice the kit behind this one. A small, square container with a few thin syringes inside, wrapped in plastic.

The ship shakes, and I hold on to the cubby door. A loud noise like suction rattles through the hold. My feet slide beneath me as Beechy lifts us off the deck. I grip the cubby tighter.

I glance at Oliver. He's half free of the wires.

My fingers stretch and take the first syringe they find. Lettering on the plastic reads SLUMBER INJECTION.

I rip off the plastic and roll the thin, white syringe over in my palm while with the other hand I try to keep from falling. Oliver screams behind me. He spits the gag out all the way.

The ship turns and throws me sideways, against the wall. I cough and suck in air. My wounded jaw is on fire again.

With a grip on the corner of the compartments, I ignore the pain and heave myself to Oliver. His wild eyes look ready to kill me. If I wait two more seconds, he'll get his hands loose enough to do it. He's almost there.

I don't want to hurt him. I want to make him better, but I can't, I can't.

I steady his thrashing head with a hand and punch the needle into his neck. My thumb on the plunger, I press until it's all the way down, and all the liquid is inside Oliver's jugular.

It sets his body seizing.

No, no, no. I panic. Did I give him the wrong thing?

I remove the needle, snatch the plastic covering, and reread the lettering: SLUMBER INJECTION. Unless they mismarked it, I didn't screw up. This must be what it does.

I run my fingers through my hair, waiting and waiting for confirmation.

A moment later, he falls limp.

I press a hand to his wrist to check for a pulse. Relief seeps through me. He's still alive, still breathing. But his neck is bleeding.

The ship tilts as I reach for the medikit. I hit the wall again and cry out. I struggle to unscrew a small vial of disinfectant and dab it on a bandage. When the ship evens out, I slap it onto his neck wound, hoping that'll do the trick. If he dies because of me, I will never, ever forgive myself.

"I need your help!" Beechy calls.

"I'm coming." I scramble to my feet, grab another strip of bandage for my still-stinging jaw, and shove the medikit and its contents back into a compartment.

39

In the main cockpit, Beechy swivels in the pilot seat, tapping buttons and pulling levers on the dashboard. We're flying over the last ships on the hangar. I glimpse people running below us. Officials in black armor scramble into fighter jets. Two of them might be helping a limping Charlie.

"Buckle in," Beechy says as we speed up through the short tunnel. The Pipeline is ahead. "Some of them are gonna follow us. I might need you to blast them for me."

"I don't know how."

"Just sit down. I'll show you."

I swallow and slide into the copilot seat just as we careen up into the Pipeline. I grip the arms so I won't fall. The chair shakes from all the rumbling, and it's too big for me. When I pull the straps over my chest they don't feel tight enough.

On the control panel, between all the buttons and knobs and monitors, a small screen at the very center flashes the blinking countdown:

1:22:40

"The clutches control the direction of the ship's main guns." Beechy points to two black levers on the dashboard in front of me. "Turn the red knob to activate the rear gun. Then press the clutch buttons to fire. Do it quickly, please."

I bite my lip and twist the knob clockwise. Over my head, a screen slides down from the ceiling, showing me a pair of long, silver guns on the back of the ship and what lies in the Pipeline beyond them. A fighter jet zooms out of the hangar tunnel, followed by another, then another. They don't head down to the Core; they make for us.

"You want me to blast them?" I ask.

"Just slow them down, if you can."

My fingers are slippery from sweat and blood as I grip the clutches. The system must read my body heat because right away a green grid appears on the screen with circles that follow the maneuvering pods. I move the clutches, and when the guns aim at the right spot, the circles start beeping.

Beep-beep-beep-beep-beep-beep-beep-beep-beep-beep—

I press the buttons too late, and the jet of blue light disappears into the darkness.

Focus. It's okay.

I try again. This time the blue laser skims the side of a jet, making it swerve out of the way.

It doesn't shoot back. Of course not. No one wants to hit the KIMO bomb.

But they wouldn't be flying after us without a reason. To cut us off and force us backward? If that's the reason, they might be able to. They're having no trouble keeping up.

"You can't go any faster?" I ask.

"Would you like us to crash?" Beechy asks. "Believe me, I'm as anxious as you are. Once we're almost clear of the Pipeline, I'll put us in hyperdrive."

I tap my fingernails on the clutches, as if that'll speed up time when there are miles and miles of Pipeline ahead of us.

Focus. Breathe.

I'm pressing the clutch button to fire again when a jarring noise fills the cockpit. Like someone pulled an alarm and then cut it off abruptly.

"What—" I start.

The ship lurches to the side, skimming too close to the wall of the Pipeline. Gravity slams me back and against the arm of my seat. Beechy's yelling, trying to keep us steady. I'm struggling to breathe because my seat strap's pressing into my neck, cutting off my air.

Beechy veers us out of the way at the last second. I force the straps away from my throat and suck in all the oxygen I can manage.

"What happened?" I ask.

"*Vrux,*" Beechy says, tapping buttons on the dashboard. "They're hacking the ship's system."

Odd lines of code fly across the monitors, replacing the timer reading, the pressure gauge, the fuel gauge, the speed odometer.

"Autopilot instigated," a computerized voice says.

We're slowing down. No no no no no. We should not be slowing.

"We have to stop it!"

"I can't from here." Beechy growls in annoyance. "I need you to find the engine room. It should be back down that passage heading to the bunk rooms. I need you to look for a module with red and blue wires—more specifically, for a silver one. Cut the silver wire, and that should disengage us from the main flight control system."

I quickly unlatch my seat straps. "You're sure?"

"No." He jams a lever forward with both hands, and we speed up a little. But not nearly enough. "I'm hoping they built this ship like all the others. Please hurry. It's very difficult to fight auto-pilot."

I scramble out of my seat.

Back down the corridor, I spare a second's glance at Oliver to make sure he's okay. He's still unconscious, still strapped to his seat. His head's flopping over.

The ship careens and I smash into the wall of compartments. Pain shoots up my arm.

I don't have time for this. Charlie's gonna turn our ship around and then he's gonna kill me.

He's gonna kill Logan.

He's gonna kill everyone.

I slip my fingers through the holes in one of the compartments to keep from falling again, and pry open a cubby. I need something sharp to use to cut the silver wire.

I fumble in a kit and find nothing but medical gauze.

I reach for another. This one's empty. I curse loudly.

The ship tilts again, and my feet start to slide and I grip the compartment harder.

There! A small pair of scissors is in the kit behind the empty one. I hope they're sharp enough. I snatch them and run down the corridor with the bunk room at the end of it. I pass a door to a tiny galley before I come to the one labeled ENGINE.

I slap my palm over a button in the wall, and the door zips open. Inside, the light's already on. There's a glass window in the floor through which I can see steam, probably from the engines. The walls are covered with buttons and wires and modules, from the floor to the ceiling that stretches a good five feet over my head. Whoever built this room must've built it for a giant.

I start skimming the walls. Wire after wire. There must be a thousand. Red wires and green wires and black wires and blue wires. Where's the silver?

Beechy is better at this. He should be doing this, or Oliver. I'm useless when it comes to ships. I never wanted to be a pilot.

The rumbling picks up again. I press against the door and hold on to the handle—thank the stars there's a handle on this side of it—and force my eyes to keep moving, to keep looking. I have to find the silver wire. Where are you, you stupid thing?

There—that might be it. A thin silver wire pokes out of a black panel near the ceiling, beside a clump of red wires mingled with blue.

But it's too high for me to reach. I'm going to have to climb.

Finally, something I'm good at.

I push away from the door and quickly decipher every crack in the wall, every button that could be used as a foothold, as long as I'm careful not to press it. I slip the scissors between my teeth and bite down hard. If the ship tilts again or I fall, I don't want them to slip and get lodged in my throat.

I reach and dig my nails into a crack between two modules, and heave myself up, placing my foot on top of a bigger button. Carefully, carefully.

I reach again and find another crack, and pull myself up to the top of a thicker panel.

The wall trembles and I clutch the crack with everything I have. Breathe. It's okay.

One more step and I'm high enough to reach the wire if I hang on to the wall. If my fingers or my feet don't slip.

I let go with one hand, my heart thrumming, and pull the scissors out from between my teeth. I stretch my hand up and work the wire between the scissor blades. I try to keep my breathing steady.

I squeeze the handle, listening for the snap that'll tell me the wire is broken.

It doesn't come.

Come on, *please.*

I try again, squeezing the scissors faster this time. Sweat trickles down my forehead.

It still doesn't work. The blades must be dull.

I scream through my teeth.

I squeeze the scissors with no pause in between, again and again.

The ship jolts and I cling to the wall and keep trying. I can't give up. I have to fix this.

The ship careens sideways again, and my fingers slip and I'm

falling,

falling,

landing hard on my back, and I'm slipping across the floor and crashing into a wall module because the ship is still turning. Charlie must be turning us around.

I gasp for breath. It feels as though knives and needles are sticking into my back, and I'm trying not to cry, but I see something that makes it better. It makes me dare to think maybe everything will be okay.

A piece of silver wire is stuck to the blade of my scissors.

When the ship rights itself, I reach for the door handle and heave myself up, ignoring the pain shooting through my body. I have to know if it worked. I have to know if Charlie's still controlling the ship, or if it's ours again.

The hallways don't tilt anymore. The ship still rumbles, but it's smoother, like it's supposed to feel.

I stumble into the main cockpit. "What's happening?"

"They turned us around for a minute there, but we're back on target," Beechy says, breathing heavily.

"It worked?"

"It did."

I look out the window. He's right. We're flying straight through the Pipeline, even faster than before. I can almost see the end of the tunnel. The fighter jets are falling behind us.

"We have an hour and eight minutes," Beechy says. "It might be enough time to escape the bomb's range once we deploy it out in space. We'll see."

I sink into the copilot seat, smiling even though I probably shouldn't yet.

"Think we could make it all the way to the moon?" I ask. "We could explode the acid generator. Knock out two evils at once."

Beechy chuckles. "I'm afraid that might be too far, if you want to make it back home. Maybe we'll take a trip there with a different bomb once all this is over."

"Fred could make another one like this, I'm sure."

There's a crackling sound from the ship-com on the dashboard. I freeze. So does Beechy.

A voice spills out of the speaker—a screaming, strangled voice: "Turn the ship around!"

It's Charlie.

"I-I thought I disconnected us from him," I say. My eyes are wide. I'm not smiling anymore.

"Ship-coms run on a different connection. It's okay. I can turn it off." Beechy reaches for the switch.

"Wait." I put a hand on his arm.

Charlie's still talking. I want to hear what he's saying: "You've ruined everything. They're coming for us—Marden is going to attack and it will be *your fault*. Everyone will die because of you."

He sounds desperate. We've stumped him.

He has nothing left to use but his lies.

I reach for the comm and press the TALK button. His voice cuts out. "You're a liar, Charlie," I say. "You're the one trying to attack Marden. I know about everything. Fred told me."

"Then he told you I was having him build the bomb to destroy the acid generator, yes?" Charlie's voice is fast but shaky. "That was the original plan. The acid is still a threat, Clementine."

"The shield's protecting us. It's not going to stop anytime soon."

"You believe that, don't you." His hollow laugh sounds worse through the crackling speaker. "You think you're so clever. You think you've *won*."

"We have, Charlie," Beechy says. "We're not turning around."

There's silence through the ship-com. I bet Charlie turned it off on his end so we can't hear him crying.

"Crazy old man," Beechy says, shaking his head and smiling. "Now hold tight. We're gonna speed up."

The tunnel opens ahead of us, showing me a sky half full of moon. Pink acid drips and swirls onto the shield. It almost looks beautiful.

I grip the arms of my seat as we burst from the Pipeline. Rocky mountains rise around us. Over their snowy peaks, I glimpse the horizon where some of the dark is starting to wash away.

I close my eyes and let the air flowing in and out of my nose relieve the ache in my back, and the dull throbbing in my jaw, and the fear in my heart.

Just a bit longer, and all of this will be over. The bomb won't be a danger anymore. I'll be back with Logan.

All of us rebels will expose Charlie for what he is, and we will end him.

There's a dull crackle. The ship-com.

"Not again," Beechy mutters.

"You made me do this," Charlie says in a clipped voice.

That's all he says.

"Do what?" I ask, but the comm isn't crackling anymore. He can't hear me.

"Don't listen to him," Beechy says. "He's trying to scare you."

I dig my nails into the armrests. Maybe he is, maybe he's kidding. Or maybe he's going to do something bad. He's always doing something bad. He's always killing someone.

But who could it be this time? Someone I care about, maybe.

It hits me like a blade to the chest: *He still has access to Logan.*

No, no, no. It can't be that. I shake my head. He's not doing anything. Beechy's right; Charlie's trying to scare us into turning back.

But we won't turn back. We can see straight through his lies.

I close my eyes again and take deep breaths, until my heartbeat returns to a more normal rate. I count seventy-two beats per minute.

I open my eyes and focus on the world outside the window, on the acid shield that's almost beautiful. It shimmers in places, looking like a giant dome enclosing our planet. It traps the pink fog where it can't harm us; it keeps us safe.

But suddenly the shield flickers and goes out. It vanishes, exposing the clouds and the land and the people to an acid sky.

I stop breathing.

40

The acid doesn't rush toward us in waves like it did in the simulations. It slowly sifts through the air, mingling with the highest clouds. It paints them pink, the color of death.

I can't believe this is happening. Charlie cut the shield.

"No. He can't have done this. He *didn't*." I stumble over my words. My voice rises in pitch. "We're just dreaming, right? We'll wake up and everything will be better, right?"

Beechy is too quiet beside me, his wide eyes staring at the acid floating free in the sky.

I open my mouth again, but this time I choke on the words. I can't swallow.

The acid will make its way down into the air people breathe, into the water they drink, into the wind they walk through. It will constrict their throats, burn their eyes, and eat away their skin.

Those inside steel buildings and underground will last longer than those out in the open air, but not forever. The acid can corrode glass, and it will slowly leak through cracks in the steel until it reaches every single person still alive.

Everyone is going to die.

"What do we do?" I ask, clenching my hands as if that'll keep my voice from trembling.

Beechy doesn't answer for a moment. He just stares out the window. When he speaks, his words are soft and slow. "This ship will hold up. It was built for that. We can try to make it to the generator, to destroy it with the bomb, so this doesn't get any worse. Charlie will put the shield back up."

"How do you know that?"

"He doesn't want to die. He wants to make us turn around so he can go through with his plan and get the Core warship in space.

That makes sense. But . . .

"You said the generator's too far."

"It might be. We have to find it first."

I dig my nails into my arm and look back out the window, understanding. Even if we can reach the generator before the detonation timer hits zero—fifty-one minutes from now—there's hardly any chance we'll have enough time to deploy the bomb and flee the fire. It will explode while we're still in range, taking us with it.

We will never see Logan or Sandy again.

"We didn't get to say good-bye to them," I whisper. I hope Beechy knows who I mean.

"No, we didn't. I'm not giving up yet, though." Beechy reaches for my hand and squeezes it. "Either way, we'll end this together."

I squeeze his hand back. "Okay."

He gives me a tight smile. "Now, hang on."

With my free hand, I lock in my seat straps and grip the armrest.

Beechy slams a lever forward, and we lean back and back, heading straight toward the moon, speeding through the clouds. I hang on to his hand and my chair for dear life. My seat straps aren't tight enough, and I'm afraid I'll slip out and crash into something. Oliver better be safe back there.

Oliver.

I have to wake him up. He has to know what's going on before we all die.

He has to hear me say I'm sorry we didn't leave him there on the hangar, where maybe he'd be safer.

But I can't tear my eyes away from the view just yet. We leave daylight, as well as the Surface, far behind. We rip through the place where the atmospheric shield used to be and head out into space.

The moon grows bigger outside our window. It's bigger than I ever imagined. Heat waves rise from its surface: clouds of pink acid. Deadly, but they are beautiful.

Beyond the moon, there are stars and stars and endless stars. They're pink and gold and bluish-green, dotting the galaxy with light and color. I see them, and I don't feel trapped anymore. I see them, and I'm sure there's someplace out there better than the world I left behind.

My bare feet make no noise on the ground of the corridor. We're still moving fast, but out here in the vacuum of space it doesn't feel like it did in the Pipeline, when the force of gravity kept me pinned to my seat. It's more like we're floating.

In the passageway by the cargo lift, Oliver sits wrapped in wires and strapped to his chair, his head flopped onto its side against the wall. There's blood on some of his hair. It's still wet when I touch a finger to it. He must've banged his head when we were flying fast back there.

I swallow hard to keep my throat from tightening. We shouldn't have brought him here. We should've taken him out of the ship on the hangar, even if officials shot at us, even if Logan and Sandy found out what we were doing.

Turning away, I find an antibiotic vial in one of the medikits, unscrew the cap, and squeeze a dot of gel onto my finger, hoping whatever germs are on my hands won't screw up Oliver even more than I already have. With unsteady hands, I ease his head forward and gently rub the gel into his hair.

I want to wake him up, but I don't know how. I gave him a slumber injection, and those are pretty powerful.

I've made so many mistakes.

If he doesn't wake, he won't know what I did to him and he won't feel it when we die. Maybe that's a good thing, except he won't hear me say I'm sorry. I need him to hear it.

"I *am* sorry," I whisper. "I swear it."

I'm sorry. I'm sorry. I'm sorry.

I wish there were some way I could hack into the KIMO control system and reset the timer. Or put the escape pod that's carrying the bomb on autopilot so we could detach it from the main ship and it could fly to the generator on its own.

My heartbeat picks up. Its thuds fill the silence in the corridor.

Autopilot might require a passcode I don't have, but manual piloting might be possible. Someone could detach the escape pod from the main ship and transport the bomb to the generator on its own.

Me. I could fly it. Then Oliver would live, and so would Beechy.

It's so simple. Why didn't I think of it before?

Running through the scenario in my mind, the problem hits me. There's no way the pod could reach the generator fast enough on its own, especially carrying a missile half its size. It needs the bigger ship to get closer first.

But I could detach it once we're close. I could wait until we're almost to the generator, until I'm sure the pod can carry me the rest of the way. I'd buy the ship an extra minute or two, at least, compared to the time it would take if we waited to deploy the missile from the main ship console. Hopefully, I'd buy enough extra time for Oliver and Beechy to clear the detonation range.

I turn and stare at the passageway to the ladder. As for me, I'd be all alone in that pod. I'd be all alone when the bomb ripped me to pieces. There's no way I'd escape the missile's range in a ship that small. We have to make sure we hit the generator straight on, and that requires a close shot.

"Clementine?"

I jump, startled.

Beechy stands in the cockpit passage doorway with his hands in his pockets.

"Don't you have a ship to pilot?" I ask.

"I set us on a course. We should be okay for a couple minutes." He gives me a crooked smile and comes over, looking at Oliver. "Are you trying to wake him?"

I nod, pressing my lips together. "I don't know how to, though. I gave him an injection to put him to sleep. Anyway, he's probably still subdued. He'd still try to kill us if he woke."

"Hmm." Beechy walks past me and opens one of the wall compartments. He rummages through the kits inside.

My eyes stay on him. I wonder if he's had the same ideas as me, about piloting the escape pod. I wonder if he was planning to sacrifice himself for me and Oliver, but wasn't going to tell me.

I'm not going to tell him. I know he'd try to stop me.

"Here we are," he says. He holds up a syringe in a plastic wrapper. It looks like the slumber injection I gave Oliver before.

"What is it?" I ask.

He holds it out so I can read the label as he moves to Oliver. ENERGY INJECTION.

"I'm surprised you never asked me how I manage to fight the monthly injections," he says, ripping off the wrapper.

I frown. "I guess I forgot." Other things seemed more important.

"Well, I use one of these." He pops off the needle cover. "See, the monthly injection calms the mind—it makes it easy to manipulate. To combat it, you do the opposite and make the mind frenzied with a high energy boost. But that causes confusion, which is why it takes a strong mind to fight submission off completely." He rips off the plastic. "Oliver, here . . . Well, I don't think there's any harm in trying."

I chew on my bottom lip, thinking of Oliver after our first Promise Elevation. How subdued he seemed, even then. "Are you sure?"

Beechy nods. "It's been some time since he had the injection, anyway. It should be starting to wear off. Here, hold this."

He hands me the syringe. I hold it by the tips of my fingers, as if it's poisonous. Beechy works the wires off Oliver, freeing him.

The ship rumbles. Beechy glances toward the cockpit. "You've got it, yeah, Clem? I don't want us to crash. Just stick the needle right into his shoulder."

"But—"

"It'll work." He throws me a smile and disappears down the passageway.

I grip the syringe, staring at Oliver. What if it doesn't work? What if he wakes up and he's even worse?

But I guess I owe it to him to try. He deserves to know what's happening and why before he dies.

I hurry forward before I can change my mind, and peel his shirt back a little to expose his shoulder. I count to three.

I jab the needle into his shoulder, and press the plunger.

He moans, and his eyelids flutter.

I pull the syringe out. Take two steps back.

He blinks once. Twice.

Looks at me.

I tense instinctively. I wait for him to start screaming again or lunge at me now that he's free.

He blinks again. Faster.

His eyes widen. "What's going on?" he asks, sounding a bit panicky.

I let out the breath I didn't realize I was holding. He sounds like Oliver again. He's okay. He's better.

He has no idea what's going on.

I hesitate. "Charlie subdued you," I say slowly, still afraid I'm going to set him off. "But we snapped you out of it. Do you remember anything?"

He nods, pressing a palm to his sweaty forehead. "He made me help fly the hovercraft to the site. He told me I was special, that I got to stay behind to protect the bomb and make sure no one messed it up. I don't know why I agreed to that."

"It was the injection. It wasn't you."

"But I knew I was gonna die."

"Well, you're not dead." I want to add: And you won't be because I'm going to save you.

"I'm not." He blinks, processing the information. "Where am I? What happened after I tried to stop you and Beechy?"

So he remembers that. I bet he remembers me knocking him out with the slumber injection, then.

"Uh." I shift my eyes away from him. "How about I show you? That would be easier."

"Okay." He pushes off his seat, trying to stand. He wobbles on his feet and reaches for the wall.

"Here, I'll help you." I let him lean on my shoulder.

"Thanks."

We join Beechy in the cockpit.

"Hey," Oliver says.

"Hey," Beechy says. "How are you feeling?"

Oliver doesn't answer. He's looking out the window, staring at the moon for the first time in his life. It's thick with the fog of moonshine. It's hard to tell whether there's even a solid surface underneath, or just fog and fog and more fog.

I prefer to look at the stars. They shimmer reds, purples, and blues in the distant reaches of the universe. They're tiny specks of light, but each one is a sun or a planet. Marden must be somewhere out there. I can't tell which speck it is, though.

"Why are we flying to the moon?" Oliver's voice cracks. He clings to my shoulder like he's scared of the moon and I can protect him.

"Charlie turned off the acid shield because we hijacked the bomb," Beechy says. "Now we're transporting the bomb to the generator that makes the acid, so we can blow it up."

Oliver's eyes have never been wider. He opens his mouth and

closes it twice, no doubt trying to figure out which question to ask first.

"Generator," he repeats. "What generator?"

"That generator," Beechy says, pointing out the window.

41

There's a spot on the moon's surface where the fog clears a little. It's far away and tiny, but I can still make out something unnatural there, something with a color darker than the fog. It might be the top of a massive structure. A generator that pumps acid into space, for some of it to float into Kiel's atmosphere and kill people.

Kill me. It's going to kill me.

"You knew about this?" Oliver asks, pulling away from me. He looks from me to Beechy and back again.

"No," I say. "We had no idea. I found out in Karum."

"You're serious? Someone just built a generator on the moon. That's where all the acid came from."

"Why don't you sit down," Beechy says. "I'll explain."

Oliver grumbles, but I can tell he's having trouble standing anyway. So he slips into the chair I was sitting in, the copilot seat.

I stand there behind the two of them while Beechy starts telling him about Marden and Charlie's war and everything we discovered. I wring my hands and swallow the lump rising in my throat. It refuses to budge.

I glance at the timer on the dashboard:

$$00:19:01$$

Nineteen minutes.

We're going to be close enough soon. We're going to be close enough for me to detach the escape pod and transport the missile to the generator without the timer running out. I think. I hope.

But I have to slip away first. I have to figure out how to fly the escape pod.

I have to say good-bye to Oliver and Beechy without really saying it.

The seconds tick by. I pretend Beechy's smiling instead of staring out the window with emotionless eyes. I pretend Oliver's hoarse voice is laughter. I pretend we're flying to the moon to see the sights instead of on a suicide mission.

I'd pretend forever, if only I had more time.

But the timer is down to seventeen minutes and thirty-five seconds.

I tuck the curls behind my ears and take a shaky breath. "I'm going to check if there's a restroom," I say, interrupting Beechy.

"Okay," he says. "There should be one attached to the bunk room."

"Thanks." There's a lump in my throat, and my voice almost cracks, but I fight it. I glance at Oliver one last time. His cheeks are pale. He thinks these seventeen minutes are all he has left.

But there's wonderment in his eyes too—dull, but it's there. Because of the stars, I bet. He always wanted to see them. He always wanted to fly in a spaceship.

I think he's going to be okay.

Beechy continues talking. My heart thumps against my ribs. It might shatter one or all of them if I keep standing here, so I turn and hurry away.

I don't look back.

I press the button on the wall, and the doors to the escape pod slide open, one after the other.

There's the screen where I tried to type in the code to disable the bomb and failed. There's the window showing me the moon. There's the floor separating me from the missile, from the weapon Fred built that will blow me to smithereens in fifteen minutes and seven seconds, and, I hope, the generator too.

I sit in the pilot seat and put my head in my sweaty hands. My whole body is shaking.

I need more time. Fourteen minutes isn't enough, not at all. I need to say good-bye to everyone. To Logan especially. He said he'd wait for me on the hangar, but I left and I'm not coming back.

Logan, oh Logan, I hope you're okay. I hope you're not dead.

I wish I hadn't left him. But then he'd be dead for certain; he would've been blown up with me when the bomb went off. This way, maybe I can save him.

Please, please, let me save him.

Outside, I can see the top of the generator now. It's a tower, thin and rectangular, peeking through the clouds. A red light flashes on the top of it. It could almost be my school building on the Surface, or that tower I tried to climb the day I met Laila.

When I die, I'll be with her again. That's something good, at least. I'll die out here with the stars and the dust in the moonlight. The bomb will take me out. That's better than dying from the acid. I won't feel any burning; I'll just be gone. My ashes will float off to the stars. To Marden, maybe.

Maybe that won't be so bad.

The dashboard starts beeping. I stare at the timer. Ten minutes.

Focus.

I have to figure out how to fly this thing.

I scan the dashboard. Most of the buttons and controls look the same as the ones in the main cockpit, there are just fewer of them.

I flip a switch and a dim blue light comes on overhead. I flip another and the dashboard powers on. The buttons light up yellow and red and purple like the stars.

"What are you doing in there?" a voice says.

Oh, no. I haven't shut the transport doors yet. I think I was waiting until the last second.

I turn my head. Oliver is at the top of the ladder down the short passageway, staring at me, bewildered.

He shouldn't have come looking, but part of me is glad. Part of me is relieved. Now I can say good-bye to him.

I swallow. "I'm gonna do it myself. I'm gonna fly this pod to the generator, so I can deploy the bomb and you two can get away. We're close enough now that I'll reach my target."

"No, you're vruxing not," another voice says. Beechy hoists himself up the last rung of the ladder.

"Yes, I am." I reach for the button to seal the doors.

Oliver blocks the entranceway. "You can't."

"You're not." Beechy pushes past Oliver.

"Get out." I press hard against my seat, afraid one or both of them will rip me out of it. "Please leave me alone."

Beechy grabs my shoulders. I kick hard against his legs, forcing him back a step. Then Oliver grabs me too. I'm not stronger than both of them. They wrench me to my feet. They're ruining this. They're ruining everything.

"Stop it!"

They don't stop. They drag me out of the transport into the passageway.

"Let me *go!*" I yell. I didn't want this to happen. I wanted to save them both. "We're running out of time!"

"If anyone's going to sacrifice himself," Beechy says calmly, "it's going to be me. Oliver, please help Clementine down the ladder. You two can fly the ship home."

"No!" I shake my head, panicking. "No, no, no, you can't do that. I'm supposed to do that. You have to let me."

"You can't fly the pod."

"You can tell me how!" I push against him and kick as hard as I can. Oliver has let go of me, so maybe this is working.

"Clementine, *stop,*" Beechy says.

There's a loud sound of suction. I stop struggling and whip my head back to the transport door.

The escape pod has been sealed shut.

Oliver is inside it.

Beechy lets go of me now. Maybe they planned this, maybe he knew this was going to happen because he doesn't move. Or maybe he doesn't know what to do.

I run. We're right near the doorway, but I can't get there fast enough.

"Oliver!" I scream.

He's sitting in the pilot seat. He runs his trembling hands through his hair. I can't see his face. I need to see his face.

I jam a finger on the button and press it. I pound a fist against the cold glass. The door won't budge.

"Stop!" I scream again, hitting the glass so hard my hand might break.

He leans over the dashboard, tapping several buttons in consecutive order. A faint *whir* catches my ears. The engine turns on.

"No, please . . ." I blink fast.

He glances at me with red, watery eyes. "It's okay," he says. The glass muffles his voice to almost nothing.

"It's not."

"Someone has to do this." He takes a shaky breath. "Beechy has Sandy and his kid. You have someone, but me, I've got no one."

"You have me."

"I'm glad," he whispers.

I spread my fingers apart on the window. "I'm sorry," I tell him. "I'm sorry for everything."

"Don't be."

There's another sound of suction, louder this time. The escape pod detaches from the part of the ship where I'm standing, revealing its round black body with K-I-M-O painted on one side and the missile head poking out of the other. There's only one glass door left between me and the vacuum of space.

I don't hear Oliver crying, but I can see the tears running from his eyes. He turns away and grips a lever to maneuver the pod to the left, toward the generator, until I can no longer see his face or his ship from this window. Until he's left me behind.

I spin around. Beechy's gone; he must've already gone back to the cockpit to fly us away.

No no no no . . .

One rung at a time, I haul myself down the ladder until my feet touch the floor. The world tilts. I think it's just my head. But I don't stop running.

Beechy sits in the cockpit, fiddling with dials and easing back the flight clutch. His hands fumble; there are dots of sweat on his face, or maybe they're tears. Our ship turns away from the moon and the generator. The one-man transport flies past us to the right and pushes onward.

The numbers on the dash read:

00:05:03

"We have to stop him."

Beechy doesn't say anything at all.

I don't take my eyes off the window. When our ship turns around all the way, I switch the weapon monitor to the rear guns so I can still see the pod.

In my ears, the beep of the countdown grows louder and louder. Amidst the hazy pink darkness of space through the monitor, the round ship moves farther and farther away, ever closer to the steel tower surrounded by mist.

I can't tell when he gets there, when he reaches the generator. I pray he got close enough.

A cloud of gray smoke erupts from the generator site, consuming everything around it, all the acid gas and the space dust too. The smoke spreads far, far out, and I'm afraid it's going to swallow us whole. But we're moving fast enough to escape it.

Oliver isn't. He's gone.

When we're safely on course, Beechy stands and wraps his arms around me, and I shake my head over and over and sob into his shoulder. I don't know if he gets it. I don't know if he understands.

Oliver is gone forever, this isn't another test. Oliver, who tried to save me from Sam. Oliver, who helped me feel better when I was scared about everything.

It's partly my fault he's dead.

Words tumble into my head and play over and over, and make me cry even harder:

>*To the krail's caw, to star song*
>*In the field, love, we'll dance*
>*'Til the moon is long gone*
>*Until the world ends*

42

Our ship rockets away from the moon, back to Kiel. I see the stars in the rearview monitor and picture Oliver's body floating among them. But in truth, his body is broken. He's gone someplace I can't follow.

I cry until I have no tears left. I imprint his face in my head because I don't want to forget it: his messy brown hair; the eyeglasses he insisted on keeping; his wide eyes the color of a blue sky.

I hope he's someplace better. I hope he's safe, wherever he is, maybe even happy.

I hope Laila and Ella will take care of him.

We're nearing Kiel's atmosphere when I see it: a shimmering dome enclosing our bluish-golden planet. The acid shield is back up.

But beyond the shield, the sky is still riddled with acid. It paints the clouds a dark pink color, like a deadly sunset. I wonder how much acid seeped into the atmosphere before Charlie turned the shield back on. I wonder how long it will take for all of it to clear from the air.

I wonder how many people already died.

Not Logan, please. I swallow hard and count to three hundred to fight back the worry.

The mountains below us grow larger through the window, until I could touch the snow on their peaks if I could reach the glass.

"Where are we going?" I ask Beechy.

"A rendezvous point in the mountains," he says, easing the clutch sideways so we won't hit the snow. His jaw is tense, and his eyes red. "Whatever rebels are left will meet us there. And we'll figure out what our next step is."

I stare at the acid shield in the rearview monitor, my stomach churning with acid of its own. I already know what I'm going to do. I'm going to kill Charlie.

I'm going to make him pay for everyone he stole from me, and all the lies he told.

Below us, the mountains dip to form a river valley lit by rays of red sunlight. White rapids swirl in the water, tumbling over rocks. Trees with black leaves and thick, gnarled branches form a small forest.

This valley looks untouched by humans, almost impossible. Like something out of a dream.

We hover to a landing in a forest clearing beside the river. Beechy turns the engine off, and the cockpit falls silent.

My heart still beats too fast. One hundred and thirty-two beats per minute, I count, and breathe to try to slow it down because it's not good for me. I must continue to focus.

"Could we wait for them outside?" I ask. It seems like it's been a long time since I've felt wind or sunlight.

"Okay, but we'll need safety suits first," Beechy says, pushing out of his seat, "unless you want to fry in that acid. There should be several on board."

I follow him down the passageway, along the corridor with the bunk room and the engine room. Inside the bunk room, he opens a cupboard in the wall and pulls out two white suits that look like space suits, but lighter.

We pull them on over our clothes and zip them up. The fabric feels smooth and cool against my skin. He helps me secure the clear helmet over my head, and I help him put on his. I press a button on the suit, and the small machine attached to my back lets oxygen flow into my helmet.

For a second I'm back in the Core room with the water tank, about to dive down deep to visit the vul. Oliver is alive again.

I blink and he's dead.

Back in the main passageway, Beechy uses the control panel on the wall to open the cargo lift. As the door zips open, wind whips into the ship. I half expect it to carry me away, high up into the sky, back to the moon maybe. I almost wish it would.

But Beechy's gloved hand grips mine, keeping me from flying away.

We walk down the ramp onto the grass. The clouds are darker than they should be. Rain might be coming. Even with the protective suit on, the wind is cold. I shiver and Beechy puts his arms around me, pulling me as close as he can with these bulky suits on. My eyes scan the sky for flight pods or hovercrafts. I listen for the sound of their engines.

"What if they don't come?" I can't hide the crack in my voice.

"We'll find them," Beechy says. "We're almost out of fuel though, so we'll have to get more. There's a place within walking distance where we can get some."

"What sort of place?"

"A camp. A hidden base where some of the rebels have been staying, preparing to fight Charlie."

I almost don't believe him. A place like that sounds safe, and I didn't think there were any safe places on the Surface, except maybe the adult city.

A drop of water hits my helmet. Then another, until the rain drenches us and the grass and I'm grateful for the suit. It might be my imagination, but the water seems to have a pinkish tint to it. Acid.

It's not going to be safe to walk outside without these suits for a while.

The whir of a sky engine reaches my ears.

I pull away from Beechy, every nerve ending raw. It might not be Logan. It might be Cady or one of the other rebels, but it could be him. I need to see him. He needs to be alive.

Please.

Please.

Please.

The flight pod slows, hovering lower and lower until it lands not far from us in the grass. The wind from its rotors rustles the fabric of my suit.

And I see him.

Logan scrambles out of his seat, wearing a suit like mine. He fumbles to open the door.

I'm already running.

I reach the pod at the same time he emerges from it.

Then he's here and holding me again. There's blood clotted in his hair and too many scrapes on his cheeks, but he's alive and he's touching me and we're both shaking because we can't believe this. I wish we didn't need these stupid helmets. I want his lips on my mouth and his hands in my hair. I want to kiss him forever and ever and ever.

"I didn't think we'd make it back."

"I thought you were gone," he says. "I thought you blew up, or the acid got you. What happened?"

Tears well up in my eyes, and I don't stop them. "We flew to the moon. We destroyed the generator. But Oliver's gone, Logan. He was my friend, and he's gone."

"I'm sorry."

"It's Charlie's fault—we have to stop him. He'll try something like this again—I know it."

"We will."

Behind him, Beechy climbs into the pod, and Sandy throws her arms around him. Her laughter mingles with her tears.

Logan slips his gloved fingers through mine, and we move to join Beechy and Sandy in the pod. We're going to the rebel base now. The others are already there, waiting.

Inside, I slip into the passenger seat beside Logan and take off my helmet. He takes off his.

We kiss as the pod lifts off the ground. His hands tangle in my curls. Our breaths mingle. He tastes like hope, like every good thing I've ever lost.

I am never letting him go.

I lean my head against his shoulder and clutch his arm. I breathe in through my nose and out through my mouth until my heart isn't skipping beats anymore.

Until I can almost believe everything is going to be okay.

But I know this won't last. Charlie will come up with another plan to bring war to Marden, one that might involve too much death.

He'll realize I didn't die up there. He'll come for me or he'll send Sam to put a bullet through my head.

But I'll be ready.

＊

Outside, one of the mountains rises like a giant before us. Its peak is too high for me to see it through the clouds, but I'm sure there's snow up there. We hover low above the trees, making for the mountain wall close to the ground.

I'm almost afraid we're going to crash into it, but there's an opening in the rock. A gap where a skinny branch of river slithers into the mountain.

The opening is just big enough for us to enter. We fly slowly into the darkness. The blue lights of our pod flash on the cave walls, onto places where water drips on the rock, onto narrow entrances to passageways where bad things might be waiting.

Then there's a speck of light ahead. It's as small as a star at first, but it grows in the window, until I see that it's not just one light but many: a row of lights dotting the cave walls on either side. These walls are made of steel.

There's another wall at the end of the tunnel. A giant doorway with words written on it. The letters look like someone painted them, but it must've been a long time ago because the paint has faded.

With the help of the other tunnel lights, I can piece together the words:

K.I.M.O. CORPORATION

EST. 30 RC

WE FIGHT TO JOURNEY HOME

ACKNOWLEDGMENTS

This is the book of my heart. It would not have been possible without the help of numerous individuals.

First, I owe a planet of thanks to my agent, Alison Fargis, who believed in me when I was close to giving up. Equal thanks are offered to Kathy Huck, my brilliant editor. You both helped me turn this story into the one I truly wanted to tell.

Thank you to the whole team of designers, marketers, publicists, and book lovers at St. Martin's Press for helping me share my story. Thank you also to the lovely ladies at Stonesong for your support and enthusiasm.

All the words in all the books cannot express my thanks to Jennifer Rhee, my best friend and confidante. Thank you for your patience, your guidance, and your laughter. Emma Castor and Karen Casteloes, thank you for reading my work, even when it was horrible. Ashley Harger, thank you for being one of my first readers, and my very first friend.

My deepest gratitude to Kelly Kehoe, John Hansen, Marcy-Kate Connolly, and all the others who saw *Extraction* through its good days and bad days, and helped it grow. Ríoghnach Robinson, thank you for your wit. I'll never forget that your words inspired this novel.

Many thanks to the wonderful community at Agent Query Connect, and to all my fabulous Twitter friends.

Thank you to the teachers who encouraged me to pursue my dreams over the years, especially Gloria Ciriza, Robert Kaechele, John Graber, Peter Cirino, and Stuart Voytilla. Thank you to the teachers whose lectures I failed to pay attention to because I was writing. (I truly apologize.)

Mom, Dad, Daniel, Elisabeth, Julianne, and extended family, thank you for your endless love and support. Michelle, thank you for the stories you shared with me when we were young, which inspired me to become a writer.

Thank you, God, for I am nothing without you.

And thank you, reader. I hope this book will help you as much as it helped me.

DON'T MISS THE NEXT INSTALLMENT IN THE
EXTRACTION SERIES

REBELLION

Available in 2015